THE PICOBE DILEMMA

Steve Legomsky

To Lorraine,
To Annie and Will,
To Katie, Mike, Kai, and Marco,
And, as Kai used to say,
To the "all flammey"

ACKNOWLEDGMENTS

Heartfelt thanks to Don Abel, Linda Ballard, Carol Boggs, Ben Dolnick, Linda Fried, Lorraine Gnecco, Jane Keating, Annie Legomsky, Diane Legomsky, Katie Legomsky, Barb Rea, Julianne Statham, and Michael Toolan. You all slogged through a very rough first draft, and your tactful, thoughtful suggestions helped me turn it into something passable.

PROLOGUE

Tuesday, December 30, 2025

I'm a brain surgeon. Seriously. I always laugh when that term is used pejoratively, as in "he's no brain surgeon." Some people seem to think you must be especially brainy if you make your living cutting into other people's brains, a lot smarter than the surgeons who operate only on "dumb" body parts like knees or gall bladders.

That said, I must admit with all due humility that I actually *am* very smart. And not just smart, but on the verge of a scientific breakthrough that will transform the world we live in and move humankind closer than we've ever been to the dream of eternal life. At least I *will* be on the verge of accomplishing this if the folks who claim to care about me will stop berating me about my "obsession" with this project, or about my becoming "detached from reality."

I'll give you the details later, but my journey began when I discovered that the human brain electronically stores every memory it has ever processed. And it stores them permanently – even after death. I have now figured out a way to extract those electronic memory data from the brains of deceased humans and preserve them digitally. Soon I will be able to translate them into English. I will be able to reproduce a person's whole life and save it forever. *I am about to test this on the brain of my own mother.*

The moment I grasped the enormity of what I had taken on, I knew I would need to chronicle these events in real time. Warts and all, the highs and the lows, the technical and the personal. I'm baring my soul to the world because I want those who study the history of science to be able to retrace the path that led me to this revolution. Hence, this journal.

I confess I also have a secondary motive for recording these events. Biographers have always relished writing about the personal lives of those who changed the world. As soon as I go public with my discovery, they will be dissecting my personal life in every which way. The world will want to know how I even came up with the idea. They'll want to know what inspired me to keep going in the face of continual setbacks and amidst deep skepticism from the few around me who knew what I was up to. They'll want to know everything about my core philosophy, my values, my life experiences, and how they shaped my life's work. Only through this account can I hope to preempt some of the more irresponsible speculation.

As you're reading this, you might be thinking I'm narcissistic, maybe even delusional. I would strongly advise you to reserve your judgment until you see for yourself what I have achieved. I think you will be embarrassed that you ever doubted me. As will the others.

But in order for any of this to make sense, I first have to tell you a little about my early life. When you get to chapter 2, you'll understand why.

CHAPTER 1
THE SEEDS ARE SOWN

It happened on my very first day of high school in University City, Missouri, an inner suburb of St. Louis. The year was 2005.

I remember it vividly. The high school was a typical 1950s brick building with long, dark, cavernous hallways and linoleum floors, flanked on both sides by endless rows of metal lockers and combination locks. I was in Mrs. Aruna's 2 pm English class on a hot, muggy August afternoon. The air conditioning had failed. My seat was in the leftmost aisle, about halfway back, next to a west-facing window through which I could see the black asphalt parking lot filled with teachers' cars and with the sun blasting against the side of my head.

Joanie, who sat in back of me, and Carla, who sat next to her, were whispering things to each other and giggling virtually nonstop. Mrs. Aruna either didn't notice or pretended not to. At every brief pause I hoped they were finally finished, but within seconds their conversation would resume, and it was really getting on my nerves. I was sweating profusely and very sleepy. I kept checking the clock, but its creep toward the end of the period was ever so slow.

At some point, a secretary entered the room and handed a note to the teacher. The secretary was an obese middle-aged woman, and some of the boys snickered to each other. One of them, Alan Olson, whispered something crude. I saw him at my fifth high school reunion, and he denied ever having said that, but I know he did because I heard him.

Mrs. Aruna read the note slowly, nodded, and asked that Jason Stramm please come to the front of the room. That's me. I walked up to her desk. She told me in a soft, kindly voice that the guidance counselor needed to see me.

I didn't know where the guidance counselor's office was. Mrs. Aruna told me the secretary who had just handed her the note would escort me there.

The secretary was very kind as well. I asked her what this was about. She just said it would be better if Mr. Marson told me. I asked her who Mr. Marson was. She said he was the guidance counselor. And she said my mother was with him in his office.

I assumed my doting mother had come to the school to give the guidance counselor all kinds of information that would help my teachers "understand" me and my "special needs" (which, for the record, were in fact quite normal). So I wasn't alarmed – just embarrassed.

But the moment we entered the office and my mother saw me, she burst into tears. Mr. Marson rose and handed her a tissue. He then turned to me.

Mr. Marson was a handsome man, tall and trim, I would guess in his 40s. His short-sleeved white shirt exposed dentist-like hairy arms. I couldn't make out his features well, because the sun was streaming through the window from behind him, directly in my eyes. For some reason I was surprised when his voice turned out to be high-pitched and somewhat scratchy. "Hello, Jason. I'm Mr. Marson, the school guidance counselor. Please have a seat."

My mother, still sobbing, told me that something terrible had happened.

"Your father was on his way to meet a friend of his for lunch today. He was running late, and he ran across a busy street. The car couldn't stop. It hit him. An ambulance rushed him to the hospital. Daddy didn't make it, sweetheart. He passed away about two hours ago."

And then she gave me a very tight hug that she desperately sustained for what seemed like a very long time.

The whole episode was so other-worldly. I was in this strange new building, in a strange office, with a man I didn't know and my crying mother telling me that my healthy, vigorous father, whom I adored, had suddenly died. Just like that. It was the first time I had experienced the death of anyone close to me. Not even a pet.

The whole thing wasn't registering. I remember asking my mother whether I should go back to class now. She said no, I should come home with her and we need each other now more than ever. She told me how much my father loved me and again burst into tears.

I loved my dad dearly. He was an easy-going, smiley kind of guy, with an odd-looking, asymmetrical mouth that seemed to extend further toward his left side than his right. He had reddish hair, which he kept very short.

Dad was on the short side, but he had a muscular athletic build. One time I saw my mom smile and tell him he had great abs. He usually wore polo shirts or T-shirts that were always neatly tucked in, which made him look like a gym teacher.

Everyone liked him. He and my mom seemed to have a good relationship, though every once in a while she would comment to me that he was not an "ambitious" sort of man. She said this in a tone that suggested at least mild disappointment.

He was a very engaged father. During baseball season we were forever playing catch. He taught me how to hit. "Keep your eye on the ball until the very last moment. Don't worry about the bat. It will go where it needs to go. Same when you're fielding. Watch the ball, not your glove. And get down low. There's no excuse for letting a ball go through your legs."

Dad used to say I was a chip off the old block. In some ways, I am. I too am short and on the slim side and have red hair, though I wear my hair longer than he did and I definitely don't have his muscular physique. I also wear glasses; he never needed them. And I'm asthmatic; he was always in perfect health. Anyway, I'm a very different person -- more ambitious, more intense, a bit fidgety, sometimes uncomfortable in social situations, and not physically graceful the way he was.

I've always had an exceptional natural aptitude for anything mechanical. By age six, I was continually disassembling and reassembling kitchen appliances. My mom started storing these gadgets on the high shelves that I couldn't reach. I built a ladder out of some wood and nails that I found in the garage, and I used it to reach those shelves. It's true. Age six.

I especially loved anything electrical. I had just turned seven when my parents scheduled a handyman to come and fix an electrical short that was preventing the hall light from turning on. When they went out that night, I persuaded the baby-sitter to let me get into the wiring and fix it before the handyman came, which I did. The next morning my parents told me never to tamper again with anything electrical, because it was extremely dangerous. They also never hired that baby-sitter again. I knew they were proud of me, though, because I would occasionally hear them telling other adults about how I had fixed the electrical wiring. And after they had scolded me for doing this, my father smiled and gave me a hug. It was a humid summer day, and he had been outside mowing the lawn, so he had that outdoor sweaty smell, but the hug still felt good and for some reason I remember the feeling vividly.

Strangely, with all the time we spent together, my father to this day remains an enigma to me. We never talked about his life. As a child, it never occurred to me that either of my parents had had a childhood or that as adults either of them had a life outside of being parents. It never crossed my mind to ask about their histories, or their families, or their reflections on life, or what they did all day when I was in school.

I'm still not even sure what my father did for a living. He never talked about it, and he was home a lot. I once asked my mother what Dad's job was. She said he was a consultant. I had no idea what that was. "He advises people about different things." I asked what things he advised people about. "It's kind of hard to explain," she said. "All sorts of things."

My mom would talk a little more about her life and would share a little more of her feelings. Unlike my father, who had only one sibling – a sister who died at age 4 from an untreated ear infection, of all things – my mother came from a large family. She was the youngest of six kids, all of them still alive as I write this part of the journal.

They all appear to be on civil terms, but we never really spent much time with them. Three of them lived on the East Coast. We would visit once in a while. I didn't particularly enjoy those visits, as only the youngest of them – my uncle Alex – had any kids even close to my age. And that child, Bartholomew (his real name, his parents reportedly having loved the children's story about the boy who kept taking hats off his head), was two years older than I was and made no attempt to conceal his unrelieved lack of interest in playing with me.

My mother's other two siblings were my Uncle Hal, who lived in California and whom we almost never saw, and my Aunt Betsy, the only one who lived in the St. Louis area. She and her husband,

Uncle Norris, lived in an affluent suburb called Ladue but still sent all three of their kids to private school because the public schools were not capable of meeting the "special needs" of their "unusually gifted" children. My parents were happier living in racially diverse University City and sending me to public school.

Both of my dad's parents died before I was born, but happily I got to know my mom's parents very well. Grandma and Grandpa lived in Olivette, another suburb of St. Louis. I loved them. They visited us often, and as a child I spent a lot of time at their house. I remember they had a huge back yard, and they had set up a swing and a slide just for me. Grandma used to make brownies for me, but she always baked them too long, which made them more like cake instead of the chewy kind that I really love. I never told her that, to spare her feelings.

I'm skipping ahead now, but my grandparents died in a car accident during my sophomore year of college. It was some drunk driver, who escaped unscathed. I was very upset when my mom called me with the news, and she was inconsolable, sobbing nonstop as we talked. Neither of us felt anger, though we would have had a right to. All we felt were a deep sadness and a sense of permanent loss.

I came home for the funeral. We both cried on and off throughout the whole service, and she periodically held my hand. I think that was probably the saddest day of her life, even sadder than the day my father died. Losing one parent was hard enough. Losing both of them unexpectedly and simultaneously was too much to bear. I had to return to college a couple days later. I still remember how lonely she seemed on the day I went back, and how guilty I felt about having to leave her in that state.

My mom went to medical school at the University of Rochester and became a dermatologist. You might have heard of her. Her name is Martha Love. She started all kinds of programs for children with melanoma, for which she was once written up in a New York Times Sunday Magazine article.

Dermatology was a good specialty for her (and for me), because she rarely had emergencies to attend to and consequently was able to enjoy what today we would call a "healthy work-life balance." It also meant that I always had to wear sunscreen when I went outside, even in the old days when no one else did. After a while I got used to the other kids calling me "Whiteface." Davis Davis Jr. (his real name) was a year ahead of me and the high school's star athlete, an all-state defensive lineman. He was the one who came up with that nickname, and he thought it funny enough that he would call me this every time he saw me and tell everyone within hearing range "hey, say hello to Whiteface." Every time.

Health-conscious as she was when it came to skin, my mother otherwise took poor care of her own body. She was a heavy smoker for many years, even during her pregnancy and my childhood. You could smell it on her whenever you got close. Mrs. Luccino next door would never even come into our house, because of the second-hand smoke. My mother never exercised and ate all the wrong things. Somehow she nonetheless managed to maintain a pretty good weight, and my sense is that men found her attractive. She was about 5 feet 9, I believe.

Even though her work hours weren't oppressive, they were still longer than those of my father. That didn't mean my father did much housework. My mother still did most of it, including all the cooking. That was a shame, because the same unhealthy food that she fed herself also made up the bulk of my diet and that of my father. To this day, I marvel that despite this diet all three of us were on the thin side. High metabolisms, I guess.

If I had had any siblings of my own, I imagine they would have had these high metabolisms too. But I was an only child, which was fine with me.

Anyway, I've always regretted that my impressions of my parents were and remain superficial. I never really knew what made them tick – what forces shaped their lives, what they cared about, what their frustrations and regrets were, what they wanted or expected out of life, or even what their relationship was like. I've always wanted to know more about their thoughts, ideas, and feelings. I wanted to know *who they were*. And not just who they were in general, but who they were at different stages of their lives. Because I don't believe that the person you are when you're young remotely resembles the person you become later in life.

I got to know my mother better as I got older, but my father died too soon. I never had the chance to ask him the important questions. Or if I had the chance, I squandered it. Too young and stupid.

Those regrets are a large part of what has prompted my lifelong work and what has driven me to stick with it even at those points where the prospects of achieving concrete results looked especially dim. If I'm really "obsessed" with this work, as my wife always used to tell me (and I'm not, I'm just very serious about it – there's a difference), that's a big part of why.

But that's not the only big thing that's driving me. There's something else.

My parents never exposed me to any organized religion. It wasn't a big deal. But in the aftermath of my father's sudden death, I became a confirmed atheist. I didn't buy any of the traditional accounts of a supreme being. I couldn't find any way to solve the perennial contradiction of a god who is simultaneously all-powerful and all good, but who nonetheless allows the world's people and other creatures to commit such unspeakable cruelties and endure such horrific pain. I could accept the theoretical possibility of a supreme being who was either all-powerful or all-good but not both, though frankly I saw no convincing evidence of even that. True, I had no way to explain how else the universe could have been created, but positing the existence of God simply shifts the inquiry to who created God.

I especially scoffed at the idea of heaven and hell or any other form of an afterlife. Without a supreme being, I didn't see how this was possible. I thought consciously about it. I felt certain that human life – or any other life for that matter -- ends when the body gives out. When the heart stops pumping and the lungs stop breathing. That is it. There's no more. And that's still what I believe.

I wish I believed in an afterlife. That would be comforting. But I can't make myself believe something just because I think I would be happier if I believed it.

All this unnerves me. Like most kids, I never gave a thought to *how* quickly life passes. That was something I didn't grasp until well into adulthood. But I did understand, early on, that whatever its speed, life is finite. I even understood that it was infinitesimally short relative to the universe. Infinitesimally short even relative to the microscopic slice of the universe occupied by recorded human history.

There is an emptiness in me when I contemplate the brevity of life and the suddenness and completeness of its finish. I can't bear the thought of my existence simply ending forever.

In the days and months that followed my father's death, this became a steadily deepening preoccupation. I thought about it all the time. My mother told me that this is not normal. "Lots of people fear death, and many of them are doubtful about there being an afterlife," she said. "But to become so obsessed with it – especially at such a young age – is worrisome." She thought I was showing signs of depression or obsession or both. She wanted me to see a therapist.

But I knew I had no psychological disorder. I had an active mind, and my father had just died unexpectedly. This was a natural subject to dwell on. So I refused to see a therapist. There was no need. And despite what some people around me seem to think, there *still* isn't.

To her dying days, I don't think my mother ever stopped worrying about my stability. Her fears were sincere, but they were groundless, and her constant harping about it was aggravating. Much later, my wife would start in with the same theme and would be equally off base. My second post-doc lab assistant, a young man named Marvin about whom you'll read much more later, also implied I had some issues that I should seek counseling for. I wish everyone would just leave me in peace and stop trying to "help" me.

Anyway, if I had to identify the forces that have driven me to pick memories out of dead brains, I guess it would be mainly those – my craving to know more about my parents, and the need to find as close a substitute for eternal life as biology will permit.

With all that, high school was a blur. Girls really weren't a big part of my high school experience. I was physically gawky. I don't think my personality was particularly nerdy, but my interests and activities certainly were, so that didn't help either. And partly too, I was just shy around girls. Not painfully so, but enough that even when I had a desire to ask a girl for a date it would take me forever to summon up the courage.

I did have a few dates in high school, including taking Sandra (I can't remember her last name) to the junior prom. I never did manage to get a date for the senior prom, which made me extremely self-conscious. I tried to pretend that I had consciously preferred not to go to the prom because proms were stupid, but the real reason was that I couldn't think of anyone I wanted to ask to the senior prom who I thought wouldn't turn me down. In any event, I probably had about four dates in all of high school, and no two with the same girl.

College was better. I went to Cal Tech, where I majored in mechanical engineering. I loved class. I even loved studying. Most of all, I loved the lab. I was truly in my element.

I had a couple of brief but meaningful relationships with fellow students during those four years. One was with Melissa Pasternak, but I broke it off after a couple months or so. The other, my senior year, was coincidentally with another Melissa, Melissa Santos. She was beautiful and very sweet, the first girl I was unequivocally in love with. I could never quite believe that she was interested in me, but she really was, at least for a while. She said she loved my enthusiasm and my excitement when I was talking about things I was in the process of inventing. She said my vibrancy in those moments was infectious. She even told me once that I was handsome, especially my eyes.

But after about three months she broke my heart. I was a very nice person, she told me, but we would both be graduating in just a few months and would be better off in the long run if we explored other relationships, which I later learned she had already gotten a head start on.

By my senior year I had decided that as much as I liked mechanical engineering, what I really wanted to be was a surgeon. I had taken tons of required and elective science courses, so I was prepared for medical school. I ended up attending the excellent medical school at the University of Rochester, just as my mother had done.

Those four years were intense, but I came away with a medical degree and a wife. She was Jessica Polinski, from the unlikely town of Oatmeal, Texas. That's a real place, you can look it up. Oatmeal is the second-largest town in all of Burnet County, about an hour's drive from Austin.

We first met during rounds one day at a children's hospital. I asked our supervising doctor a question that must have impressed Jessica, because she smiled warmly to me when I had finished. At the end of the rounds she invited me to go out to lunch with her. I was smitten. I found her attractive in an exotic kind of way. She was extremely thin (she's filled out since then), with an aquiline nose, large green eyes, a pretty smile, and long, jet-black hair. She was smart and possessed of a delightful sense of humor. We dated for the last two years of medical school and got married the summer after graduation.

I'll tell you more about Jessica later, but for now I'll just mention that we were lucky to both get residencies at Houston Methodist Hospital. This was the highest-ranked hospital overall in Houston, and it was very good for both of our specializations – neurosurgery for me, ophthalmology for Jessica. She liked the fact that it was only a 3-hour drive to Oatmeal, where many of her family members still lived. Most importantly, it enabled us to be in the same city.

Our residencies were pretty typical. Extremely long hours, major sleep deprivation. Mine was especially rough. Neurosurgical residents are constantly getting summoned to the hospital in the middle of the night to treat head injuries, usually from car accidents or gunshots. And Jessica's and my rare times off almost never coincided. We completed our residencies in the summer of 2019.

I had long been regaling Jessica with the wonders of the St. Louis area. It wasn't just that we had an Arch and everybody else didn't. St. Louis was actually a great city in which to live, and especially suited to raising a family, which was our intention.

As it turned out, Jessica learned that her medical school classmate and good friend, Marilyn Benedict, was also finishing up her residence in ophthalmology and was planning to move to St. Louis with her husband. Jessica and Marilyn agreed to start a practice together, conditioned on my getting a position in St. Louis.

And I did. I wanted to be a research neurosurgeon, and happily I was able to get a three-year post-doc at Washington University in St. Louis. It's one of the country's premier medical schools. I was working in the lab of an eminent neurosurgeon, Dr. Rajesh Patel. Between the university and an NIH grant specifically for academics starting careers in medical research, I was earning a decent income. So was Jessica, as her and Marilyn's practice got off the ground spectacularly fast.

We thought about renting a house or apartment for the first year, so that we could take our time looking for a more permanent home. But we learned from a friend about a wonderful house that was on sale in the University Hills area of University City, the same inner suburb where I had gone to high school. This area of the town is a quiet, middle-class, very beautiful neighborhood with elegantly curving streets and lots of trees. Like most of the surrounding homes, ours was a four-bedroom, two-story brick house built around 1940. It had a spacious living room with a nice fireplace and lots of light, a relatively modern kitchen, two recently renovated bathrooms, a cozy TV room, and a finished basement. There were lovely front and back yards, the latter with a large but overgrown flower garden.

The house was much bigger than we needed and was much more expensive than we could then otherwise have afforded, but my mother was willing to lend us the down payment. Even though my post-doc was only for three years, we planned to stay in St.

Louis for the long haul and to have children, so the investment made sense.

Jessica and I both loved our jobs, and even the work hours were reasonable, for both of us. For the first time in years, we had a life. Our relationship was idyllic. We would have dinners together. We often got away on weekends and explored the scenic rivers and streams of the Missouri hills. We worked out regularly together at the neighborhood gym before work.

And just in case you're wondering, our sex life in those early years was wonderful. I'm not going to go into detail about that, because frankly sex is something that I've always felt awkward and self-conscious talking about. I'm not a prude – not by any means. I just don't see a need to dwell on it, so I won't say much about it in this journal.

I don't think we were ever happier than during that first year in St. Louis. It was like the TV commercials where they show young couples in love, always flashing big white toothy smiles to each other even while they're on adjacent treadmills, eating breakfast cereals, or brushing their teeth.

Our precious son, Zeke, was born on September 30, 2020, about a year after our move to St. Louis. He arrived on a beautiful sunny day, healthy and happy. Unfortunately, the labor was extraordinarily difficult, so much so that the obstetrician cautioned us that a second childbirth would be very dangerous. We never did have the additional children we had once planned on.

I was always excited to get home and play with Zeke. He was such a happy, good-natured baby. It's trite to say it, but all parents light up at their baby's first smile of recognition and all parents delight in watching their child's sense of wonder and process of discovery. Zeke started crawling when he was about (I think) seven or eight months. That's when things got especially interesting. He and I would crawl around the house together as he explored the terrain of the living room, kitchen, and dining room with Daddy by his side. And I could tell that it gave Jessica a great deal of pleasure to see her boys having so much fun together.

Our lab, which now consisted of Dr. Patel and three of us assistants, was focused on the way the human brain processes memory. Like many other researchers around the world, we hoped to find ways of preventing or at least delaying memory loss due to aging.

This isn't the time for false humility, so I won't deny that I was clearly the golden boy among the three assistants. This became apparent about a year into my post-doc, when I made a scientific discovery that impressed Dr. Patel enormously. I didn't know it then, but that discovery would turn out to be the starting point for the lifelong work that will soon make me the most famous scientist in the world.

If you're a lay reader, there are just a few things you have to know about neuroscience in order to understand my early discovery and its later significance:

The human brain is divided into regions. The region most associated with memory is called the cerebral cortex. The cerebral cortex, in turn, consists of four "lobes." Of these, the most important to my research is the temporal lobe.

There are different kinds of memories -- memories of specific events, memories of facts, visual memories, auditory memories, somatosensory (touch) memories, emotional memories (including social and sexual memories), unconscious "procedural" memories that guide bodily movements, and so on. If, for example, you are attacked by a robber with a knife, you might remember what he looks like, the sound of his voice, the words he spoke, and the fear you felt. These different kinds of memories are temporarily stored in different parts of the brain.

The hippocampus is the part of the brain that binds these into a single memory. The hippocampus also stores that unified memory for up to a week and then sends it to another part of the cerebral cortex for longer-term use. Researchers call this process "systems consolidation."

The brain contains approximately 100 billion "neurons," or nerve cells. There are different kinds of neurons. Some are transmitter neurons. Their job is to sense external stimuli like sights and sounds and transmit the messages to other neurons. The neurons that receive these messages are called "receptor" neurons. A single receptor neuron can receive these messages from hundreds or even thousands of different transmitter neurons.

The connections between the neurons are called "synapses." These are the pathways by which the transmitter neurons send information to the receptor neurons, thereby creating memory. Crucially important here – remember this – the neurons contain certain proteins that are essential to this process.

One last thing: Memory is not static. Neuroscientists have known for many years that the synapses are strengthened, and the memory more easily accessed, every time you recall that memory. They have also long known that memory is constantly being edited. That's one of the reasons memory is often unreliable. What you think you remember, even clearly, might be different from what you originally experienced and different even from past *recollections* of what you had originally experienced.

But here's the big question: Is memory actually stored on a long-term, or even permanent, basis? Or do the neurons and synapses that process memory have to reconstruct the same memories every time a particular thought or experience is recalled? In 2019, the prevailing view among neuroscientists was the latter -- that memories have to be continually refreshed in order to be preserved in the brain. The assumption was that the brain does not store the original memory, or even edited versions of that memory, for very long.

I wasn't convinced. So with Dr. Patel's blessing, I spent almost my entire three-year post-doc trying to find out once and for all whether the brain stores each memory permanently and, if so, how.

In this lab we didn't study the brains of cadavers. All of our investigation was done with brain scans taken from live patients. Electrodes would be attached to the skull of the subject patient. For some patients who were undergoing brain surgery, the electrodes would actually be attached directly to the brain, giving a more detailed picture. Electrical stimuli were then applied to targets within the cerebral cortex, and we would contrast the patient's recollections of past events with and without the electrical stimuli.

During some of these experiments, the electrical stimuli enabled the patients to recall events that had occurred many decades earlier and that they had previously forgotten. That result wasn't new or unusual. We had seen it many times in our lab, as had other researchers.

What was new was my discovery that some of the electrical stimuli that enabled people to recall these long-forgotten memories were in places where I couldn't locate any sign of proteins. Yet it was already common knowledge that the proteins are essential to the formation of new memories and the editing of old ones. Without them, the memories could not have been refreshed. Besides, refreshing would require the person's conscious recollections, and these patients assured us that they had not thought about these particular events since childhood. Those assurances were credible, because many of the newly-discovered memories were of innocuous events that the person would have had no occasion to recall consciously –

for example, what he or she had had for dinner on a particular day.

The inference I drew was that at least some of the memories I had just pried loose must already have been stored there for several decades, not re-constructed anew.

To be clear, I never doubted that long-dormant memories might be hard or impossible to recall *consciously* without periodic recent refreshing. But intuitively I had always believed that every memory remains imbedded at least unconsciously in the brain regardless of whether, how often, or how recently it has been refreshed. And now my discovery that old memories remained intact even in places where I couldn't find any sign of the proteins that would be needed for reconstruction – and without any indication that the person had consciously recalled the experience since its original occurrence -- lent some empirical support to my belief.

Admittedly, that inference wasn't inevitable. Maybe the proteins were there after all, and my equipment just wasn't exacting enough to detect them. But that seemed unlikely, because the same equipment was easily able to detect proteins in other areas that were no more accessible and in some cases even less so.

Another possibility was that our electrical stimuli substituted for the proteins – that they performed the same functions. That too seemed unlikely, because there was no reason to expect these electrical stimuli to precisely mimic the same chemical reactions as the proteins. They had nothing in common with the molecular structures of these proteins.

By process of elimination, this left me more convinced than ever that memory is very likely stored permanently in some form. I couldn't be sure what that form was. It might be a chemical substance. But my bet, instead, was that memory is stored as electrical energy that has been permanently trapped inside some of the nearby receptor neurons.

So I initially named the neurons that store these memories for the long term "micro-batteries" – micro because they are so tiny and batteries because they (probably) store electrical energy. I quickly changed the name to "pico-batteries." Pico means one-trillionth. I thought that would be more exotic than micro, which conveys only the pedestrian one-millionth. But "pico-batteries" kind of sticks in the throat, so I shortened it to "picobes."

I shared my conclusion with Dr. Patel, who encouraged me to write up my findings and publish them in a medical journal. I was hesitant, because at that point my inference still wasn't much more than a guess. To show that these picobes exist, I would eventually have to actually find them and prove that that is what they are. We had been stimulating the brain by injecting electricity from an artificial external source, but I would need to find the actual neurons that I believed already contained these trapped electrical signals – my picobes. Dr. Patel understood this, but he urged me to publish my findings anyway, with proper qualifiers about the need for physical verification and my intention to attempt it.

It didn't occur to me at the time, but a lesser person than Dr. Patel might have claimed the credit for himself. It was his lab, after all. But he was a man of integrity, had nothing left to prove, and, I think, sincerely enjoyed helping young researchers succeed in their careers. Either that, or he was just risk-averse and worried that his colleagues would find this to be a crackpot idea that he wouldn't want to be considered the author of.

At any rate I took his advice, wrote up my findings, and submitted the article to the prestigious Journal of the American Medical Association (JAMA). To my delight, after intensive peer review, they published it. Soon after that, the equally prestigious New England Journal of Medicine published my follow-up article. My reputation spread quickly. I became an instant rock star in the neuroscience community.

For the remainder of my post-doc I worked hard to locate these elusive picobes and the electrical data they permanently stored. It wasn't hard to find all sorts of electrical fields in many areas of the brain, but I needed to isolate the individual neurons that I was convinced were trapping this electricity. I did not succeed. I still believed it likely that they exist, but I was becoming less optimistic about my ever finding them. And in my honest moments I knew there was a real possibility that my theory might simply be wrong.

If it was, then I would have wasted several years of time and energy pursuing a phantom.

I frequently thought about cutting my losses and starting anew with a different project. But I wasn't quite ready yet to give up the hunt.

Dr. Patel easily sensed my growing impatience and personal doubts, but he emphasized to me that a discovery like the one I was pursuing can take years. I shouldn't be disheartened that I haven't struck instant gold. Yes, there might come a point when it's time to quit. But I was nowhere near that point yet. He reminded me of the rapid technological advances in magnetic, ultrasound, laser, fiber-optic, electrical, and other diagnostic biotech innovations. If picobes do indeed exist – and he agreed with me that it's likely they do – then with these new search technologies it was only a matter of time before I found them.

So I continued experimenting any way I could think of, with any kind of brain scan available to the lab. But I still kept coming up empty-handed.

In the spring of 2022, during the third year of my post-doc, the Medical School offered me a tenure-track position as assistant professor, to begin in the fall. I accepted it with great excitement. They gave me a generous package that included a good salary and research support. This enabled me to continue working in Dr. Patel's lab.

He and I collaborated on several articles. My reputation kept soaring. I was invited to speak at numerous conferences, including some in fabulous places overseas. It wasn't easy for Jessica to get time away from her practice, but on occasion she managed it and we were able to travel together and of course bring little Zeke. He didn't quite know what to make of the strange surroundings and incomprehensible languages, but he smiled a lot and seemed to enjoy himself most of the time.

As much as I liked working with Dr. Patel, and as grateful to him as I was and remain, I now wanted a lab of my own. From kindergarten until my graduation from medical school at age 26, I had been a full-time student. During my residency I had been under the strict supervision of other doctors. As a post-doc I had continued to work under the tutelage of another doctor. Even as a tenure-track assistant professor, I continued to labor in someone else's lab, constrained by the dictates of Dr. Patel's research priorities. It was time to strike out on my own.

Luckily, just a year into my tenure-track position, I was able to. Although still young, I landed a five-year research grant from the NIH. Together with the university's contribution, I had enough funding to set up my own lab from scratch and even hire my own post-doc assistant.

My lab was sleek, modern, state of the art. It still is. Everything is white – the walls, the ceiling, the white granite tiled floor, and the furniture. There is a large rectangular central area. Near one end are two long white tables at right angles. Near the other end are two similarly-arranged white tables. On the tables is an assortment of cameras, microscopes, imaging equipment, and computers with multiple monitors. In the middle of the lab, between these two sets of tables, is a space for refrigeration and chemical preservatives. Around the perimeter of this central area are white file cabinets and white bookcases. At one end of the lab is my office -- a large square cubicle that I fitted with one-way glass so that I can observe my lab assistants without feeling self-conscious about their watching me while I work. At the other end of the lab are two smaller cubicles for up to two lab assistants, both with clear glass windows.

As the lab was being set up, I began realizing that the holy grail I'd been searching for was unlikely to reside anywhere near the outer surface of the cerebral cortex. If it were there, I would have found it by now. It would be necessary to cut into the deeper recesses of the brain, and that was something I could not do with live subjects. I decided I needed to poke and prod brains that had been taken from cadavers shortly after death. My hope was that I could discover brain structures and cellular compositions that would be hospitable places for picobes. If I succeeded, perhaps I could then figure out a non-invasive way to locate them in the same places in the brains of living subjects.

Of course, these brains would have to be chemically preserved, but today that's not difficult. Formulas capable of preserving the human brain without even having to use ice have been around since at least 2001. The process is called neurovitrification and since then has been vastly improved.

By this time I had acquired decent background knowledge of biochemistry. But for the kind of research I now wanted to do, I knew I would need help from a serious biochemist.

That's when I hired Lisa Holz as my assistant. Lisa had just finished her Ph.D in biochemistry at Duke University. She had a strong academic record, some very good co-authored articles, and sterling references. I interviewed her twice. She seemed exceedingly bright, eager, and very warm. We had fantastic rapport.

She was also beautiful, with a very pretty mouth, a warm smile, high cheekbones, and thick brown hair down to the middle of her back. She had one of the smoothest speaking voices I've ever heard. I have to admit I was quite taken with her. Her physical appeal wasn't why I selected her, but I think it would be dishonest of me to say nothing about her beauty and pretend I didn't notice such things. Again, though, that truly played no part in my hiring decision. Or if it did, it was only a small part and mainly unconscious. Certainly not a major factor. I'm sure of that. She really was *incredibly* beautiful, though.

Anyway, Lisa and I worked very well together. Often I would find myself sexually aroused just thinking about her or talking with her. I'm only human. But I'm pretty sure I never let that show, and it didn't prevent me from focusing on her work and treating her like the impressive professional that she was.

From her first day, she dived into the research. At the beginning (this didn't last long), she worked long hours, with laser-like focus.

From time to time she would take a three-day weekend to visit her boyfriend, a guy named Manny who lived in Miami. Strangely, he never once came to St. Louis, so to this day I've never met him. He apparently had some kind of start-up company that he said required him to stay tethered to Miami for his customers, but at first I didn't really know anything more about him than that.

Out of curiosity, I looked up his webpage and found some of his social media communications. From his picture, I can't say he was especially handsome, certainly not as handsome as I would have expected of someone who was able to land the amazing Lisa. His pose and expression gave me the sense that he thought of himself as muscular, but to me he just looked flabby. And he had this foolish-looking clipped mustache that I thought made him look like Hitler. Not that I claim to have movie-star looks myself, but I have to say I come out way ahead of him.

I think Lisa could have done a lot better than some guy who looks like that, never comes to see her, and expects her to do all the traveling. If I had been he, I would have come to visit her as often as I could. I even told her that once, but this information seemed to unsettle her. I'm not sure whether she thought I was hitting on her (I wasn't) or whether she just didn't like my criticizing her boyfriend. Either way, I thought it best to drop the subject.

I do know that I always loved coming to work. Apart from my personal fondness for Lisa, we had a wonderful working relationship. We enjoyed both the physical and the intellectual challenges of exploring the internal tissues of dead people's neurovitrified brains, and we both felt certain we were on the verge of finding the locations that would be inviting settings for picobes.

About a week after Lisa's arrival, Jessica asked to meet her. We all got together for lunch. That evening Jessica remarked that "Lisa is very attractive, don't you think?" I'm not the most perceptive person around, but I knew enough not to salivate or say "Oh, sweet Jesus, yes!" So I just shrugged and muttered "I guess so. I hadn't really noticed." Jessica frowned and shook her head. I sensed she didn't believe me.

I knew I was developing strong feelings for Lisa. She was so beautiful, smart, warm, engaging, and genuinely kind. She appreciated my talents and accomplishments and never hesitated to let me know. And of course we were working closely together, toward a common goal that inspired both of us. Plus, we were the only two people in the lab. It would have been unnatural *not* to think about her constantly.

But I also knew I would never make any advances toward her or otherwise reveal my desires. For one thing, Jessica would be devastated if she ever found out. I would never have wanted to hurt her or risk destroying my happy marriage and losing Jessica and

Zeke. For another, romantic relationships between supervisor and supervisee were strictly verboten. Also, I could safely assume Lisa had no reciprocal interest in me and that the only thing that could come of it would be rejection, continuous awkwardness in our working relationship, and possibly her leaving. So I suppressed my feelings.

Even at that, these were happy times. My marriage was good, and Jessica and I were both enjoying our work. Back then, there were no warning signs of the difficult person that Jessica would soon become.

Zeke, now three years old, was really coming into his own. He could ride his little scooter, read a few short words, throw a tennis ball, do somersaults, and put his head under water at the swimming pool. And he was still young enough to think his mom and dad were superheroes.

It's funny. As I write this, I'm finding unusual pleasure in recounting those happier periods of days past. I'm feeling a serenity that I have not felt for many years. In those youthful days, I had no inkling of how my life would unfold. I certainly had no premonition that my personal life would unravel in the way it has or that I would become so fragile – or, on the other hand, that I would soon be within reach of becoming the most famous scientist in the world.

How could it be that not that long ago I had such a complete sense of well-being, and yet today, on the verge of finally completing perhaps the greatest scientific discovery in recorded history, all I feel is this relentless anxiety and sense of foreboding? Where did all that happiness go? At this moment I should feel elation. But except for right now, while I'm reminiscing about times past, I don't. Just the opposite.

Why?

CHAPTER 2
THE LIGHT BULB TURNS ON

Wednesday, October 23, 2024

Eight days ago, my laptop died. Yes, I'm a dinosaur. I have continued to use my old laptop, with its own internal hard drive. But now I couldn't even turn it on. The IT folks at the medical school took one look at it and pronounced it DOA.

How could I have known that this innocuous event would flip a switch that would ultimately enable me to transform human life in ways previously thought unimaginable?

I guess history is full of both positive and negative upheavals that would not have occurred but for fortuitous events. What if Hitler's parents had not had sex nine months before his date of birth? How many millions more people would have died of bacterial diseases if Alexander Fleming had decided to become a musician instead of a scientist? What if John Lennon and Paul McCartney had never met each other?

But I'm getting ahead of myself. The panic hit when I remembered how lax I had been about backing up my files. I normally create files on my laptop's hard drive. I know I should back them up, but I seldom do. Would these data be recoverable? If not, I've permanently lost years of work.

The IT guy I approached was Tim. He was in his forties, prematurely bald, probably around 6'3", and very thin. He had a wispy blond mustache and wispy beard. He wore jeans and, most days, the same Woodstock T-shirt that his grandfather had proudly handed down through the generations. Somehow it was still intact.

I sought out Tim because in prior interactions he had come across to me as the smartest of the IT crew. So it stunned me when he told me that this time my laptop was beyond repair. But it had lasted a long time, he said, so I shouldn't feel bad.

"Can you retrieve the data?"

"I don't know. Aren't your files backed up?"

"No."

"They're not backed up anywhere? Not even on the server?"

"No."

"Shit, man."

"That's your answer, 'shit, man'"?

"I'm not a magician, Professor. I'll try. Gimme a few days."

"Tim, this is like life or death for me. I've got years of work that could be lost."

"Bummer. But like I said, I'll look at it in a few days."

"Please try everything. This is really horrendous."

"Got it. I'll call you when I know something."

And so I left the computer lab with a knot in my stomach. I actually felt physically ill. I had emailed a few of the files to Lisa, and I was pretty sure she had saved those, but the vast majority of my last two years' work resided, if at all, solely on the hard drive of my now-dead laptop.

Lisa consoled me. "I'm so sorry," she said. "But you know how good Tim is. I'll be shocked if he doesn't get your files back."

At home that evening, Jessica consoled me too. She didn't know Tim, but I told her that he was really good and she kept my focus on his exceptional skills. Still, I felt very uneasy.

The next few days passed slowly. I bought a new computer and began using it, but I wasn't very productive. So much of the work I was doing built on what was on those earlier files, and in any case I couldn't keep my mind on anything but Tim and my lost work.

After a week I still hadn't heard anything from Tim, so I called him.

"Tim, have you had a chance to look at my laptop yet?"

"Oh, yeah, everything's cool. I've been meaning to call you. I downloaded all your files to a portable drive yesterday morning. You can pick it up any time. But dude, you need to back up your files."

I didn't know whether to kiss him or strangle him. I wanted to say: "You asshole!!! You saw how distraught I was. You did this yesterday morning? When were you planning to call me?"

Instead I said: "Oh my God! I can't believe it. Thanks so much. Thank you, thank you, thank you! You're a genius! I'm coming over right now."

I retrieved the portable drive, got back to my lab, and uploaded all the files to my shiny new computer.

Sure enough, all the files were there. All was right with the world.

I shared the good news with Lisa. She smiled her amazing smile and gave me a hug. It was the first time we had ever hugged. It lasted only about two seconds, but they were two of the best seconds of my life. She told me how happy she was for me. And she added: "From now on, you're going to back up every single file you create or edit, right?" She didn't say it in a nagging way. She said it in a kind of teasing way, almost a coquettish way. Had she sensed how much her hug had meant to me? Did it mean anything to her?

Late that afternoon I realized that I needed to call Jessica too. She had seen how down and how anxious I'd been the past week, so I had to let her know that everything was now all right. I reached her at work, and her sigh of relief over the phone was audible enough that I was sure everyone in her office had heard it.

"I'm really happy for you," she said. "I'm going to bake some brownies tonight for you to bring to Tim. That would be a nice thing to do. So when did you find out?"

I was so unprepared for that question that I answered it truthfully.

"First thing this morning. Tim did this yesterday but never called me. So I had to call him, this morning. If I hadn't, I'd probably still be waiting. Can you believe that?"

"You got this great news hours ago, and you're only calling me now?"

"Well, I figured you'd be tied up with patients."

"Why would I be tied up with patients this morning but not now?"

"I don't know, Jessica. I guess I was just excited to get all the files back and wasn't really thinking straight. What's the difference? The important thing is that everything is OK now. I thought you'd be really happy for me."

"I am. I already told you that. So how did Lisa react when you told her?"

Now I saw where this conversation was going.

"Lisa? Oh, she was very pleased."

"What did she say?"

"I don't remember her exact words – something like 'Oh, that's great news.' Why are you grilling me like this?"

"I'm not grilling you. I'm just surprised that you told Lisa right away but waited several hours to tell me. Anyway, I've gotta go. I have a patient. I'll see you tonight."

And she hung up. She was clearly miffed. And, I think, troubled. That was puzzling. Surely she wasn't worried that someone like Lisa would ever take up with someone like me?

But I guess that was a slight faux pas on my part. It seemed like a small one, though, and after a few minutes I stopped thinking about it and got back to work. I arrived home that evening, just a few minutes after Jessica, and everything seemed normal, which was a relief.

Jessica's reaction did get me thinking, though. She's a woman, so if she believes I'm attractive enough that someone like Lisa could plausibly be interested in me, is it possible that Lisa might size me up the same way? Maybe I've been shortchanging myself.

Anyway, that was yesterday. When I left for work this morning, I had a bounce to my step. I dropped Zeke off at pre-school and drove to the lab.

At the lab I greeted Lisa, grabbed a cup of coffee, and checked my email. I was still euphoric about regaining my files, and I was also soaking in the warm feeling of Lisa's hug. But I knew I had to force myself to stop exulting in the retrieval of the files and stop daydreaming about the lovely Lisa. I had to get back to the important memory work that had been driving both of us for, now, more than a year. So back to the old files I went.

And then it hit me.

My old laptop was dead as a doorknob. There was no electricity or any other energy pulsing through its veins. Yet the memory that it had been storing was perfectly intact. Nobody had to keep refreshing the data for fear they would otherwise vanish.

Well, if the memory stored on the hard drive of a laptop retains its integrity even after the unit that houses it has died, is it possible that the same is true of the human brain? Might the brain retain its stored memories even after the rest of the body has died, at least until the brain tissue substantially deteriorates?

And if the answer is yes, then just as the data on the laptop's hard drive can be both extracted and copied to another physical storage device, could the data stored in the brain be similarly accessed and digitally stored? This would preserve the memories long after the brain tissue has wasted away, maybe eternally. The central challenge would then be reduced from finding, accessing, and preserving the data to simply decoding them.

Once the data are transferred to a permanent storage device – and backed up, I won't make that mistake again – mathematicians, computer scientists, and perhaps linguists could take the time they needed to do the decoding. The implications are limitless!

Of course, if this is true, then Lisa and I have been wasting our time cutting up dead brains with scalpels in a pointless search for tissues and structures that might somehow be likely places for picobes to hide in live humans. Really, I've never been entirely sure we would recognize such properties if we fell on them. What we should be looking for are the picobes themselves. Until now, it hadn't occurred to me that they might not only exist, but persist even in dead brains.

And if my intuition is correct and the memory data they store are in the form of electrical energy, then we should be probing with much more sensitive instruments in the hope of detecting either the electrical signals themselves or some other evidence that they are there. For that, there is a whole range of new-fangled sensing devices at our disposal.

On further reflection, I decided I had been too quick to dismiss our past work with dead brains as a waste of time. We had actually eliminated whole areas of the cerebral cortex as likely landing spots for picobes and had found some areas where for various reasons the prospects were more favorable. Those findings would help us a great deal in figuring out the optimal locations for the more targeted probing that we would now get started on.

This was huge. I knew I needed to talk it over with others. But I also knew the whole idea would sound like the rantings of a mad scientist. Whom could I trust? Lisa? Jessica?

Certainly not my colleagues in other labs. They would either appropriate the idea themselves or dismiss me as the lunatic who tried to pick memories out of dead people's brains.

Same for the NIH. If the bureaucrats there ever got wind of my using their grant money for this purpose, they would think I had gone off the deep end and would likely forbid the use of any of my grant funds for this project. I could also probably kiss good-bye to any chance of their renewing the grant when it expires a little less than four years from now, or for that matter ever getting another NIH research grant for any future project. And I'm not sure I would blame them. The whole thing does sound macabre.

But it makes sense. If memory is stored, and stored as energy, why would it vanish into thin air just because the blood is no longer circulating? Sure, death will prevent the formation of new memories, but why does it have to destroy the old ones?

One thing was immediately clear. For a project of this magnitude I would now need the expertise of a real biochemist more than ever. And of course that had to be Lisa.

Before approaching her, I wanted to think this through a little more. I at least wanted to formulate a broad overview of the major steps this project would require. Piece by piece, the plan materialized rapidly.

I couldn't wait any longer. I went over to see Lisa, insisted on absolute confidentiality, and described my idea to her. She seemed befuddled.

"We're going to extract memories from dead human brains?"

"Yes. And we need to talk about what kind of probing we can do to find out. What do you think?"

She stayed calm.

"Well, it's a really interesting thought. But scaling it back a bit, I'm thinking that if you can verify your earlier theory that memory really is permanently stored rather than merely reconstructed – and I think we're already very close to doing so -- that alone would be a major breakthrough. It would settle a longstanding controversy. Researchers will learn a lot more about how memory is both formed and stored, with possible implications for treating neurological diseases, especially those involving memory loss. But what you've just described goes way beyond that. You're talking about the brain actually preserving these data after death, and if that's not enough, you're then going to somehow access these data, then upload them onto some kind of hard or portable drive, and then translate them into a language that we can understand."

"Exactly."

Lisa laughed. I loved it when she laughed. It was even more joyful than when she smiled. And this particular laugh was one of pure affection. At least I think that's what it was. Actually, maybe it was more of a nervous laugh. Now I'm not sure.

She said she loved my sense of adventure and my vibrancy when I was talking about creative projects. That was déjà vu. Those were almost the identical words that my senior year girl-friend, Melissa Santos, had used, and with uncannily similar warmth and sincerity. It was a nice flashback, but mostly it was wonderful that it was Lisa who was expressing this affection. Still, I sensed she didn't think there was any serious chance of my project actually working.

"You think I'm crazy, don't you?"

"No, of course not. It's just that I worry that you could devote your entire career to this project and just be setting yourself up for continuing frustration and ultimately failure. Not because of any inadequacy on your part, but because there are *so* many seemingly insurmountable obstacles. It just all seems like sci-fi to me. Wouldn't it be better to concentrate on locating and actually examining the picobes that all your research seems to suggest exist in live humans? That would be huge."

"Listen to me. I have a specific plan. The project will have four phases. Phase 1 is actually finding these picobes in dead brains in the first place. With what we've found already in the way of potentially hospitable brain tissue, we can pretty quickly start the process of probing for electrical signals deep within the recesses of the temporal lobe. Once we find them, we enter the next phase, which is physically accessing them. For those first two phases your biochemical expertise will be vital. The third phase is transferring these electrical signals to an electronic storage device, because once the person dies, the brain will no longer be producing the proteins that enable the synapses to work, and then it really would be only a matter of time before the memories are lost. And the final phase is decoding all this information once it's electronically stored. That will require a math whiz. But every one of these steps is doable."

I could tell from her expression – and her silence – that she was still dubious.

"Lisa, if we succeed, we'll be altering the whole course of humankind. We will have changed the very meanings of life and death."

Now she seemed more than just dubious. She seemed troubled. But I persisted.

"Look, if we fail, we fail. But this is my dream, and I'm not going to stop until I either realize that dream or reach a point where it's clear that there's no path forward. And Lisa, I need you with me for this. I need your expertise, but even more, you're an important person in my life and I need your support.

And if this succeeds, imagine the lifelong thrill of having been part of it – or how regretful you'll feel later if you had a chance to be part of it but declined."

"Jason, can I ask you a personal question?"

"Of course."

"I've seen how passionate you are when you're on the verge of a scientific discovery. But this seems different to me. I've never heard you talk before about things like changing the meanings of life and death. That sounds more like theology or philosophy than science. Is there something else that's driving you?"

I was dumbstruck. It took me a few moments to realize it, but Lisa had penetrated a part of me that I myself had not previously understood. It was a little like one of those trite detective shows where the brilliant sleuth struggles in frustration to piece the evidence together – until his dimwitted friend makes an offhand comment that triggers the critical insight. The detective excitedly says "that's it! You're a genius" and races from the room to pursue the lead, leaving his befuddled friend scratching his head.

But that's kind of what happened today – an innocuous question that finally helped me connect the dots. My expression must have looked strange, because Lisa looked concerned. She asked me if I was all right.

I was still processing this.

"Jason?"

"Yes, I'm fine. I'm more than fine. I think I'm getting what's driven me these past few years to spend my entire career trying to figure out how memory is processed and stored, and what's behind my zeal for this project. You're right. It's not just the thrill of scientific discovery."

"Tell me."

"Well, it's actually two things. I want people to know who their deceased loved ones were. I mean who they really were. What they thought and felt deep down. What they experienced. We never think to ask them those questions while we still can, and even if we asked, we'd probably get only the most superficial responses. Our loved ones wouldn't even be conscious of everything they've ever thought or felt. And even most of their conscious thoughts and feelings are usually long-forgotten. For that matter, some other thoughts and experiences might be ones they don't want to share, but which their families badly want to know about."

"But Jason, if that's the case ..."

"Wait, there's a second reason I need to do this. I've never believed in God, and definitely not in an afterlife. And it distresses me to think that at any unforeseen moment, and within a few decades at the latest, my existence will simply end. No one will remember me. It will be as if I never existed at all. I want to stay alive forever. But what does it mean to be alive? I think it's experiencing thoughts, and emotions, and physical sensations. That's what really constitutes meaningful life. I mean, really, what else is there besides those experiences? So if we can preserve those very thoughts and feelings forever, isn't that the functional equivalent of eternal life? This is what I've been searching for since childhood."

Lisa fell silent once more. Then she spoke very softly and very deliberately.

"Jason, I'm very fond of you. You've been so kind to me from the moment I arrived. But now you're scaring me. It's as if we're tampering with the universe. It's playing God.

"And I'm also thinking about you. This is such a mammoth undertaking. I know you. I can easily see you becoming so immersed in it that it swallows up your entire life. And if that happens, and the results you're hoping for never materialize – and maybe even if they do -- I fear it will destroy you."

"That's not gonna happen. I have an amazing life, and I'm never going to let it slip away. I know I tend to get passionate about things, but that doesn't mean I can't stay grounded. And I'm sensible enough to know when it's time to throw in the towel if it comes to that. But it's something I have to try. Will you help me?"

"Yes. But if I ever reach the point where I think we're going nowhere, or this is getting out of hand, or my moral qualms prevent me from continuing, I want your word that I can withdraw with your blessing."

"You have my word."

And with that conversation Lisa was on board and we were ready to do some serious planning. That was also the point at which I started writing this memoir. I know there will be skeptics at every turn – even Lisa, until she sees our forward progress. But I myself have no doubts at all. Because the outcome will be so momentous, I am going to write these journal entries as we go along.

Since secrecy will be essential until I'm finished, I'm typing these entries on a separate, personal computer that I have brought from home solely for this purpose. I will never connect this computer to the web. Nor will I connect it to the university's or any other network. It will now be a completely isolated, self-contained unit that no one will ever be able to hack into. And I have not just one, but two complex passwords that I've committed to memory and haven't written down anywhere. I will print each installment after I write it, and that will be my only backup. Email and anything else that requires the web, the network or any other externality will be performed on a separate lab computer.

This memoir isn't just for me. It's for the biographers and historians who will bury themselves in every detail of my life – both scientific and autobiographical. They will debate for years from what inner source a man could summon the vision for such a project and what external events could inspire him to persist.

You might have noticed that the date of this entry is October 23, 2024. Make a mental note of that date. It will become known as the day that Dr. Jason Stramm conceived the idea for inventing eternal life in a laboratory.

CHAPTER 3
HUNTING FOR PICOBES

Thursday, October 24, 2024

For some reason, I didn't mention any of yesterday's news to Jessica when I got home last night. I guess I was afraid of her reaction. Even Lisa had initially resisted. Jessica would be more direct. I didn't want her bursting my balloon. Not that night.

On the drive to work this morning, I was thinking I'd need to come up with a good name for this project. Everyone has heard of the Manhattan Project, so named because it originated in New York. I didn't think the "St. Louis Project" had quite the same ring. I liked "Enigma," but that name had already been taken and I also didn't want my project to be associated with the Nazis. And I definitely didn't want a military name, like "Operation Seize Memory," or a boring technical name like the "neuron and synapse systems consolidation project."

I suppose I could simply call it the Stramm Project. Would naming it after myself make me appear vain? I don't think so, really, when people think about how revolutionary this is. In fact they might take it as a reflection of my extraordinary modesty that I would give this world-changing discovery such a simple name, rather than a flashier name. I'll run this by Lisa. She usually has good instincts for these sorts of things.

I'll also have to get used to the public spotlight. There will be lots of awards. The Nobel Prize in Physiology or Medicine is not a stretch. There will be media interviews, keynote speeches, and the like. I can't deny that the fame will be exhilarating, but I've always been a nervous public speaker and hope that with enough repetition I'll be able to get over that fear.

I'm probably getting ahead of myself. I can worry about all this once we're further along.

Lisa and I met later this morning to map out an overall plan and figure out precisely what we would have to do at each stage. By lunchtime we had come up with the basic outline. It would largely follow the plan I had mentally mapped out yesterday. There would be four stages: finding and studying the picobes, accessing the electrical signals they were storing, capturing those signals and transferring them to an electronic storage device, and decoding them.

Tuesday, December 10, 2024

For the past several weeks, we've been researching the various probing technologies, hoping to find one or more that would enable us to detect extremely faint electrical signals. What makes this so hard is the needle-in-a-haystack problem. The picobes we're looking for will occupy an infinitesimally small proportion of both the mass and the volume of the temporal lobe. Finding a needle in a haystack would actually be easier. This is more like looking for a molecule in a haystack.

But today, after weeks of research and discussion, we settled on a plan for phase I. The first priority is to find some sign of electrical activity in these dead brains. If we can't do that, we're finished. Once we detect any electrical signals in a given area, no matter how faint, then we can safely assume that my picobes exist and can hone in on where they are.

To find them, we finally settled on a combination of two techniques. The traditional EEG that you've probably had in doctors' offices detects and measures electrical activity, but the electrodes are attached only to the outer skull. We're expecting the picobes to be too deeply embedded in the cerebral cortex for a traditional EEG to give us precise enough information.

We can do better. We'll be working with the brains from cadavers, not those of live patients, so we can dig deeper. We'll be able to cut into the areas of the temporal lobe that we've already identified as the most likely homes for the picobes, implant the electrodes there, and move them around using a technique called "intracranial EEG." That will hopefully enable us to pick up electrical signals that are too weak to be detected by electrodes that are placed on the skull or even on the surface of the brain.

Still, all of these technologies measure only the total electrical activity in a particular area of the brain, not the electrical activity of individual neurons. To better pinpoint the location of any picobes that we detect, our plan is to follow up the intracranial EEG exploration with another technique called magnetoencephalography, or "MEG."

MEG measures the magnetic field generated by electrical activity in the brain, and today's version of it produces even better spatial resolution than the intracranial EEG. It doesn't work especially well until you're very close to the electrical activity that you're looking for, but once the intracranial EEG detects electrical signals in a given area, we hope to combine that information with what we can learn from the MEG to zero in more closely on the locations of individual picobes.

Once we're satisfied that we know precisely where the picobes are, we'll then need to use other advanced technology to actually see them. We'll want direct, close-up optical images at the cellular and molecular levels. I have some ideas about the best technologies for doing so, but let's not worry about that just yet.

It will take some time to acquire the necessary equipment, so I placed the order for the intracranial EEG today. I didn't order the MEG equipment, because they said that would take only about two weeks, and I figured we wouldn't be using it until we first detect the picobes electronically and spend a good deal of time probing the areas around them. Money, luckily, is not an issue, at least for now. I've carefully conserved my grant money and still have plenty of it left.

Wednesday, December 11, 2024

Up to now, I still hadn't told Jessica about any of this. She knew that Lisa and I had been probing dead brains to identify the most likely places to find picobes later *in live humans*. And that had indeed been our original plan. She had no idea that we were now expecting to find live picobes in the dead brains themselves.

At least unconsciously – maybe consciously as well – I guess I had been avoiding telling her for fear that she would ridicule the idea. But I knew that I couldn't put this off forever. So last night I explained to her what we were doing.

As I had expected, Jessica was incredulous. Just like Lisa when I first sprung this on her, only less diplomatic.

"You're serious."

"Quite serious."

"I'm sorry, Jason, but this is one of your nuttiest ideas yet. The brains you're taking from cadavers aren't alive. That's why you're able to take them. There's no heart to keep blood circulating. The brain isn't getting any more nutrients. It takes energy to sustain these electrical signals. All the energy is long gone."

"Actually, I don't think so. I think something is locking in the electrical signals that were there when the person died – something that's sealing their escape route. And the equipment we've ordered will help us find out once and for all whether I'm right. If I am, this will be huge."

"And how long do you think it will take to find out?"

"I can't say. It could happen the first day, or it could take months. But I'm not going to give up until I'm nearly certain that these picobes don't exist."

"You're still calling them 'picobes'? That's cute."

Then she laughed and added further insult.

"By the way, if I die before you, don't do this with my brain – I wouldn't want you to discover all my evil thoughts."

"Don't mock me. This is something I've thought about for a long time. I've been looking at all kinds of evidence, and I think the chances of these picobes surviving the person's death are very high. Lisa has been examining the evidence too, and after some initial skepticism she agrees with me that the odds are very good. So I'm not going to let somebody who has no idea what she's talking about ridicule the idea. I now regret that I even told you."

"Well, as usual, you told me months after telling Lisa. I'm obviously not the confidant that she is."

"Is that what this is about? You can't stand the fact that I discussed this with my co-worker, who knows the ins and outs of this research and respects it, before I told you?"

"I don't know what your relationship with Lisa even is. You two seem awfully chummy. I'm lucky if you ever tell me anything about your life outside this house."

"I don't like where this conversation is going. Lisa is my assistant, nothing more. There's a reason I share things like this with her first. And if you have to know, there's a reason that I waited this long to tell you. I knew you would trivialize my work, as you always do. And you've confirmed that I was right."

"Fine, Jason. If you want to waste the next several months of your life hunting for these imaginary treasures – which, amazingly, none of the thousands of brilliant neuroscientists who have been studying the brain for decades have ever stumbled upon – have a good time. Just don't delude yourself into thinking you're doing something worthwhile."

There was a lot of anger that I wanted to hurl at her at that moment, but I suppressed it. I would never have demeaned her work in the way she's demeaning mine. But really, I don't even care. I could give a flying fuck what she says or does. If her goal is to drive me further away from her and closer to Lisa, she's succeeded.

I didn't sleep well after that, and in the morning Jessica and I didn't speak – not a word. I took refuge in spending a little extra time with Zeke before driving him to pre-school.

When I arrived at the lab, I was still upset over the previous night's argument. Like any married couple, we had argued about small things from time to time. But never had our arguments been this vicious. There's no way I'm ever going to speak to her again until she apologizes. And means it. And if she wants to think I'm having an affair with Lisa, fine. I'm not going to disabuse her of it. Let her think it if she wants to.

Anyway, I'm now putting this whole thing out of my mind and concentrating on my work. Unfortunately I've just learned that it will take about six weeks to receive the intracranial EEG equipment. We'll use that time to do additional physical exploration of the areas that we expect to probe electronically, but it will be a long six weeks.

Thursday, December 12, 2024

I know I said I wouldn't speak to Jessica again until she apologizes. But when I got home from work last night, I couldn't stand the tension any more. Besides, we couldn't maintain this silence without completely discombobulating Zeke.

So I took the high road and spoke first. I explained to her calmly that the things she was saying the previous night had been very upsetting to me. She burst into tears and apologized. She said she realizes she had said some hurtful things, she truly does respect my work, and she is really sorry. I started to mist up too and told her I was sorry I hadn't handled it better. We hugged. Order was restored, though I still had this uneasy feeling that when my project heats up, as I know it soon will, this charged atmosphere could return. For now, though, I'm determined to just focus on the short term.

At the lab this morning, Lisa and I brainstormed (no pun intended) further on how to prioritize the next several weeks as we await the intracranial EEG equipment. We agreed that most of our time will be spent continuing to physically probe the tissue in the temporal lobe. But I also told her that if she would like to take some vacation this would be a good time to do so. She was grateful and arranged to take off two weeks to spend with her boyfriend in Miami, starting on the 23rd. I immediately regretted that I had offered her the time off.

Thursday, December 26, 2024

Yesterday was Christmas. We all had a nice time at home. Zeke was old enough to understand that he would be receiving lots of presents on Christmas Day, and for several days leading up to it he would ask us how many more days until Christmas. When the time came he was very excited, and we opened presents first thing in the morning.

It turned out to actually be a bit of a cranky day for him, but in between short bouts of whining and fussing he enjoyed most of his presents and even seemed to like it when Jessica and I gave each other presents. My mother always spends Christmas Day with us, and this year she gave Zeke a highly sophisticated talking elephant, which he loved.

I know I shouldn't be dwelling on this, but Lisa has been gone since last Friday and won't be returning from her vacation until a week from Monday, another eleven days not even counting today. I really miss her a lot, and I feel particular distress when I think about her and her ungrateful boyfriend putting their bodies together. There's no way that Nazi bastard deserves her.

Monday, January 6, 2025

Today is the day Lisa returned to the lab. I arrived at work earlier than usual, around 7 a.m. Lisa was due to arrive at 8:30. I had bought her a little welcome-home gift, a box of Marshall Field's chocolates, which I knew she loved.

Lisa is always punctual, so at 8:30 I expected her to walk in at any moment. But she didn't. By about 9:00 I was starting to worry. What if she's decided to stay in Miami? Surely she would have told me. She would never simply not show up. Then again, maybe she realized I had developed these strong feelings for her, and she couldn't bring herself to tell me.

At 9:15, she walked through the door to the lab, out of breath and apologizing for being so late. Her car wouldn't start after two weeks in the cold winter weather here, and she had needed to find someone to give her a ride.

No matter. She looked stunning. She had spent time on the beach in Miami and had a beautiful tan to show for it. My longing for her was overwhelming now, but I tried to appear as casual as I could, telling her not to worry. And I have battery cables, so I offered to drive her home at lunchtime and get the car started. She said thanks but no need, because her next-door neighbor was going to do that for her after work.

I gave her the chocolates, and she rewarded me with her amazing smile.

"Oh, that is *so* sweet! Thank you so much. You remembered that I love these."

I was hoping she would give me another hug, but she didn't. Instead she went straight for the chocolates and said they were delicious. I told her it was great to have her back and asked her whether she had had a good time in Miami.

"Yes, it was wonderful. It's the first time we've had more than a three-day weekend together since I started here. I also met Manny's parents for the first time. That was a bit scary, but they seem very nice, and I think we really hit it off. How was your Christmas?"

I *really* didn't like the fact that she was meeting his parents. That sounds serious. I had been hoping she would leave that asshole. Now it sounds like just the opposite. But I couldn't let on that this was bothering me, and she had just asked me about my Christmas.

"Great. We didn't go anywhere, but it was nice to get away from the lab for a couple days and spend some quality time with Jessica and Zeke. Glad to hear you had a nice time."

"Fantastic. Well, I should check my email and get back to my work."

And with that, she smiled again and went off to her cubicle.

Thursday, January 16, 2025

The equipment arrived this afternoon, several days early! The company provided the initial setup. The guy who did the setup was meticulous and took the time to explain how to use it. The system was set up so that Lisa and I could use it simultaneously and on our own separate brain specimens.

I could tell the setup guy was immediately enamored of Lisa and in no particular hurry to leave. He was really pouring on the charm, which I found irritating. But she didn't encourage him in any way, and when he left we both stood silently for a moment admiring the brand new equipment that would soon send us off on our adventure.

Friday, January 17, 2025

This is our first day actually using the intracranial EEG equipment. Although the device has been around for decades, it has become steadily more sophisticated over time. The spatial resolution has become so much higher, and it's become capable of penetrating much more deeply into the brain tissue than ever before.

Unfortunately, with those enhancements it has also become much more complicated to operate. It took us the better part of today to start feeling as if we know what we we're doing. By the end of the day, though, we felt we had a handle on it. We were both eager to start some in-depth electrical scanning on Monday. It's killing me that after waiting for weeks for the equipment, I now have to wait around for another three days to start using it.

Saturday, January 18, 2025

I couldn't wait until Monday. This was just too exciting. So I came to work. Jessica wasn't pleased, because today is the first day in a couple weeks that we've had sunshine and mild temperatures, and she had hoped we could go on a family walk.

"Normally I'd love to, but I'm really anxious to see how this next phase of the project will work. Couldn't we go for a family walk tomorrow? I'll only be away a few hours and I'll come home as soon as I can."

"But won't you need Lisa there in order to get started?"

"No, this is something I can begin by myself. She'll be able to pick up on it when she gets in on Monday."

And off I went. In the car, I wondered whether Jessica's question had been her sneaky way of finding out whether Lisa would be joining me at the lab today. But I don't think so. I've been very good at concealing my feelings about Lisa, and I'm pretty sure Jessica is finally over that concern. I think she was just hoping to persuade me that a nice family outing would be preferable to working at the lab.

Ordinarily it would be, but not today. I got settled in at the lab and immediately went to work using the intracranial EEG to probe the brain tissue in the areas that both Lisa and I had agreed afforded the most fertile ground for my picobes.

All morning, I poked and prodded, with nothing to show for it. But I wasn't discouraged. I've known from the start that finding any of these tiny needles in this massive haystack would likely take weeks or even months. I grabbed a quick lunch and resumed the probing in the afternoon.

At one point I thought I had detected something, but it was a false alarm. That kept the adrenalin flowing, though, and I kept moving the electrodes ever so slightly to nearby areas. Still nothing. I kept probing.

When I eventually looked up at the clock, it was 9 pm.

Shit!!! I had told Jessica I would be only a few hours. I called her to tell her I was about to leave for home. She told me in a fairly icy tone that Zeke had been waiting for me, but that he had ended up falling asleep about two hours ago, and so now I won't see him until the morning. I said I was sorry, time just got away from me, but I promise we'll do something fun tomorrow.

Monday, January 20, 2025

As I had promised, Jessica, Zeke, and I went for a nice family walk yesterday along a nearby nature trail. Zeke had a great time picking up sticks and breaking them in half.

But I have to admit that every few minutes my mind would refocus on the prospect of finding my elusive picobes. I've been fantasizing about finding them for several years, and now that I had a serious chance to discover them even in brains that were otherwise dead, it wasn't possible to put the project out of my mind for very long.

So I got to work early this morning, beating Lisa by about two hours. I immediately resumed my probing with the intracranial EEG, as did Lisa when she got in. We both labored all day, but unfortunately no glimpses of picobes just yet.

Tuesday, March 4, 2025
We've now been at this for more than six weeks and have found not a single encouraging sign of picobes. Every day we both come to the lab and poke and prod with our fancy equipment. As excited as I was about coming to work when I first conceived the idea – and for weeks afterwards – that's how much I've hated coming to work these past few weeks.

It's not just the oppressive boredom of probing, coming up short, moving the electrodes, probing some more, coming up short again, moving the electrodes yet again, and again, and again. That's bad enough. It's more the feelings of frustration and fear. I fear that Jessica was right – that my life dream, in which I've invested so many precious years and so much labor, opportunity cost, and emotion – has been a fool's errand.

Despite how much I now hate coming to the lab, I've been working longer and longer hours in what I'm starting to regard as an increasingly futile search for something that just plain doesn't exist and never has. When I first started probing with the intracranial EEG, I typically left for home around 6 pm. But with each day of failure, I convinced myself that at any moment I could strike paydirt. So I started staying later and later. These days, my typical lab time runs from around 7 a.m. till 10 or 11 pm. I've been grabbing a quick lunch, skipping dinner, drinking more and more coffee, and getting 5-6 hours of sleep if I'm lucky. I've come in on a few Saturdays, but no Sundays. I know I've lost some weight, though I haven't stepped on a scale to measure how much.

I really can't blame this on anyone else. Dr. Patel encouraged me to pursue this project, but in fairness he never suggested that my picobes would survive in the brains of cadavers. Then again, he did assure me that with enough persistence I would at least find them in the brains of living subjects. Did he really believe that, or was he just too cowardly to tell me my hypothesis was ridiculous? If it was the latter, I'll never forgive him. I've relied heavily on his encouragement in deciding to stick with this for so long. If he didn't really mean it, he's done me a real disservice.

Lisa too. Yes, she was skeptical at first, and she was honest enough to tell me so, which I appreciated. But she ultimately led me to believe that she shared my optimism about this project, and she knew I couldn't have gone this far out on a limb without her support and active assistance. Was she sincere? Maybe yes, maybe no. It's entirely possible she went along because she didn't have the fortitude to tell me to my face that she thought this whole thing was a pipe dream, knowing that I might lash out at her for having so little faith in me. Or maybe she worried I would even fire her if she didn't feign optimism. If that's what's going on, she's someone I'll never forgive either. If she cared about me with one-tenth of the passion she apparently reserves for her fucking

"Manny," she would never have sent me off on this futile, directionless hunt for an imaginary treasure.

She also has no hesitation in going home each day at 5 pm. Once the clock strikes five, she's gone. God forbid she should stay until 5:05, let alone till late at night as I do.

I can tell that this impasse is taking its toll on her, though. She had always been such a warm, cheerful presence. Her smile always lit up what was otherwise a pretty drab laboratory environment. That smile seems to be gone. Maybe it was a fake, a forced smile from the outset, and I was too taken in by her physical beauty to see through the façade.

Or maybe I'm being too hard on her. Maybe my own mood is affecting hers, and the poor woman is getting just as discouraged as I am.

Anyway, last night Jessica and I had another argument. I didn't get home until close to midnight, and I must have awakened her when I came in the door.

"Nice of you to show up."

"I really don't need any of your sarcasm just now."

"Can you see what's happening to you? This project of yours is becoming an obsession. It's unhealthy – dangerously so. And it's not just you. You're crowding out every other person and every other thing in your life. Including your family."

"You're getting a little hysterical. I spend plenty of time with my family. This project isn't the only important thing in my life. But it is extremely important to me. It has the potential – I would even say the likelihood – of being transformative. I'll make Copernicus seem like an irrelevancy by comparison."

As I said those words, I knew I wasn't being honest. The truth was that my doubts had grown very large. But I wasn't about to admit that to Jessica, not with the way she was talking to me now.

"Are you listening to yourself? You're comparing yourself to Copernicus? And *I'm* the one who's getting hysterical?"

"Now listen to me, just for once. I'm a scientist. Scientific discovery is what turns me on. I get pleasure and enormous fulfillment out of it. I set ambitious goals for myself and I work toward those goals. I like making tangible progress and ultimately achieving those goals. That's who I am."

"So this is just your way of passing the time?"

"Now you're trivializing my work. Again. Why do you always have to argue with me about my work? Why are you always trying to minimize it? I know you think it's all a bunch of bullshit. If you want to think that, go ahead. But you know that I believe in it, and you know how important it is to me. Why are you being so cruel?"

At that, she softened a bit.

"OK, Jason. I'm not trying to minimize your work. I'm really not. But you have no idea how much this is hurting me and Zeke. I'm very worried about the effect all this is having on our family, especially Zeke. He needs an engaged father. And I need an engaged husband. You're rarely home, and even when you're physically here, you're off in your own world."

"Fine. I still think you're exaggerating the amount of time I spend in the lab. But I'll try to spend more time at home."

"Jason, it's not just the family life I'm worried about. It's you. I don't begrudge you being passionate about your work. To the contrary. That's always been one of the things about you that's so exciting. But I think you've crossed the line from passion to obsession. You've blocked out all the people who care about you and all the things that give meaning to the only life you have. It's getting out of control. I think you need to see somebody."

"I'm mentally ill, then. That's what you're saying?"

"I didn't say that."

"Not in so many words. But you just said I should 'see somebody'? What the hell does that mean?"

"Jason, I know I've said some harsh things to you. I'm sorry for all of them. But I remember how happy we were in our early days together, and I see all that going down the tubes. I worry all the time that you're headed in a very dangerous direction and that you've become so preoccupied with this project that you're not able to see it yourself. That's why I think counseling could be helpful."

I took a deep breath.

"I hate all this arguing. I really, really hate it. I'll try to be a better husband and a better father. But you're wrong about this becoming an obsession. This project means a lot to me, and yes, I'm passionate about it. But I'm not detached from reality. I recognize that it's taking a huge amount of my time, and I've been willing to put in that time because it's something I believe in and because this intense time commitment is short-term."

I continued.

"Remember Houston? My hours right now aren't any worse than they were for both of us then. If anything, it was worse then. But we were OK with that because we both knew that was a short-term sacrifice, just like this. It's going to be a little while longer, just until I can determine whether my picobes exist. Then I'll know whether this whole project is even a go. Once I find that out one way or the other, I'll finally be able to exhale and my work schedule will return to normal. I promise. Just give me some time. And some space."

She clearly wasn't convinced. I'm sure she didn't believe that my work schedule would ever return to normal, and I don't think I persuaded her that I don't need to see a shrink. But at least, for the first time in a while, we were able to discuss this with each other civilly, even tenderly. That made a big difference.

Still, I can't overcome my doubts that I will ever achieve this dream. I also continue to hate the monotony of this relentless poking at dead brains and the demoralizing results that repeat themselves day after day after fucking day. And I really hate the fact that Jessica can't tell the difference between passion and mental illness. Jesus!

Monday, March 24, 2025

It's now been about three more weeks of the same. I know I had promised Jessica that I'd start working more reasonable hours, but something keeps sucking me back into the lab, in one last desperate search for my picobes. If anything, my hours have been even a little longer than before and my stress levels have been even more heightened – if that's possible.

Jessica and I have started bickering again. None of the arguments have been as biting as some of the earlier ones, but there's a lingering tension that I can feel whenever I'm home. This past weekend was no exception. I'm really getting fed up with this. Her manner with me is very abrupt. She seems to speak to me only when there's some practical need to do so, like telling me that she'll need my car to get to work one day this coming week because hers needs a repair, and so I'll have to take a bus to the lab that day. And when she does speak to me, there's no warmth or joy in her voice. It's all very matter-of-fact, even a bit icy. All indications are that she despises me. I can't say I feel any warmth toward her either.

I think Zeke is picking up on this. He seems a little more clingy than usual, always wanting to be in the same room as his mother or me and frequently looking up, probably to make sure one of us is still there. And I notice he's more serious than usual, not his normal smiley, laughing self. I really have to make sure I spend more time with him. I will definitely do that, as soon as I get past this critical juncture in my project, which is approaching the point where I'll have to make a concrete decision whether to continue or give up.

Lisa and I had a candid discussion today about exactly that. We agreed that we're not making any headway at all. We accepted that there is a point at which our continuing failure to detect any electrical signals will require us to abandon the project, and we agreed that that point was fast approaching.

Lisa was very subdued during that conversation, as she has been over the past few weeks. The warmth in her manner doesn't seem to be there anymore. I hope I'm just imagining this, but I'm starting to think that the changes in her personality and in our relationship aren't due entirely to our collective disappointment in our work. I'm sensing that she's starting to find me personally off-putting, just as Melissa Santos did when she broke up with me in college and maybe as Jessica now feels.

This seems to be a pattern. The women in my life find me interesting and even appealing at first, but once they get to know me, they're invariably disappointed. Lisa is very perceptive, and I suspect she's figured out by now that my feelings for her go beyond our work relationship and even our friendship. That might be what's putting her off. And the more distant Lisa becomes, the more I seem to look for excuses to go over to her cubicle and talk with her. I'm probably just pushing her away even more, but I can't seem to help myself.

Sometimes life gets to be too much. Last night, after Lisa had left and I was all alone in the lab, I turned off all the lights, sat down in a chair, and cried nonstop in the darkness of my solitude for half-an-hour. Not just sniffling and sobbing, but tears pouring out in a torrential rain.

Tuesday, March 25, 2025
In one instant today, everything changed.

It happened at about 11:00 a.m. Lisa came to my cubicle and excitedly told me to come to her work station right away. She looked as if she'd just won the lottery.

When we got there, she pointed to the indicators on the intracranial EEG. Then she spoke deliberately.

"All morning I wasn't getting anything at all, just like the last several weeks. The tissue was dead. And then suddenly, look!"

She had definitely picked up something. The monitor was registering what appeared to be some electrical signals. They were faint, to be sure, but they were the very first time we had detected any electrical energy in dead brains. And they were consistent with the way we expected electrical signals to register. Afraid of false hopes, we talked hurriedly about whether they might be something else, or whether there could be a flaw in the equipment. But for a number of reasons we felt able to eliminate those possibilities.

We carefully marked the spot where the electrodes that picked up those signals had been placed. Just then, my phone rang. I ignored it. We stared at the monitor a little longer and then decided to move the electrodes ever so slightly. My heart was pounding now. The electrical signals stopped for a split second and then picked up again, with the same magnitude. We marked that spot too. And then another move. This time we lost the signals. We moved the electrodes once more. Still nothing. Then we moved the electrodes again. Now the signals returned. Another move. This time, the signals not only stayed with us continuously, but intensified. We were surely getting closer to the source.

Lisa teared up. And then I teared up. She smiled for what seemed like the first time in weeks, took out a tissue, wiped away the tears, and, before I realized what was happening, kissed me. On the lips!

"I'm so sorry, Jason! How embarrassing! I know that was completely unprofessional. Don't get the wrong idea. I'm just so happy about all this! And I'm really, really happy for you."

I wanted to respond in kind, but for some reason I didn't. Fear, I think. I just stood there awkwardly and mumbled something about how happy I was too and how much I've appreciated everything she's done.

Lisa's spontaneous reaction came as a shock – a particularly exciting one --but after that we both focused on the intracranial EEG process. For hours we continually moved the electrodes tiny distances and recorded the responses, getting a pretty fair mapping of the most electricity-rich pockets of tissue in that same small section of the temporal lobe. In some areas we detected exceptionally strong electrical signals. In other areas they were weak or nonexistent.

These were my picobes, my babies. I felt a surge of grateful appreciation for Dr. Patel, without whose encouragement I might have given up long ago. And I felt even greater warmth for Lisa, who I now think never doubted that I was on to something really big. And I realized that while I had been a little down the past few weeks, it really hadn't been that bad – just the expected few steps backward before today's giant leap forward.

I knew we would now need the MEG equipment soon, and the company had told me shipping would take about two weeks. So I immediately placed the order.

Once the intracranial EEG enables us to identify the rough proximity of the picobes, the MEG will give us additional information. Combining those results will help us better pinpoint the locations of the picobes.

But I also knew we would need more than that. Even the combination of the intracranial EEG and the MEG won't get us optical images of the individual picobes, much less their molecular structures in the required level of detail. For that, we'll need something far more high-powered.

That brings me to Dr. Lihong Wang. In 2011, Dr. Wang, a biochemical engineer then based at Washington University, invented a game-changing technique that he named "TRUE." This was an acronym for "time-reversed ultrasonically encoded" optical focusing. Together with more recent breakthroughs in electron microscopes, mainly in the early 2020s, TRUE can now give researchers and clinicians vivid optical images of cellular and molecular structures that are buried deep inside previously obstructive tissue.

I'll elaborate on TRUE a little more when we get to that stage, but for now I'll just mention that today I also put in an order for it and the accompanying super-high-power electron microscopes. These are the most powerful microscopes currently available. They are much better than light microscopes, and a quantum leap above even the most advanced microscopes available ten years ago. They will enable us to actually see the tiniest parts of the picobes up close once we pinpoint their exact locations.

So mark this date down too: March 25, 2025. That's the day Dr. Jason Stramm discovered stored memory in dead people's brains and set the stage for replicating eternal life.

Wednesday, March 26, 2025

The euphoria of yesterday's discovery made it very hard for me to leave the lab at a decent hour, but I did anyway, surprising Jessica at about 5:30 pm. For one thing I couldn't wait to share my news. I suppose I had a strong "I told you so" desire, but honestly, that really wasn't it. Now that I felt better about myself and my work, I guess I felt a renewed warmth toward Jessica. We had been together now more than six years, had brought a wonderful little boy into the world, and still knew each other better than anyone else knew either of us. And despite the cold war that had been brewing for several months, I believed the mutual affection was still there.

I startled her when I walked in and looked straight at her.

"I have something to tell you."

Now she looked nervous, even frightened. I didn't want to keep her in suspense. In fact it crossed my mind that she might have been expecting me to say I was leaving her. But I have to admit I relished the melodrama. In the car on the way home I had practiced how I would tell her the news. I spoke calmly and quietly.

"Today we found my picobes."

"Oh, my God!"

Pause.

"How sure are you? I mean, is this a definite finding?"

"Yes. We are 100% certain. The intracranial EEG doesn't lie. We detected electrical signals coming from lots of places in the temporal lobe. We checked and re-checked and re-checked. It's been years of work and years of uncertainty. And now this is actually happening. This is like a dream, only it's real."

Jessica now had tears in her eyes. She said she was so very happy for me, and we hugged.

While holding her, I told her about the despair I had felt the night before.

And then I couldn't stop chattering about all the gory details of the discovery. I began speaking in rapid-fire, excited tones.

"There's still a ton of work to do, but the important thing is that I've discovered for the first time ever that this electrical energy is preserved in the brain even after the person dies. This is fucking huge! And now that I know for sure that my picobes exist, I feel this all-consuming relief. I'm no longer going to feel this compulsion to work crazy hours. I can have a normal family life again and still feel fulfilled at the lab as I progress step by step. Everything is going to fall into place now. I can't believe how good life is going to be."

"Jason, I know that as you're saying these words you really mean them. But I also know you. As you get closer and closer to the finish line, you're going to get more and more excited and want to spend more and more time at the lab. Please promise me you'll fight that temptation and force yourself to come home at a decent hour – and think about things other than work when you're home. It won't come easily to you. You'll have to focus consciously on making that your daily routine."

"I promise. And it won't be as hard as you think. It's what I really want."

That was last night. This morning was another one of those mornings where I couldn't wait to get to work. Neither could Lisa. In the roughly two weeks that it would take for the MEG and TRUE equipment to arrive, our goal was to do everything we needed to do with the intracranial EEG to identify the areas where we would focus MEG and then TRUE for the optical images.

Working with a different brain specimen, I was able to reproduce the same discoveries that Lisa had made yesterday with the brain she was working with. This was a key finding. It means that the same geographic patterns in one person's brain are present in the brains of other individuals.

That discovery also enabled us to parcel out our respective assignments. We divided up the areas of the temporal lobe that we would each be responsible for mapping. We set up a schedule, so that by the time the MEG and TRUE equipment arrived, we would together have identified all the areas that we could then target with greater precision and observe up close.

Today we both found that our mapping was going very well – slightly faster and more smoothly than we had predicted. I reminded myself of last night's promise to Jessica that from now on I would come home regularly at a decent hour. I didn't want to break that promise just 24 hours later, so even though in my renewed excitement I would have preferred to keep going longer, I came home even earlier than the night before – around 4:30 pm. Jessica didn't get home until her usual 5:15, so I was able to discharge our nanny early and have some one-on-one time with Zeke. When Jessica got home she was very pleased.

Thursday, April 3, 2025
This afternoon we finished all of our preparatory work, a little ahead of schedule. And we did it working normal hours. I've kept my promise to Jessica

and I'm really enjoying having time at home with her and Zeke.

Monday, April 7, 2041

All the equipment for both the MEG and TRUE arrived today as promised. I was pleased that the setup guy wasn't the same one who had set up the intracranial EEG system. This one was an older man, I'd say in his 60s, and he was all business. There was none of the irritating flirting with Lisa like last time. That had really pissed me off. I should probably have reported him, but I let it go and it no longer bothers me. It's water under the bridge.

But I have to say that if that same guy had returned this time and carried on the same way, I would have dressed him down with strong language. And I would purposely have done it in front of Lisa, just to humiliate him. Luckily the occasion didn't arise, and as I said, I really don't even think about that incident anymore. It's just that it was so unprofessional and obnoxious. He really was a total asshole.

Anyway, the new guy got both systems up and running, and before he left he made sure we both knew how to operate them and felt comfortable with them. After he left us, we practiced with the MEG. The real work of probing the priority areas will begin tomorrow.

Tuesday, April 8, 2025

I can't believe it. Yesterday everything was fine. Today, we had been using the MEG system for no more than an hour when it completely broke down. It just plain stopped working. I don't know whether it was something we did or a problem with the equipment itself or a problem with the installation. This is really aggravating. I called the company and they agreed to send somebody out, but the soonest he can get here is Thursday.

Thursday, April 10, 2025

The maintenance man showed up this morning and fixed the problem. It was actually something fairly minor.

There are billions of these picobes, so obviously we're not trying to isolate every one of them before we get to the next stage. These are basically trial brains, which we've been using just to make sure the picobes exist, see what they look like, discover their properties, and hopefully access the electricity that they contain. We don't need all of them for those purposes. All we need is a representative sample, and we expect to have that within a couple weeks at the most.

Thursday, May 1, 2025

Well, it took us a little longer than expected to finish the MEG work. There were a couple more equipment failures along the way. The company was responsive, but it still set us back a few days.

I think we've now done as much as we need to do on that front. We've zeroed in on almost 300 picobes in lots of different areas, so we have a fairly representative sample. And I'm confident that we've been able to mark their locations with enough precision to zoom in on them with TRUE.

I mentioned earlier that TRUE was invented in 2011 by a Washington University biochemical engineer named Lihong Wang. TRUE combines ultrasound and light beams in an ingenious way. Here's a brief explanation:

Ultrasound imaging is one way of getting a picture of something inside the body. High-pitched sound waves are beamed, usually through a person's skin, at the target area. They bounce back from that target and are collected by a probe (called a transducer). The probe is attached to a computer. Based on several factors – how loud the sound is when it returns, how high-pitched it is, how long it takes the sound to return to the probe, and various properties of the body parts that it had to pass through – the computer creates a visual image of what the targeted area must look like. That image is then displayed on a monitor.

Ultrasound is a valuable resource. For one thing, it doesn't involve radiation and so is extremely safe when used on live patients, but since we're working with dead brains, that's not an issue for us anyway.

The other benefit, which is highly relevant to our work, is that it can produce accurate images of targets that are much more deeply embedded than those which light beams can provide. Light beams don't travel well through tissue; they scatter as they go through. Sound waves don't scatter very much at all, so they can produce much more detailed images of deeply embedded targets.

Still, the ultrasound image is artificial and indirect. The computer in effect is guessing what the object probably looks like based on the characteristics of the sound waves as they bounce back. It's a pretty good guess, but not the same as the kind of actual picture that light beams can give us.

Dr. Wang gave us the best of both worlds. His TRUE device uses ultrasound to mark out a path to, and then back from, the target. It produces what he has called a "guide star." The light beam then follows that exact path and bounces back. Normally, by the time it bounces back, a light beam that is targeted at an area buried deep within the body becomes so scattered that the resulting picture has very poor resolution. But the genius of Dr. Wang's invention is that, by traveling along the exact path already built by the ultrasound, the light beam bounces straight back to the original focal point, thus creating a real-time optical image far more detailed than what either technology could produce alone. The way I picture it is that I can't shine a flashlight into soil that's beneath the surface, but if I first dig a tunnel into the ground I can then focus the light through that tunnel.

Even better, scientists and engineers in the early 20s made spectacular strides with microscopes. By fitting TRUE with these higher-powered-than-ever electron microscopes, we can now use this combined technology to examine the cells and even the molecules of picobes that are located deep within the cortical folds.

Since we're dealing with dead brains rather than live subjects, you might be wondering why we don't just cut into the brain tissue until we reach the target areas. But that would mean losing lots of tissue in the process, and we ultimately want to be able to scan wider swaths of the brain than we could if we had to destroy some of the picobes in order to examine others. So combining TRUE with the most powerful microscopes available enables us to have our cake and eat it too.

We started eating that cake today. This was exciting beyond belief. Imagine spending your whole professional life searching for a treasure – not just any treasure, but one that will change the world -- and then finally, one day, getting to hold it in your sweaty palms.

Of course I can't physically hold my picobes. But that's what it feels like. It was thrilling enough a few weeks ago when I was able to detect the electrical activity that betrayed their existence. It was wonderful later to discover exactly where they live. But now I'm actually seeing the creatures themselves, with my own eyes. And not only seeing them, but zooming in on their tiniest innermost parts.

It reminds me of how I felt when I first saw an ultrasound image of Zeke in utero. All along I had known he was in there, but actually seeing him with my own eyes brought my excitement to a new level.

And before you get judgmental about my analogizing picobes to human children, or take this as still "more" evidence of my moral decay or my falling off the deep end, let me state for the record: I am fully aware that picobes aren't children. But they're both my babies and it was wonderful to meet them for the first time, even though I couldn't yet touch them. That's the only point of my analogy, OK?

It was clear that we were looking at individual neurons. After years of research, I know what neurons look like, and that is positively what these are. I can see their cell bodies, their axons, and their dendrites. I can see their membranes. This is just how I've always imagined they would look. They are beautiful.

I can tell Lisa is awed as well. I hear multiple offerings of "wow!" and "Oh, my God," and at least one "Oh, my sweet Lord!," with one "Holy shit!" interspersed. My reactions were similar, though I'm not sure what the atheist equivalent of "Oh, my God" is.

I really can't find the words to capture the ecstasy that I feel as I look at more and more of my picobes. I know they're just body parts, not independent live organisms, but I can't help feeling paternal toward them.

Neither of us could contain our excitement long enough to take even a short break. Even Lisa, who is normally out the door by 5 pm at the latest, stayed until about 7:30. I knew I had promised Jessica that I'd be coming home at a normal time from this point on, but there was no way I could have torn myself away at that hour. I knew she would understand that this is the first day I've gotten to view my picobes up close and how gratifying that is, and of course I planned to emphasize that this is just a one-time relapse and that I'll be back on schedule starting tomorrow.

So I called to tell her all this and let her know I'd be home late. I forgot to tell her the part about this being only a one-time thing, but I got out the rest. She was understanding, as I had expected, but encouraged me not to stay *too* late because I would need my sleep the next several days and it was important to pace myself. "This is a marathon," she reminded me, "not a sprint."

As it turns out, I ended up staying extremely late tonight. The more picobes I looked at, the more addictive it became. And even when I finally forced myself to stop, I wanted to write today's journal entry before the events and the emotions become as distant a memory as the data stored in my picobes.

Friday, May 2, 2025

Today was pretty much just more of the same, but without the monotony that had been so oppressive at earlier stages. Knowing that the picobes exist, and in fact being able to actually see them, have made the difference between giving up on the whole project and going forward with optimism and exhilaration. The effect on my mood has been indescribable.

I wasn't able to keep my promise to Jessica. Tonight I worked until 9:15 and got home at 9:45. She wasn't pleased, but we didn't have an all-out brawl either. I think she's beginning to realize how momentous this is and what a crucial stage we're at – and that I'm constitutionally incapable of leaving earlier when I'm as immersed in the project as I now am. So at least for a while, I think she's going to tolerate my hours.

Wednesday, May 14, 2025

I know I have to heed Jessica's reminder that this is a marathon and not a sprint – and not just for my own health but for the sake of our family unit. So once I start making some tangible headway into the next leg of the project, I'm going to discipline myself.

That next leg started today, and it involves solving a puzzle: Why doesn't the electrical energy in these neurons just escape? Why doesn't it leave through the same door it entered?

Every neuron has a cell body that is encased in a thin fatty membrane, a kind of bag that holds the cell together and keeps unwanted material out. The cell also has an axon and usually many dendrites. These are long, thin structures that extend out from the cell body.

Proteins live in the membrane. The proteins are of different types, and they perform different functions. Their main function is to facilitate the flow of nutrients and ions (electrically-charged atoms and molecules) through the membrane and into the cell body, and the flow of waste material and undigested material out of the cell body.

I would have expected that all this internal electrical energy would cause the pressure inside the cell body to exceed the pressure outside. On that assumption, I would have thought the electrical energy that is storing the memories would simply escape from the cell body and disperse. Am I wrong about that? Is there a simple physics explanation? For example, maybe the tissue surrounding the picobe is denser than the environment within, so that it's simply harder for the electricity to get out? Or is there some other explanation?

I guess I must have intuitively expected the electricity not to escape all along. Otherwise, how could I have been so confident that the electrical signals would still be contained within the picobes once I had located them?

Anyway, my first hypothesis is that the answer has something to do with the membrane that encloses the cell body. That's where the holes are. I need to find out why the electricity doesn't simply flee through those holes.

This is where Lisa's biochemistry background was critical. She explained to me, in more detail, how the various substances travel in and out of the cell body. Some of this I had already known. Other parts were new. Here's how Lisa explained it:

"OK, there are lots of different substances that have to travel into and out of the cell body. Nutrients have to come in. So do ions, in order to create the electrical charge essential to memory. Other things have to leave – waste products, undigested material, and so on."

"I get that. But explain to me exactly what propels these things in and out. Is it electrical forces? Chemical? Mechanical?"

"A little bit of each. You've seen the holes in the membrane. They're the protein channels. The lining of these holes is made up of proteins. Nutrients and ions travel passively, without the use of energy, into the cell body through these protein channels.

"Then there are protein transporters. They do require energy. They transport all these substances through the membrane.

"And finally there is a process known as endocytosis. It too requires energy. The outer surface of the membrane physically engulfs the substances it's transporting – it kind of swallows them up – and pushes them through the membrane and releases them into the cell body. The reverse process is exocytosis, where the membrane engulfs the waste products while they're inside the cell body and pushes them back out to the free world."

"But Lisa, the thing is, the electricity is somehow trapped inside these cells. I realize the proteins are no longer there, so they can't actively transport the electricity outside or anywhere else. And since the exocytosis that you just described also requires energy, that's not going to happen in a dead brain either. That, I get. But the holes are still there. We can see them. Why doesn't the electricity just escape through those holes?"

"I don't know. I'm baffled too. The first thing I can think of is that these protein channels are all substance-specific. Maybe the open ones are meant only for the passage of waste products, or undigested material, as opposed to electrical energy."

"But whatever they're designed for, they're still holes. Why wouldn't the electricity naturally head out? Now that the person is dead, I imagine the physical pressure that the ions exert inside the cell body is greater than the pressure outside the cell, right? In addition, ions have charges, and now that the rest of the brain is dead I'm assuming the fields outside these cells have become electrically neutral. So wouldn't ions – whether they're positive or negative – naturally flow into that neutral environment?"

"I'm sorry. I feel as if I should be able to answer that question, but I can't. I'm just hoping we can discover some clues as we see more and more of the molecular structures of these cells."

And with that, Lisa and I both decided to call it a day and think about this some more tomorrow.

Monday, May 19, 2025

The past week I've been consistently staying at the lab until late at night. I've been desperately trying to analyze the holes in the membranes of my picobes, more convinced than ever that they hold the secret to the mysterious ability of the cell body to keep the electrical signals in tow. But so far neither Lisa nor I have made any headway.

That's OK. I didn't expect the answer to be that easy. I just wish I could see some indication that we're further ahead than we were a week ago.

Meanwhile, Jessica and I had another "discussion" last night. This discussion shed less heat and more light than some of the previous ones. To my surprise, this one also wasn't mainly about my hours or my health or my selfish subordination of family life to work. For sure, she was again concerned with my recurring periods of obsession, and indeed she led with that theme. But her primary concern, she said, is even more serious.

"Your project disturbs me at a more fundamental level. What is this all about? I've seen you passionate about your work before, but never like this. What's going on?"

That question made me realize something. I had explained all this to Lisa, but only when Jessica asked me this question straight out did it dawn on me that I had never actually shared my motivations with my own wife.

So I offered an explanation. I told her of my lifelong craving to know more about my parents. And I explained how my belief that there is no afterlife, with the consequence of complete nonexistence upon the occurrence of death, has also been at the core of my psyche since adolescence. But, I told her, I've come to believe that in another sense a person can exist for long after he dies. I now think a person exists for as long as there are memories or other recordings of that person – whether passed on via oral narrative, written down, electronically recorded, or in any other way. As long as someone is thinking of you, you still exist.

It's a continuum, though. Memories start to fade, there comes a point when other people no longer think of you or even know you once lived, and at that point your prior existence becomes meaningless. In that sense, your existence ends. It might not be at the moment of death, but except for a handful of famous individuals, that point is typically reached after one or two generations at the most.

"But, Jason, everyone who has ever breathed has altered the world to that extent and in more profound ways. Do you no longer exist just because no one knows of your experiences or your accomplishments or any of the other ways in which your life made the world a different place?"

"You existed in the past, yes. But I don't care whether you say the person no longer exists or his existence no longer matters. To me, that's just semantics. Either way, one's existence eventually becomes meaningless. So if you want a loved one to exist for a long time, you have to record whatever you can about him or her in the most durable form possible. The more information you record, the longer that person will exist. And you can't record what you don't know. That's what's so wondrous about my discovery. I'm prolonging the person's life by decades, maybe centuries – maybe forever, or at least as long as the universe lasts. And in the process I'm creating a way for others to do the same for the people they love."

"Aren't you the one who's playing with words now? This discovery – even assuming it succeeds, and I think you have to admit that's not a slam dunk -- doesn't enable anyone to continue to exist in any real sense."

"When I say the person continues to exist, I'm not saying they themselves have interests that are worth preserving. I'm just saying they continue to exist in the minds of others. And with my discovery, instead of that existence lasting only another generation or two, it can potentially last to eternity. Isn't that recollection of what another person has done the true meaning of life?"

"So you've discovered the meaning of life? Does that not seem a bit presumptuous?"

"You don't understand me at all. I'm not a philosopher. I'm a scientist. I'm not trying to figure out the meaning of life. Scientific discovery is what turns me on. All I've been trying to say is that without a real afterlife, my work has the potential to make a person's life eternal in a different way."

"But what's the point of eternity without meaning in life? If life doesn't have any meaning for however many years you're considered alive, what's achieved by stretching it out longer?"

"I didn't say life doesn't have any meaning. I'm just saying I don't have any particular interest in trying to isolate that meaning or put some verbal label on it. I'll leave that to the philosophers and the linguists. I'm actually quite sure that life has meaning, at the very least for the people and other sentient life forms that are living it. Yes, it's a fleeting meaning, but it's a meaning nonetheless."

"Fine, let's assume life has meaning and that you don't care what that meaning is. And let's further assume that eternalizing that life prolongs that meaning. Let's even assume your project succeeds completely and you devise a way to preserve these memory cells for eternity. The point is, you yourself, when you die, will never be conscious of it. Other people might discover something about you, but that won't affect you at all. You won't be aware of anything. What good does it do to live forever – if that's what you think this is – if you're not even sentient?"

"Well, I've thought about that. My first thought was that unfortunately this is the best I can do. Think of it as cutting my losses. At the least, it enables me to know *now*, while I'm still sentient, that my memories and the thoughts and feelings they reflect will persist long after my heart is no longer beating and my lungs are no longer breathing. Since there's no afterlife, that's better than nothing, isn't it?"

"But …"

"Wait, there's more. Lately I've been thinking about this at a whole different level. I take back what I said a moment ago. I guess in a way I really thinking about the meaning of life. What exactly does it mean to be alive? Are we human beings really anything more than the thoughts, emotions, and physical sensations that together comprise the whole of our experiences? Those are what we feel. Those are what we think. And if that's basically who we are, and if those thoughts, emotions, and physical sensations last forever, isn't this eternal life in a more direct sense? I'm starting to think that this discovery is about more than simply existing in the minds of *other* people. It's actually about your essence – what you feel and experience – continuing to exist eternally in *your own* mind as well."

"I don't know, Jason. For one thing, I think I'm more than my inner thoughts and feelings. I think I'm also the flesh and bones that make up my body."

"The only reason your flesh and bones matter at all is that they sustain your bodily functions, so that you can actually have those thoughts and feelings and physical sensations and life experiences. Your body is just a means to that end. It has no independent significance whatsoever."

"Let's say I accept that. It's still not really your thoughts, feelings, and physical sensations that are being preserved, is it? It's just the *memories* of those things. Even while I'm alive, I might clearly remember that I felt lots of pain a few years earlier when I fell and broke my arm. But that doesn't mean I'm feeling that pain now."

"What I'm on the verge of discovering is different. I'm resurrecting the original memories, not just the recollections of those memories. Or at the very least, the original memories as they've been edited during the person's life. I'm effectively reconstructing the complete person by reassembling all those impulses that mattered when they occurred. And I'm doing it in a form that can be preserved forever. That's as close to eternal life as any of us are ever going to get, and it's a lot closer than where existing technology can take us."

"I'm exhausted, Jason. Let's go to bed."

And we did.

Monday, June 2, 2025

It's now been almost three weeks since we began probing the component particles that my picobes are made of. I guess I have to say there's been no forward progress during this time. I don't think we're any further along than we were three weeks ago.

That's demoralizing. Until I can learn more about the structure and composition of these tiny neurons, I'll never be able to come up with a way of accessing the electrical signals – the memory data -- that they're storing.

I'm continuing to work ridiculous hours, even longer than before. I can't help myself. I have to get to the bottom of this, and that won't happen when I'm not in the lab. I'll have plenty of time to recuperate later, but right now I have more pressing priorities.

Of course that hasn't stopped Jessica from resurrecting her tired old song about how I'm endangering my health and destroying the family, even losing touch with reality. To the contrary, the reality is that I'm on the verge of a world-changing discovery and I just need to put in a little extra time to achieve it. But she can't see past her own nose. All she can see is that I'm working long hours. And when she starts in on me, all she's doing is causing me more stress and more sleeplessness.

I'm starting to think this isn't just about my being away from the family for more hours during this temporary period. I've come to realize there's a certain amount of professional jealousy operating. Jessica graduated from medical school and with her colleague, Marilyn, has developed a commercially successful ophthalmology practice. But anyone with a medical degree could pretty much do what she and Marilyn have done. She knows that she has never even attempted anything as monumental as what I am on the verge of, let alone achieved it. And she never will.

I think that's really at the heart of it, and I get disgusted when I think about how petty she's being. Of course she'll never admit that, even to herself, but it's becoming pretty clear that that's what's going on.

Even Lisa has been telling me I need to slow down or I'll run myself into the ground. She said it in a nicer way than Jessica did, but I still didn't appreciate it, especially when she told me I should "step back and take a deep breath." I really don't think I need this kind of patronizing "advice" from my young, inexperienced research assistant. And I told her so.

She seemed stung by my words, and she claimed that she had just said that because she was concerned about me and had meant to be supportive, not condescending. I took that as an apology and have now let it go, though I won't be so forgiving if she ever pulls that shit a second time. If she wants to talk that way to her beloved "Manny," that's her business, but that's not the way you talk to an eminent scientist.

Tuesday, June 17, 2025

A couple more weeks have passed since my last journal entry, and still no progress on our microanalysis. I don't know *what the hell* is preventing those electrical signals from escaping.

Meanwhile, just for sport, Jessica continues to berate me about my work hours and my health. Lisa, fortunately, hasn't said a word about it since my stern talk with her. She's been very quiet, performing her daily probing of the picobes without a great deal of small talk or other conversation. She's back to leaving for home at exactly 5:00 on a regular basis and isn't showing the extra effort that I would like to see, but I think I'll leave that alone for now. She's still young and doesn't have the priorities that I expect she'll develop as she matures.

Wednesday, June 25, 2025

I had a eureka moment today. I don't want to get too excited about it yet, because I'll have to test it, but I now have a road map and think this could be the breakthrough I've needed.

The problem has been figuring out why the electricity doesn't escape from the picobes. Why can't it get out the same way it got in?

The cell membranes are transparent, so I can see both inside and outside the cell body. Today, for the first time, I noticed a subtle asymmetry in the protein channels. The opening on the inside end is slightly different from the opening on the outside.

My theory now is that these protein channels aren't just ordinary holes that have somehow been sealed off. Or at least they aren't ordinary seals. Somehow electricity had to be able to enter but later unable to leave. I now think these seals are really one-way valves, kind of like the valves they put on tires. Maybe this is the body's way of making sure that most of the nutrients that enter the cell body stick around until they can be fully digested, though that's just a guess.

In live subjects, as Lisa explained, the ions can enter in many ways. They can be engulfed by the cell membrane and pushed through to the interior of the cell – the process known as endocytosis. They can also be carried through the membrane by protein transporters. And they can enter passively, through the protein channels. My theory is that they continue to enter the cell body until the pileup becomes so great that either the mechanical or the electrical pressure inside the cell equals or exceeds the pressure outside. When the internal pressure builds to that level, no more electricity can enter.

Anyway, that's how the ions get in. But once the person dies, getting out is another matter. Without active proteins, the ions can't hitch rides with the protein transporters. Without the external energy that only a living organism can provide, they also can't get out via exocytosis. And if I'm correct that the protein channels are actually one-way valves, the ions can't escape through that route either. This would leave them effectively trapped forever.

Assuming these protein channels are indeed one-way valves, I still need to find out how those valves actually work. That will be critical later as we figure out how to transfer the electrical signals to a digital storage drive.

Wednesday, July 9, 2025

Well, after two more weeks of staring at my picobes from every possible angle, hoping to find some tangible confirmation that the protein channels are one-way valves, Lisa and I have solved the puzzle. Actually, Lisa deserves the credit for spotting the tiny structure that holds the key. Once she did that, I was able to figure out how these one-way valves work. It was dumb luck in a way, but with enough repetitions and variations I guess it was only a matter of time before we found what we needed.

First of all, Lisa discovered that the passageway through each of these holes isn't cylindrical. It's actually funnel-shaped. The wider opening on the exterior surface of the membrane narrows to an extremely tiny opening on the interior surface. That had not been obvious to us before, but the super-high-powered electron microscopes enabled us to see this now. That alone would explain why it's easier for electricity to enter than to exit.

Still, you would think at least some of the electricity would manage to escape through even the narrow opening. So if that were all there were to it, we would have to assume that some of the electricity has escaped and that all we're seeing is the part that remains. That would be a shame, because it would mean that some of the memory data that I am convinced they have been carrying has been lost.

Happily, there's more. Until today, researchers had thought that these protein channels were completely hollowed out, so that molecules could travel through them passively. The major part of Lisa's discovery today was that they are not hollow all the way through. There is a disk inside the passageway, the tiniest distance away from the interior opening and parallel to it. It is extremely thin and is 99% transparent. I can easily see why it has eluded other researchers.

Anyway, this disk protrudes from one wall of the passageway, like a stalagmite, and is big enough to block *almost* the entire passageway. So even the rare electrical signal that randomly manages to exit briefly through the tiny interior end of the funnel immediately hits the disk and is reflected straight back into the cell body.

This would shatter the conventional wisdom that passage through the protein channels is completely passive. It might be passive on the way in, but because these are one-way valves, these molecules need the active assistance of proteins to get out. And those active proteins won't be there once the person dies. That's why this electricity is still stuck in the cell body. At least that's my working theory.

Like Dr. Patel, I'm the kind of person who believes in crediting the work of my subordinates and giving them positive reinforcement. Lisa is the one who spotted the disk, and I praised and thanked her lavishly for this critical discovery. I could tell that meant a great deal to her. Already I can see a subtle change in her outlook, a bounce in her step. She's hopefully on a return path to her always-sunny disposition, and I think it's only a matter of time before I see that unique warmth and glacier-melting smile on a daily basis once more.

Truth be told, though, we were both experimenting with different combinations of microscope variables, so it was really just a matter of chance that she spotted it before I did. I'm not trying to diminish her accomplishment. It took a good eye to realize she had stumbled upon it. But once she showed it to me, I was the one who did the heavy intellectual lifting, figuring out that without the active assistance of the no-longer-existing proteins the ions wouldn't be able to get past the disk.

Naturally, I never said that to Lisa. I want her to feel that her efforts are contributing to this project and am happy to forego some of the credit if doing so makes her feel valued – which of course she is.

We're now ready for the next phase – figuring out how to get these hermetically-sealed electrical signals out of their shells. Lisa and I are going to strategize about that, first thing in the morning.

CHAPTER 4
OPENING THE GATES

Thursday, July 10, 2025

As much as I love my picobes, what I really value are the electrical signals they are imprisoning. The one-way valves are a godsend. Without them, there wouldn't be any electrical data left to access. But those same one-way valves that have prevented these electrical signals from running away are now keeping their father from embracing them. I need to find a way to liberate them.

It won't be enough to set them free. I have to capture them once they're out. That's the whole point. But one step at a time. There's no shortage of cadavers' brains to experiment on, and not even a shortage of picobes in a single brain. The next step will be to find a way to release the electrical signals, without worrying just yet about capturing them.

So Lisa and I separately researched the various technologies for piercing through microscopic objects. We set a goal of coming up with potential strategies by Monday, when we'll discuss which of these are promising enough to warrant further effort.

My plan is to finish my preliminary research by tomorrow and take off the entire weekend for the first time in what seems like ages. I'm softening a bit in my attitude toward Jessica. To be fair to her, I really have been working long hours, and that's left her with all the child care responsibilities. Of course, the day care center has done the vast bulk of it and even when she's home, our part-time nanny does most of the work. But still.

The fact remains that she doesn't fully understand the immensity, the complexity, or the importance of my project. So I get that she thinks I'm spending too much time at the lab. I'll take the weekend off. And tonight I'll even fill her in on the crucial discovery we made yesterday and the start of the exciting next phase.

Sunday, July 13, 2025

Last Thursday night, as planned, I told Jessica I would be taking the weekend off and described our latest breakthrough. I thought she would be ecstatic about my having some family time and at least mildly congratulatory about the breakthrough. I was wrong. Her reaction to my weekend plans was sarcastic. The import was that I'm making it sound as if I'm doing her a giant favor (which I was, actually, since I was practically bursting at the seams to get back to the research).

And there was virtually no reaction at all when I told her about Lisa's discovery and the fact that I had then figured out what prevents the electricity from escaping. There seems to be literally nothing that Jessica and I can both be happy about at the same time, except I guess Zeke, and I haven't even had as much time with him these past few weeks as I would have liked.

As it turned out, I wasn't able to fully stick to my plan to spend the weekend at home. I didn't get as much done Friday as I had hoped and, as I explained to Jessica in terms any person with an IQ over 50 would understand, Lisa and I had arranged to meet Monday to update each other on what we've found so far. Since I didn't finish my work on Friday, I had no choice but to come in Saturday. Unfortunately I didn't finish Saturday either, so I needed to spend all of Sunday in the lab as well.

None of that registered with Jessica. She claimed not to understand why it was so vital that I meet with Lisa on Monday. Her reasoning was that if my research wasn't coming along as fast as I had hoped it would, I could simply postpone the meeting with Lisa to another day. I was the boss, after all.

I was thinking "Right, just 'postpone' it." The irony here is that she was having a hissy fit that I was failing to honor my commitment to her, yet it didn't bother her in the least that if I didn't go to the lab this weekend I would be reneging on my commitment to Lisa to meet with her on Monday. Of course that subtlety too was completely lost on Jessica.

Monday, July 14, 2025

This morning Lisa and I met as scheduled this morning. Yesterday I had come up with an idea I'm excited about, but Lisa was clearly excited about her own idea, so I let her go first. I felt that my idea was likely to be the more productive path forward, and I wanted her to have the pleasure of sharing her idea before it became anti-climactic. She spoke rapidly, and her facial expressions and gesticulations were as animated as I have ever seen. This is what she said:

"OK, if I sound too full of myself, please forgive me. But after unlocking the explanation for what is preventing the electricity from escaping, and now coming up with a way to free the electricity in a dead person's brain, I feel like I'm on a roll, and I'm kind of bursting. So listen to this!

"We know that in a live human the memories are constantly being refreshed and strengthened. And we know this wouldn't happen without proteins. They're the vehicles that transport most of the nutrients and the ions. And last week we figured out that they're able to escape from the otherwise sealed-off cell, carrying waste and undigested molecules with them, by navigating around the disk that I had spotted near the interior opening.

"So I started thinking that maybe we could use proteins to export the electricity. But of course there aren't any proteins actively operating in the brains of dead people. So then I thought what if we created our own synthetic protein, modified so that it absorbs the electrical energy in the cell body before exiting through the funnel and navigating around the disk? We could then inject these synthetic proteins into the cell body through the one-way valve and let them absorb the electrical signals. When they escape, we capture them. There would be a lot to work out, but what do you think of this as a general strategy?"

I paused. She looked at me eagerly, I think anticipating that I would be heaping extravagant praise on her and jumping at the idea. But I wanted to think carefully before saying anything, because my first reaction was annoyance – even anger -- over what struck me as pure hubris. She says *she* unlocked the explanation for why the electricity hadn't escaped? *She* did it? Yes, she spotted the disk before I did, but I was the one who ran with it and formulated the explanation.

But I figured I could deal with that irritation later. On the merits, to be frank, I found her idea absurd. I know she's the biochemist and I'm not, but somehow we're going to create these modified synthetic proteins and train them to absorb electricity? Seriously? And then, after we capture those fattened-up proteins, we're somehow going to extract the electricity from them? And even if we could complete all the steps that this convoluted process would require, how many years would it take?

I'm glad she's thinking outside the box, but I wanted to tell her that sometimes there's a reason that a particular idea isn't already, you know, in the box. Saying those things would have crushed her, however, so instead I responded as tactfully as I could.

"Hmmm, that's very interesting. We'll have to think some more about that. The main challenge, I think, is that the process you've described would involve several steps, and any one of them could run into a fatal obstacle. Also, this could take a very long time, with no guarantee of success, couldn't it?"

"I thought you might say that. But from a biochemical standpoint, I believe this is plausible. And yes, there are potential roadblocks at every juncture, but really isn't that true of our whole project? We might have failed to find any live electrical signals. We might have failed to figure out why the electricity can't escape. Even now there's no guarantee that we'll succeed in freeing the electricity, capturing it, downloading it to a computer, and deciphering it. Some people would say that success on all of those fronts is not only not guaranteed; it's a longshot. And yet we're giving it a try, even though we know the odds are heavy and the time frame is long. Maybe we should give my idea a similar chance."

"Well, with your training and knowledge, it's natural that the first solution you would come up with would be a biochemical solution. But let me throw out an alternative idea. It's one that I think is more likely to produce results. It's also likely to be faster. Instead of using chemicals, why not just pierce the holes with laser beams?"

"But, Jason, there are billions of picobes. If we try my method, we can develop the synthetic proteins, create them in bulk, and let them loose to seek out the holes in the picobes. That seems a lot better than your method. Are you going to train the laser beams on these holes one at a time? That should work fine -- as long as we both live a few hundred million years."

"For your information, I have an idea that would involve a spray of millions of laser beams at a time, so that …"

"So that they can not only pierce the holes in the picobes, but obliterate the picobes entirely, as well as all the tissue around it? That's a great plan, Jason. Really brilliant."

This time I was truly shocked. I had never known Lisa to display such rudeness and sarcasm, let alone such disrespect. And I told her so and made clear this was absolutely unacceptable.

She was unrepentant.

"Maybe if you treated me with a modicum of basic respect, I would express myself differently. I have worked very hard for you for almost two years now. I've been completely loyal. I feel that I've contributed to this project in countless ways. And with all that, you've never once said anything to indicate that you think I have any skills or talents of any kind. And now, today, I come up with what I think is a really innovative strategy for releasing the electrical signals from the picobes – a strategy that will help *you* advance toward your dream of a lifetime. And your only reaction is to dismiss my idea as if I were an idiot and to focus solely on your own idea."

For a moment all my defensive anger disappeared. All I felt instead was a deep longing. I told her I was so sorry and that of course I valued everything she has done and regard her as a super-talented scientist and a dear friend as well. I asked her if I could give her a hug. She said yes and looked up at me. And then, without a second's reflection, I kissed her.

She screamed at me and backed away as if I were a leper.

"What are you doing?!!! Don't touch me! I can't believe you did that!"

That was hardly the reaction I had expected, especially since she had kissed me that time when we first discovered the picobes. Apparently what's sauce for the goose isn't sauce for the gander. Or maybe it's the other way around. I believe a goose is female and a gander is male, so maybe in this case I should say that what's sauce for the gander apparently isn't sauce for the goose. Now I can't remember which is which. I'll have to look it up.

Anyway, that doesn't matter. The point is I immediately regretted kissing her and felt very embarrassed.

"I'm sorry, Lisa. It was a spur of the moment thing. I think we're both feeling a little fragile just now. It didn't mean anything, and I promise it won't happen again."

She calmed down and said she just needed a little time to herself to regroup. I told her we could resume the conversation tomorrow if she preferred, and she said yes, that would be good. I also told her she should feel free to take the rest of the day off, and she thanked me and said she'd like to do that.

Wednesday, July 16, 2025

Last night I couldn't stay at the lab. I had a knot in my stomach over what had happened with Lisa. The truth is that I'm in love with her. It's time for me to admit that to myself. It's bad enough that that love will never be reciprocated. Worse still is that I think she now finds me creepy, maybe even scary. Work was the last thing I cared about after that.

So rather than drift aimlessly around the lab like a zombie, I went home at about 5:30 pm. Jessica and Zeke were both surprised to see me, as it was the first time in weeks that I'd come home earlier than 10 pm. I should have seized the rare opportunity to devote my full attention to Zeke, but I couldn't summon the motivation to do even that. Instead I lied and told them I was sick and just wanted to go to bed, which I did.

I didn't even get up for dinner. In fact I didn't even wake up until about 9:00 this morning. When I did, I had a major headache and the start of a chest cold. I guess that's what I get for lying about being sick. And I guess I must be more worn-down than I had realized.

I went to the lab anyway, and Lisa and I arranged to meet around 11 to resume our conversation from yesterday. There was a little bit of awkwardness, but it wasn't as bad as I had feared and it seemed to disappear entirely once we re-focused on the project. From that point, the discussion was very professional, albeit a bit stilted considering we'd been working closely together for almost two years. I picked up where I had left off before the blowup.

"OK, you were asking how we could use laser beams when we're talking about billions of isolated, individual targets and we don't want to destroy all the tissue that joins them. You were right to ask. Here's my thought. Are you familiar with electro-optical smart fibers, or EOSFs?"

"No, sorry."

"No, it's OK. There's no reason you should be. They were invented by a team of Swiss electrical engineers who started working on this about seven years ago but didn't complete and publicize their invention until last fall. So it's been out less than a year. But I'm certain it's destined to become one of the most powerful medical research weapons – and probably medical treatment weapons as well - in modern times.

"You know that for decades now optical fibers have been used in both research and industry, for conducting light. But they don't conduct electricity, so the Swiss team set out to build an analogous fiber that would conduct electricity more efficiently than any of the existing conduits.

"What they ended up inventing was something that does much more. The EOSF isn't just a conduit. It's a smart fiber. It can be programmed to sequentially aim at millions of targets that the operator identifies by their locations and properties. In this way it can send and receive both light beams and electricity to and from millions of targets, one at a time, with a single command.

"My thinking is that we can set the controls so that it targets only the holes in the membranes of receptor neurons. We'll have to figure out how to do that, and that might take some time, but I believe it can be done. These machines aren't on the market yet, but one of the Swiss team members is a guy named Michel Valierre. He's an old friend of mine from my time in Houston, when he was on leave in the electrical engineering department of the university. I'm going to contact him to see whether he'd let us test it out."

"You think he will?"

"I don't know. But I should be able to find out quickly. If the answer is no, maybe we should give your protein strategy a try, you think?"

Lisa smiled. Man, was that a relief to see!

"Thank you, Jason. Let's see what your friend says."

So I emailed him. It's seven hours later in Bern, where he is based, so I had expected that he had gone home, but I was pleasantly surprised when he responded within the hour. As it turned out, he was at a conference in New York at the time, and we ended up having a wonderful conversation, full of reminiscences.

He said he would talk with his colleagues when he returned to Bern in two days. They had several EOSFs available and he was optimistic that they would welcome my use of it, because there hadn't yet been many tested applications of it and the feedback and publicity could be helpful. Assuming his colleagues agreed, he said, we could probably receive it in less than two weeks.

The comment about wanting to publicize our hopefully successful novel application of this new technology was, however, a bit of a complication. For obvious reasons, I have kept my project under wraps. Jessica and Lisa are the only people who know about it, and they're both sworn to absolute secrecy. So in explaining to Michel why I wanted to use the EOSF, I was purposely vague. All I told him was that it would enable us to better examine the molecular structures of the neurons that process memory.

That was enough of an explanation for now. But if he really wants to publicize a new application of the EOSF, I'll eventually need to supply much more detail and perhaps even documentation of our results. I'll worry about that problem down the road.

Friday, July 18, 2025

True to his word, Michel emailed me today, and he had great news. He and his colleagues will be more than happy for me to use the EOSF for the application I described, and they will arrange to have it shipped off on Monday. I can expect to receive it about three days after that, which would be next Thursday.

To use it, Lisa and I will have to figure out how best to identify the properties and locations of the one-way valves at which we want the EOSF to aim its light beams. So we decided to develop as much of that plan as we could while we awaited arrival of the EOSF. That meant both of us reading and digesting everything we could find about the fledgling EOSF and figuring out what information we would have to input.

I must say, this is getting *really* exciting. We are now talking, realistically, about releasing actual memories stored in dead people's brains.

Thursday, July 24, 2025

More crazy hours these past few days. Lisa and I have both been working our tails off to learn as much as we could about the EOSF in preparation for its arrival. Michel and I have exchanged many emails, and those have been helpful, but mastering the best use of this extraordinary invention is very difficult.

On the home front, things have not improved. Jessica clearly feels put out that I'm not home more, and these days we seldom have opportunity to talk by the time I get home. And even if she's still awake then, honestly I'm so exhausted that all I want to do is grab something to eat out of the refrigerator and then go to sleep. I have neither the time nor the energy to argue.

We're civil to one another, including saying hello when we see each other for the first time in the morning or at night, but really that's about it. There's no warmth. I know she still doesn't appreciate what's at stake here, and at this point I'm not sure there's anything I can do about that. If she insists on putting her head in the sand and valuing her daily pleasantries more than the revolutionary impact that my project is destined to have for humankind, all I can do is lament that.

The exciting news is that the EOSF arrived at the lab today, as expected. Lisa and I had prepared for its arrival and knew how to set it up, which we did.

There's still a subtle strain between Lisa and me -- a remnant, I think, of our argument last week and the unfortunate incident that followed it. I'm hoping this will pass with time, but I really don't know whether it will. When we're talking, she seems to stand at a slightly greater physical distance from me than she used to, but it's possible I'm just imagining it. I've definitely noticed that she almost never initiates conversations with me. Whenever we talk, it's because I approached her. She's always polite, but she'll quickly say "well, I'd better get back to work – lots to do" or something like that.

I'm thinking about approaching her and talking directly about this. We're adults, after all, and we're going to be continuing to work closely with each other, so if there's a problem we should get it out into the open and address it head on. Then again, maybe some things are best left unsaid. I don't know what to do. I just wish things could return to the way they were.

Often I have this fantasy in which Lisa tells me that the reason she's been a bit distant is that she is afraid of getting too close because she has long had romantic feelings for me and knows that she can never have me. These fantasies usually end up with my pouring my heart out, letting her know how I really feel about her, and even telling her that I will leave my wife and marry her. And since it's a fantasy, she says yes and we kiss and passionately embrace right there in the lab. I end up pondering what I would do if she were actually to tell me she loved me.

And then I'm suddenly, violently jolted back to reality. This is not going to happen. And these fantasies aren't giving me any pleasure. Far from it.

Knowing they'll never happen just tortures me. I have to get a grip.

I'm mentioning this now because, right while I was in the midst of one of these fantasies, Lisa stopped by my desk with a question about the EOSF. I answered her question and then impulsively asked her whether anything was bothering her that she'd like to talk about.

"No, everything is fine."

"It's just that I'm noticing a little distance between us that I don't think used to be there. Are you upset about the other day? If you are, please tell me."

"No, it's OK. It's not a big deal."

"OK. I just hope we know each other well enough by now that if anything is bothering you, you won't feel the slightest hesitation to tell me."

"I appreciate that, Jason, but really, everything is OK. I should probably get back to work, though, because I'm kind of in the middle of something."

And with that, she smiled and went off.

I really couldn't read her. Her smile seemed perfunctory, even a bit forced. She appeared to be a little standoffish as she was speaking, even as she was saying that there were no problems between us and that the incident was not a big deal. I don't know. Maybe I should take all this at face value. Maybe I'm the one blowing this out of all proportion. I wish my instincts could be surer. I'll just carry on as usual and hope my worries are groundless.

Friday, July 25, 2025

Lisa and I are both continuing to work furiously on formulating the instructions for the EOSF to identify the picobes and train its laser beams sequentially on the desired targets. And those targets aren't the entire picobes. They are even tinier – the disks inside the protein channels in those picobes. They are the objects we have to pierce if we want the electricity to flow out.

The tricky part is describing the identifying properties of these disks with EOSF instructions that distinguish them from all the surrounding matter. We don't want the EOSF indiscriminately wiping out whole areas of the brain. Lisa's role in this part of the project is critical, because the main distinguishing characteristics of the disks are their locations, shapes, and chemical compositions.

The most obvious problem is that we really don't yet know the chemical compositions of the disks. We could make educated guesses based on the optical images, but there are too many possible answers.

Wednesday, August 13, 2025

We've now been at this for almost three weeks, with no tangible results. Lisa is completely stuck. She has performed countless experiments, and has done laborious research, in an attempt to pin down what these disks are made of. They don't seem to resemble any familiar element or compound. Every time she thinks of a substance that this could plausibly be, she discovers some property that excludes that substance.

It appears to be something she has never seen before, perhaps a substance that simply has yet to be discovered.

If I were a biochemist in Lisa's position, I would be excited at the possibility of discovering a brand new biological element or compound. But Lisa found these disks other-worldly, even a bit creepy. Unlike me, Lisa is religious – a devout Methodist – and she has actually begun to wonder aloud whether this is God's way of telling us that we are crossing a forbidden line. This recalled for me her initial reaction to this whole project, when she worried that by seeking the functional equivalent of eternal life we were tampering with the universe in a way that God would disapprove of.

I obviously found the idea preposterous, but I've been walking on eggshells with Lisa and certainly can't tell her that she's being irrational. That's about the worst thing you can say to a scientist. So I just reassured her that she was going about this in a very productive, systematic way and encouraged her to stick with it a while longer. Sometimes, I have to say, I marvel at my managerial skills.

I also didn't have much else I could productively do until we succeeded in developing instructions for the EOSF to pierce the disks and release the electrical signals from their cells. Truth be told, I liked working in parallel with Lisa because it gave me much more time with her. It also immersed me in her specialized world, enabling me to talk with her about subjects that she was the expert on, for a change.

Thursday, August 28, 2025

Today Lisa's determined efforts (and my positive reinforcement) paid off. She conclusively identified a calcium compound as the material that the disks are made of. I was with her when she saw the results of the test that confirmed her finding. This was the happiest I've seen her in a long time. There were no kisses or hugs this time, but her whole body language was different, much more like the Lisa of old. It was a joy to behold.

I teased her about her earlier worry that God was displeased with our tampering, thinking that she would laugh about it now that she knows how silly she had been to think that. I seem to have offended her, though. She didn't find my teasing amusing, and she said politely that religion was something I shouldn't make jokes about because God was the most serious entity in her life.

That reaction totally surprised me, and I immediately apologized. But I must say I just don't get how highly intelligent, educated people – especially scientists -- can take this superstitious nonsense so seriously or be offended by innocuous little jokes or comments like the one I had just made. Whatever happened to sense of humor? I guess I'll never understand it. And that's probably a good reason never to say anything again along those lines, and certainly not to Lisa.

Friday, August 29, 2025

Today we worked together, translating Lisa's newly-found knowledge about the chemical composition of the disks into language that we could add to the EOSF instructions. We finished at 8:00 pm and called it a day. But we were now both chomping at the bit to actually run the EOSF and find out whether we could finally release the electrical information in the picobes. Neither of us wanted to wait until Monday, so we decided we would both come in tomorrow and see whether this works.

I know I won't sleep much tonight, and I also know Jessica will say something nasty when I tell her that I'm planning to go to work tomorrow. But I don't care. This is too incredible to put off.

Saturday, August 30, 2025

We had expected all along that these EOSF instructions, like most other complicated software, would not work seamlessly on the first try. Add in the fact that we're feeding the software into brand new, revolutionary hardware, and there would surely be bugs to work out. So we expected that this would take multiple refinements and a fair amount of time.

Sure enough, our first EOSF run failed. Forty-three different bugs, some of them undoubtedly related, appeared. Starting today, we began systematically addressing them one at a time. This probably sounds like boring work, but each bug presented its own interesting logic challenges, and I actually enjoyed solving them. I think Lisa did too.

Wednesday, September 3, 2025

We got through the last of the 43 bugs this afternoon and ran the program again. This time only six bugs appeared, all of them new. Progress.

Friday, September 5, 2025

We solved all six bugs today, or so we thought, and tried again. Another failure, but this time with only two new bugs. We worked on those this evening and thought we had solved them, but when we ran the program again, the same two bugs appeared. Hmmm.

Saturday, September 6, 2025

The two bugs are definitely related. Lisa and I worked on them all day today and I think we have now just about solved them. There's a little more to get through, and we hope to finish this tomorrow and try another run.

Lisa agreed to come in tomorrow morning right after church, but it's possible I'll be able to finish this even before she arrives. If I do, I'll wait for her before actually running the program. She too has worked very hard on this phase of the project, and I want to share with her the thrill of actually seeing the electrical signals break out of their prison cells for the first time.

In the meantime, it had occurred to me early this morning that I hadn't checked my phone voicemail messages for ages. Nobody leaves voicemail messages anymore, so I hadn't thought about it. But when I checked, I found a few stray unheard messages.

All of them except one were innocuous or otherwise not necessary to respond to. But the one exception was a message from my mother back in March. Yikes! It was the same day – in fact, just minutes after -- Lisa and I for the first time had experienced the thrill of detecting electrical signals in the brain specimens that we were working with. I remember now that in the middle of all this, my phone had rung and I had ignored it. In her message my mother had just asked me to call her to chat because we hadn't talked in a while, nothing urgent.

It turns out that when I didn't call her back within a couple days, my mother called Jessica to make sure everything was OK and Jessica had assured her I was fine but incredibly busy at the lab. Meanwhile, Jessica never mentioned to me that my mother had called the house. If she had, I would of course have returned the call. My poor mother had been upset that I hadn't called, but after talking with Jessica she didn't want to disturb me at the lab, where I was now spending the lion's share of my time.

But since I hadn't spoken to my mother even once since then, I felt terrible about not having called her. So I called as soon as I heard her voicemail message, months late but better than never. It was good that I did, because my mother had been worried that perhaps I was upset with her about something. I assured her that wasn't the case at all, told her how sorry I was that I hadn't called her, and explained that as Jessica had told her, I had just gotten super-busy at work.

"So what have you been working on?"

"Oh, you know, the same stuff. Trying to get a better understanding of how memories are formed and whether the brain actually stores them or has to reconstruct them each time. There's a lot of new technology out there that's enabling me to get a much closer look at the molecular structures of the cells that process memory. Who knows where that will lead, but it's important stuff, so I've been sticking with it."

"So it's basically the same work that you've been doing the past couple years or so?"

That question got me wondering. Was this my mother's subtle way of conveying that my life is boring, or that I've hit a dead end in my career? That would be out of character. She's always been positive and supportive.

Worse, though, is it possible that Jessica has told her about my project and my mother was now trying to get me to tell her about it so that she could try to talk me out of it? That would be bad. Apart from the fact that this would just cause my mother to worry about me even more, especially since I can imagine the version Jessica would be giving her, I could foresee my mother sharing this information with her friends, who in turn could spread it to others.

Without knowing what if anything my mother already knows about it, I don't want to proactively tell my mother about it and instruct her to keep it secret, because if Jessica hasn't told her about it, I would then be revealing it. So I tried to sound casual and change the subject.

"Yeah, pretty much just a continuation of that. But tell me about you. Anything new?"

"Well, I had my 70th birthday last week. I didn't want a big deal event, but it was nice to get together with a few friends who came over for coffee and cake. You remember Doreen, from across the street? She came over along with her sister who was visiting from Illinois – a delightful woman, though extremely tall. I'll bet she was over 6 feet. Marcia came too. Also Pat and Cynthia. Alice couldn't make it because her husband was undergoing surgery. Apparently he has heart problems. Poor man – he's a really nice guy. Have you ever met him?"

"Actually no, but please tell Alice they'll be in my thoughts. And I can't believe I forgot your birthday, Mom. I'm really sorry – I've just gotten so caught up with work."

"That's OK. I'll pass your good wishes on to Alice. She's known you since you were a baby, and you know she's always been very fond of you."

"Well, it's great to talk to you, but I should probably run. I'm actually at the lab now, even though it's a Saturday, because we're at a fairly critical stage in one of our experiments. But I'll be sure to call more often."

"You said 'we' – are you there with someone else?"

"Oh, yeah. I have a very good post-doc who's been assisting me. But I really do need to get back to work, so let's be sure to talk soon, OK?"

"OK, good-bye, darling. I love you, and please call whenever you can."

"I will, Mom – bye for now."

And we both hung up. I know I shouldn't be so grudging about spending time talking with my mother. She's been such a consistent source of love and support in my life, and it was bad enough to forget her birthday and completely indefensible not to get around to calling her for so many months.

It's just that, these days, I can't seem to work up any interest in anything except this project, and of course Lisa. I have to admit that even little Zeke, who of course I wish I had more time for, hasn't really been on my mind. Thankfully, we're making steady progress here at the lab and it's only a matter of time before I'll be able to resume a normal family life.

Of course, it doesn't help that my sex life with Jessica has basically been over for some time now. What an amazing coincidence it is that every night when I get home she just happens to be asleep! Or more likely, she's faking being asleep so she won't have to do anything as repulsive to her as having sex with me. Honestly, though, I could care less.

I'm not entirely sure that Jessica and I will ever be able to regain what we once had, because so much vitriol has now been spilled. It will be hard to put that genie back in the bottle. But I'll try. If it doesn't work out, it certainly won't be my fault.

Sunday, September 7, 2025

Today was possibly the most emotional roller coaster ride I've ever been on. It went from the depths to the heights and then back to the depths.

The day began with a horrible argument with Jessica. This time I was the one who started it, but for good reason.

"My mother called you months ago to ask about me, and you never told me. I would have called her right away. Instead, I never found out until yesterday, when I heard the voicemail she had left on my phone back in March, and of course I called her immediately. But she had been fretting that maybe I was upset with her and that's why I hadn't called. I let her know that wasn't the case at all, but I wish you had told me she was trying to get hold of me."

"Are you for real? Yes, I must have forgotten to pass on the message. I'm sorry! But you don't bother calling your mother for months and you have the gall to blame that on me? This is something I should have to periodically remind you to do? Seriously? Maybe if you'd stick your head out of the lab for two minutes, you wouldn't do these things."

"Yeah, well, that's not going to happen today. I'm going back in this morning."

"No, you're not. You told me on Friday that you were going to take Zeke to the playground this morning. And when I told him that, he was very excited. You've spent appallingly little time with him these past few months, and I'm not going to let you disappoint him yet again."

"I forgot. I'll take him to the playground. But then I'm headed to the lab. We're hoping to reach a major milestone today, and I'm not willing to wait till tomorrow."

"You said 'We.' I take it Lisa is coming in too?"

"Yes. Do you have a problem with that?"

"It's your life."

"That's right. It *is* my life. And I'll run it the way I want to."

"You always have."

"I don't have time for this. I'm going to get Zeke."

"He's already eaten. All you have to do is get him dressed, as if you were a real parent."

Jessica's nastiness and sarcasm sucked all the joy out of what should have been a nice fun time with Zeke. And since I've had so little time with him, I'm resentful that she would ruin it. But I had to make sure my anger wasn't visible to Zeke.

Jessica was right, though, that Zeke was excited about our outing to the playground. For about 45 minutes we had a wonderful time. Until I said he could go down the slide one more time and that we would then need to go home. By this time I was looking at my watch. I knew that Lisa would be arriving at the lab any minute, and I was anxious to finish the EOSF software so that we can free our electrical signals at long last. And of course I was anxious to see her.

Zeke took what was supposed to be his one last ride, but then he refused to budge. He said he wanted three more times on the slide. I said no, we really have to go home, "but tell you what, you can have one more ride." He said OK and went down the slide again.

But he didn't honor the bargain. He started heading for the slide yet again, and I had to remind him that I had said that would be the last time. He threw a horrible tantrum. He threw himself down on the ground, crying, screaming, and repeatedly saying "I don't want to go home."

In the end, I had to pick him up and carry him, wriggling around fiercely trying to get away and screaming at the top of his lungs, all the way to the car, and then battle physically to get him into his car seat. I was furious, and for the first time that I can remember in months, I yelled at him. Loud. This didn't quiet him down at all, and he screamed all the way home.

When I left him in the house and went back to the car, I could still hear him screaming as I drove off. It was awful. I get a rare chance to have what should have been some wonderful one-on-one time with my little boy, and it ends up like this. All after putting up with another sarcastic tirade from Jessica.

I was determined not to let those events spoil what I knew could be one of the most eventful milestones in my project. I got to the lab and focused on the two remaining bugs from yesterday. As I had hoped, I was able to figure out the remaining modifications to the software instructions shortly before Lisa arrived. I was pretty optimistic that this fix would work and that we would now succeed in piercing the barriers that were trapping the electrical signals inside my picobes.

To give us some physical assurance that the electricity was actually leaving the brain, I decided that before we run the program I should attach the electrodes of the intracranial EEG to the outer surface of the brain. That way, when the electricity escaped and created a new electric field, the intracranial EEG would reveal it. I managed to hook that up and waited eagerly for Lisa's arrival.

I also decided that when we succeed with this operation – and I fully expected that would be today – I would not try to give Lisa a hug, no matter how ecstatic we would both be. I didn't want to take any risks along those lines.

She got in just before noon. I couldn't wait to start up the machine.

"Are you ready?"

A big smile from Lisa. She was very excited. If there were still any problems in our relationship, they sure weren't evident at this moment. She said "Let's go for it."

I turned on the machine. It took a couple minutes to boot up. I called up the software and made the minor modifications to the program. I clicked on "run." We held our breath.

It took about 30 seconds more. Those were 30 very long seconds. Suddenly lights began flashing and it was clear that something was happening. For the first time, there were no error messages. The intracranial EEG that I had hooked up to the surface of the brain to detect the formation of a new electric field was going wild. The electrical signals were clearly escaping.

Lisa had tears in her eyes. I was pretty choked-up too. We looked at each other, both of us beaming broad smiles, and we shook hands. I know that sounds like a strangely muted form of physical celebration for two people who had been working so closely and who had just made a dramatic breakthrough, but somehow it seemed natural at the time. There was genuine happiness all around.

I was feeling pretty giddy, but there were still a couple things we needed to do to make sure Operation Liberate Ions was successful and complete. One was to repeat this process a few more times, changing the instructions slightly so that the EOSF aimed at new, neighboring parts of the brain. We did this immediately, and the results were always the same. There were no error messages, and lights were flashing on the intracranial EEG.

The other remaining task was to detach the electrodes of the intracranial EEG from the surface of the brain and reattach them to one of the same spots that the electricity had just escaped from. Just as we had hoped, the receptor neurons where we had once discovered trapped electricity were now empty. The EOSF had indeed enabled that electricity to escape.

There was now no doubt that we had succeeded in this crucial phase of the project. There was some cleanup work to do, and some write-ups as well, but another dramatic breakthrough was now complete.

We know that huge challenges remain. It was one thing to pierce the disks that had blocked the electrical signals from escaping. Harder still will be figuring out how to capture them and upload them to a permanent storage device. Even then, there will remain the excruciating challenge of deciphering the messages that those signals contain. But for the moment, we were content to just exult in what we had now accomplished.

Unfortunately, it was only for a moment, because a few minutes later Lisa dropped her bombshell.

"Jason, there's something I need to talk to you about."

I waited, suddenly feeling extreme nervousness bordering on panic. I sensed something ominous. She didn't disappoint.

"I've been thinking about this for a while. I've known that once we succeeded with this phase of the project, there wouldn't be much more I could contribute. The process of capturing and uploading the electrical signals, and then decoding them, aren't the kinds of things that a biochemist can really help with. For those, you need a computer science person, or maybe a mathematician, or both. I've really loved being part of this project, but it's time now for me to do some additional research and writing of my own. I want to apply for tenure-track positions myself, and I need to beef up my own research credentials, so that's what I'll be focused on doing. I also want to have more than a commuter relationship with Manny, and that means moving to Miami."

I fell silent. I just didn't know what to say. Lisa didn't seem to know how to handle that awkward silence, so she kept on talking, more and more rapidly and nervously, and somewhat repetitiously, to fill the gap.

"I mean this has really been an amazing experience for me, and I have a world of respect for you. You've done phenomenal work, I can't believe I've been part of it. And I hope you'll succeed. I mean I fully expect you to succeed. It's just that there's really nothing left for me to do on this project. And I need to be with Manny and have a more normal relationship. And I need to get started preparing for when I'll be applying for tenure-track positions."

"Lisa, I get all that, but this is kind of a shock. I suppose I should have seen this coming, but honestly I didn't. I have to tell you, I really can't face the thought of coming to the lab every day and you not being here. You can't imagine the hole that will leave in my life. Please stay. Please. I'm sure we can think of some really interesting and fulfilling things for you to do here."

"Jason, I can't. I really have made a final decision. I know this is coming as a surprise. It was stupid of me not to let you know earlier that I've been thinking along these lines. I'm so sorry. And I also think I've hurt you. I'm so sorry for that too. But I promise you're going to be fine. With your reputation, you'll be able to recruit a super post-doc for the remaining phases of the project, and I know you're going to succeed. It's going to be so exciting when you do."

"I don't think you're getting how much I would miss you if you left. I don't just mean because of your biochemistry expertise. I think you know how I feel about you on a personal level."

"I do know that, Jason, and I feel the same way. You're a valued friend."

Lisa's last phrase stung. A "valued friend"? She was much more to me than that. I had hoped I was much more to her than that, even though in my saner moments I understood how unlikely that was. I'm sure she knew very well that I thought of her as much more than a "valued friend." I would make one more attempt.

"Lisa, please, please, please. I don't want to sound pathetic, but please stay. How about one more year, and then we can reassess?"

"Jason, no, I'm sorry. This is truly a final decision. But I didn't mean I was leaving this minute. We still have some cleanup and some write-ups to do on the phase we just completed, and I've been planning to stick around until that's done. That should keep me here another two or three weeks, I would think. I'm certainly not going to leave you in the lurch."

So that was it. I couldn't think of anything else to say and, already embarrassed by my pleading and whining, I just lowered my head and fell silent.

After a few seconds, Lisa told me one more time how sorry she was and said it was best that she go home now.

This day is finally over. From the hell of horrendous arguments with Jessica and then Zeke, to the ecstasy of succeeding with the liberation of the electrical signals that almost surely carry human memory data, to the unspeakable despair upon hearing from Lisa that she will be leaving, this day is over.

I don't know what to do next. It's 3:00 on a Sunday afternoon. I can't bear the thought of staying here in the lab alone. And I can't bear the thought of going home. I can't even force myself to cry. I'm beyond being able to do even that.

So I went outside for a walk. I walked and walked, thinking and talking to myself. I must have walked for miles, because when I next looked at my watch, it was after 8:00. I knew I should grab something to eat, but I wasn't hungry.

I came back to the lab and wrote up this account of the day while the events were still fresh in my mind. I'll go home as soon as I finish. Zeke will be asleep, but Jessica will be there. I don't want to talk to her and I have no idea what I would say if I did. I have never felt so despondent in my life.

CHAPTER 5
TRANSFERRING THE PRISONERS

Monday, September 8, 2025

I don't think I slept for a single second last night. So much was rushing through my brain – the oppressive environment at home, the excitement of yesterday's breakthrough at the lab, and the devastating news of Lisa's leaving. And of course the planning for the next phase of the project. I tossed and turned, eventually got up, ate something, tried to fall asleep again, gave up and got out of bed again, tried once more, and eventually got up for good at 5:00 and went to the lab.

Jessica slept through the whole thing, oblivious to my physical movements and to the storm going off in my head. She was probably surprised to see that I was gone when she woke up, though she didn't call the lab or do anything else to confirm that I was still alive.

But one thing you do when you can't sleep is think. I did a lot of that. Despite my exhaustion, or maybe because of it, my mind was racing. I felt as if I had just downed ten cups of coffee, even though I hadn't drunk a drop since yesterday afternoon. And believe it or not, this sleeplessness turned out to be extremely productive on at least two fronts.

First, I had an idea for a last-ditch attempt to persuade Lisa to stay on. I know she said that part of her thinking was that she wanted to be with Manny in Miami. But that was just one of the reasons, and she didn't sound as if it was the primary one. Mainly, she said, she didn't think there would be anything left for her to do here, and she also needed time to work on her research to prepare and publish papers that would support her eventual applications for tenure-track positions.

Well, what could be a more ideal place to do her research than at my lab? She would have a great workspace and lots of equipment, and I could promise her continuing financial support. As long as her work related to memory in some way, and I was sure it would, I could easily justify using some of my grant money to support her research. She wouldn't need to work on my project at all; she could devote herself full-time to her own work. Plus, I would be there for her to bounce ideas off of. I decided I would make that pitch to her when she gets to the lab.

And second, I came up with a plan for phase 3 — capturing the freed electricity and uploading it to a permanent digital storage device. All along, I had been thinking of this as a two-step process. I had been assuming that the first step would be capturing the electricity in some kind of vessel and storing it there temporarily. And the second step, I had assumed, would be later, somehow, transferring those electrical data to a permanent storage device.

But last night, in my agitated state, I started thinking that I might be able to use the EOSF to do both things simultaneously. Up to now, we had been using the EOSF to do just one thing — shoot light beams at the disks in the picobes' protein channels.

The EOSF, however, can do so much more. For one thing, it can conduct not only light, but also electricity. In fact that was its main purpose -- to do for electricity what optical fibers have long done for light. In addition, it can conduct either of these in both directions. So in this next phase, in addition to using the EOSF to shoot light beams at the disks in the protein channels, we can position it so that as soon as the disks are shattered, the escaping electrical signals will be reflected straight back through the fiber into the storage device. We'll seal off both ends of the fiber – one end inside the brain and the other end by the storage device – so that the fiber will be their only available path out. That means we won't lose any of the electrical data.

Not only that, but the EOSF is capable of creating a vacuum. And since we're sealing it off at both ends, we'll be able to preserve that vacuum along the entire length of the fiber. That's a major advantage, because in a vacuum both light and electromagnetic waves can travel at their maximum speed of 300 million meters per second. That in turn is extremely important; after all, we have billions of these picobes to extract electricity from. And we can do all of this with a single set of commands. The vacuum will also eliminate any distortions that air would otherwise introduce.

We'll still have to develop new software that will enable the storage device to recognize and receive these electrical data. That will be a challenge, one that I'll need a computer science whiz for in any event. But this approach will at least simplify the process by combining everything into one step.

I don't want the electrical signals to pile up in the fiber and cause a traffic jam. So it will have to be a process of firing off one light beam, waiting for the storage device to record the arriving electrical signal, and then firing off the next light beam. This means we'll need to calculate how fast the storage device can record these signals, and that will determine how long we tell the EOSF to wait in between firing off light beams.

But the important thing is that I now have a plan. And it's a plausible plan. I must say I am quite proud of myself and relieved to know I have a realistic path forward.

As soon as Lisa arrived at the lab, I told her excitedly that I had an idea that I thought she would really like. She seemed pleased that I was now in a buoyant mood, just the opposite of the state she had left me in yesterday. We sat down at one of the lab tables with our cups of coffee, and I offered her the opportunity to do her research at this lab, with full financial support, my help and advice whenever she needed it, and no responsibilities for my main project. She could focus all her efforts on strengthening her credentials for tenure-track positions.

I'm not sure what I was expecting from her when I made this offer. Gratitude? Excitement? An immediate, complete change of heart?

None of that happened. She shook her head and turned me down right on the spot. She didn't even say that she would need time to think about it.

"That's very generous of you, Jason. It truly is. But I really have made up my mind on this. That just wouldn't work for me."

"But why?"

A long pause.

"Well, for one thing, a big part of my thinking is that I want to be in Miami with Manny, as I told you yesterday. Our commuter relationship is tolerable in the short term, but I worry about whether it can be sustained in the long term. At a certain point Manny deserves someone who is actually going to be there for him, and I think he feels that way as well. And I can't blame him."

"Lisa, I don't want to butt into your personal relationship with Manny, so forgive me if you think I'm crossing the line. But you have to think about your own needs too. Believe me, any man would be crazy to blow a relationship with you. The real question should be whether *you* can accept a commuter relationship for a while longer, not whether Manny can."

"I know you're meaning to compliment me, Jason, but I think my relationship with Manny is something he and I have to work out on our own."

"I'm sorry. Again, I didn't mean to cross that line. I just find it hard to conceive of anyone not being willing to do *anything* that's necessary to have and keep you as his partner. And I'll just leave it at that. Is that the only reason for turning down the offer I just made? Because I think it would make a great deal of sense from a professional standpoint."

"Jason, I just don't think this will work. Thank you again for being so generous. And supportive. But it's time for me to finish up here and move on. I'm really sorry."

With that, Lisa returned to her cubicle. I sat at the lab table for a few minutes and then returned to my own cubicle.

This was a major setback. And a surprise. I had been sure she would accept this offer. I can't help wondering whether she's being completely straight with me. The only reason her refusal would make any sense is the Manny issue, and I still don't think that's what's driving her. There has to be something else.

Is it me? Is she starting to doubt my mental health, just like my mother and Jessica? Does she think I've become too obsessed with this project? She's been pretty excited about it too lately, so I would have thought that my passion for it would be a draw, not a drawback.

Or maybe she's starting to feel uncomfortable around me because lately I've made so little effort to conceal my feelings for her? Have I been too aggressive in pouring out how I feel, to the point where practically every encounter is awkward and stressful for her? Am I making a complete fool of myself? She has to know I'm in love with her, and if her feelings for me don't rise to that level, I can see why this might be a difficult situation for her.

Plus, I'm married. Even though my marriage seems to be on the rocks, she might think that any show of amorous feeling on her part would be wrong. She is very religious, after all.

Actually, there's another possibility, one that I don't like to think about. She knows all the secrets involved in this project. She needs to publish something innovative in order to bolster her academic qualifications before she starts applying for tenure-track positions. Is she thinking about violating her promise of confidentiality and publishing the results we've achieved to this point, maybe even claiming primary credit for them? That sure doesn't sound like her.

Then again, she did say something yesterday about staying here another couple weeks in order to write up what we've done. At the time I assumed she was doing this for my benefit, looking ahead to publication of the project. But now I'm wondering whether she has something more sinister in mind. That would be such a betrayal. I've placed so much trust in her and have done so much for her. To turn around and do something that cruel, and that selfish, would be truly wicked. I wish I could read her more confidently.

Tuesday, September 9, 2025
I'm resigned to Lisa leaving. I've tried everything, and it's a done deal. It's time to accept that reality and move on. It's just so hard to do that. Thinking about her departure leaves such an ache in my heart. I mean

that literally – I can actually feel physical pain in my chest.

I decided not to waste any time in hiring the new post-doc. Lisa was clearly right about one thing. I need a computer science whiz, someone who can write the software that will enable the storage device to understand and record the electrical data that the EOSF will be sending its way. Down the road I'll also need someone to decode those data, and I don't know whether the same person will be equipped to do that, but I can defer that decision for now.

For this next stage of the project, the candidate has to be the perfect person. The task at hand will be extremely technically complex. It's a huge challenge that will require a first-rate mind, a solid grounding in data properties, a willingness to work long hours, great creativity, and the personal makeup to take on a challenge that inherently carries a high risk of failure but the potential for spectacular results.

This person doesn't have to be my best friend, but since we'll be working so closely, he or she has to be pleasant and collegial. I'm not into power plays, but I insist that the person also be someone who will show the proper deference to a supervisor. I value honest and constructive feedback, but once I make a final decision about any aspect of this project, I don't want a lot of argument or resistance. The way Lisa spoke to me that time I had the nerve to reject her nutty idea about creating synthetic proteins was disrespectful, unprofessional, and entirely unacceptable. I simply won't tolerate that. I just won't. And of course this must be someone with absolute integrity, someone I can trust completely to keep our project confidential until I publish the end product.

So I drew up an ad, ran the draft past Lisa for her input, and posted it on the web. The position is a post-doc, with full financial support and an expectation, though not a guarantee, of a three-year term. The only formal requirement is a Ph.D in computer science or a closely-related field.

With Lisa responsible for writing up the process and results of phase 2 of the project, and with so much of phase 3 dependent on the work of the new post-doc who hasn't been hired yet, there actually isn't a whole lot I can do in the meantime. The main task I'm setting for myself for the next few days is to start writing the instructions that the EOSF will need in order to perform the procedure that I conjured up yesterday.

The logic will be even more complicated than what was required for the previous phase, for lots of reasons. We're now going to be transporting both light beams and electrical signals, rather than light beams alone. Furthermore, we'll be doing both at the same time, and they'll be traveling in opposite directions.

Over the next few weeks, until the new post-doc arrives, that and the interviewing of candidates will really be the only things I need to do. So I'm thinking now that this is the perfect time to ease off briefly, spend more time at home, and try to catch up on sleep and health.

I've set the alarm on my watch to go off every afternoon at 4:45. I'll finish up what I'm doing, write the journal entry for that day, and then force myself to leave the lab no later than 5:00. Things will heat up again once we get going in earnest on phase 3, so I need to take advantage of this interlude to recharge for the next round. If Jessica was right about anything, it was to remind me that this is a marathon and not a sprint.

Wednesday, September 10, 2025

Jessica seemed surprised when I arrived home at 5:30 yesterday. I told her that the project will be slowing down for the next few weeks and that during this period I'm committed to working normal hours, coming home around this same time on weekdays and taking the weekends off completely.

Her reaction was matter-of-fact. There was no gushing, no dramatic show of excitement. That didn't surprise me, because she probably thought that despite my best intentions this relaxed work schedule would be history much sooner than I planned. I have to admit that has happened in the past.

Still, I was surprised that she wasn't the least bit curious about why the project would now be slowing down. Most likely, she didn't care. She did tell me this is a good decision and added that I need to take this opportunity to get reacquainted with Zeke. Of course I didn't need her to tell me that, so her "advice" was irritating, but I let it go. I really didn't want another argument on the first day of my far too long-delayed period of normalcy.

I also have no illusions that this brief respite will turn her around and restore the kind of relationship we once had. Too much blood has been spilled. I don't think things will ever return to the way they were. But I do hope we can at least avoid the overt hostility of the past several months and interact civilly and respectfully – if not for our own sakes, then at least for Zeke. We haven't had any loud shouting matches in front of him, but he is a sensitive little boy who I think can pick up on even very subtle signs of friction.

Monday, September 15, 2025

I have stuck meticulously to my plan. Since last Tuesday I have left the lab no later than 5:00 every day. I've made steady progress on the EOSF instructions, and Lisa seems to be making good headway on her write-ups. Her last day in the lab will be Friday September 26. If she lets me, I'll take her to lunch at a nice restaurant on that last day. I want us to remain on friendly terms. You never know what the future will bring.

To my delight, more than 70 applications for the post-doc position have arrived so far, and I expect to receive more this week. I've been reviewing them. Amidst the many clear non-starters, a few look really promising. I've tentatively identified at least two candidates and possibly a third whom I'd like to interview, but before scheduling them I'll give it another couple days to see what else comes in.

Meanwhile, things are going as well as expected at home. I can't say that relations with Jessica have been loving or even warm, but they have been cordial, which I suppose is the most I could reasonably have expected. If this relationship is ever fully repaired, it will take a good deal of time. We have, however, had family dinner each night since last Tuesday, and that's been good. Last night I decided I should probably fill her in on the recent developments at the lab.

"I have some news at work. Lisa and I finished up the second phase of the project, which was figuring out a way to release the electrical memory data that had been trapped inside the picobes. I'm now starting the planning for the next phase, which involves transferring the electrical signals from the picobes to a permanent storage device. And since that's not something that a biochemist like Lisa is really trained for, we've agreed that she would be moving on. I'm in the process of hiring a new computer science post-doc for the next phase."

"When's her last day?"

"A week from Friday."

"So what is she planning to do?"

"She's going to move to Miami, where her boyfriend lives, and do her own independent research. She wants to apply for tenure-track positions and needs to solidify her scholarly record."

"Wow, how did this come about?"

"Well, we both talked about it and agreed this move made a good deal of sense for both of us. There really isn't much more she can contribute at this point."

"You must feel really sad about her leaving."

I know Jessica well enough by now to know when an innocent-sounding question is more than that. I was determined not to call her on this explicitly. I thought the best response would be one that comes across as casual but not so uncaring as to be implausible.

"Of course. I've worked with her for about two years now, and she's been a great colleague and a nice person. I wish her well. But it's definitely time for her to move on. And I'm excited about getting a genuine computer science whiz for my next post-doc."

Jessica just nodded. I'm certain she feels some relief that Lisa will be leaving town, though I'm not sure why, because it's not as if Jessica still has any feelings for me. I'm less sure whether my casual tone was convincing. Partly to change the subject, and partly as a peace overture, I asked her how things were going for her at work. Frankly I could care less about her work, but I wanted to at least make it sound as if I did.

I don't think she interpreted my question as a sincere expression of interest, because she just said that things were fine, nothing new. And that was pretty much the end of our conversation.

Zeke and I had some quality time this past weekend. We went to the playground again, and this time I let him stay for two hours, at which point he decided he had had enough and wanted to go home. There were no apparent remnants of the previous weekend's blowup, no traumatic effects that I could discern. I guess that's the nice thing about being four years old. Actually, now that I think of it, his birthday is coming up in just two weeks. My little boy will soon be five years old. Jessica told me he had just missed the cutoff birth date for kindergarten for this year, but he'll be starting next year when he's almost six. My goodness. How did all this happen so fast?

Wednesday, September 17, 2025

I've been doing some additional thinking about how far I can trust Lisa. I think it's more likely than not that she's on the up and up and that she'll honor her pledge of confidentiality. It would take an exceptionally horrible person to betray me by revealing our project to the world, let alone claiming credit for it just to bolster her shot at a tenure-track position. And I really don't think Lisa is that kind of person.

At the same time, she has been acting strangely these past few months, and I'm not so sure I know her anymore. Again, I think she's most likely trustworthy, but the reality is I can't be certain.

I'm thinking that allowing her to meet her potential successors might be risky. Even if she isn't planning to steal our work for her own ends, she might feel a perverse obligation to warn the interviewees about what our project really entails. If she did that, then they – and especially those individuals whom I interview but don't hire – certainly couldn't be relied on to keep the secret.

In addition, I'm not confident that she won't tell them I'm strange, or volatile, or even mentally unstable. I don't think I'm any of those things, but God knows what Lisa's current perceptions are, and if the candidates were to ask her what I was like to work with, and her true impressions are negative, she would be capable of saying anything. So to be on the safe side, I decided to schedule all interviews for the week following her departure.

That still doesn't solve another basic problem: What, exactly, should I myself tell the interviewees? They'll need to know what work they'll be doing, and obviously they'll ask me directly if I don't proactively tell them.

I can't reveal that I have extracted live memories from dead brains. That news would spread like wildfire, and others would either steal the idea if they find it credible or dismiss me as a nut job if they don't. But I have to tell them something.

I decided that in the interviews I'll be as general as possible without sounding evasive. I'll need to convey that my work focuses on human memory and that in this particular project I'm studying the electrical signals that the brain transmits when processing memory. And then I'll explain that their job would be to develop software for inputting these electrical data to a storage device. I won't outright lie, but I'll word it in such a way that they assume I'm talking about brain scans from living subjects.

Once the person is hired, I'll have to be much more specific. In any event they'll see for themselves what's going on in the lab. Which is why I have to be absolutely certain that the person I hire merits complete trust. I'll interview them rigorously, have very detailed conversations with their references, and then just have to trust my instincts.

Friday, September 19, 2025

I've continued to maintain my 5:00 departure time, and things have remained the same at home. The détente with Jessica is still in place, and evenings playing with Zeke have been wonderful.

Yesterday at the lab I finalized all three interview dates for the week after next. Lisa will have left by then, and since she doesn't know the identities of the people I'm interviewing, I don't have to worry about her poisoning their minds or revealing our secret to them. I'm probably being a bit neurotic about that, but it's still best not to take chances.

I also told Lisa that I'd like to take her to lunch on her last day, and she thanked me and said that would be great. I can't believe that day is only a week away.

I'm making progress on the EOSF instructions, though that has been a little slower than I had hoped. That's OK, though. I'm still committed to my current, sane work schedule and think the instructions will be in pretty good shape by the time the new post-doc is on board. Until then, I can't run the program anyway.

Wednesday, September 24, 2025

I reminded Lisa about how critical it is to keep this whole project secret. If word were to get out, anyone could steal the idea, anyone could believe I'm crazy, the NIH could put restrictions on my grant and/or decline to renew it, or the medical school could terminate my position if they find the project upsetting.

"Jason, you know I would never breach confidence. Are you worried that I might do that?"

"No, of course not! I'm just so invested in this, and so much is at stake, that I thought the confidentiality was worth emphasizing and reminding you about. I know you would never consciously do anything like that, but it would be easy to accidentally blurt out something that gives it away. When you go to apply for tenure-track jobs, they'll be sure to ask you about your work here, so I'm just encouraging you to think carefully and deliberately about how best to describe it without revealing anything about the dead brains."

"You don't need to worry. You know me better than that."

"OK, no reason to belabor this. See you tomorrow."

Friday, September 26, 2025

I don't think the reality of Lisa's impending departure fully registered until today. This morning she gave me her write-up of phase 2. I read it over, and it was fine.

As planned, I took Lisa to lunch to celebrate her last day. She loves Thai food, so we went to a wonderful Thai restaurant just off the U City loop, a stretch of road that for several decades now has been chock full of interesting cafes, restaurants, and shops. This restaurant isn't fancy, but neither of us cared about that. The food is great and the atmosphere relaxed.

At lunch I tried not to get too serious or sentimental. I wanted to come across as someone who liked Lisa as both a friend and a colleague and of course would miss her, but at the same time not let it show that I thought this was the end of the world. Our conversation was actually pretty relaxed, as if nothing consequential was changing. The same was true during the ride back to the lab.

We had one final talk at around 4:00, just before she left. At that point I could no longer pretend this wasn't a big deal, and after all that had passed she would never have believed that anyway. So I thought the best thing was to just tell her that I will miss her more than she will ever know but that I genuinely wish her all the luck in the world, both professionally and personally. And of course I told her to make sure we always stay in touch.

I was glad I had finished on a high note, and I could tell she was too. She said very nice things to me in return. We hugged for the last time. Then I watched her walk out the door.

Monday, September 29, 2025
This is my first day back in the lab without Lisa. Something made me walk over to her cubicle and look inside. I had been fantasizing that she had decided to come back after all and to surprise me in the process. The shock of seeing her empty cubicle jolted me back to reality. Part of me finally accepts that she is gone.

Another part of me can't help but think that one day, perhaps years from now, she will be back in my life.

For now, though, I need to concentrate on the present. Here at the lab, I have work to do on the EOSF instructions. And this evening we're going to celebrate Zeke's fifth birthday. Jessica has already made a cake, which she hid from Zeke's view. We've bought him several presents, including a bicycle. Wrapping it was a challenge, but we got it done last night after he was in bed, and he's going to go wild once he unwraps it and sees what it is.

Tuesday, September 30, 2025

Last night's birthday party was fantastic. Zeke loved his presents and especially his bike, just as we knew he would. But he kept breaking away from it for another helping of cake, and for a while we indulged him. You only turn five once. In the end, he had way too much chocolate and despite our best efforts didn't fall asleep until after 10:00. He was a pretty cranky guy when we had to wake him up this morning for pre-school.

Friday, October 3, 2025

Earlier this week I interviewed two of the post-doc candidates. Both were OK but not special.

Today I interviewed the final candidate, a young man named Chen Zhenpang. He had immigrated here with his parents from China at age 2 and had taken the nickname "Marvin" because it's easier for Americans to pronounce. Even before he arrived, he was the candidate who on paper I was the most excited about. For one thing, his credentials could not have been more perfectly tailored to the task at hand, which was the main reason I'd invited him to interview. His Ph.D dissertation at Columbia had been on new ways of understanding digital language.

As an extra bonus, he had double majored in college – mathematics and linguistics. I was practically salivating. Here is a candidate who could take the lead in both of the remaining phases – the inputting of the electrical signals and their subsequent decoding. Still, you never know how someone will come across in person.

He hit it out of the park. His intelligence was abundantly on display. We talked about his dissertation, and it was clear that this is a person who has not only a first-rate analytical mind, but a creative one as well. As he described the thesis and objectives of his PhD research, there was no doubt that he loved exploring new territory. He was deferential, easy to talk to, and warm without being unprofessional.

Our interview had been scheduled for two hours, but we talked for three and then went off to lunch to continue the conversation. I felt an instant bond and a strong sense that this is someone I can trust. He was also very positive about moving to the Midwest. His wife is from Chicago, he told me, and she has long wanted to return to this part of the country.

The only awkward moment came when he questioned me about the work he would be doing and how it fit in with my overall research project. The other two candidates had been satisfied with my general and deliberately cursory description of the project, but Marvin was more sophisticated. He asked a couple of thoughtful and nuanced follow-up questions that put me on the spot. I was impressed but uneasy, as I hadn't wanted to reveal too much at the interview stage. I kind of stumbled around in my answers without letting on that I was working with the brains of dead humans, and he was polished enough to know when to stop probing. For a moment I felt as if I were the one being interviewed.

When it was time for him to return to New York, I told him how much I had enjoyed meeting him and that from my perspective the interview had gone extremely well. I didn't want to extend an offer immediately, though, because I still needed to talk with his references. They had all written glowing letters of recommendation, but I couldn't afford to take any needless chances and wanted to hear from them orally.

I called all three of them this afternoon. All were in New York, where it's an hour later, but I was able to catch two of them still in their offices. Both of them described Marvin over the phone as glowingly as they had in their letters. One of them, a professor who had been at Columbia for 25 years, said Marvin was one of the two or three most brilliant students he had ever had, and a fine person to boot. I couldn't catch the third reference in time, but I left him a voicemail message and an email message as well.

The exhilaration of finding the seemingly ideal post-doc assistant for the next phase of the project, and hopefully beyond, at least temporarily overshadowed the pain of Lisa's departure. If the third reference is similarly raving, I will definitely extend the offer to Marvin.

Monday, October 6, 2025

Another nice weekend. I'm realizing now how much I needed this down time – for my own health and feeling of well-being, for the sake of my little boy, and for the sake of my marriage. Yes, even Jessica seems to be a little less on edge when she talks to me. For months I'd been assuming that our marriage is going to end in a bad way and that it's only a matter of time.

I'm no longer resigned to that possibility. We're both going to have to work at it, especially me. Really, it's my work hours that precipitated all this. I can't tell you how healthy I suddenly feel being able to admit that. Even after the project gets intense again, as it will soon after we begin phase 3, I'm going to make a determined effort to maintain these normal work hours. That will mean taking a little longer to finish the project, but I can see now that that tradeoff is more than worth it.

This morning Marvin's third reference called me back. As expected, his evaluation was just as glowing as the other ones were. So with that final piece in place, I emailed Marvin, letting him know that I would be offering him the job and asking him to call me.

Marvin called me back just minutes later. I offered him the position and told him how much I had enjoyed the time we had spent together on Friday and how exciting a project this will be. I spelled out the formalities, including the salary, which I set at the very highest level I thought I could justify under the terms of the grant.

He said he's incredibly happy and honored to receive this offer and that he had returned home from St. Louis very excited about this job and working with me. He asked me, though, whether he could have a week or so to make a decision. It turns out he had interviewed for a post-doc at Cornell just a couple days before meeting with me and that they had told him they would get back to him sometime this week. Would that timeline be OK?

This was disappointing and a little unnerving. I had thought that the exceptional rapport we had, the chance to work on such a ground-breaking project (though he didn't know yet *how* ground-breaking this will be), and his wife's desire to move back to the Midwest would be an irresistible combination. But I replied that of course he should take the time he needs to make what I appreciate is a major decision.

He thanked me and promised to get back to me by the end of the week.

Thursday, October 9, 2025

The last two days have been suspenseful and stressful. I had reservations about both of the other candidates whom I'd interviewed and was increasingly seeing Marvin as the key to my succeeding on the next two phases of the project.

I was also disappointed that his decision whether to accept my offer depended on whether Cornell offered him a position. I'm not surprised that he would attract the interest of many other universities, but after our day together last Friday, I had interpreted his enthusiasm as a pretty sure sign that I would be his first choice. It now appears I'm just a fallback.

So when the phone rang this afternoon, and Marvin called to accept my offer, my spirits soared. It was excitement at the prospect of attacking the final stages of my project with a person who I knew would give me the best chance of success, and relief knowing I would not have to settle for either of the other two interviewees. Both would probably have been all right, but I would never have felt the same degree of enthusiasm or optimism.

I told him how happy I was that he had made this decision and that I know it will be great to work together. He said similarly generous things. We agreed that his starting date would be October 27, which is two weeks from Monday. We firmed up the arrangements by email. I immediately emailed the other two interviewees to thank them for coming and let them know that I had selected another applicant.

I even called Jessica at her office to tell her that Marvin had accepted. I don't usually like to disturb her when she's with patients. In fact I think the last time I called her at her office was when I had phoned to let her know that Tim had successfully retrieved the files on my dead laptop, and her reaction then was that I should have called her sooner since I had told Lisa hours earlier. But she knew how anxious I'd been this time, about finding the right assistant, so I figured I'd let her know right away. And she actually seemed happy for me that Marvin had accepted my offer.

After I hung up, it occurred to me that maybe she was happy because I had hired a male. She never was comfortable with my working so closely with Lisa.

I also started thinking a little more about Marvin. I was happy he had accepted, but I wondered whether Cornell had rejected him and I was his second choice, or whether he had decided that I was his first choice after all and so had withdrawn from consideration at Cornell. Obviously it doesn't matter. The important thing is that he's coming. It would be nice to know, though. But I don't really care, I'm just curious. I suppose I could ask him once he arrives, but if Cornell rejected him, my question might cause him embarrassment. I think I'll just drop it. Or I suppose I can just play it by ear.

Monday, October 27, 2025

Marvin arrived at the lab today on schedule, and I set him up in the cubicle that Lisa had occupied. He seems a little discombobulated, because he and his wife had arrived in St. Louis only last night and the apartment that was supposed to be ready for them wasn't. So they had to find a hotel for a couple days before they can move in, and all their furniture is in a U-Haul trailer hooked up to their car. I can't wait to get started on our project, but I offered the poor guy a little time to settle in. He thanked me but said that really isn't necessary and that he too is gung ho about getting to work.

So we sat down and talked about the project in detail. I first secured his promise to keep everything confidential for reasons that I said I would explain, which I did. When I got to the part about the dead brains, he was stunned. He couldn't believe that the brain would continue to store electrical energy containing memory data even after a person dies.

He was also astounded that we could use the EOSF to pierce holes in the tiny disks that had been blocking the release of these electrical signals. Amazing to me was that he was immediately able to piece all this information together, combine it with what I had told him earlier about his job of uploading electrical data to a storage device and decoding it, and grasp the implications of the project.

"Dr. Stramm, it sounds as if your plan is to retrieve the actual memories of dead humans in a form that we can understand?"

"Please call me Jason. And yes, that's exactly what this is about."

"This is unbelievable! All along I'd been assuming you were talking about electrical signals coming from the brains of live subjects. I mean, if we can pull this off, it will be one of the great scientific breakthroughs of all time! The implications are boundless! I just can't believe it! Incredible! Oh, my God, when can we start?"

I was in heaven. This kid is even better than I had thought. He seems like a younger version of myself. He figured this out in seconds and, instead of reacting with caution or skepticism like Jessica and even Lisa at first, he was excited. I could tell he was barely able to stay in his seat. The tougher the challenge and the more innovative the project, the more passion he displayed for doing it. I have a soulmate. This is really going to be fun.

So I brought him up to speed on all the details. I spent a particularly great amount of time teaching him about the EOSF, which he had heard of but did not yet know much about. That technology too got him excited.

I proposed a division of labor. Generally, I will be the EOSF guy. I'll continue to work on the EOSF instructions. I've been making progress but still have a number of complicated logic problems to sort through. Once I finish writing those instructions, my intention is to try to run them, working out the bugs as I go along. In addition to getting the EOSF to shoot light beams sequentially at the disks in the protein channels (as we had done before), I'll need to get the EOSF to then create a vacuum in the fiber and usher the electrical signals back through the fiber to the storage device at the receiving end.

The storage device won't be able to record the arriving electrical signals until Marvin finishes writing the recognition software, but I can at least get the procedure working up to that point. I'll be able to puncture only a relatively small number of disks for now, because, without the released electrical signals actually being absorbed by the storage device, they'll get backed up in the fiber. But that's OK. At this stage I just need to make sure our procedure is ready to go by the time Marvin completes his assignments.

Marvin has two immediate priorities. The first is to make sure we have the fastest computers, and the drives capable of storing the greatest quantity of data, that we can afford. His second priority, and the one I assume will present the greatest challenge, is writing the software that will enable the storage device to recognize and record the data carried by the electrical signals. Marvin confirmed my assumption that there is no existing software that can be modified very easily to do that. But he expressed confidence that he'll be able to create it.

And so, with our respective assignments in hand, we got to work.

Wednesday, October 29, 2025
Today Marvin finished researching computer options. He believes that the portable drives that we currently use are actually fine. The computer science revolution of the past seven or eight years has produced portable drives that can store previously unthinkable quantities of data. Our existing portable

drives can easily accommodate all the electrical data that we'll be able to transfer from a single brain.

It's the processing speed that needs a major upgrade. We'll be extracting electrical signals from billions of neurons one at a time. We'll need a computer with a processing speed several times greater than that of our existing computers. These are available, he said, and he doesn't think the project will be realistic without them unless our only goal is to download a small amount of memory data so that we can prove the theory. But they are *extremely* expensive (his emphasis).

Fortunately, and to Marvin's great delight, I have enough grant money to cover the costs of this new computer. I placed the order today and then resumed working on the EOSF instructions. It will take about three weeks for the computer to arrive.

Friday, October 31, 2025
Jessica reminded me that tonight is Halloween. For many years this had become a dead holiday, as parents stopped letting their children go trick-or-treating. There were too many dangers. But in the last few years, and particularly in our neighborhood, that tradition has seen a resurgence. She decided that I would take Zeke trick-or-treating, as I have had practically no time with him for weeks. She will stay home and hand out candy to the children who come to our door.

This meant leaving the lab no later than 4:30 this afternoon. That was tough for me, because shortly before that I was just starting to break through one of the more tenacious logic barriers I had encountered in writing the EOSF instructions. But I dragged myself away from the lab and got home in plenty of time to take Zeke around the neighborhood. We had a great time, except when some of the adults expected Zeke to actually talk to them. He was either too shy to do that or too impatient to get to the next house, so I didn't make him talk except to say thank you.

Monday, November 17, 2025

Over the past couple weeks, I've continued to put in very long hours, not getting home until after Jessica and Zeke are asleep. It's been a major struggle to finish writing the EOSF instructions. The logic has gotten really complicated, and I'm getting frustrated that I haven't been able to finish it yet. But I'm getting closer every day and think I'm now seeing some light at the end of the tunnel.

When I finish writing the instructions, my next step will be a trial run to see whether my instructions actually work. It doesn't really matter that it's taking me a long time to complete these tasks, because we won't be able to go further with this project anyway until Marvin finishes writing the recognition software, and that will surely take more time to finish than my part will.

Jessica now seems resigned to the reality that for a little while longer I'm going to have very limited family time. There haven't been any major blowups, just a relationship of unspoken peaceful coexistence.

She should understand by now that this project is immensely important and that its complexity requires my exclusive focus for a few short, discrete periods. There's not a lot I can do about that.

The other day I even came up with an analogy that I thought would drive this point home. Military personnel routinely have to be away from their families entirely, and for much longer periods of time. Their family members accept this, and are supportive, because they are unselfish enough to appreciate that military service entails sacrifice for the good of the country and the world. Their families are willing to share in that sacrifice. It's the right thing to do, and it's an act of love. I'm similarly doing something that will bestow untold benefits on humankind, and it's not even requiring the same level of family sacrifice as military service. I'm not risking my life, and I'm home often, not away for a year at a time.

None of this sunk in. Jessica just nodded and walked away.

Marvin has also been working furiously and staying late at the lab. I still miss Lisa, but she never showed the level of commitment I'm seeing from Marvin. Having a colleague who is as driven as I am to devote long, intense hours to this project is a true delight. He's clearly very excited about it.

I asked him yesterday whether his wife is OK with his work schedule. He confided that she's feeling a bit lonely at the moment. She doesn't have a job yet, and having just moved to a brand new city she doesn't have any real friends here, so of course she misses having Marvin around. He feels bad about this, but once he makes a breakthrough with the software that he's designing, he'll be able to dial it down a bit. So as Marvin sees it, this is a short-term problem.

I told him I agree and mentioned that my wife has similar concerns, but I didn't let on how acrimonious our relationship has become. I don't want to scare him or discourage him from continuing to focus on his work, which is so vital to the whole project.

The good news is that the new computer arrived today. We were both happy about it, but Marvin was practically drooling. For him, it was like opening his presents on Christmas Day and finding the dream toy that he had always wanted. His enthusiasm always makes me smile. He spent most of today getting it set up and reading about its many revolutionary features.

I think he would have spent the whole night here playing with his new toy but for the fact that today was his and his wife's wedding anniversary. He had promised her that they would go out for a nice dinner. Given his long absences from the home since arriving in St. Louis, he felt this was a promise he had to keep. I told him I understood completely and that he should go out and enjoy himself.

But all this made me realize that I had completely forgotten about my own and Jessica's anniversary this past July -- four months ago. That was around the time that Lisa and I were working feverishly to figure out how the picobes were able to trap the electrical signals. By then, also, my relations with Jessica had already deteriorated quite a bit. So I guess the last thing on my mind was our anniversary. The funny thing is that she never said a word to me about it. Maybe our anniversary no longer matters to her either.

Monday, December 1, 2025

This morning I solved the last remaining logic problem and completed the first draft of the EOSF instructions. That was a great feeling. This task had proved to be much tougher and more frustrating than expected, but now I had a good enough set of instructions for a trial run.

Since Marvin hasn't yet finished writing the software that will enable the computer to recognize the arriving electrical signals and record them on the portable drive, the electricity will have no place to go once it reaches the computer. That means the electrical signals from the multiple picobes will pile up inside the fiber. So at this trial stage, I had to instruct the EOSF to do only a small number of repetitions to ensure that there would be plenty of room for the electricity.

Shortly after lunch I took my maiden voyage, running the EOSF with my hot-off-the-press instructions. There were 73 error messages. I had certainly expected some bugs on the first run, but I was disappointed there were that many. Upon closer inspection, many of them were related. Some bugs will automatically disappear once I solve some of the other bugs. Still, there were many independent glitches to work through, and this afternoon I set to work methodically addressing them one at a time.

Tuesday, December 2, 2025

Marvin feels he's making steady progress on the recognition software and is now extremely confident that he will ultimately succeed. He has also now done enough to estimate the maximum speed with which the new computer will be able to process and record the electrical signals from the picobes. He has determined that the computer will be able to process the signals from about 4000 picobes every second.

I had rightly assumed all along that the processing speed of the computer – not the time it takes for the freed electricity to travel to the computer – would ultimately determine how long it will take to upload all the memory data from a single brain. But now that Marvin has given me the maximum processing speed of the computer, I can do the actual math.

The key here is that I don't want the light beams traveling in one direction while the electrical signals are traveling in the opposite direction through the same space, because the light could distort the data carried by the electrical signals. So the EOSF will have to wait until one set of electrical signals has been recorded on the portable drive before it fires off the light beam that will release the electrical signals from the next picobe.

In a vacuum, light travels at about 300 million meters per second and electrical signals travel at almost that same speed. The fiber that will connect the brain to the portable drive is about one meter long. So the round trip – light traveling to the picobe and electricity then traveling to the portable drive – will be two meters.

This means that in theory the EOSF could fire off approximately 150 million light beams per second. With an estimated 10 billion receptor neurons in the temporal lobe (that's the most recent estimate according to the 2025 scientific consensus), it would thus take only about 67 seconds to empty all the electrical signals in the entire temporal lobe!

That's the theory. In practice, though, that figure is meaningless. At least two things will limit our speed in a much more serious way.

The first is the maximum processing speed of the computer. At the rate of 4000 picobes per second, it will take us 2.5 million seconds (about 29 days, going continuously 24/7) to record the electrical signals from all of the 10 billion picobes in the temporal lobe.

The other limitation is the capacity of the EOSF. I'm estimating that it can be programmed to target a maximum of 30 million different sites with a single command. At the computer's maximum processing rate of 4000 sites per second, each command will therefore keep the EOSF busy for a little over two hours. And with 10 billion sites, that also means setting it up about 333 times.

Marvin and I aren't going to be in the lab 24/7. So there will be many times when everything is idle. We'll have to figure out a schedule. If we take turns coming in to re-set the commands, maybe we could do it, say, six times a day, seven days a week? That would be 42 times per week. At that rate, the uploading would take about eight weeks, which would be fine.

There might be some brain tissue deterioration over that period, but with modern neurovitrification techniques any data loss should be minor. I'll have to talk with Marvin about how often he'll be able to come in to change the commands.

He won't have to wait the whole eight weeks to get started on the decoding. As more and more data pour in, he'll hopefully be able to begin looking for patterns. But all that is still well down the road. This is once again beginning to look very, very exciting.

Friday, December 5, 2025
I'm making some pretty good progress in de-bugging my EOSF instructions. After a few more test runs, I'm down to 36 error messages. I need to complete my job of getting the EOSF to sequentially pierce the disks in the protein channels and enable the escaping electrical signals to travel through the fiber to the computer. Only after I get that process working will Marvin be able to do a test run on the recognition software that he's currently writing.

This afternoon, during a coffee break, Marvin and I had a very revealing conversation. As he talked about his work, I could readily see his love – there's no other way to describe it – for mathematics and science. For him, this is one wonderful gigantic logic puzzle, and it is pure pleasure to try to solve it.

I too love those kinds of challenges, but for me the main driving force in this project has not been the potential for scientific discovery. That has merely been a means to an end. My goal is nothing less than the replication of eternal life. I want to alleviate the pain of knowing that one's existence ends when the body dies – for myself, yes, but for the larger society as well. So I sat Marvin down to explain to him where I was coming from. I gave him the abbreviated version.

"Marvin, I've talked about this with Lisa and with my wife, but I don't think I've ever explained to you why this project is so important to me. I don't believe in a supreme being or an afterlife, and the prospect of immediate nonexistence upon death has always left me despondent. I've come to feel that human life, in its essence, is nothing more than the sum of what we think and feel. So if we can enable those thoughts and feelings to survive in a permanent form even after a person dies, I think we're doing nothing less than preserving the essence of that person's life. The person's thoughts and feelings can live forever. Do you agree?"

Marvin listened attentively but seemed unmoved.

"That's interesting. Yeah, that makes sense."

"I'm curious what your religious beliefs are. You don't have to tell me if you'd prefer to keep that private."

"Me? Well, my wife and I aren't super-religious, but we do go to church most Sundays. We both did that when we were kids, and we're kind of keeping up that practice as adults."

"But do you believe in God? Do you think there's an afterlife?"

"I'm not really sure. I can't say I've thought much about it. Oh, by the way, you'll love this. I discovered a feature of this new computer that I think will be incredibly useful as I program it to recognize variations in the electrical signals that it receives. It turns out there are more variations in those signals than I had first assumed. This new computer is amazing. It will be able to break those variations down in ways that I could never have imagined."

At that, Marvin described this exciting new feature to me in minute detail. I have to admit I was only half-listening. Marvin was now in his own world, lost in the ecstasy of this new treasure.

I was feeling a bit let down. From the moment he arrived, I had begun thinking of Marvin as a younger version of myself. I saw his analytical brilliance, his work ethic, and his unbridled enthusiasm for mathematical and scientific inquiry.

But this conversation disappointed me. He's not my younger incarnation at all. His lack of interest in the larger cosmic implications of this extraordinary project was astonishing. As impressive as his analytical skills clearly are, he lacks the broad vision that a scientist who wants to achieve path-breaking results has to have.

I'm still thrilled he's here, no question about that. His work in this project might easily make the difference between success and collapse. But he's missing something important. And he's not me.

Monday, December 8, 2025

This morning Marvin kind of jolted me again. This time, what he delivered was a reality check.

"Jason, I know that right now my priority is supposed to be finishing the recognition software so we can get these electrical data onto the portable drive and keep them safe. But I've also been thinking ahead a little about the decoding that I'll eventually need to do. And it occurred to me that maybe I could learn something from the way they deciphered the hieroglyphics on the Rosetta Stone. So I did a little research on that. It was just a couple hours, I hope you don't mind."

"No, of course not. I'm glad you're thinking ahead. What did you find out?"

"Well, it's not good news. It actually kind of worries me. It took them more than 20 years to decode the Rosetta Stone. And that job was a cakewalk compared to what will be required to translate these electrical signals. The big thing – they could never have pulled this off otherwise – was that the inscriptions on the Rosetta Stone appeared in three language versions, which they could assume were all saying the same thing. And one of them was ancient Greek, which was a known quantity. So they had a reference point for translating the hieroglyphics. We don't have that. There's no known language to measure our electrical signals against. And we don't even know anything at all about the lives or the thoughts of the people whose brains we're extracting information from."

"True, but ..."

"Wait, there's more. The guy who made the final breakthrough with the Rosetta Stone was a Frenchman named Champollion. He wasn't working from a clean slate. By the time he came on the scene, there had already been some key breakthroughs by an Englishman named Thomas Young. Until Young came along, everybody had been assuming that the three languages on the Rosetta Stone were all phonetic. But Young made a key discovery about one of them – not the hieroglyphics or the Greek, but a third language that they later called the Demotic script. He figured out that that language actually contained *both* phonetic characters and ideographic symbols, though it apparently didn't occur to him that the same might be true of the Hieroglyphic version. Young had also managed to translate a few specific Hieroglyphic characters, though he never compiled the comprehensive language that Champollion would later develop. My point is that we don't have any of that kind of work to build on. We're starting from ground zero."

"OK, I hear you. I never thought this would be easy. But don't forget we have all these tools now that those guys didn't have more than 200 years ago or whenever that was. The big thing is that we have powerful computers that can process massive gobs of information. They didn't. We can process more data in five minutes than people 200 years ago could have processed in a lifetime. And we can synthesize that information to expose patterns. We also have decades of experience developing mathematical models for breaking codes. They didn't have any of those either."

"I guess. I'm still kind of concerned about this, though. I just don't know."

"Well, let's not worry about this just yet. Right now you need to focus on the recognition software so we can safely store all these data while we're figuring out the decoding part."

That conversation threw me. For one thing, it was the first time I'd seen any lack of confidence in Marvin about anything. But more than that, he made some good points. What if it really does prove impossible to crack the code? Or what if we crack the code, but it turns out these weren't memories at all, just some residual electrical activity in the brain?

Up to now, I've been ecstatic about how everything just seemed to be falling perfectly into place. But if we can't crack the code, the whole project will have been futile. I'll have wasted years of time, effort, and emotional investment. And probably squandered my marriage in the process.

CHAPTER 6
PARENTS ARE MORTAL

Thursday, December 11, 2025

I got the news this morning, as I was about to leave for lunch. Jessica called me at the lab.

"Jason, I just heard from your mother. It's nothing to worry about yet, but she's been having a little trouble breathing, so she went in to see the doctor. They took X-rays and did an MRI or a CAT-Scan, she wasn't sure which, but she definitely has a tumor in her left lung and they think it's likely that it's malignant. The good news it's just a small shadow, and they think they caught it at a very early stage. But they can't be 100% certain until they operate. They've scheduled the surgery for Monday morning. You need to call her."

"Obviously I need to call her! You don't have to tell me that. Why did she call you and not me?"

"She said she planned to call you tonight. She didn't want to disturb you at work. I told her that you'd want to talk to her right away."

"I'm going to call her right now. Bye."

And with that, I called my mother. She was adamant that it was not going to be a big deal. She repeated, several times, that the doctors were very confident they had caught the cancer early on and that it would just be a matter of removing a small mass. They didn't even think she would lose a lung or need radiation or chemo.

She then talked about how stupid she had been to smoke, and how this is actually a blessing in disguise, because it's forcing her to stop smoking once and for all while there's still time to repair the damage. Really, she insisted, the prognosis is excellent, and I shouldn't worry. But she was grateful that I called, and how was my work going, and it's always a joy to talk to me.

This development shook me for a while. My mother is now the only adult in the world who loves me. Jessica no longer does, I'm sure of that. And Lisa most likely never did. Of course there's little Zeke, and I'm going to make sure that from now on I give him the time and attention that we both need – and deserve. As soon as I get past this next phase of the project, successfully running the EOSF. I'm now getting very close. The instructions are basically written, and I'm zeroing in on a successful run.

Monday, December 15, 2025
At Jessica's suggestion, which was a good one, I drove my mother to the hospital. Jessica had said it would mean a lot to my mother for me to be there with her before and after the surgery. And she was right. My mother was extremely appreciative. On the short ride to the hospital, she told me that she loves me and wants me to be happy. And in turn I assured her that the doctors wouldn't be painting this rosy picture of her prospects if they were at all worried.

Honestly, during the ride over, I wasn't even thinking about work. My attention was focused on keeping my mother calm.

After all the prep work, they eventually wheeled my mother into the operating room. They told me they would call me as soon as they had anything to report and that I would be able to see her in the recovery room soon after the operation.

Two hours later, the surgeon came out to the waiting room. He told me that he was both surprised and sorry to report that once they opened her up, they could see that my mother's cancer had spread to several critical organs. It was inoperable. They didn't try to remove any of it. They just sewed her back up and brought her to the recovery room. I would be able to see her in about 30 minutes.

I'm a doctor, so of course I understood what the surgeon was saying. But I must have been in a state of either shock or denial, because I asked the surgeon what this means. He looked at me as if I were an idiot and explained that this means my mother is not going to survive very long. I pressed him on how long, and he told me it was very difficult to predict an exact timeline. I said I understood that, but he must at least have an estimate – weeks, months, years? He said this was something to discuss with the oncologist, who will go over all the options with my mother.

I thought he was being awfully brusque, but there really wasn't anything left to say. He told me that a nurse would see me shortly to bring me to the recovery room, and then he left.

My mind raced back to that first day of high school, when my mother had to tell me that my father had died a couple hours earlier. This was just as unexpected. I had understood that the doctors wouldn't be able to provide a really reliable prognosis until they actually operated, but I had been optimistic based on their earlier assurances. I don't know how they could have led us along when they knew very well that at that point they had no way to assess how serious my mother's condition was. They were just guessing. I felt cheated.

In the recovery room my mother was still woozy. She didn't ask me how everything had gone, and I was relieved she didn't, because I didn't want to break the news to her while she was still recovering from the surgery. I told her that she needed to get some rest and that I would come back this evening to visit her in her hospital room.

I called Jessica to fill her in. She was supportive, but the whole time all I wanted to do was get off the phone. I grabbed a quick lunch in the hospital cafeteria and then went to the lab. As I was driving, my mind kept flitting back and forth between the news about my mother and the work I needed to do.

Marvin was out at lunch when I arrived, so I was alone with my thoughts for a little while. He returned shortly, though, and I filled him in. He was very nice. He told me how sorry he was to hear this and offered to help in any way he could.

I returned to my task of solving the remaining bugs in my EOSF instructions and actually made some decent progress. Marvin appears to be at a temporary impasse in writing the recognition software, but I'm certain he'll come through before long.

Tuesday, December 16, 2025
Last night I visited my mother in the hospital. The anesthesia had worn off, and she was fully alert. Her oncologist had visited her about an hour before I got there and had delivered the bad news. So by the time I arrived, my mother had had a little time to absorb what this meant. That made our conversation easier.

The oncologist also scheduled an appointment with her for tomorrow morning to discuss her options. My mother told me she would like me to come to that meeting. I said of course. She asked whether it would be OK with me if Jessica were there too, and I said yes.

Wednesday, December 17, 2025
The meeting with the oncologist didn't last long, maybe 15 minutes. The oncologist was a nondescript Malaysian man, probably in his 40s, with a kind and empathetic manner -- unlike the surgeon. He was also completely candid. He told my mother that without further treatment she probably had 3-6 months. He said that with a combination of chemotherapy and radiation she could prolong that timeline, but that that would probably buy her only about three additional months at most.

He advised her not to make any decisions today, but to think about what she'd like to do, talk with her family, and then let him know whether she would like to proceed with the chemo. She shouldn't wait too long, he added, because if she decided to have the chemo, they would want to start soon.

After that meeting the nurse wheeled my mother back to her room and I drove Jessica to her office. Jessica told me that my mother should stay at our house while she's recuperating. Otherwise we didn't say much.

When we arrived at Jessica's office, she patted me on my arm, told me in a kindly way that she was sorry this has happened, and reassured me that life will go on and that everything will be OK. I was pleased that with all the harsh words we had recently exchanged, she could not bring herself to be cruel to me during this emotional time.

That evening I again visited my mother in her hospital room. She told me she had made a firm decision to forego chemo. She said she didn't need any more time to think about it. The few additional months that chemo would buy her would be miserable, and she wanted to enjoy or at least tolerate her remaining time as much as possible.

She was very happy when I told her that Jessica and I wanted her to stay with us during her recuperation and was especially excited that she would be able to see more of her little grandson. That reminded me that we need to figure out how to explain all this to a five-year-old.

Tuesday, December 23, 2025

My mother has been staying with us since her discharge from the hospital. The surgical wounds are healing about as well as expected, and she's now pretty close to the point where she'll be able to return home, which she seems anxious to do. As much as she likes having the three of us around, she said she really wants the comfort and the normalcy of being in her own house.

I hope that's all it is, and that she's not picking up on the stress in my and Jessica's relationship, because that's surely something that my mother doesn't need right now. I'm certain I'm not doing anything that would give that away, and hopefully Jessica isn't either. We haven't told Zeke yet that his grandma is dying. That can be put off until we're closer to the time.

Meanwhile, I know I should now be spending more time at home, especially with my mother and Zeke. And just in case I hadn't been able to figure that out on my own, Jessica is frequently reminding me.

But our project in the lab is well behind where I had wanted it to be, and I keep focusing on the fact that Marvin won't be able to test his recognition software until I finish my job of programming the EOSF to send the electricity from the picobes to the computer. He hasn't finished writing the recognition software, so I haven't slowed him down yet, but he seems to be getting close, so I really need to finish my part.

The past few days, that has meant once again working long hours, sometimes without any progress to show for an entire day. By the time I do get home, it's usually about 10 pm or so, and everyone except Jessica is asleep. In tones she hopes my mother won't overhear, she whispers to me that this is the worst time I could possibly pick to work my "insane" hours. I'm too tired to argue with her, so I usually just ignore her and plop down in front of the TV to unwind while I grab a quick dinner before going to bed.

All that said, I have made considerable progress. The original 73 bugs in the first draft of my EOSF instructions are now down to 4. Those remaining four bugs aren't intractable, exactly, but they are challenging. I'm confident I'll be able to solve them, but I don't know how long that will take.

On another front, though, another light bulb just turned on. This idea is just half-baked, and it might sound shocking at first, but I'm writing it down in this journal so that I can think about it some more in the coming days. It has to do with Marvin's concerns about the challenges that the decoding will eventually present. He compared our project to the deciphering of the Rosetta Stone. He talked about how difficult that was and why the decoding challenges we face will be even greater.

The main reason he thought our job would be harder is that we, unlike the folks who worked on the Rosetta Stone, have no preexisting reference point. We don't have a Greek language version that we can compare our electrical signals to. And we don't know anything about the lives of the people whose brains we're examining. If we did, we'd have our reference points.

Well, as it turns out, I know a great deal about the life of one person who is about to die – my mother. I also know that my mother long ago consented to the use of her body for research when she dies. If we were to extract and store the electrical signals that contain the memories in my mother's brain, we might very well be able to start identifying the thought patterns that correlate to particular signals.

Again, I know this idea will be shocking to some. I'm not clueless. But it holds real promise and wouldn't hurt anyone. I'm going to need to give this more thought and then talk it over with Marvin.

Thursday, December 25, 2025
It's Christmas Day. All four of us – Jessica, Zeke, my mother, and I – spent the day at our house. It was nice to spend the whole day with Zeke, though he didn't seem overly excited about his presents -- not even the child-sized electric car that he could actually sit in and steer. I would have loved to have a present like that when I was a kid. By the end of the day I would have disassembled it and put it back together again five times.

We knew this would be my mother's last Christmas. I feel bad that I haven't spent more time with her these past few years, but she knows that I love her and understands that my work schedule has been crazy. I also want to be sure I don't make the same mistake with her that I made with my father – failing to ask all kinds of questions while it's still possible.

That led me to a plan. Although my priority at work has been to finish debugging the EOSF instructions, I have to think ahead to the decoding phase. Mindful of Marvin's observations about the need for reference points, and well aware that my mother's condition leaves me only a narrow window to gather information about her life, I decided I would meet regularly with her, probably on a daily basis. I would visit with her during the day, when Jessica was at work, so that we could talk in privacy.

Obviously I won't tell my mother that I plan to keep her brain after she dies and extract memories from it. For one thing, she would be horrified. In her current vulnerable state she would never understand the scientific benefits and would find the whole idea upsetting. For another, she might not want me to know everything she has done or thought. Moreover, if she knew why I was asking her all these questions, she might withhold crucial information.

I also wouldn't want her to think that professional gain is my only reason for spending time with her during her dying days. And it isn't. I will truly treasure my limited remaining time with my mother, and I want her to feel the comfort of knowing that her son is there with her. So I told my mother that I plan to come home from work every day around lunchtime to visit with her. Predictably, she was very happy.

Later in the day, while all of us were together at dinner, my mother told Jessica about my intention to visit her at lunchtime every day. Jessica seemed surprised and extremely pleased. So much so that I began reconsidering my decision not to tell Jessica what I planned to do upon my mother's death. But first I want to talk this over with Marvin to make sure the information I acquire from these visits – I suppose "interviews" would be a better word – will actually be useful to him during the decoding phase.

Friday, December 26, 2025

When Marvin arrived at the lab this morning, I couldn't wait to tell him my idea and hear his reaction. Once he'd gotten settled into his cubicle, I walked over.

"So I've been thinking some more about our conversation the other day. You were right to point out that the people who deciphered the hieroglyphics on the Rosetta Stone had a reference point to start with. They had the Greek language version available. We don't have anything like that. But you made an interesting comment. Remember you said it's not even as if we knew anything about the lives of the individuals whose brains we were extracting data from."

"Yes?"

"Well, as it turns out, maybe we do."

"You found out who our brain specimens came from?"

"No. But as you know, my mother is dying."

A very long pause.

"Are you saying what I think you're saying?"

"Yes. And I'll be spending a good deal of time with her in the coming weeks and months, learning as much as I can about her life and her thoughts. She consented a long time ago to donate her remains for scientific research, and my thinking now is that my knowledge of her specific life events will be to us what the Greek language version was to the decipherers of the Rosetta Stone. Is that amazing, or what?"

"I'm not sure what to say. I understand this from a scientific standpoint, but are you sure you're prepared to do this? I mean this involves mutilating your mother's body and spending months probing her brain. Isn't that going to creep you out?"

"To be honest, no. I would never harm my mother, but after she dies, that body isn't her. It's just the container that she was in while she was alive. And I think she would be very pleased to know that that container can be used to create such an extraordinary gift – eternal life – for humankind. In fact it would be used to create eternal life for my mother herself, preserving the thoughts and sensations that were, and now will always be, her life."

"I hope I'm not getting too personal, Jason, but you say she 'would' be pleased to know this. Does that mean she doesn't actually know?"

"I haven't told her, because I don't want her to feel inhibited when I have these conversations with her about her life. But I'm sure she would approve if she knew."

"Again, I'm not trying to be a downer, but is this even legal? I mean, you can't just do whatever you want with a person's remains, can you?"

"Well, you raise a good point. I've been assuming it's legal. I'm her only child, so I would guess I have the right to decide how best to dispose of her remains. I mean, children are always making decisions about cremation versus burial, and so on. But you're right that this is something I should check into. Assuming it's legal, though, are you OK with it?"

"I have to admit I was shocked a minute ago when you first told me. But I guess there's not really anything wrong with doing this as long as it's legal. And it would be really nice to have a reference point. That could make the difference between cracking the code and failing. Or it could shave months or years off the time for doing so. But it's totally up to you, obviously."

At lunchtime, as planned, I drove home to visit my mother. It's now been ten days since her surgery, and she was starting to rebound from it, so she insisted on making lunch, which was ready for me when I arrived. We started with small talk, and then I popped the question.

"Mom, you know I always felt bad that while Dad was alive I never asked him any questions about his life, and now I'll never be able to. I would like to learn as much as I can about your life, if you don't mind sharing your experiences. I want to be able to pass these down to Zeke when he's older, and I also want to know about them for myself. Would it be OK if I interviewed you from time to time during these lunchtime visits? I promise I won't bother you whenever you're feeling tired or weak, and I'll stop as soon as you want me to."

"That would be lovely, dear. I know how much of a place your work takes up in your life, so it makes me very happy to think that you have the time and the desire to know more about me. Of course, ask me anything you want."

My mother's answer was bitter-sweet. Naturally I was thrilled that she would let me interview her and glean as much information as I could. But I knew that I was deceiving her. I never revealed, and she had no way to know, my true purpose in interrogating her in this way. I felt more than a tinge of guilt. I was using my dying mother as a prop for my work project.

Still, it's not that black and white. I was perfectly truthful when I told her that I had always felt bad about knowing so little about my father. And I really do feel a need to know more about my mother, and not just because that will help me in my research. I was truthful also when I said that I wanted to be able to pass all this family information down to Zeke.

True, I didn't include the detail about using this as a reference point for deciphering the electrical signals that carry memory data, but that probably wouldn't have altered her willingness to be interviewed. I also have to make sure she's not so inhibited that she holds back on things. And the bottom line is that the scientific breakthrough that this will permit, or at least facilitate, will benefit all of humanity, not just me.

I actually don't know why I'm beating myself up over this, because it's not as if I'm hurting anyone in the process. So I have no reason to feel guilty. Anyone in the same position I'm in now would reach the same conclusion if they gave the issue two seconds of thought. As a matter of fact, it would be selfish of me to tell her the whole story and thereby jeopardize the success of the project. If anything, that's what I should feel guilty about – the fact that I was selfish enough even to contemplate telling her just to make myself feel less guilty.

So that's settled. I'm going to start the interviewing process tomorrow. This afternoon, when I return to the lab, I'll start writing down some questions that I need to ask her. At some point I'll also have to do some research and figure out whether there are any legal hurdles to worry about. I wish I could go to a lawyer for advice on that, but I can't risk a leak – not at this critical stage.

Tuesday, December 30, 2025

Since you have gotten this far into my journal, you will already have read the prologue and chapter 1. I wrote those over the past two days and inserted them at the beginning so that all the succeeding passages would make sense.

Thursday, January 1, 2026

Jessica isn't happy that I'm working on New Year's Day, but I have no choice. I had been planning to work normal hours during the current phase of the project, figuring I had plenty of time because we wouldn't be able to go forward anyway until Marvin had finished writing the recognition software. But over the past week two things have forced me to return to long hours at the lab. One is that Marvin thinks he is just about finished writing a testable draft of his recognition software. He'll be ready very soon to start running it, but he won't be able to do that until I complete my task of perfecting the EOSF instructions, so that the electrical signals he needs to upload will actually be able to travel to the computer. I don't want to hold him up.

The other development is that I have more work to do than I had anticipated. In addition to the final debugging of the EOSF instructions, I'm now spending about two hours a day going home for lunch and debriefing my mother.

On top of all that, the legal research has proved much more time-consuming than I had expected. All I want to know is whether, as her only son, I can legally extract my mother's brain after she dies and then return the rest of the body to the undertaker. That seems like a straightforward question, but nothing is easy. I now have a lot of information, though, and hopefully I'll be able to pull it all together by tomorrow.

I'm getting a little nervous about timing. I don't know how much more time my mother has left before she dies or becomes too weak to continue the interviews. And I have so much more information to get from her. I want to know about her experiences and thoughts from her whole life span, as much as she can remember. And time is running out.

But I also have to finish the legal research while she's still alive and then make advance arrangements with the funeral home. Plus, I want to be sure we can start downloading the electrical signals from her brain as soon as possible after her death. I'll use all available chemical preservatives to minimize the deterioration of the brain tissue, but I still can't be sure how much data I'll lose if I have to wait a long time for the downloading. In addition, the downloading of her brain can't begin until Marvin finishes testing his recognition software on our existing brain specimens, which he can't even start doing until I finish the EOSF instructions.

This is getting very tense. I'm already back to working seven days a week and not getting home until late at night. I doubt that I'm physically capable of sustaining any more hours than that.

Friday, January 2, 2026
I can't believe this. I apparently wasn't feeling enough time pressure. Now, on top of everything else, I received an email this morning from my department head. He claims he emailed me a month ago for my annual progress report and still doesn't have it. I was

late last year too, he added, and the tenure committee "is not amused."

I have *zero* recollection of receiving the earlier email. It wouldn't surprise me if he forgot to send it and now wants to shift the blame for the delay to me. But I can't be sure. I have to admit I've been preoccupied and might well have missed it. I've been missing a bunch of other things, it seems, so maybe he's right. I'm starting to think I'm losing it. He says he absolutely needs it by Tuesday.

I don't know what to do. It's not just the time it will take to write it. It's the secrecy. I can't reveal that I'm extracting the memory data from dead brains, for lots of reasons that I explained earlier. And I haven't published anything for ages, since the time this project started heating up. But I have to demonstrate tangible progress, or I could literally lose my job and my lab.

I'm going to have to fudge a little. Years from now, when the biographers are writing their stories about me, it will seem comical to them and to the readers that I had to fudge my progress reports in order to keep my job and continue this project. But right now, before the work is finished, getting caught falsifying my progress report would itself be cause for instant dismissal. I have to be extremely careful.

I won't share any of this with Marvin or anyone else, and I'll keep my account as close to the truth as I can without giving away any secrets. That will be my weekend work. Which means I needed to make some real headway today on all the other stuff.

But I wasn't able to do even that. That's because, three hours after receiving that email from my department head, a similar email arrived from the NIH. That letter said I was two weeks delinquent on the annual progress report that I owed them as a condition of my grant.

This is turning into a nightmare. I have the same problem with them that I have with my department head – not being able to reveal what my project entails and the progress I've made to date. And it will take even longer to fill out that report once I've figured out what to say, because there are a million forms, they have to be completed online, and there is *always* some glitch with the program. I don't know why the *hell* they can't get it right.

This also means I'm going to have to skip today's lunch interview with my mother. She'll be disappointed, and more important, she doesn't have many weeks left and there's still a whole warehouse full of information I need to get from her.

I'm also finding it very suspicious that the requests from my department head and the NIH just happened to arrive the same day. Obviously, they have been in touch with each other, unbeknownst to me until now. That is truly weird. Why would they do that? My world is coming apart at the seams.

Saturday, January 3, 2026

Last night I made a massive mistake. I told Jessica about my plans to extract and keep my mother's brain and to download memories from it. I figured she would eventually find out anyway after the death occurs, because she'll need to know about the funeral and related arrangements.

She went berserk. It was one of those surreal conversations, where she somehow managed to scream at me in whispered tones so as not to wake up Zeke or be overheard by my mother.

I don't need this extra stress. I really don't, especially now. Her main grievances were that I was talking about "desecrating" my mother's body and that I would be "violating" her. And on top of that, I was deceiving her about my intentions. What kind of son would do that to his own mother, and while she is dying, etc, etc.

I didn't know whether to argue back or just crumble. I ended up doing neither. I was simply numb. It felt as if there were nothing at all going on in my brain. I just mumbled something about going to bed. She told me this conversation is not over.

I woke up early this morning, drank three cups of coffee instead of my usual one, and willed my body to the lab. The last thing I wanted to spend time on was my two progress reports, but I had no choice. If I didn't complete them by the already late second deadline, I risked losing everything. The whole project could go down the tubes.

As it turned out, I was able to finish and submit both reports. I had to stay until after midnight to do it, and I had to take some minor liberties with the truth, but I'm pretty sure these reports will satisfy all concerned parties.

I wrote that I had made real progress working with dead brains and that I am close to determining which areas of the brain hold out the most promise for later finding picobes in living subjects. That is actually true. The only things I didn't mention were that I had actually located picobes in dead brains, that I've figured out why electricity doesn't escape from them, and that I was able to use the EOSF to shoot light beams into the disks inside the protein channels and capture the escaping electrical signals.

Since there are written and electronic records of the EOSF having been delivered to my lab, I had to come up with some kind of explanation as to what I was doing with it. So I wrote that I was using it, with the embedded super-powered electron microscope, to shoot light beams into the dead brains and more precisely locate the areas whose properties seem most conducive to housing picobes in live humans. I just have to hope that nobody asks for physical documentation.

I had to skip my lunch visit with my mother today in order to finish these reports, but I'll resume those tomorrow. I can't afford to miss any of the visits from this point on, because there's no way to predict how much longer she will be alive and strong enough to continue.

Meanwhile, Marvin was also in today. He now comes in regularly seven days a week just like me, though he doesn't stay nearly as late. As he had predicted, he finished the first draft of his recognition software and is now ready to test it on the new computer. That was great news, but it means that now I absolutely have to finish debugging the EOSF instructions so that he can get started with the testing he has to do. I'm going to make a concerted effort to complete the EOSF instructions tomorrow.

Sunday, January 4, 2026

I have *got* to get to the lab before too long if I want to have any chance of finishing my EOSF testing today. As promised, however, Jessica cornered me in the kitchen and told me we needed to talk about my plans for my mother and that it has to be now. "We can't keep putting this off," she said.

Normally I would have ignored her and gone to the lab, but her mood suggested she was now able to discuss this calmly and rationally, so I figured I should seize the moment even though my mind was solely on the EOSF task. We went outside for a walk so that we could discuss this in privacy.

She had to start with a really stupid, flip comment.

"Wasn't there a famous baseball player who died a long time ago, and his son cut off his head so that one day his father could be cloned?"

I'm a baseball fan, so this was really irritating.

"A 'famous' baseball player? This was Ted Williams, the greatest hitter who's ever lived. That's like saying 'wasn't there a famous Revolutionary War general who became the first US President?' I mean the man had a lifetime batting average of .344. And he was the last .400 hitter. Nobody's done it in the 100 years since. And then he missed five years at the peak of his career serving in the Marines during wartime and still managed to hit 521 home runs – as a left-handed pull hitter in Fenway Park, with its cavernous right-center field. Jeez!"

"Sorry! I hadn't realized you were so emotionally attached to this Ted Wilson person."

"*Williams!* Ted *Williams!* But that's not the point. The point is, don't compare me to the cryonics folks. They're whack jobs. They think that if they freeze someone's body they'll eventually be able to restore the whole body to life and then clone it, once the necessary technology just magically appears. All I'm doing is preserving the memory cells in the brain, the same way a computer continues to store data even after the computer dies."

"Jason, this is grisly. You're talking about cutting up your mother's body, decapitating your own mother. You can't pass this off as just a science experiment. It's grotesque."

"My mother's body is not my mother. It will soon be nothing more than a vessel that used to perform the function of keeping all her life functions in working order. Once she dies, it's just a decaying mass of chemicals. It will have no life and nothing of meaning – except for her brain, which contains the physical matter that enables me to reconstruct her thoughts and her feelings. And those will remain the essence of who she is and was."

"What about her privacy? Shouldn't secrets remain secret? If your mother didn't want to share something, shouldn't we respect those wishes? We all think evil thoughts from time to time. What separates people on moral grounds is only whether we act on them. Would you want our son to know these things about his grandmother? For that matter, would you want him to know everything *you've* ever thought – every bad or even embarrassing thought, every sexual impulse, every picking of your nose when you thought you were alone, everything you've ever done that would diminish his pride in you or his respect for you, or even make him ashamed? Isn't there a fundamental right to privacy, at the very least for your innermost thoughts that you've chosen not to share with anyone else?"

"We're talking about what will happen after my mother dies, not what's happening now. She will never know that others will learn about her private thoughts. Revealing her secrets doesn't harm her in any way. But it does preserve her for others, and again, it preserves the very things that constitute who she was and is. I don't mean to sound like a broken record, but that is the reality."

"But once this discovery becomes public and accessible by others, every living human will know that their most private thoughts can potentially be disclosed against their will and that there is nothing they can do about it."

"Not true. There are laws that allow people to specify what is to become of their remains. If they make clear that they are to be buried or cremated intact, with no body parts removed, the law requires that their wishes be respected. I actually went online to confirm that. So even after my project is completed, no one will have to live with the worry that their private thoughts and feelings will be exposed to others, if they don't want them exposed."

The truth was that I hadn't actually completed my legal research, but that was what I preliminarily understood as the law. I'll confirm that as soon as I can. In the meantime, I knew I needed to get to the lab.

It was good I did, because I finally finished debugging the EOSF instructions. This is a big milestone. I managed to get the light beams to pierce a small number of disks and enable the freed electrical signals to arrive at the computer. I repeated the test several times on different areas of the brain and succeeded each time. I was now confident that my instructions worked.

I then made one modification to the instructions, so that they would now permit the EOSF to operate at the maximum capacity that the computer could handle. I finished all this at about 11:00 pm and emailed Marvin to let him know that he could now proceed to test his recognition software.

This is a huge relief, though the work that had to be finished this weekend prevented me from interviewing my mother two days in a row. That's a big deal considering her remaining days are so limited. Tomorrow I'll get back on schedule and also resume my legal research to make sure I can find a legal way to extract and keep my mother's brain after she passes.

Monday, January 5, 2026

Because of all the time-sensitive work that wiped out the last three days, I actually haven't seen or talked to my mother at all since Thursday, even though we're now living in the same house. I've been leaving the house early in the morning when she's still asleep and returning late at night when she and everyone else have gone to bed for the night.

This morning, however, she had a scheduled appointment with her oncologist. Jessica demanded that I drive my mother there and take part in the meeting, which of course I would have done anyway.

When I saw my mother this morning, though, I was shocked. In just four days she had badly deteriorated. Her face was drawn, she had lost weight, and she seemed very weak. All she wanted to do was sleep. I had to practically force her to get dressed and into the car so that we could see the doctor.

The doctor's news was grim. He had originally estimated that without further treatment her expected remaining time would be 3-6 months. Even at the low end, that would have given her until about mid-March.

But now, less than three weeks after providing that estimate, he told us that new test results have forced him to revise his estimate downward. He now thinks she is in her final few weeks and that she can expect to require heavier doses of painkiller, and therefore longer bouts of sleep, as time goes on.

He suggested we start making preparations for hospice care. My mother said she wanted the hospice care to be at our home. She wants to spend her remaining days with her family. The doctor said he understood that but advised her that there could well come a point, soon, when her physical discomfort becomes substantial enough to require the skilled care and facilities of an external hospice.

This was sobering news, and on the drive home my mother was extremely quiet. When we arrived at the house, she held onto my arm for support as we went in, and I asked her what she would like me to make her for lunch. She wasn't hungry, she said. All she wanted to do was take a nap. But I insisted that she eat something to maintain her strength.

I also figured she had to eat lunch at some point anyway, and as long as I was there then and hadn't interviewed her at all since last Thursday, and since the window for getting vital information from her was now closing rapidly, lunch seemed like as good a time as any for our next interview. Not an ideal time, I realize, but I knew I had to do this while it was still physically possible.

"Mom, are you strong enough now to talk about your teenage years? We kind of skipped over that period last time."

"I'm sorry, dear, but I don't think I can do it just now. Maybe after my nap."

"Well, the thing is, I'm going to need to go back to the lab right after lunch, so if we could talk for even a few minutes, that would be really good. It's very important that I learn as much as I can about your life."

"OK, but just for a couple minutes. I don't think I can do much more."

"Understood. I know you were a top student in high school. But what about your social life? Did you do a lot of dating?"

"Oh, yes, as a matter of fact, I did. I was actually very pretty then, and quite popular with the boys."

"I'm sure you were. Do you remember the names of any boyfriends?"

"Yes, during my entire junior year I dated Robert Navin. He was a very nice boy, and we had a great time together, but after about a year or so, it all kind of fizzled out and we ended up going our separate ways."

"Did he take you to the junior prom?"

"Yes, he did. That was the first time I had ever drunk alcohol. I think I had two beers. My parents smelled it on my breath when I got home and grounded me for a week. They also told me I was never to see Robert again, though we ended up sneaking around for several weeks after that. It didn't really matter, though, because by then I think we were both starting to lose interest. Robert ended up going into the military after graduation. Sadly, I learned about a year after the fact that he had died in a freak shooting accident during basic training. Even though I no longer had any romantic attachment to him by then, I felt terrible, because he was a good kid who died way too young."

"That really is a shame. What about your senior year?"

"Actually, dear, I'm really tired now. I think I have to go to bed. Could you please help me?"

"Of course. But can you just tell me briefly about your senior year? Was there anyone special you dated that year? Was there anything else big going on, like college applications or visits? Did you go to the senior prom?"

"Yes, I did. In fact that was the very last senior prom at my high school. They were starting to go out of fashion everywhere, and the following year my school decided to just not do them anymore. But I really can't keep my eyes open one minute longer. Please help me get to my bed now, dear."

So I started walking my mother to her bedroom. But the details about the proms are important, because I can later find out the exact dates of the proms, so the more detail I can get from my mother now, the more data Marvin and I will be potentially able to match when we get to the decoding stage. I felt bad badgering my mother on this when she was so tired, but since she had to be awake anyway as we walked to the bedroom, I tried one more time to pin her down about the details of her senior prom.

"What was the name of the boy you went to the senior prom with?"

"I think it was Robert Navin."

"Mom, you said he was your junior year boyfriend and you broke up at the end of that year. So your date for the senior prom must have been someone else."

"Oh, yes. I got a little confused just now."

"Do you remember his name?"

"Robert's?"

"No, your date for the senior prom."

"I told you, it was Mark Toricelli. Please, no more questions."

And that was the end of the conversation. I helped my mother into bed and covered her with a blanket. Within seconds, she was asleep. It was OK to leave her alone, because I was confident she would be asleep until well after Jessica got home, but I put a glass of water on her night table in case she woke up and was thirsty. I then drove to the lab.

Upon arrival, I got the bad news from Marvin. He had done the first test run of his recognition software. There were 455 error messages!

This was a major setback. Marvin had been confident that the first draft of his program was solid and that his first run would reveal only a few minor bugs at worst. Many of the error messages were incomprehensible, even to him. He could not for the life of him figure out what had gone wrong.

I told him about my mother's negative turn, and he told me he was sorry to hear this. I'm not sure how sincere his expression of sorrow was, though, because he seemed very distracted.

I explained to him that it's really important to have the recognition software up and working by the time my mother dies. I would use every available chemical preservative to minimize the deterioration of her brain tissue, but the longer it takes before we can start the uploading, the more brain tissue, and therefore the more data, we will lose. As it is, the uploading itself will likely take about eight weeks, so any delay before we can even begin it will be exacerbated. We need to be ready to upload my mother's memory data to the computer the moment she dies, which is now going to be sooner than we had previously thought.

This all seemed to unnerve Marvin even more, so I reassured him that he was doing great work and that I was confident he would solve the error messages. This was hard for me, though. I had to control my own anxiety, which is growing with every hour.

I now knew I had two immediate priorities. One is to finish my legal research so that I could be sure that when the time comes I'll be able to take custody of my mother's remains and perform the necessary surgery.

The other priority is jotting down as many questions as I can think of to put to my mother during our few remaining interview sessions. The key is to focus on those events that I'll be able to match up with specific dates or other specific information, especially any frequently recurring events or recollections that might later match up with any commonly recurring electrical signals from the brain. The more reference points we have, the better our chances of decoding.

I spent the rest of the afternoon on the legal issue. I still don't know why lawyers have to make everything so complicated, but after carefully reading everything I could find on the subject, here's what I learned:

Generally, the law says that the wishes of the decedent have to be honored unless there's a good reason not to. My mother long ago specified in her will that she wished to donate her organs for research, that her remains should then be cremated, and that I, as her son, should carry out those wishes in the way that I thought best. Which is what I plan to do.

It turns out there's also a law called the Uniform Anatomical Gifts Act. A variation of it is in force in every state. It lays out who is allowed to actually donate an organ for research, who is allowed to receive the organ, and who is qualified to remove an organ from the dead body.

I meet all the requirements. An adult child of the deceased may decide who to give the organ to. I just have to make sure I either express that intention in writing or make an electronic oral recording, and this afternoon I wrote and signed the required document.

Those who are allowed to receive an organ for research include hospitals, medical schools, universities, certain private organizations, and any "other appropriate person." Since I am a neurosurgeon whose research requires the brains of cadavers, I'm obviously an appropriate person. And nothing in the law says I can't donate the organ to myself.

And finally, any physician who is medically qualified to remove the organ from the body is allowed to do so. Again, that's me.

So I'm now certain there aren't any legal obstacles. This means I can now make the necessary advance arrangements with the funeral home. I'll arrange for my mother's body to be brought to the lab as soon as possible after she passes, remove and preserve the brain, and then have the funeral home pick up the remaining body and transport it to their facilities for cremation. I can also reassure Marvin that everything is legally on the up and up.

Meanwhile, I'm hoping Marvin can turn things around. I badly want him to have the recognition software up and running by the time my mother passes. I'm not at all confident he'll be able to do that. Not *at all* confident.

Tuesday, January 6, 2026

Last night Jessica woke up when I got home and scolded me for leaving my mother alone yesterday. It should have been obvious to me, she said, that my mother was too weak to be able to take care of herself. And all that on top of just receiving the terrible news from the doctor. I wasn't much of a son. She hoped Zeke will turn out be a better son than his father is.

I really don't know what Jessica thinks I could have done for my mother during the few afternoon hours that I left her alone. My mother was sound asleep. I suppose I could have called Jessica and asked her to come home from work to stay with my mother if Jessica thinks it was so critical to have somebody there while my mother slept. But I never heard Jessica even hint that she would have been willing to do that. I'm sure that if I had called her, her excuse would have been that she was too busy with her patients. But my being busy with my own work, even with the unusual urgency I was now operating under, is irrelevant, because my work is so unimportant.

She's incredible. There are times when I wonder how she ever graduated from college, let alone medical school.

This morning, though, we both agreed that we should hire an aide to stay with my mother during the day from this point on. Jessica volunteered to make the arrangements since, as she sarcastically noted, I was "so busy." And she actually knew the perfect person, a woman named Doris who had just finished caring for another elderly patient who had died last week. Doris was looking for work, was trained and highly competent, and in Jessica's opinion would fit the bill perfectly.

Jessica called Doris later this morning and Doris was happy to start right away, meaning tomorrow. Jessica then called her office and cancelled all her appointments for the day so that she could stay home with my mother this one time.

I looked in on my mother before leaving for work. She was sleeping peacefully. Lately Jessica has been the one to drop Zeke off at pre-school, because by that time I'm already at work in the lab. But today she couldn't, since she was staying with my mother, so I ended up waiting around and then taking him. Actually I'm glad I did. It made me realize how little time I've had with him recently, and I gave him a big hug when I left him with the teacher and the other kids. He squirmed away and ran immediately to the teacher for a hug. That made me feel bad, but I'm glad he loves his teacher.

Back at the lab, the first thing I did was call the funeral home to make the advance arrangements. Since my plan is so unusual, I feared that the funeral home would react with shock, as Jessica had. In that event I wanted to be sure we had time to address any of their concerns now, rather than in the chaos that will follow my mother's death.

As I had expected, the woman who answered the phone seemed shocked and puzzled. Maybe she was also disgusted, I couldn't tell. She asked me to hold for the director.

I was on hold for several minutes. I'm sure she was telling the director that there was some wacko on the phone who wants to cut out his mother's brain when she dies and wants us to make the arrangements. I don't know where they get these people. Eventually the director picked up the phone.

"Hello, Mr. Stramm, is it?"

"Dr. Stramm, yes. Has your assistant filled you in on the reason for my call?"

"Yes, she gave me a brief summary. Let me say first that I'm very sorry to hear this sad news about your mother. I hope she's resting peacefully during this terrible illness."

"Thank you. I wanted to talk with you in advance because I appreciate that the arrangements I'm planning are very unusual and I thought it best that we discuss them in case there are any problems that we need to take care of at this stage."

"Yes, I'm glad you called. I don't mean to make you rehash everything you've already explained to my assistant, but if you could run through the whole situation once more, I'd appreciate it."

"Sure. I'm an academic neurosurgeon. I run a lab at the Wash U Medical School. My research is on the way the human brain processes memory. For that purpose, my lab works with brains that have been taken from dead bodies and chemically preserved. It's very important work, because it could hold the key to eliminating or at least stalling dementia in elderly patients. There's particular benefit in my being able to work with the brain of someone I knew, because I would have a better idea of what to look for. My mother's will says that her organs are to be donated for research and her body then cremated, and it says I should be the one to make the organ donation arrangements. My father passed away a long time ago, and I'm her only child. Your funeral home did a very nice job when my father died, and I'd like you to do this for my mother as well."

"Thank you, Dr. Stramm. I'm very happy to know that you were pleased with the funeral arrangements for your father. Can you tell me a little more about the logistics? What exactly would you like us to do?"

"Well, as a neurosurgeon, I myself am qualified to do the actual cutting, to remove the brain from the body. But timing is critical. In order to prevent deterioration of the brain tissue, it's paramount that I remove the brain as soon as possible after death occurs and immediately preserve it chemically. So as soon as my mother passes, I would plan to call you and ask you to transport the body to my lab. I will then remove the brain surgically. It will take several hours, and as soon as I finish, I'll call you to transport the remaining body back to your facilities. Since I'm a doctor, I can also provide the death certificate. You could then take care of any other legal formalities and, when the time is right, cremate the remains. I'd then like to schedule a memorial service a couple days later."

"Dr. Stramm, I understand what you're saying, but as you've recognized, this is highly unusual. I'll just need to make sure we're complying with all the legal technicalities. I don't want to cause you any extra stress at this difficult time, but I'll need to think about this a little more."

"I've researched the law very carefully, and this is perfectly legal. If you like, I can send you all the legal information so that you can see it for yourself. And of course if you still have any doubts, you can always run it by your own attorneys. But my mother has very limited time left. She could die any day and almost certainly won't make it more than a few weeks, so I have to ask you to please decide as soon as possible."

"I will do that and get back to you very promptly. And yes, if you could send me the legal information you've found, that would be extremely helpful. Again, please accept my advance condolences. I know this is a very difficult time for you and your family."

After we hung up, I typed a summary of the legal considerations and emailed it to him. And then it was back to work organizing more questions to put to my mother.

At lunchtime I went home. Jessica seemed surprised to see me, even though she knew that my daily routine included lunch with my mother. She told me my mother had had a rough morning but had fallen asleep an hour ago and we needed to let her sleep.

This was frustrating for me, because I still had work to do at the lab and couldn't just sit around for hours waiting for my mother to wake up. So I tried to explain to Jessica that it was important to both my mother and me to have time together during her brief remaining life. I said I would wake her up so that we could have lunch and talk about her past. Yes, she'll be tired, but she can immediately go back to bed after lunch. She would feel terrible if she missed me.

But talking to Jessica is like talking to a wall. Her response was that I was being selfish "beyond belief," that I could care less about my mother's welfare, and that I just wanted to use her as a data source for my "ghoulish" scheme to cut out and somehow decode her brain. And if that weren't enough, I wasn't even willing to spend the half-hour or so that a round-trip drive to the lab would require and come back this afternoon once my mother was awake. I would rather subject my dying mother to all this needless discomfort than lose a precious half-hour of my time. And on and on. You get the drift.

I so wish I had never told Jessica about my plans. Yes, of course, I want to maximize the information that I can obtain from my mother for use in my project. But in the first place, none of this is for my own personal benefit; it's for the joy and peace of mind that the replication of eternal life can bring to humankind. That's a little more important than the temporary discomfort of one individual.

In the second place, I wasn't making this up. It really *is* important to my mother – and to me – to have some time together.

And in the third place, who the hell is Jessica to make this decision? This is my mother, not hers.

So I woke up my mother and asked her what she would like for lunch. It took a little while for her to sort out what was happening, and when she did, she told me she wasn't hungry and just wanted to nap a little longer.

"Mom, I can only stay a little while, because I have to get back to the lab. I don't want to miss our lunchtime together."

"OK, dear, but I'm feeling a little nauseous right now, so I'll just sit with you while you eat. I'll eat later when I feel better."

"Actually I'm not all that hungry either. So let's just talk for a few minutes and then you can go back to sleep when you're ready, OK?"

"OK. How is everything at work?"

"Oh, it's fine. But I wanted to talk to you about Dad, because we haven't had much of a chance to do that yet."

"Yes, I still miss your father. He was a very kind person. And he was a loving husband and father. If you're the kind of husband and father he was, you can be very proud of yourself."

"Well, tell me more. Where and when did you meet?"

"We actually met at Swarthmore, I think in our junior year. We both graduated in 1967. But we didn't date then. We were just in the same group of friends. And then we ran into each other at our tenth college reunion, so I guess that would be 1977. Wait, I said that wrong. We graduated in 1977, not 1967. So that means our reunion was in, oh, I'm so tired. I'm getting a little confused."

"That's OK, Mom. I know you're tired. Take your time."

"OK, right, we graduated in 1977, so the reunion would have been 1987. We liked each other right away, and I remember being surprised at how handsome he was and wondering how I hadn't noticed that before. Anyway, he seemed to like me too, and after the reunion dinner we broke away from the crowd and went for a walk. It was a beautiful, warm May evening, and I hope this won't embarrass you too much but we ended up making out a little on our walk. Nothing heavy, just kissing."

"You can probably skip over that part, Mom. So then what?"

My mother was now getting a second wind.

"Well, I had to return to my dermatology practice here, and your dad was living in Philadelphia at the time. He had stayed in the area after college. But we both wanted the relationship to continue, so we started to take turns traveling between St. Louis and Philly to see each other on many weekends. After a few months of that, your dad quit his job and moved to St. Louis so that we could live together. I thought that was pretty nice, though it did cause me to wonder a little about how serious he was about having a career. Remember by that time he would have been, um, about 32, and I was kind of hoping he would be starting to think more seriously about what he wanted to do with his life. But we were very happy together, and we got married two years later, I guess that would be 1989."

"It was a nice wedding?"

"Oh, it was a wonderful wedding. It was at the Botanical Garden. June 11, 1989. Your grandpa and grandma were there. They both loved Dad right away. Really, everyone did. All my brothers and sisters came to the wedding too. And lots of our friends and some of our parents' friends. Dad's father died very young, about a year before the wedding. And as I think you know, Dad's only sibling – his little sister – died when she was four years old. So Dad's only relative at the wedding was his mother, and sadly she died just a few months before you were born. I'm sorry you never got to know your paternal grandparents. For that matter, I never got to know them either. I always regretted that, because I think that would have helped me better understand your father."

"What didn't you understand about Dad?"

"There was a part of him that I couldn't relate to. I could never understand why he didn't care at all about having a successful career or accomplishing tangible things. He cared deeply about being a good husband and father, which he more than was. But he was perfectly content to just let time go by and enjoy the pleasantries of life one day at a time. I don't think he had any more specific life dreams."

"Were you disappointed in him?"

"No, because he had so many other wonderful qualities. Well, maybe a little. It's just that I would have liked to see a little more substance, and I guess I have to admit there were times when I kind of lost interest. But he was such an extraordinarily decent person, so who am I to demand more than that? You know, sometimes we get bored and end up thinking or doing things we're not always so proud of later."

"What do you mean, Mom? What aren't you proud of?"

"Oh, nothing shocking or particularly interesting. Anyway, I think I've bared my soul enough for one day. The main thing is I would never want you to feel disappointed about your father. He was smart and kind, and he loved you more than you can imagine. You should be very proud of him, just as he was of you. And now I really am feeling very weak. Can you help me walk back to bed?"

"Of course. How about just a few more questions first, though? Like do you think Dad sensed that you wished he were doing more? And I don't mean to press you, but are you saying you did things you now regret?"

"Jason, that's enough. I'm too tired now. I'm sorry. Please help me get back to my bed."

Until then, my mother's manner had been warm and kindly. That last utterance seemed to come with a sharper tone. I think she was getting tired of having to keep telling me how tired she was. So I dropped the subject and walked her back to bed. Just like yesterday, she fell asleep almost the moment her head hit the pillow.

I was actually a little hungry now, so I went to the kitchen and made myself a sandwich to eat in the car as I drove back to work. Unfortunately Jessica was also in the kitchen. She glared at me and shook her head with a disapproving frown, as if to ask "How low can you sink?"

Then she started in again about the privacy thing.

"Let me say this in terms that even you might understand, Jason. Forget about your mother's private *thoughts*, ones that she purposely wanted to keep secret. How would you have liked to be in your parents' bedroom when they were having sex? How would you have liked to be in the bathroom when your mother was taking a crap?"

"First of all, keep your voice down, for God's sake. What if she were to wake up and hear you? And what the hell are you talking about? Stop it. You're being crude. And stupid."

"No, I'm trying to get across to you that that is exactly what you're talking about doing. You're invading her private space. You have no right to do that."

"You're making a ridiculous comparison. This is totally different. She would be aware of me being right there in her private moments. That would have been distressing for *her*. What I'm talking about won't happen until after she's dead. She won't be aware of anything, Jessica. She won't *care* about anything. Because she'll be dead. Get it?"

"Fine, I'll change the example. The bedroom door and the bathroom door have peepholes. You can watch all this and she'll never know. That would make it OK? What she doesn't know won't hurt her? That's what I'm hearing you saying."

"Do you hear yourself? You're being truly disgusting. I'm not going to listen to this shit."

"You're right. Watching your mother through a peephole would be absolutely disgusting. And that is exactly what you're planning to do."

"It's not even close to what I'm going to do. I'm not physically watching my mother do any of those things. All I'm talking about is retrieving her memories. It's a clinical process, taking electrical signals and translating them into English. That's not the same as in-person, physical observation."

"Once you retrieve the memories, you're going to have a visual image in your mind. It will be the same visual image as you would have if you were watching her contemporaneously. It might be even more vivid, because between her conscious and unconscious thoughts, you'll now have access to every graphic detail, not just the ones you physically see and notice."

"This is absurd. This conversation is over."

"Be careful what you wish for, Jason."

As aggravating as that conversation was, my thoughts as I drove back to the lab were focused on something my mother had said at the beginning of today's conversation. She described my dad as a loving husband and father but then added: "If you're the kind of husband and father he was, you can be very proud of yourself." I think those were her exact words.

The word "if" stuck in my mind. Was she subtly implying that I have *not* been the kind of husband and father that he was? I realize that lately I've had to spend inordinate amounts of time at the lab. And I have to admit that even when I'm home my mind tends to wander back to my work. But that's a very recent thing, and it's short-term. As soon as this project is finished, these crazy work hours are definitely going to stop. I've always made that clear to Jessica.

I don't think it's too much to expect a devoted spouse to understand that sometimes circumstances demand short-term sacrifice. Of course Zeke is too young to understand that, but he will when he's older, and by then things will have returned to normal. Maybe I'll never be as good a husband and father as my own dad was, because he was exceptional, but I still think I've done a hell of a good job on both fronts.

I was also thinking about what my mom had said toward the end of our conversation. She tried to minimize it, but she was clearly disappointed in my father's lack of initiative. I would have liked to hear her say that by the same token she was proud of the energy and initiative I've always shown.

I'm not sure why she didn't say that. Maybe she doesn't want to encourage me to go further in that direction. She might want me to tamp this down if anything, and concentrate more on my marital and parental responsibilities. Maybe she thinks I'm like the mirror image of my father – that he was a loving husband and father but a disappointingly low-achiever, and that I'm the opposite, a stunningly successful professional but a detached husband and father.

And then she made that comment about thinking or doing things she's not proud of. Not just thinking, but doing. What was that about? When I pushed her on it, she clammed up, saying it was nothing dramatic and that now she had to sleep. But it was obviously something. I don't doubt she was tired, but was her sleepiness just an excuse not to talk about it, or was it really and truly no big deal? Sometimes I have a hard time reading my mother.

When I got back to the lab I immediately wrote down everything I could remember from today's conversation. I keep a special loose leaf binder just for this purpose. I've been recording all of these conversations immediately so that I don't forget anything. When it comes time for Marvin to start work on the decoding, I'll share this with him.

The next thing I did was check with Marvin on his progress. So far there's been none since yesterday. He's still trying to understand the error messages.

Wednesday, January 7, 2026

Our nurse's aide, Doris, arrived this morning, right on time. My mother was awake, so we were able to introduce them to each other. Jessica had told my mother yesterday that Doris would be starting today, and my mother remembered, so there was no surprise. She will regularly arrive at 7:30 a.m., so that Jessica will have time to drop Zeke off at pre-school and then drive to work in time to see her first patient.

Around 10:00 a.m., the director of the funeral parlor sent me an email saying their lawyers have some "concerns." He said he appreciates that the timing is sensitive and will get back to me with something more definitive either today or tomorrow.

God help us! What "concerns" could they possibly have? I laid out the laws for them and they're perfectly clear. The lawyers probably want to make it sound as if they're having to put a lot of time and thought into this so that they can charge the funeral home more money. I'll give this guy until tomorrow afternoon, and if he doesn't agree to my proposed arrangements by then, I'll take my business elsewhere. I really don't need this hassle.

Thursday, January 8, 2026

Sure enough, the funeral director emailed me to say that he was very sorry, but that on the advice of his lawyers he was not able to participate in this arrangement. He again expressed advance condolences about my mother.

I emailed him back to ask him what the legal problem is. I explained that I need to know because I will now have to approach another funeral parlor and will want to understand what his lawyers think I can and cannot do. He was good enough to reply right away, but his answer was vague. So I emailed again to ask for the names of his lawyers. I said I'd like to talk with them myself so that I can get a better understanding of their concerns and how I might cure them. I even said I'd be happy to pay the lawyers for the time they spend with me on the phone.

By late afternoon he hadn't replied, so I called the funeral home. This time a different receptionist answered the phone. I asked to speak with the director.

"Who's calling, please?"

"This is Dr. Jason Stramm. I've been corresponding with the director, and he knows what this is about."

"Thank you. Please hold."

A few minutes later she was back on the line.

"I'm sorry, Dr. Stramm, but the director is not available today. May I take a message?"

"When will he be available? This is extremely important."

"I don't actually know when he'll be available."

"Is there someone there who would know?"

"No, I'm sorry. But I'm happy to take a message."

"Is he really not available, or does he just not want to talk to me?"

"Sir, he is unavailable. Would you like to leave a message, or not?"

"Please just tell him that I emailed him yesterday to get the names of his lawyers, and I expect the courtesy of a reply."

This really pisses me off. My mother is dying, this guy is a funeral director, he refuses to deal with me, won't tell me why, won't give me the names of the lawyers who he says are telling him he can't deal with me, and won't even show me the respect of responding. If he were simply unavailable for a few minutes or even hours and the receptionist had said he would call me back, I would have taken all that at face value. But when she claims not to know when *if ever* he'll be available, he's obviously avoiding me.

I'm starting to wonder whether his lawyers really advised him not to do this – or for that matter, whether he even consulted any lawyers. He probably just thinks this situation is weird and is too cowardly to risk possible adverse publicity. Either way, this is very aggravating.

So I called another funeral home and asked to speak with the director. This woman was much more accommodating. She didn't have the oily manner of the first guy, with his feigned sympathy. She did gasp a bit when I got to the part about extracting my mother's brain, but as I explained the reasons, she seemed to understand and even appeared to be intrigued.

I also assured her that I have researched this carefully and that it is perfectly legal. Unlike the first guy, she immediately said that would be fine. She didn't need any time to think it over, but the more advance detail I could give her about the arrangements, the less there would be to do when the moment arrives. She said she would get back to me tomorrow with the cost estimate if that is OK, which I assured her it was.

One complication I want to avoid is having to wait for another doctor to come to the house to confirm my mother's death and sign the death certificate. Once my mother passes, I will have no time to spare before removing and chemically preserving the brain. I want to keep any deterioration of brain tissue to an absolute, unavoidable minimum.

So I will sign the death certificate myself. As an MD, I have the legal authority to do that. I looked it up on the web to be sure. I can do this online and will do so as soon after the death as I can.

Friday, January 9, 2026

Just as she had promised, the funeral director emailed the cost estimate to me this morning. It was a little higher than I had hoped, and it didn't include the costs associated with the memorial service because we hadn't yet worked out what the service would entail, but the quote seemed reasonable and I immediately accepted. I can't believe how much easier this was than dealing with that asshole from the first place – who even now, by the way, hasn't gotten back to me.

One thing I realized I needed to do immediately is order all the equipment that I will need to perform the required surgery on the appointed day. Of course most of the things you find in a standard operating room won't be necessary here. I obviously won't need an anesthesiology setup, IV stands, blanket warmers, or any of the other items required for surgery on live patients. And I already have a table that I can easily use for this purpose.

But I will need a few things that I don't already have. This is a research lab, not an operating room. I'll need sheets to cover the operating table and receptacles for disposing of medical waste. I already have instruments for making fine incisions into brain tissue, but I still need instruments for cutting through bone and scalp, as well as a few other miscellaneous things. So today I ordered all this equipment. It should arrive within a week.

Meanwhile, I can't say I've noticed any change in my mother's condition over the past few days. She seems to be on a kind of plateau, nearly always tired but pretty much pain-free and lucid. Maybe we'll end up having more time left than we had previously thought.

Our lunchtime interview sessions have continued, and she's been able to give me heaps of information about her childhood starting at around age 5. She can still remember her fifth birthday party. It was a picnic in her back yard, and there were lots of other children and their moms. She remembers nothing before that.

I jumped ahead to a day I can remember very well and knew Mom would too. It was the day her parents died in a car accident and she had to call me with the news. I still have their obituaries, so I know the exact date. It was February 17, 2011. It hurt her to recall this, which made me feel guilty for putting her through that pain again, but she was able to convey her sadness without any apparent trauma.

She added that on that day the memory of my father's death had come flashing back to her as well. She said she still finds it hard to accept that her parents and her young husband all perished so suddenly, without warning -- and all three in senseless car accidents.

I wanted her to focus on happy moments as well, so I simply asked her to name her happiest days. That's easy, she said. When she gave birth to me, when Zeke was born, and her wedding day, in that order.

I haven't been going in any systematic chronological sequence. I'm just trying to hit as many rough age ranges as I can. If I run out of time to get everything I want, I'd rather learn a little bit about each of the major age ranges of her life than learn every day-by-day detail of the early years only to miss everything that came later.

I've had to continue pushing her to stay with me longer than she would ideally prefer, because the remaining time is so scarce, but I sometimes feel bad badgering her to keep talking when she is exhausted and just wants to sleep. I still feel I'm doing the right thing. There will be plenty of time for her to rest soon enough. I know that must sound insensitive, but I think you understand what I mean.

Unfortunately, there also hasn't been much change in the status of Marvin's recognition software. He's still puzzling over the error messages and I've had to keep biting my tongue. I'm very surprised that someone as smart and computer-savvy as he clearly is can't figure out how to even get started debugging his software.

But he's working ferocious hours and showing visible signs of stress. Pressuring him wouldn't accomplish anything. Still, it's hard to say nothing and pretend I'm taking this calmly, because my insides are in turmoil. We are dangerously close to running out of time.

Thursday, January 15, 2026
All the operating equipment that I ordered was delivered today. I set it up in a space in the middle of my lab so that I will be ready to go without any further preparation. Its arrival was yet another reminder of my race against time.

Friday, January 16, 2026
I feel as if I'm in a helicopter, suspended in the same location in mid-air. Nothing is changing. My mother's condition seems exactly the same as a week ago – no better, no worse. We met with the oncologist yesterday. He could see that my mother's stamina had not diminished in the past week, but he said the prognosis and timeline are still the same.

My lunchtime interviews with my mother continue. We're beginning to fill in more and more phases of her life, including the past few years, which I've been concentrating exclusively on since Wednesday. This routine is actually becoming a bit monotonous. And Marvin is still stuck at 455 error messages.

Saturday, January 17, 2026

I stayed home today. There isn't a whole lot for me to do now at the lab. The legal research is finished, my supply of questions that I still want to ask my mother is probably already greater than our remaining interview sessions will allow, and the arrangements with the funeral parlor are all set.

By staying home, I was also able to take advantage of the breaks in my mother's naps to do four more interviews, not just the lunchtime one. I don't need to push her to answer a few additional questions when she needs to sleep, because I know I'll be here to resume the questioning the next time she wakes up. By keeping the interviews shorter and more frequent, I think I'm also getting more accurate information. Once she starts getting sleepy, her memories aren't as reliable.

Staying home also means more interaction with Zeke. He's not happy when I have to suddenly break off whatever game we're playing because Grandma just woke up, but I always promise him we'll play again shortly and I'm able to keep those promises, so I think he's OK. Jessica said she badly needed to get away, so she's out somewhere with her friend Raynette.

Late this evening, Marvin called. He was very excited. He told me that he finally, finally had made a breakthrough. He had identified and fixed a single glitch that was causing about half of the error messages. The original list of 455 errors was now down to 236. That's still a lot, but for the first time he feels confident that he will be able to whittle this list down very quickly.

I could hear the relief in his voice. I told him how pleased I was but cautioned that he can't let up now, because there is less and less time left and we remain dangerously close to not finishing in time. I also reminded him that even after he has fixed all the remaining errors and successfully run the program, we would need to do several additional test runs with slightly different variables to make sure this is really working perfectly, before we use it on my mother's brain and risk irreparably losing memory data.

That seemed to shake him up again, and I immediately realized that was a stupid thing to say. He was sorely in need of positive reinforcement, and today's breakthrough should have been rewarded with praise, not an ominous forecast of all the work that still lies ahead. Honestly, I don't know why I say these things.

Thursday, January 22, 2026
Until today there was still no noticeable change in my mother's condition. But this morning, for the first time, she complained of chest pain. It wasn't severe, she said, but it was definitely uncomfortable. I called

the doctor and he asked me to bring her in immediately, which I did.

After some additional imaging he advised that the cancer had migrated a little bit since the last visit. This was something he had been expecting all along. Again it was impossible to know how much more time my mother had, but this was not a good sign.

My mother reacted very badly to this news. During the drive home, she was uncommunicative. I would say something and there would be no response. I would ask her whether she was OK, and at most she would nod her head slightly, sometimes not even that.

There was obviously no point in interviewing her when we arrived home. She declined food and just wanted to go straight to sleep. My mother is typically stoic, so her behavior today is the first sign I've seen of intense physical pain.

I knew I would need to record that suffering in my notebook and include the exact time, so that Marvin and I will later have a possible reference point for decoding the electrical memories of suffering. But I took no joy in this. I was now thinking more about the pain that my mother, whom I dearly love, was experiencing than about my project. I know this has not always been the case, and for that I am starting to feel a deep sense of shame.

When Jessica got home from work, with Zeke in tow after she had picked him up from pre-school, I filled her in on the day's events. She went straight to my mother's room to check in on her. My mother was asleep. Zeke wanted to play, but I had a pit in my stomach not knowing whether I was about to receive more icicles from Jessica.

I guess she must have sensed that I was suffering from today's news, because she didn't scold me for not doing more or for treating my mother as a research tool rather than as my dying mother. Still, there was a chill in the house, and we just both methodically worked on preparing dinner while Zeke quietly entertained himself.

I know Jessica thinks I have lost all human emotion, but she's wrong. It finally struck me today that my mother – the only remaining person who has loved me since the moment I was born -- would soon be gone. I finally felt some empathy for her, understanding the physical and emotional pain she was experiencing and knowing that it would only get worse.

For some reason I couldn't bring myself to confess any of this to Jessica, let alone tell her about the shame I have started to feel. Even though I am certain she would respect me more and treat me with more kindness if I revealed all this, I can't seem to tell her. I don't know why.

At the lab, Marvin has made considerable progress over the past few days. He's now down to 89 errors. Whether he can finish in time is still not clear, but this is a good sign. I'm not feeling the elation that this progress should bring me, though. Right now all I can think about is the imminent loss of my mother and the mess I've made of my life.

I'm thankful that I still have Zeke. And as much tension as there is between Jessica and me, I can't deny that she's a stabilizing presence. When we're together in the house, the ill feeling that grips me is tempered by a sense of security. When I'm in the house and she's not, I worry that she too has gone away and left me alone.

I know all of this is probably irrational, but it's how I feel. Maybe my problem is simply lack of sleep. For weeks now, I toss and turn for hours every night before falling asleep, and then I wake up 3 or 4 hours later. I'm betting that's why I'm feeling so emotional right now. I just don't know how to fix it.

Thursday, January 29, 2026

My mother's condition continues to worsen. Her pain is now more intense, and she is much more heavily medicated. This has drastically reduced the amount of productive interview time.

This morning Jessica called me at the lab. She said Doris had just called to tell her that my mother's breathing had become very labored and that my mother was feeling a lot of pain even with the medication. Jessica called an ambulance, which by then had arrived and was taking my mother to the hospital as we spoke. She told me I needed to go there at once. She said we might be nearing the end. She would meet me there.

By the time we both arrived at the hospital, the nurses had given my mother additional painkillers, and she was now stable and relatively comfortable.

Tests revealed no further metastasis, but the doctors wanted her to remain overnight so that they could monitor her. Jessica and I both told her we would be back to visit and that she needed to sleep, which she immediately did. We both left then. We decided we would both return this afternoon, but at different times so as to minimize the periods that she would be alone.

I'm once again becoming conscious of Marvin's race against time. In the past week he has continued to progress, reducing the errors from 89 to 36. He says some of the remaining 36 errors look fairly easy to solve, but several others will be tougher nuts to crack. And of course we still don't know how much more time we have before my mother's passing.

Friday, January 30, 2026

This morning my mother was discharged from the hospital. She is stable for now, but she will need even higher doses of painkiller than before. Jessica and I brought her home, and she has been resting comfortably pretty much all day.

Jessica asked me whether I had been keeping my mother's siblings updated on her condition. I realized I hadn't contacted them at all. I don't think they have any idea my mother has cancer. Jessica told me disapprovingly (because that's now how she tells me most things) that she had urged me to do that weeks ago. I have no recollection of her telling me that and suspect she never did. And if she really had thought of this weeks ago, nothing prevented her from picking up the phone and calling them herself. I guess she finds it easier to blame this lapse on me.

In any event, I agreed we needed to notify them. As busy as I am, I methodically called each of my mother's siblings and advised them to be on standby, since I would let them know as soon as my mother passed and we knew the funeral arrangements. I was hesitant to make that promise, because I knew that as soon as my mother died I would be under intense time pressure to rush her to my lab and perform the necessary procedure. But I didn't see any alternative.

None of my mother's three East Coast siblings were home when I called, so for them I had to leave voicemails. That was extremely annoying because I wanted to finish all this and not have to have lengthy conversations later.

To minimize the chances of their calling back, I left a fair amount of detail. I also gave them Jessica's phone number and suggested they call her if they had any questions. My Uncle Hal in California has now retired, and he was home to answer the phone. He said he was very sorry to hear this and will try to come in for the funeral if he can.

My Aunt Betsy, the one who lives nearby in Ladue, wasn't home, but her husband, my uncle Norris, answered the phone. He didn't seem especially sad. Mainly he was indignant that I hadn't called Betsy weeks ago. He was certain she would have stopped in often to visit and help out, and she will be very upset and angry that I hadn't called earlier. Not that he's surprised that I hadn't been thoughtful enough to call, he added.

I tried to explain that, unlike Betsy, I work during the day and have had to put in long hours at the lab while simultaneously taking care of my mother. It's not as if I've had a whole lot of free time to think about calling aunts and uncles.

He told me I was being insensitive, which I found not just obnoxious but ironic, since any normal person would see him as the one who was being insensitive. It's my mother who is dying, for God's sake. Anyway, I told him that Aunt Betsy should call Jessica if she has any questions. He then said "Thank you for calling" and hung up. I started to remember why I never liked him.

Meanwhile, Marvin had a spectacular day at the lab, resolving all but three of the remaining error messages. The race against time continues, though. It's beginning to look like a photo finish.

Sunday, February 1, 2026

My mother is now going downhill fast. Yesterday Aunt Betsy came to visit. Uncle Norris, who had been so morally self-righteous on Friday, didn't bother to come. I'm perfectly happy that he didn't; it's his hypocrisy that I find irritating. Anyway, Aunt Betsy seemed shocked at the sight of her now-emaciated sister. Mom has eaten very little the last couple days. She is clearly on her last legs.

I stayed home today to spend time with my mother and tried several times during the day to get some additional information from her, but she was too weak to converse meaningfully. Each time, Jessica would admonish me to let her rest.

Marvin and I are going to have to do the best we can with the information I've been collecting from the interviews up to this point. That's OK, though, because over the past several weeks I've actually obtained lots of data points from all the major phases of my mother's life.

The big news is that at 11:15 this morning – I noted and recorded the time because this is a huge milestone – Marvin successfully ran the recognition software. He was able to get the computer to recognize, and record on the portable drive, the electrical signals that the EOSF was sending its way.

We have now accomplished nothing less than figuring out how to transfer memory data from a dead human brain to a digital storage device! And not just figuring it out, but actually doing it. There will remain the enormous challenge of deciphering these data, but we now know how to capture it and hopefully preserve it indefinitely so that we can soon get to work on the decoding.

I congratulated Marvin and told him that he should immediately try to run the program again on different parts of the same brain and then on another brain specimen. If the program continued to work in those other places, we could be confident that it will work when we attach the EOSF to my mother's brain. And then he was to call me the moment he had any results.

A couple hours later, he called. He had successfully run the program on other parts of the same brain and then on the other brain specimens. This was too good to believe, and all day I have felt complete happiness and excitement about this latest development and what it augured.

I admit I feel a little guilty exulting over this during my mother's final days or perhaps even hours, but I can't help myself. This has been my dream, the most important mission of my life, and it has been consuming practically all my waking hours for the past several years.

While my mother was sleeping, I told Jessica the news. I spoke to her in a solemn voice so that she would be able to see that while I was excited about Marvin's progress my innermost thoughts were still with my mother during this sad time. I think she doubted my sincerity, because her reaction was to express horror that I was still committed to this "ghoulish" plan, as she likes to call it.

She can't stop me, she acknowledged, but she hoped that I still have enough "moral fiber" left to call off this "monstrous scheme." And if I don't, she doesn't want to hear another word about it. Her sole priority at the moment is making my mother as comfortable as possible, and that should be my sole priority as well.

I just walked away, aggravated but not surprised. Of course I care about making my mother comfortable. What kind of monster does she think I am? But that doesn't mean I can't also be excited about the imminent realization of a life dream.

I didn't even bother to say that to Jessica. By now, I know her well enough to know that once she gets an idea in her head, no matter how preposterous it is, trying to change her mind is like talking to a wall. And I was determined not to let her ruin the elation that I can't help but feel at this historic moment.

CHAPTER 7
THE MOMENT ARRIVES

Monday, February 2, 2026

Life sometimes has a strange way of meeting deadlines for you just in the nick of time. When I left for the lab this morning, I was still reveling in yesterday's developments. I could not have known that the phone call would come this very next day, while I was out on the street picking up my lunch from the food truck.

Mark Twain was right. Truth really can be stranger than fiction.

It was Jessica. Doris had just called her to say that my mother's breathing had become very labored. She was gasping for breath and her death now appeared imminent, like any minute. Jessica told Doris not to call an ambulance. There was no point, she said, in prolonging my mother's suffering with yet another hospital stay. I need to rush home right now, Jessica said. There is still a chance I could say good-bye to my mother while she's able to hear me.

I told her I would leave immediately. But before leaving, I quickly called the funeral home to put them on standby, so that they could pick up her body promptly and transport it to the lab as soon as I tell them the time has come. I then drove home straight away.

When I arrived, Jessica and Doris were with my mother. She was still breathing faintly but was now unconscious. An hour later, my mother stopped breathing. I checked her pulse. It had stopped. Her body was still warm, but she was gone. I noted the time of death so that I could enter it on the electronic death certificate that I will submit online when I get to the lab. It was 1:45 pm, February 2, 2026.

I don't know why it had taken so long to register, but the moment I mentally noted the time of death, the impact of my mother's death finally hit. It all came out. I began to cry uncontrollably. I hugged my mother's still body and rested my head on her chest. In between sobs I kept blurting out "Mommy, I'm sorry. I'm sorry. Please forgive me." This went on for several minutes. Jessica tried to console me, stroking my head.

When I finally returned to my feet, I felt unsteady. Jessica quickly grabbed hold of both my upper arms to save me from falling. She had tears in her eyes. Doris did too, but mostly she seemed embarrassed at the spectacle I was making of myself. And even then, my tears continued to pour out as I pondered the reality that my mother was never coming back.

It took about a half-hour for me to collect myself, but when I did, I went to the bathroom so I could have some privacy for the phone call I knew I had to make. The funeral director picked up the phone herself and told me they have been ready to go and would be there in less than 20 minutes.

I then called Marvin, filled him in, and asked him to be ready to assist when we arrive at the lab. He said he was sorry for my loss and assured me he would be ready as soon as I needed him. When I returned to the room where my mother lay lifeless, I saw that a blanket now covered her body, including her face.

I didn't warn Jessica or Doris that the funeral home employees would soon be arriving, which they did about fifteen minutes later. Although I had long ago apprised Jessica of my general plan, I hadn't mentioned that it would entail taking my mother's body and transporting it to the lab just minutes after the moment of death.

So the knock on the door surprised her. There were four men. They all expressed their condolences and conducted themselves respectfully. When I gave them the go-ahead, they carefully placed my mother's body on a stretcher, secured it, and carried it to the van that was parked in the street.

Jessica and Doris said not a word. Doris of course had known nothing about my plan, so the look of bewilderment on her face was plain. Jessica just stared at me in disbelief. I walked outside, got in my car, and drove to the lab, followed by the van that was transporting what used to be my mother.

As soon as I arrived, I got on my computer and submitted the electronic death registration. It took only about five minutes.

Just as I finished, the men from the funeral home arrived with my mother's body. They placed it on the operating table, conveyed their sympathies once again, and quietly left.

With Marvin watching and available in case I needed him, I proceeded with the surgery. I had not performed any actual surgery since my days as a resident, but the skills and the knowledge were still there and I felt confident that I could carry out this procedure competently.

If you are squeamish, you should skip the next two paragraphs. They contain a few graphic details.

There was no need to remove the blanket, which I simply pulled down so that it was no longer covering my mother's head and neck. Nor was there any reason to remove the clothing from the body. Out of habit I washed my hands thoroughly and put on my surgical gown, even though I was not operating on a live patient.

I carefully severed the head from the body, wiping away the blood as I went along. At that point Marvin asked if he could be excused, and I said OK but asked him to stay within earshot in case I needed anything. I cut my mother's hair. Then, piece by piece, I removed the scalp, until I was left with only the brain and part of the brain stem. I immediately immersed the brain in a chemical preservative called "formalin-plus." This is a 20s enhancement of the formalin compound that neuroscientists used in former times.

I know that this clinical description of the procedure I had to perform will have made many of you uncomfortable, and for that I apologize. If it seems unfeeling or unnatural – even inhuman, another word Jessica once used when I apprised her of my plans – please remember that the object on which I was operating was not my mother. It was merely an inanimate object, the vessel in which my mother once lived. It would be like removing the roof of the house where my mother used to live, nothing more.

Remember too that I am a scientist and a surgeon. I was able to concentrate all my thoughts on the end goal and the surgical process. The entire procedure took about three hours, and during that time I didn't once think about my mother's death or the fact that this body once belonged to her. If I felt any emotion at all while I was doing this, it was the exhilaration of knowing that by the end of the day I would be only a short step away from the greatest scientific achievement in recorded history.

When I finished, I called the funeral home to come and transport the remains of my mother's body to their facilities in preparation for her cremation. I knew we still had to set a day and time for the memorial service, notify the relatives, and figure out a program. I also knew I wouldn't have the time do any of those things and wouldn't do them well in any case, so I decided I would call Jessica and ask her to sort that out with the funeral home.

Before I did that, however, I summoned Marvin so that he and I could immediately get to work hooking up one end of the EOSF to the interior of my mother's brain. The other end was already connected to the computer. Marvin obliged. With the cleanup work I had done, he could now view the brain without feeling nauseated, though he was extremely quiet – strangely quiet, with a facial expression that I guess I would have to describe as almost uncomprehending.

The process of inserting one end of the EOSF into the temporal lobe of the brain took longer than I had expected. We wanted to be sure we started off in exactly the right place. Unlike when we were experimenting with other brain specimens, I needed to be certain that we would be able to move the brain end of the EOSF from spot to spot in a systematic way, so that by the time we were done we would have extracted the entirety of my mother's memory data.

Before we could finish locating our specific target and hooking up the EOSF, the same four men from the funeral home arrived to remove what was left of my mother's body. Keeping her covered with the same blanket, they again placed her on a stretcher and carried her out to their van. And that was that.

When we completed the EOSF hookup, Marvin fired up the recognition software that he had finished testing just yesterday. I emphasize "just yesterday" because it seems impossible that so much could have happened in roughly 24 hours.

Marvin and I held our breath as we waited for his program to complete its initial preparation work. Less than two minutes later, the monitor showed that the program was working, just as it had the past two days. My mother's memories – the thoughts, emotions, and physical sensations that she had experienced and recorded and that were, in essence, her life – were now flooding onto our portable drive at the rate of 4,000 picobes per second.

I didn't want to waste any time, so as soon as we were confident that the program was running successfully, I called Jessica to ask her to make the necessary arrangements for the memorial service. She spoke calmly and didn't ask about what I had done at the lab. She merely asked where the body now was. I informed her that it was en route to the funeral home to be prepared for cremation, which she was aware my mother had requested.

She agreed to make the arrangements for the memorial service and to notify the siblings. She said she would also speak with one of my mother's friends and ask her to spread the word to her other friends.

As she was about to hang up, she told me that I should write an obituary. That was the last thing I had time for just now, but I could hardly refuse. Jessica was doing all the other work, and I was the one who now knew the most about my mother's life. And she was, after all, my mother, not Jessica's.

When our conversation ended, I started walking over to my cubicle. For some reason, it was then that for the first time in ages I thought about Lisa.

She's now been gone more than four months. I thought about how lovely she is and about all the groundwork we had done together to bring this project to the point where it now is. She had faith in me when even my own wife had already been dismissing me as a heartless nut job. She had been a source of human warmth and understanding when I most needed it. I still miss her terribly. It is a deep longing, not just one of those "it would be nice if she were here" kinds of feelings. I thought about calling her to tell her my exciting news.

But something was holding me back. I think it was mainly fear of rejection. All indications are that she has no special feelings for me and for that matter has no desire even to stay in touch at all. She hasn't contacted me once in all this time. Part of my hesitation is pride. I didn't want her to think I was so desperate that I had to keep chasing her. And maybe part of it is not wanting to rekindle something that hopefully I'll eventually get over if I can just avoid contact for long enough.

It's a shame, really. It would probably mean a lot to her to know that the project on which she had labored so long and to which she had contributed so much was chugging along brilliantly. Also, a live conversation might give me a sense of whether she has any feelings for me that I shouldn't completely give up on. It might also give me a chance to feel her out a little bit on whether the secrecy of our project is still intact. I want to be able to trust her, but I can't be sure I can.

So I called her. She wasn't home, but it was very nice to hear that familiar soft, melodic voice in her recorded message. I left a voicemail:

"Hi, Lisa, it's Jason. It's great to hear your voice. I'm just calling to catch up. I'd love to know how everything is going with your work and your job search and all that stuff, but also I have some great news to share on the project we were working on. Give me a call when you get a chance, OK? Bye bye."

While I awaited her call back, there were two more things I had to do before leaving the lab. One was write the obituary, which I was able to do quickly. I emailed it to Jessica so that she could take care of getting it published in the St. Louis Post-Dispatch, the city's main hard copy newspaper, and posted on ArchCityObits.com, the main website for local obituaries.

The other thing I had to do was arrange work schedules with Marvin. I had calculated a while back that in order to cover all the relevant areas of the brain, we would have to move the brain end of the EOSF, and update the corresponding EOSF instructions, about 333 times. And a given placement and set of instructions would last approximately two hours.

Earlier I had calculated that if we could do these updates, say, six times per day, seven days per week, we would be able to finish the data transfer in about eight weeks. Marvin had agreed to this in principle, but now we had to arrange a specific schedule where we could take turns coming in to the lab for the continual updating.

We agreed that with everything going on with my mother's funeral arrangements, Marvin would do all of the updating for the next few days, six times each day. After that I would do the lion's share of it, so that he could get a head start researching the most current mathematical models for deciphering codes.

By the time he finishes this preliminary research, a fair amount of data will already have been uploaded to the portable drive. At that point, he can study the binder in which I recorded my mother's information, compare that information with the electrical data on the portable drive, and start looking for patterns. I'm not a trained mathematician, but I'll able to help at that stage too. I actually won't have much else to do.

It was now getting late in the afternoon, and I decided to call it a day. Today's events have left me drained. I need to go home and sleep. By this time also, Jessica will have brought Zeke home and probably explained to him that his Grandma is no longer there.

Tuesday, February 3, 2026

Last night, Jessica and I had our most unsettling conversation yet. There was no yelling and screaming. She spoke quietly but with a nervous, anxious demeanor that I don't ever recall seeing before. There was something very different about her, or at least about the way she related to me. We spoke in the living room, sitting on armchairs that were only about three feet apart, but there was an unmistakable distance between us.

Whenever I leaned forward to say something, she would instinctively arch her back and shift the top of her body away from me. At times I thought she was afraid of me. At other times, she seemed repulsed. At certain points the impression she gave was that she was talking to someone who was either stupid or mentally deranged.

She was also very businesslike. She informed me that a secular memorial service was set for 12 noon on Thursday. She has already sent out the obituary and has notified all my mother's siblings about the time and place of the service. She had mapped out a proposed outline of the service.

After the service, family members and any other well-wishers would be invited back to the house for a buffet lunch. She had already made arrangements with the caterer. She was not planning to tell anyone about the extraction of the brain, because there was no need to upset them. All they needed to know was that my mother had been cremated according to her wishes. Jessica asked me whether I had any questions. I did not, and I thanked her for doing all this.

She started to say something else, but in her nervousness she squeezed too hard on the stem of the glass she had been drinking water from. The glass shattered, cutting her thumb and drenching her right leg with water.

I got up to get a paper towel to temporarily blot the blood in her thumb and a couple dish-towels to dry her leg. But when I tried to take her other hand to help her get up so that we could walk over to the kitchen sink, she flinched at my touch and let out an audible gasp. "It's OK," she said, "I can do this myself."

I felt like a leper. She didn't want me anywhere near her and definitely not touching her. Whether it was revulsion or fear I still couldn't tell, but I suddenly felt very frightened myself and more than a little confused.

This morning we both took off from work. Her demeanor was the same as last night. Whenever we found ourselves in the same room, she would always find a reason that she had to be somewhere else. She had errands to do, or she needed to vacuum a different room, or she needed to make a phone call.

At no point did she let me get within a few feet of her. And whenever it was necessary to speak, she would display the same nervousness. A couple times she seemed to tremble physically just a little. She tried to pretend nothing was wrong, but something had clearly changed.

Thursday, February 5, 2026

Nothing in Jessica's demeanor has changed since Monday. If anything, I sense even greater anxiety and even more determination to keep me at a physical and personal distance.

For the first time, I'm also noticing that Zeke has been unusually quiet and also a bit anxious. I don't know how much of it is dealing with the death of his grandma, who he now seems to understand will never be coming back, and how much of it, if any, is that he's picking up on the strain between his parents.

Being home these past couple days has given me a chance to spend a lot more time with him. He went to pre-school as usual through yesterday, but I took him back and forth and got to spend time with him both afternoons and early evenings. Today, Jessica said she thought it best that he stay home for the day and come to the memorial service, and I agreed.

Uncle Hal from Los Angeles called yesterday to say he would be unable to come in for the service because of some things that had come up. So did two of my mother's East Coast siblings. But the third East Coast sibling, Aunt Harriet, flew in last night. She's the mother of my cousin Bartholomew, who was kind enough to join her. They will be at the service, as will Aunt Betsy and Uncle Norris.

My mother's good friend and neighbor, Doreen, will also be there and assured Jessica that she would call as many of my mother's other friends as possible, because they too will want to be there "for her." Of course, it's not really for my mother. She won't ever know who was there. It was really for themselves and possibly for the family. But I didn't say anything.

At the service, the funeral home director presided. She asked me moments before it began if I could say a few things about my mother, as the remaining family was so small. Although I have had to give occasional lectures to medical students, I have never been comfortable with public speaking, and in my current state, with everything that has been happening, I am more nervous than usual. So I told her I'd prefer not to.

She said she understood but noted that no one else has indicated an intention to speak, and suggested I might feel bad afterwards if no one says anything. I agreed to say a few words. But when the time came, I didn't know what to say, so I simply thanked everyone for coming on this sad occasion and read, word-for-word, the obituary that I had written earlier.

At the house there was a decent showing, consisting mainly of my mother's friends. Doreen told me how fond she was of my mother, and I told her that I know my mother felt the same way about her. And I thanked her for spreading the word to their other friends.

Aunt Betsy was actually very warm, telling me she knows how much of a loss this is for me and telling me to be sure to call her if I ever wanted to talk or needed anything. I know Mom had always said she and Betsy had different values, and most likely they did, but Betsy seemed like a good person. That's more than I can say for Uncle Norris, who avoided me the whole day. The asshole never once came over even to convey the most perfunctory condolences.

And it was lovely to see Aunt Harriet and even Bartholomew, my older cousin who had treated me disdainfully when we were kids. They too were both very nice and seemingly genuine in their empathy. We agreed we needed to stay in closer touch.

Jessica had to sit near me at the service (at a still safe distance, with Zeke in between us), but otherwise she continued to avoid me as best she could. I don't think the gulf that separated us was evident to the others, but it was clear as day to me, and it distressed me all day long, even more than the death of my mother.

This evening, after all the guests had left, Zeke having gone to bed, and the house now cleaned up, I decided to confront Jessica directly. She was in our bedroom, fussing with something on her dresser. I must have startled her, because she jumped a bit when I entered the room.

"Jessica, we need to talk. Something is wrong. Tell me. Please."

"Nothing is wrong. There's just a lot going on right now."

"No, it's more than that. You seem scared to death to be anywhere near me. You seem nervous all the time. Every conversation is awkward and tense."

"I told you. There's nothing wrong. I'm just very busy, between work and all the funeral arrangements, and taking care of Zeke."

"Is it my project? My extracting my mother's brain?"

"You know how I feel about that."

"Is that what's going on?"

"Jason, I've told you twice now. For the third time, there's nothing to talk about. Please just leave me alone. I have a lot to do."

So I left the room. But I found myself puzzling over her language. The first couple times she had simply said there's nothing wrong, which obviously isn't true. But the third time she worded it differently. She said "there's nothing to talk about."

That's very different from "there's nothing wrong," even though she tried to make it sound as if that were what she had been saying all along. "There's nothing to talk about" is like saying "*We* have nothing left to talk about," which implies that there's no real relationship any more.

Maybe I'm parsing her words too much. Maybe she really does mean there's nothing wrong and she's just busy. I don't think so, though. She's had lots of busy periods before, and I've never seen the kind of physically-manifested anxiety that I'm seeing now. There's clearly something she's not telling me.

I also suddenly realized that Lisa never called me back. It's been three days now. It's possible she's out of town, but I had called her on her cell, which she always keeps with her.

I'm starting to see a pattern now. Both Jessica and Lisa are making concerted efforts to avoid any communication with me that they possibly can. In Jessica's case it's very possible that she's still horrified by my project, but that's not true of Lisa, who worked hard on behalf of this very project and in any event knows nothing about the part involving my mother. And it's not as if I've been haranguing Lisa; I hadn't contacted her in months.

The possibility that I haven't wanted to think about is one that I now have to seriously entertain. Jessica and Lisa are the only two people in the world – except for Marvin, of course – who know about my project. Lisa has a motive to share it – the potential professional gains that could come from claiming a substantial share of the credit.

Jessica has a different motive. She's horrified by it, and might well be thinking about spilling the beans to my department head, the NIH, the police, or anyone else who she believes might be in a position to stop it. For all I know, she has already done so. If my suspicions are right, it would stand to reason they would want to minimize any communication with me, for fear – and fear is precisely what I see in Jessica –

that I might ask them something for which their reaction would be a tipoff.

I'm not saying any of this is necessarily the explanation for their distancing themselves. But it's a possible explanation, and I need to stay on the lookout for any signs that others know about the project. If they do, it could come only from them – or Marvin.

Of course the people at the funeral home know I've severed the brain from my mother's remains so that I can use it for research purposes. But that's all they know. They shouldn't have any idea that I've come up with a way to extract actual memories from a dead brain and transfer them to a computer, where the next step will be translating them into a language we can understand. And they certainly have no way to know that the end product of all this will be the replication of eternal life.

I suppose I could ask Jessica directly whether anyone else knows about this. If I confront her when she's not expecting it, and she has told someone, she might deny it but will probably be flustered enough that her lie will be obvious. Then again, once I ask her, she'll know I'm on to her and that might just make her and whoever she's told more discreet. She's very clever, after all, and she would certainly be capable of doing this and not getting caught. I'll have to think about this very carefully.

Oh, shit!!! I just realized that the message I had left for Lisa said nothing about my mother's death. All I had mentioned was that I had news about the project. If I had told her that my mother had died, she would have felt obligated to call back to express her condolences. How could I have been so stupid?

That gave me the idea to call her again, this time leaving the additional information about my mother's death if a voicemail proved necessary. And I also decided I would call from Marvin's phone so that she wouldn't recognize my phone number and would hopefully answer. He still has his New York area code, so there wouldn't even be the familiar 314 St. Louis code to tip her off.

I told Marvin that my phone was out of charge and asked to borrow his. Unfortunately, when I called Lisa, I once again got her voicemail. But rather than leave another message, I hung up. I knew she wouldn't recognize the phone number, so I could now call her a third time later today or maybe tomorrow, from my own phone, and she would have no reason to suspect that today's call had been from me. If she doesn't pick up when I call her the third time, then I can always leave the message about my mother.

Wait, I might have screwed myself by hanging up. What if she sees that someone has called her from Marvin's number and calls that number back out of curiosity? Maybe Marvin would simply say no, he hadn't called. Then again, Marvin might remember that I had borrowed his phone and figure out that the call must have come from me. He might then suggest she call me.

In fact, if Lisa identifies herself when she calls Marvin, he would recognize her name. He knows she was his predecessor here in the lab. They would then have quite the conversation, and in addition she would know I've now called twice and had hung up the second time, which is starting to sound like stalker-type behavior. I can't believe I hadn't thought of that in time.

At any rate, Lisa didn't call me back today or this evening, and as far as I know she didn't call Marvin either. I'm sure he would have told me. I'll try her again tomorrow.

Friday, February 6, 2026

I got to the lab early today and immediately performed the first EOSF update of the day. I didn't want to call Lisa too early and wake her up, because that would just make her angry, so I waited until 10:00 a.m., which was 11:00 a.m. her time. I called her from my own phone. I decided that in case I got her voicemail again, I would write out my message in advance rather than leave it to chance. I rehearsed it until I was satisfied that my tone would sound casual. Sure enough, I got her voicemail once more.

"Hi, Lisa, it's Jason again. I'm really sorry to bother you, but I realized that in my first message, in my excitement over the breakthrough in our project, I neglected to tell you that my mother died this past Monday. She had cancer. It was pretty tough on all of us. Anyway, please do call me when you get a chance. No big deal, it would just be nice to catch up. Bye."

Would you believe it? Lisa called back just a few minutes later. Her voice was warm and kind. If there were any remnants of the irritation or discomfort she had seemed to feel toward me when she left, they weren't evident.

"Hi, Jason. It's Lisa. I just received your message. I'm so sorry to hear about your mother."

"Hi, Lisa, thanks so much for calling back. It's great to hear from you."

"Same here. I'm sorry it's taken me this long to return your first phone call. I've been really busy lately. But when I heard the news about your mother, I wanted to call right away to see how you're doing."

"I'm actually doing OK, thanks for asking. We've known for a couple months that this was coming. I miss her, but she had a good life."

"I gather from your message that your project is going well."

"Yes, it's great. My new assistant, Marvin, is terrific, though of course he isn't you. Since you left, we've figured out how to use the EOSF to capture the electrical signals as they escape from the brain, and direct them onto a portable drive where they can be permanently stored. In fact, we've already begun transferring the memories from one of our brain specimens. It will take a while, probably several weeks, but we're expecting to transfer virtually all the existing memory data from a single brain. After that, we'll get to work on the decoding. This is really happening."

"Wow, that's phenomenal. Was that Marvin's work, figuring out the uploading process?"

"Well, mostly, yes. He's the computer scientist. But I had to do a lot of it, mainly figuring out how to use the EOSF to get the electricity to travel to the computer. All he had to do was write some software so that the computer could recognize and record those signals as they arrive. Not minimizing that part of it, of course – he did an excellent job."

"That's wonderful, Jason. It sounds like it's working out just as you had dreamed it would. Anyway, I should probably run. I have a meeting I have to get ready for. But it's been great talking to you."

"Wait, do you have time to fill me in on what's going on with you? Are you having any luck with your research, or with job applications?"

"Well, the research is going well, but the job hunt is actually pretty slow. There don't seem to be that many positions available at the moment. But I'll keep plugging."

"And Manny? He's doing well?"

"He's fine, thanks for asking. But unfortunately I really do have to run now. Again, it's been very nice to talk with you, and I'm so sorry about your mother. Take care, Jason."

"OK, bye, Lisa."

And that was it. All right, first of all, yes, I deliberately didn't tell her that the brain we're taking the memories from is that of my mother. I remember Jessica's disgusted reaction when I told her. And for that matter, even Marvin had seemed to think it was pretty grotesque, at least at first. I saw no benefit in risking Lisa thinking I was doing something grotesque.

But second, Lisa seemed to be minimizing my achievements in this project. Her question about whether the uploading was essentially Marvin's work was grating. Marvin and I both worked on that, and frankly the basic idea has been mine from the outset.

Third, she was awfully cryptic about Manny. I asked how he was doing in the hope that she would reveal something about how their relationship was progressing. All she said was that he's doing fine. Are they even still together? I have no idea.

And fourth, and most importantly, it was evident that Lisa couldn't wait to get off the phone. She pretty much had to return my call once I told her my mother had died, but as soon as she had completed the obligatory "I'm sorry to hear about your mother" and "how's the project going?," she said she had to run. And when I nonetheless asked her to take a moment to tell me how her research and job queries were going, she answered as cursorily as humanly possible and then repeated that she couldn't talk any more.

She obviously has about as much interest in connecting with me as Jessica does. Or as Melissa Santos did in college. That's fine. I could care less. The only reason I even called her was to look for clues as to whether she has disclosed our secret project to anyone, including potential employers.

Monday, February 16, 2026
Today marks two weeks since my mother's death and the start of our downloading project. Jessica's

behavior hasn't changed. She still avoids me like the plague and still claims nothing is wrong.

Meanwhile I'm having a very tough time at the lab. Every two hours I move the brain end of the EOSF and update the commands. Between Marvin and me we've now done this more than 80 times. At this rate, we're still on schedule to finish this phase of the project around the end of March.

My problem is that I no longer have much to do in between those brief bi-hourly tasks. Marvin is busy as hell. He's continuing to study the variations in the electrical data being stored on the portable drive in the hope of discovering patterns. I had expected to work on those patterns as well, but the exercise is becoming increasingly mathematical and I'm a bit out of my league. As planned, I've given Marvin a copy of the looseleaf binder that contains entries from my interviews with my mother.

From time to time, especially when I'm bored, I wander over to his cubicle to share some additional data about my mother's life that I've just thought of. He is always polite, writing down this new information, but he clearly doesn't want to spend time talking about it. He's focused on the data themselves and has told me diplomatically that he really needs complete concentration in order to start synthesizing this massive quantity of data and to begin spotting patterns.

All this free time has given me more opportunity to think about the overall project and the secrecy that it necessitates. There are so many security vulnerabilities. I really don't have any reason to doubt Marvin's commitment to confidentiality, but I have no way to be sure.

And I am increasingly concerned about Jessica. She is a totally different, and strange, person. I can no longer tell whether her avoidance of me is purely personal or whether she might be sharing information about my project with others and avoiding me for fear that in a conversation she could accidentally let something slip.

For that matter, my own mother had asked me a couple times about my work. Were these just innocent questions? Or had Jessica told her what I was planning, and had my mother then alerted anyone who she thought could stop me? Probably not, because no one did intervene, though it's possible that anyone who knows about it will wait until later to step in. They might think I'll never get to the decoding stage and that early intervention would therefore be unnecessary.

Of course Lisa also remains a mystery, in so many ways. She too might very well be leaking information to others, out of whatever motives, and I would never know. I'm glad I at least didn't tell her about my mother's connection to this project.

Again, I don't know that any of this is happening. I don't want to sound paranoid. It's just the uncertainty of it all. Any of these leaks could be occurring without my knowledge. I need to find something productive to do. I'm starting to feel like a useless appendage in my own project.

Monday, February 23, 2026

Jessica left me today. Marriage to me, she said, was like not being married at all. Also, she explained, I'm not the same person as the man she married. I'm almost not like a person at all. I'm more like a non-human laboratory creation. She would ordinarily be sorry and sad to be hurting me, and she truly doesn't want to be cruel, but she no longer thinks I'm even capable of feeling enough emotion to be hurt by her leaving or by her words.

She and Zeke will be packing up and leaving the house today. They will temporarily stay with her colleague Marilyn and her husband. Jessica would appreciate it if I could move out and let her and Zeke move back to the house once I find a place. That would be better for Zeke, and since there are two of them and only one of me, that arrangement would make the most sense. Of course I should feel free to visit Zeke from time to time. I should just email her in advance to schedule those visits.

She told me all this in the morning, as I was getting ready to go to work. She finished by simply saying "Goodbye, Jason."

I don't quite know how to describe my reaction. Consciously, I hadn't seen this coming. Deep down, though, I suppose I had known it was inevitable. Our relationship had effectively ended months ago, maybe years ago. And at some level she was right about my reaction. It felt a bit surreal, but I didn't feel hurt. It was more like just receiving new data.

At another level it left me feeling empty, curious intellectually if not emotionally about how our relationship could have gone from normal and loving to weird and uncaring. Even the knowledge that I would no longer be living with Zeke didn't seem so horrible, because I could still visit him and, practically speaking, would most likely end up spending just as much time with him as I do now. Maybe "disorienting" is the right word. Something feels off.

I went to the lab and fell back into what has become my daily routine these past few weeks. I made the usual EOSF adjustments, got a cup of coffee, read my email, and checked in with Marvin for an update. He had nothing to report. He was still studying patterns. I returned to my cubicle and started to read some of the mathematical literature on decoding, but it was a bit too advanced and I was having a hard time keeping up my concentration. I looked at my watch and saw it would be another hour and three-quarters before it was time to update the EOSF again.

And then I remembered the events at the house this morning and pondered the reality of Jessica and Zeke being gone. I needed to give some thought to the practical things I now needed to do, like food shopping, cooking, and laundry. Even though both Jessica and I were working, Jessica had been doing all these things, mainly because my work hours were so much longer than hers.

I'll now have to fend for myself. I guess I also have to get started looking for an apartment to rent. It would be nice if I could find a place within walking distance to the lab. Parking here has become a nightmare, and besides I can use the exercise.

By late afternoon, I was feeling very much off kilter. I couldn't focus on the mathematical stuff and really had nothing else to do except update the EOSF every two hours.

I didn't want to stay in the lab. But I also didn't want to go home. The house will be empty. What am I going to do all evening? I can kill some time by making something for dinner, but I'm not at all hungry. Anyway, then what? I truly can't think of a single thing that interests me.

I ended up staying at the lab until about 9 pm so that I could get in a couple extra EOSF updates. Then I drove home. The house that greeted me was dark and empty.

Tuesday, February 24, 2026
I woke up in the middle of the night. My mind just kept racing. I couldn't seem to stop it. I finally gave up hope of falling back to sleep and got out of bed. I've been waking up early for months now, long before it's light outside and long before anyone else is up, so finding the house dark and quiet probably shouldn't have seemed any different.

But it did, because I was acutely conscious of Jessica's and Zeke's absence. It wasn't just that I couldn't see them. They really weren't there and never will be again, at least not while I'm here. It's unsettling.

I arrived at the lab around 4:30 a.m. and did my usual morning routine – updating the EOSF, making a pot of coffee, and checking my email. In the past, checking my email was an annoying chore. I frankly had no interest in corresponding with anyone, and slogging through my email was delaying my getting to the work I really wanted to do.

But now that I'm looking for things to fill up my day, I actually hope for lots of messages in the morning. And of course this morning there wasn't a single message. Not one person had written to me. There wasn't even any spam.

I now had absolutely nothing to do until the time for updating the EOSF again, and that wasn't for another hour and 50 minutes. So I got on the web and checked the news, but I had no interest in the news either. After about ten minutes of trying to find something interesting, I gave up.

That's basically how my entire day went. I didn't have the energy to work on the math today, and I couldn't think of any excuses to bother Marvin. As it is, I'm certain that my visits to his cubicle are irritating him, even though he's too polite to tell me. It's now 8:00 pm, and I really can't account for how I spent my time today, other than the five minutes that it takes me every two hours to update the EOSF.

I'm not a people person, but right now, if I can't have an actual conversation with anyone, I'd at least like to be around them. So instead of going home, I went out to a Mexican restaurant for dinner. I ordered enchiladas but had little appetite and ended up bringing about three-quarters of my meal home in a doggie bag. Then I went to sleep for the night.

Sunday, March 15, 2026

I've been really tired these past few weeks, and there actually hasn't been anything significant to report anyway, which is why it's been so long since my last journal entry. I come to the lab seven days a week, and I stay here from the wee hours of the morning until well into the evening, basically just rattling around. I continue to update the EOSF every two hours, counting the minutes till the next updating time.

Marvin has been working only six days a week, as he promised his wife he would take Sundays off. I don't blame him for that. It's just that I wish he were making speedier progress on the decoding.

One benefit of sleeplessness and having nothing else to do is that my long hours at the lab have enabled me to update the EOSF about nine times per day rather than the six I had planned on. As a result, the transfer of my mother's memories to the portable drive is proceeding well ahead of schedule. Instead of a March 31 target date, I now expect to finish all the uploading within the next few days.

That does mean, though, that I'll no longer have even the one thing that currently occupies at least a fraction of my time, the updating of the EOSF. This is crazy. I'm going to have to force myself to get more involved in the decoding or I'll go nuts.

Every night for the past several weeks I've returned to that same Mexican restaurant for dinner, and every time I order the same enchiladas. I know that sounds boring and maybe even strange, but the routine is comforting and the waiters there now know me and greet me. I don't even have to look at the menu. They just ask "the usual?" and I say "yes, please."

Sometimes I hear the waiters snickering in the kitchen, where they think they won't be overheard. I can't be certain I'm the object of their ridicule, but that seems like a safe bet. I don't care, though. People in Mexico eat three meals of Mexican food every day, so I don't know what's so strange about my eating it once a day.

The only thing I found disconcerting – and it happened only once – was that one of the older waiters, after taking my order, asked me what kind of work I do. That struck me as an odd question for a waiter to ask a diner whom he hardly knows. Again I don't want to sound paranoid, but I can't rule out at least the possibility that he is on to my project.

There are lots of scenarios in which he could find out. Marvin goes out for lunch most days, and it's entirely possible he's come here on occasion, as this place is only a ten-minute walk from the lab. He could easily have let something slip. Or – and I don't think this is likely, just possible – Marvin could be deliberately leaking information about the nature and import of our project and exaggerating his role in it, just for bragging purposes.

For that matter, Jessica, if determined to sabotage my project, could well be working with a government agent or private investigator. That person would need to be undercover. Posing as a waiter, in a restaurant where I'm a regular, would be quite a clever cover.

I want to emphasize I'm not at all certain that anyone is plotting to do any of this. I'm simply saying it's possible and I need to be extra cautious about whom I talk to and what I say.

Monday, March 16, 2026

This morning Jessica called me at the lab. She asked whether I'd had any luck yet finding an apartment. Marilyn and her husband have been very generous in letting her and Zeke stay there this long, but it was meant to be a short-term arrangement and she can't stay there forever.

I actually had forgotten about this and haven't done any searching at all. I couldn't tell Jessica that, so I said I haven't found anything yet but have some leads now that look promising. And I'll get back to her as soon as I know anything.

She probably didn't believe me, but she asked me to prioritize this and I said I would. She also noted that I hadn't seen or called Zeke these past few weeks and was surprised that even now I hadn't asked her how he was doing.

Without realizing it, I had somehow put Zeke out of my mind entirely. I'm not sure why. I just lamely told her that I assumed she would have let me know if he were having any problems. She said it's not just a matter of problems. She can't understand why I wouldn't want to spend time with my son. I told her that of course I want to spend time with him. It's just that I've been incredibly busy during this critical phase of my project. I assured her I would be calling him soon and told her to tell him that.

As is typical, she still wouldn't let it go. She said she's not going to get Zeke's hopes up by telling him I'll be calling unless I really do plan to call him in the next couple days, no more excuses. I then told her in no uncertain terms that this conversation was starting to aggravate me. When I say I'm going to call my son, I'm going to call my son, and I don't need an inquisition from someone who has just left me and taken my son with her.

This seemed to strike a nerve, because she then paused a moment and said "Jason, it was you who left me. You just haven't figured that out yet." That was her melodramatic and pretentious way of telling me that I was the one who had withdrawn emotionally from our relationship. Which is total bullshit. I wasn't the one who drove my spouse away by constantly demeaning him and his work.

Anyway, the conversation ended on that sour note. But while there was no excuse for her belligerent tone, I have to admit she was right about the apartment. I have kind of dropped the ball on looking for it. And also on seeing Zeke.

In a way, that conversation kind of energized me, because the apartment search gave me a new project to work on while I was waiting for something to do on the big project. So as soon as we hung up, I updated the EOSF and then got to work combing the apartment listings. I quickly located listings for two furnished apartments less than a 15-minute walk from my lab and arranged to visit one of them right after lunch.

So as not to delay the EOSF work, I asked Marvin to please do the next couple EOSF updates. I haven't told him yet that Jessica has left me and don't see any need to share that with him, so I just said I had some errands to do, which was true.

It was a modern one-bedroom furnished apartment on the fifth floor of a new high-rise in an area of town called the Central West End. It looked fine. The price seemed a little high but still within range, so I took it. It's vacant and ready now, which means I can move in any time. We did all the paperwork this afternoon, and I'll make the move tomorrow. I don't see any point in looking at other apartments or delaying the move. I don't even need to hire a mover, because the only things I have to transport are my clothes and a few other things. All the furniture, kitchen equipment, and everything else are there. I think the realtor said the kitchen cabinets are oak, though I could care less what they're made of as long as they work.

When I got back, I called Jessica to let her know about the apartment. She was very pleased – and shocked. She hadn't imagined I would arrange all this the same day as her call. I reminded her that I had told her I had some leads on apartments, and said all I had to do today was finalize this. It really hadn't been necessary, I suggested, for her to call me this morning, because I was already on it. I didn't want to give her the satisfaction of knowing I had fallen down on the job and needed her reminders. Given how she had treated me, I had no moral reservations about embellishing the facts a little.

I also asked her whether I could take Zeke out tomorrow after school. I wanted to show him my new apartment. Jessica said that would be perfect. And I have to admit she was actually pleasant about it, even somewhat warm.

I started to wonder whether she was thawing, and whether she might be reconsidering her decision to separate. I'm just curious. I don't want to get back together with her even if she does. She likes to think I'm the problem and that I'm not the same person she married.

Well, if she wants to stay mired in that delusion, let her. Maybe it eases her guilt. The reality is that I'm the same person I've always been. She's the one who has changed, and not in a positive way.

I hadn't expected the apartment process to be this easy or this quick. I should be happy that it was, but after I move in tomorrow I'll be back to the same predicament of having almost nothing to do.

Still, today was good for me. It was the first time in a while that I've felt productive. And tomorrow I'll be able to kill some additional time transporting my clothes and getting set up in my new place.

Tuesday, March 17, 2026

Very early this morning, as planned, I moved everything into my new apartment. The whole thing – packing up, driving over there, unpacking, and setting up the place the way I wanted it – took only about two hours. I can't believe how easy this has been.

I got to the lab at 8:00 a.m., feeling pretty proud of myself. When Marvin arrived, I told him I'd be able to continue doing the EOSF updating today after all, until 4:00, when I needed to leave to pick up Zeke. He should do as many updates as he can after that.

I still had to figure out what I was supposed to do from 8:00 to 4:00 when I wasn't updating the EOSF. I was in much better spirits, though, because I had been so productive yesterday and this morning. While most other people were still sleeping, I had already gotten ready for the day, moved from a house to an apartment, and made my way to work.

Perhaps because of this improved state of mind, I was able to do something that had been eluding me for weeks – force myself to sit down with the mathematical materials on decoding and try to understand them. I reminded myself that I had enough mathematical aptitude to handle the physics, chemistry, and other science courses in college and medical school. I haven't suddenly become stupid. With enough time and effort I should be able to do this and actually help Marvin with the decoding project.

But that proved to be easier said than done. The math was very advanced. Trying to jump in with no previous background was simply beyond me. So after trying for about an hour, I gave up. I puttered away the remaining hours and frankly can't remember what I actually did today during the down times.

I was especially relieved, then, when 4:00 came and I could leave to pick up Zeke from pre-school. He smiled when he saw me, but it was a shy smile, as if I were a kindly stranger. I guess that's what I was. I hadn't seen him or talked to him in weeks, a very long period in the life of a five-year-old.

By this time Jessica had told him that they would be moving back to the house today but that Daddy would be living somewhere else. He had asked why Daddy wouldn't also be living in the house, and Jessica had purposely given a vague answer, which his five-year-old mind apparently accepted.

From his pre-school we drove directly to my new apartment. Zeke was quite impressed. He especially loved the elevator, which he noted was something we didn't have in our house. And since we were the only ones in the elevator, he got to press every button. At least we were the only ones in it until we got to the second floor, when a middle-aged man and his elderly father got in and were annoyed that they would be stopping at every floor. I didn't say anything, and Zeke was intimidated enough by the presence of these two large strangers in our small and previously private place that he too stood quietly. He just stared up at them, as children do, until we got off at the fifth floor.

He seemed less impressed by my apartment. There weren't any toys, and there wasn't anything else of interest either, except for the trash chute in the hall. I let him toss my trash bag down the chute even though the bag was only half-full. He clearly found that very cool.

With nothing else to do at the apartment, we went out to dinner. I took him to my Mexican restaurant, which I thought he would like. I have to admit I enjoyed showing him off to the waiters. Maybe this would even show them that I'm a normal family man, not an eccentric.

Zeke's favorite part was the bowl of warm, crisp chips that he could dip into the salsa. I realized this was new for him, as I can't recall having brought him to a Mexican restaurant before. By the time the enchiladas arrived, he was actually pretty full. I had to battle with him a little bit to make him at least try them, which he finally did, but he left 90% of his meal untouched, so I brought it home with me in a doggie bag.

When I dropped him off at the house, he gave me a big hug. I held onto him for a long time but could see he was getting tired of hugging, so I let him go and he ran off to play. I found myself flashing back to that scene in the high school guidance counselor's office, when my mother had needed a hug from me as much as I needed one now from Zeke.

Jessica was there to take this all in. She smiled and patted me on the arm. It seems that just when I'm ready to give up on her, she surprises me with a show of genuine humanity and even sweetness. Too little, too late, though.

By the time I left the house it was still only about 5:30 pm, and I didn't feel like going back to the lab, so I had to think of something to do. I remembered then that I had to go grocery shopping, to stock up on food and supplies.

That was a relief. Not only would that give me something to do, it would also take my mind off little Zeke and the fact that we were no longer living under the same roof. And probably never would be again.

So on the way home, I stopped at our neighborhood EasyMart, which is St. Louis's main supermarket chain. EasyMart had taken over the St. Louis market a couple years ago, displacing a long-established supermarket chain improbably named Schnucks.

I ended up buying six shopping bags worth of food and household supplies. It took three trips from the car to the apartment, but I got everything in, put all the items away, and then sank into bed early, exhausted from cumulative sleep deprivation.

I woke up even earlier than usual, around 2:30 a.m, and couldn't get back to sleep. When I awoke, I had forgotten that I was now in a new place and at first couldn't understand why the night table where I kept my glasses wasn't where it was supposed to be. But the confusion was just momentary, and I groped around in the dark until I could find a light switch and give my pupils a chance to contract.

At about 4:00 I left for the lab. For the first time ever, I could walk to work, though the streets were unfamiliar and at this hour dark and deserted. I was a bit apprehensive, so I felt relieved to arrive at my building and make my way to the lab.

And then I settled back into my daily routine – updating the EOSF, making coffee, checking my now very sparse email, trying to figure out what to do with myself in between updates, beating up on myself for not being able to comprehend the decoding math, and daydreaming about who knows what.

Saturday, March 21, 2026

Over the last several days my routine hasn't changed a bit; hence, no journal entries since Tuesday. Yet I've been finding myself much less despondent, because I can now see light at the end of this long tunnel. This afternoon marks another milestone in my quest to replicate eternal life. Today, March 21, 2026, I completed the uploading of my mother's memory data to the portable drive.

We are a good week or so ahead of schedule, and the enormity of my achievement is registering with me after a long hiatus. I had just taken all of my mother's memories – all of the thoughts, emotions, and physical sensations that she had ever experienced – and transferred them to a place where they can live forever.

And I had done this after her death. And without any help from a nonexistent god who had arranged some mythological heavenly fairyland for virtuous people to retire to after they leave earth.

True, we haven't yet figured out how to translate those data into a language that we can understand. But we will. Of that, I am supremely confident. And even before we complete that last step, the essence of my mother is already eternally preserved in those digital data, whether or not the rest of us can understand their meaning yet.

As for the decoding, I figure that if Champollion could do it, so can we. Marvin and I are surely at least as smart as he was, and although we don't have the Greek language reference point that he did, we have even better reference points – specific memories delivered directly by their creator to her son. And we have the most powerful computers ever invented.

It also occurred to me today that perhaps I had given up too soon on the idea of learning the mathematics that are needed for the decoding. My problem was that at too many crucial points the texts I was reading assumed an understanding of various foundational concepts that I had never seen and certain jargon that I'd never encountered. So I asked Marvin to recommend readings that would give me enough background information to study and understand the decoding materials.

He was happy to oblige, and now I'm going to become a student again, starting tomorrow. This not only gives me reason to come to work, it will speed up the decoding process with two of us working on it together.

CHAPTER 8
DECODING HIEROGLYPHICS

Sunday, March 22, 2026

It's day 1 of my new life. Last night I could barely sleep, but a combination of adrenaline and caffeine got me to the lab early this morning and ready to plunge into the math.

The sources that Marvin recommended are online, and I dived right into them. They were actually fairly straightforward, and my math skills were fresher than I had expected. I kept coming across concepts and vocabulary that I wish I had encountered earlier, before wasting so much time trying to make sense of the more specific advanced materials on decoding.

Marvin didn't come in today. He continues to take Sundays off, and I really don't begrudge him doing that. He's married, after all, and he works very hard the other six days. I'm finding myself feeling a renewed sense of affection toward him, even though at this stage of the project I can't afford to trust him or anyone else more than I have to.

Monday, March 23, 2026

Another long but exhilarating day. I'm on a good schedule now, arriving at the lab at 5 a.m. and staying until about 10 pm. That sounds like long hours, but the time goes quickly now that I have productive things to do again and am smelling victory. In any event, I'm only planning to sustain these hours for a few more days, until I'm at the point where I know enough to get started on actual decoding.

To that end, I had a great conversation with Marvin this morning. I now have a better understanding of how he's approaching this and why it's so challenging.

On the one hand, this is easy in theory. Whatever form the electrical signals were in originally, they're now stored on our portable drive in bits and bytes. If you're already into computers, you'll probably know all this and can skip the explanation I'm about to provide. But if you're not, here's all you need to know about digital data storage to understand what we're doing.

A bit is the smallest unit of storage. It can have only two values, a zero or a one. A byte is a group of eight bits, arranged in order. Think of it as a row of eight zeros and ones. There are 256 (i.e. 2 to the 8th power) possible permutations of 8 bits – for example, 00101001 is one possibility, 10000010 is another, and so on.

Every character that the computer stores – a number, a letter, a symbol, anything – is represented by one of those bytes. A whole word, or picture, or video would be stored as a series of bytes. The same is true of the electrical signals that we've now transferred to the portable drive. Each electrical signal that was released by a single picobe in my mother's brain now resides on the portable drive, appearing as a series of bytes.

That, in turn, means that Marvin should be able to write software that will enable him to search for particular combinations of numbers and thereby identify patterns. Comparing those patterns to known data, like actual memories that we know my mother had, will then enable us to create a kind of foreign language dictionary. We'll be able to match a particular series of bytes to a specific word or concept. And the more of that we do, the more reference points we'll have for adding still more entries to our dictionary.

Logically, all of that should be achievable with a computer. We're simply searching by number, the easiest kind of task for a computer. The problem is a practical one. The sheer amount of information and the millions of different combinations of bytes that we're seeing make it extremely difficult to identify the first few patterns. Once we're able to do that, our progress will hopefully snowball, but getting those first few pickles out of the jar is our immediate challenge.

Monday, April 6, 2026

Starting two weeks ago both Marvin and I have been able to devote our full energies to working on the decoding. Even before the last of my mother's memory data was emptied onto our portable drive, Marvin had decided that as soon as that moment arrived he would have the software ready to organize those data in various ways.

Because all the data were in the form of sequences of bytes, each of which consisted of some combination of eight zeroes or ones, the most obvious way to start would be to sort all the data in numerical order. That way the computer could easily find and flag any series that were identical. If there are any, this might indicate that they were storing the same memory, perhaps refreshed periodically over time.

If there are some series that are almost identical but not quite, that might mean the memories are related to the same event. Or it might be that these nearly identical numerical sequences are simply various versions of the same memory, refreshed and edited over time.

It didn't take long for Marvin to sort the data in numerical order. He did that two weeks ago, within hours after we had finished uploading the last of my mother's memory data. And sure enough, there were thousands – perhaps millions, we didn't try to count – of picobes that contained multiple identical numerical sequences.

That was the easy part. The hard part is figuring out what sense to make of these identical number sequences.

Marvin has a copy of the binder that contains the notes of my interviews with my mother, as well as his own notes of his conversations with me about my mother's life. So he now knows a lot about my mother's memories. He's hoping to spot some match between those known memories and the cold numerical groupings now exposed by the computer.

And I'm doing the same – searching for patterns and matches.

But we've hit a wall. We've used the computer in a vain attempt to match the numbers to the known memories. We'll keep at it, of course, and I'm hoping that at some predestined, magical moment one of us will shout eureka and we'll be on our way.

That is kind of what has happened at earlier stages of this project. There's no reason it can't happen again. We are two smart people, working long hours, with lots of reference points and a powerhouse computer.

Monday, April 20, 2026

No eureka moment yet. And I've decided to expand my work hours. By adding one more hour at each end I can now regularly get in 19 hours per day, from 4:00 a.m. to 11:00 pm, seven days a week.

This has meant setting my alarm clock for 3:15 a.m. and forcing myself to go to bed immediately after I get home, but really this entails only slightly less sleep than I've been getting up to now.

Soldiers sometimes have to do this when they're in combat zones, and I don't have to put up with anything like the hardships and fears that they labor under. I don't expect to sustain this pace forever, but in the short-term, until Marvin and I solve this final puzzle, I can do it. And I'm determined to do it.

Wednesday, April 29, 2026

I've been sticking religiously to my new work hour plan for nine days now. Except for today. I'm certain that I set my alarm for 3:15 a.m., but somehow I must not have heard it, because I slept until 5:00. That's a killer. I've lost two valuable work hours that I can't afford to squander.

The only thing I can do is make them up, which I'll do tonight. I'll work till midnight and set my alarm for 2:15 a.m. That will be tough, but it's a one-time fix and then I'll be back on my regular schedule. I can't deny that both fatigue and stress have become factors, but I've proved to myself that I can do it, and I fully intend to continue at this pace until we have a breakthrough.

I'm a bit disappointed in Marvin, whose commitment has not been at nearly the same level. He's working what in normal circumstances would be long hours – probably about twelve hours per day, six days a week – but nothing like the hours I'm putting in and nothing like what the magnitude of this project warrants.

I haven't said anything to him about it, because I know his wife is continually haranguing him to cut back his hours even more, but I've taken to recording his arrival and departure times each day on a separate piece of paper that I keep hidden away in my desk. This is just in case I ever have to let him go and I need to document my reasons. He has no idea I'm keeping tabs on him.

Still nothing to show for all this. And that's demoralizing. It's not just my impatience. If I were certain that we'll ultimately be able to translate these data, I wouldn't mind that the project is taking a little longer than I'd hoped. What's weighing on me is the very real possibility, which I've been trying not to think about, that we might never be able to solve the code.

Actually my fear is worse than that. It would be one thing if we couldn't figure out the code but were secure in the knowledge that the data on our portable drive actually represent memories. At least then I would know that my mother's memories will live forever despite the rest of us not knowing what those memories are.

But we don't really know even that. At this point, there is still no real proof that the electrical signals we have recorded are memories. They could be just useless residual electrical energy. If that turns out to be the case, this entire project will have wasted years of work and energy. And since I've sacrificed my family and everything else I cared about to achieve my dream of discovering a way to replicate eternal life, what this really will have been is a waste of my entire life.

None of this has deterred me from continuing. To the contrary, I'm finding that the longer I go without tangible results, the more hours I start putting in and the more intense my focus becomes. That kind of steely determination has always served me well and is part of the reason that this project has proceeded as far as it has. There's no way I'm going to abandon that mindset now. Not unless and until it becomes 100% clear that there is no path forward.

Friday, May 8, 2026

The eureka moment came today. I knew it was only a matter of time. And I have to give Marvin a great deal of credit.

Until now, we had both been assuming that all of the numerical sequences we've been looking at were actual memories. Marvin discovered that that's not the case. It turns out that much of what we've been looking at are metadata – information about the information.

More specifically, Marvin detected certain codes that revealed the precise moment in time when each individual memory was recorded. And I don't just mean the moment when it was uploaded to the portable drive. We can actually see when it was recorded in my mother's brain.

Of course these metadata were using their own time scale. There would be no way for the brain to know the exact calendar date and clock time of the recording, because the biological clock has nothing to do with the Roman calendar or the 24-hour increments that we arbitrarily divide the day into. In some cases my mother might happen to have been aware of the exact time and date at the time she formed the memory, but even then, that information would just be part of the memory itself and therefore would appear only in the main data, not in the metadata.

The different time scale isn't a problem, though. As long as whatever time scale the brain uses is linear, we can figure out pretty closely what calendar date and clock time any given time marker corresponds to.

I know that my mother was born on August 27, 1955 and died on February 2, 2026. So she lived approximately 70 years and 5 months. Actually, some of the memories were presumably pre-natal, so let's say that conception to death spanned about 71 years.

To discover the actual calendar dates and times when the various memories were recorded in the brain, all we have to do is see how many brain-time units elapsed from the earliest memory to the last. For example, if the earliest memory shows up on our portable drive as, say, zero, and the last memory shows up as 70 million, then we would know that each brain-time unit is equivalent to roughly one one-millionth of a calendar year.

That enables us to pretty much pinpoint the date and time of every memory. Marvin will easily be able to write and run software that will convert the brain-time in the metadata to calendar dates and times. This means we'll have a listing of the date and time of every recorded memory.

And that's huge, because it will help us decode the memories themselves. For example, we know the exact date and approximate time when my mother learned that my father had died. I know the dates and times when she was relating various events to me during our interviews. And so on. We can now search the portable drive for whatever memory data correspond to those moments. That's the first major step toward seeing the patterns that will reveal how to translate the numbers that appear on the portable drive into a language that we can understand.

This isn't just huge. It's *FUCKING* huge!!! Excuse my language. I now have no doubt whatsoever that we will soon be able to translate this numerical gibberish into English.

Monday, May 11, 2026
This morning Marvin successfully ran the software to convert the brain-times into actual calendar dates and times. So we now have dates and times for every recorded memory. For example, the data for the time when my mother was in the high school guidance counselor's office giving me the news of my father's death look like this:

August 22, 2005, 2:16 pm
00011001
01001010
11101000

And so on – this list contains several thousand additional bytes.

Now the really hard work begins. We need to figure out how to translate various combinations of those numbers into English. That will entail searching for patterns that reveal how particular combinations of bytes correlate with particular known memories.

Since there are so many permutations, this will take a long time. Which means backbreaking hours at the lab for the long haul. But I'm convinced we'll ultimately be able to break the code. And that in turn means that I absolutely will continue to put in the hours it takes to do it and will expect the same from Marvin.

Of course, now that the time pressure has reached its peak, Jessica chose today to call me. She wanted to "remind" me that "I have a son" and that I hadn't seen him or so much as called him in weeks. I tried to explain to her that I've been a little busy lately, but as usual that message fell on deaf ears.

I told her I would spend time with him next weekend. I would pick him up at 9:00 Saturday morning and return him to the house at 11:00. That would give us time to go to the playground and have a snack.

She said that would be fine and that I needed to write it down so I wouldn't forget. She's going to tell Zeke I'll be seeing him Saturday, and he will be crushed if I don't show up. I reminded her that I have never once – not ever – scheduled time with Zeke and then failed to follow through, so I didn't need her admonishing me in that patronizing tone.

This does mean giving up two more hours of work time, and it comes on the heels of my oversleeping just a few days ago. I will need to make it up, but this time I have advance notice. Working till midnight and then having to get up just two hours later the other day was a killer, so this time I'm going to be smarter and spread the diminished sleep over two nights. I'll work till midnight tonight but still set my alarm for 3:15 a.m., and then I'll do the same thing tomorrow night. That will put me back on schedule. And the nice thing is that by the time I'm with Zeke, I will already have made up for the time I'll be losing, so there won't be any future makeup time hanging over my head. I hate being in debt.

On top of all this, something unnerving happened tonight. It might be nothing or it might be significant. A little after 11:00 pm I left the lab and walked down the hall to go to the bathroom. I'm normally the only one in the building at that hour. The custodial staff finishes at 9 pm, and by then all the other researchers are long gone as well.

But tonight, not more than ten seconds after I entered the men's room and approached the urinal, another man followed me in and appeared to use the adjacent urinal. I say "appeared to use" because I didn't hear any sound of his urine hitting the porcelain, which I normally would.

Sure enough, a few seconds after I finished urinating, zipped up, and walked to the sink to wash my hands, he did the same – and at the adjacent sink, even though there was a whole row of sinks to choose from. After I dried my hands, so did he. I avoided eye contact and we never exchanged a word.

Seconds after I exited to return to the lab, I heard his footsteps behind me, all the way along the hall back to the lab even though there were two points at which he could have turned off in another direction. I entered the lab, locked the lab door, and continued to hear his footsteps as he walked away. At least he continued walking down the hall in the same direction, away from the lab. I would have freaked out completely if he had then turned around and gone back.

Again, it could well be nothing. It's just awfully unusual for someone else even to be in the building at that hour, let alone just happen to enter the men's room seconds after I did and then follow me closely until I was safely in the lab behind a locked door.

I decided then that from now on I'll keep the lab door locked all the time I'm inside, as well as every time I need to leave even for a couple minutes. I've also made a note to myself to tell Marvin to do the same.

Tuesday, May 26, 2026

It's been a couple weeks since I added any journal entries, mainly because there hasn't been anything significant to report. Marvin and I have both been searching for mathematical patterns that will enable us to translate these numerical sequences into actual memories. It's discouraging, because the quantity of data is so vast, and the series of bytes that correspond to a given moment in time don't seem to have anything in common – at least no commonality that we've been able to identify yet.

Thursday, May 28, 2026

I've been walking back and forth to work every day since moving to my new apartment, even when it's raining. That was the main reason I chose that apartment, and especially with my intense work hours I know I need the exercise if I'm to keep up my strength. To get maximum physical benefit, and also to save time, I walk at a brisk pace.

But now I'm having second thoughts. Since I get up so early, it's almost always still dark when I go to work, and typically there's no one else on the streets. That didn't bother me until this morning. As I got within two blocks of the lab, I saw what I'm almost certain was a shadow of someone ducking around the corner as I approached. It was just for a second, so I guess it's possible it was just some flicker of the street light, but I'm pretty sure it was a person's shadow. So I crossed to the other side of the street and kept walking, with frequent glances at the spot where I had seen the shadow. Nothing happened, but it was unnerving.

With my current work schedule, it will always be dark during my trips back and forth to the lab, but I tentatively decided that once I'm able to ease off on my hours, I'll drive to work on days when it's still dark outside and walk to work only when it's light out and there are lots of people around.

After further reflection, though, it's probably not a good idea to walk to work even in daylight. There are too many dangerous people on the streets, and all it takes is one who decides to assault me or even kill me, and my life would be over, just like that. It's not as if a psychotic criminal would say "I won't kill him because it's light out and there are people around." It angers me that other people who have no right to harm or threaten me can prevent me from walking, but I'm not going to cut off my nose to spite my face. And driving will actually free up a little additional time, so it's not a total loss.

The only other problem is that I still have to walk from the parking garage to my lab. The garage is underground, right below the building that my lab is in, and there's an elevator that takes me right into the main hall. But the garage area isn't well lit, and I'm always alone in the elevator. It would be easy for someone to be lurking by the elevator. In fact a couple days ago someone was doing just that. It turned out to be an elderly woman waiting for the elevator, but I couldn't know that until I got closer.

I'm not sure what to do. There's really no safe option. All I can do is play the odds, which I'm doing by driving rather than walking. When my time comes, it comes.

Tuesday, June 2, 2026

I certainly don't need additional worries just now, but several incidents have begun coalescing in my mind and are weighing on me. I've already related the strange encounter with the man who followed me into and out of the men's room and along the hall all the way back to my lab. Only two weeks later there had been the quickly disappearing shadow of a person as I walked to work in the darkness.

Those *might* both be innocuous coincidences. Maybe my mind is playing tricks on me, as I'm sleep-deprived and feeling fragile. But both events seem suspicious, and tonight there was a third one.

It happened at about 10:30 pm. I was about to make a trip to the men's room. I had my key out so that I could lock the lab door upon leaving. Before I could open the door, I heard what sounded like footsteps in the hall. As I mentioned earlier, there would rarely be any reason for any other person to be in the building at that late hour. So I backed away from the door and held off my trip to the men's room.

After about 15 minutes, I put my ear to the door and listened for any additional sounds. There weren't any, so I slowly opened the door, looked both ways along the hallway, and, seeing and hearing no one, locked the door behind me. I went to the men's room, returned, unlocked the door, came back in, and then quickly locked the door again.

To be on the safe side, I searched the lab to make sure no one had somehow managed to get in while I was gone. Fortunately, everything was fine. So I don't know whether I imagined all this or whether there is indeed something very odd going on.

Wednesday, June 3, 2026
A few weeks ago, as planned, I had told Marvin about the late-night incident involving the stranger who was following me around the building. This morning, as soon as Marvin arrived, I filled him in on the additional incidents – the suddenly disappearing shadow that I had encountered the other day on my walk to work and the footsteps I'm now nearly certain I heard last night. I re-emphasized the need to keep the lab door locked at all times.

He didn't resist, but he seemed skeptical. His take on these events was that most likely another researcher was working late hours, just as I was.

As for the disappearing shadow in the street, Marvin's theory was that it could have been anything – leaves or branches blowing off a tree between me and the streetlight, a piece of trash blown by the wind, or a dog or cat running into an alley. Or it could have been a human being who was innocently walking somewhere, just like me.

Those were all interesting theories, and I can't say they're impossible, but it still seems awfully coincidental that they have all occurred during the same relatively brief time period. I felt Marvin was being dismissive. He tried to make it sound as if I were neurotic. His assurances that "Oh, I'm sure it's nothing" and that "I wouldn't give it two seconds thought" were a bit too facile.

That conversation also brought home to me how vulnerable my project has become. I had now, unavoidably in most cases, placed my trust in several different people. Any one of them could easily leak news of this project to someone, either inadvertently or out of a variety of motives. It was time for me to think systematically about the various vulnerabilities and what I can do to minimize them.

To start with, regrettably, I have to consider Marvin. He's done nothing affirmative to raise any suspicions, but his attempt to minimize my security concerns in the face of multiple suspicious events at least raises a red flag. One who is leaking information would have responded to my concerns exactly as he did.

Moreover, his wife has been on his case about the long hours, and I suppose that he might well feel a need to explain to her why his work is so important and time-sensitive, in which event he might have shared what we are doing. If he did, it's entirely possible that she in turn has shared our secret with still others.

On top of that, if there's any foundation for my worries about someone else in the building being privy to our activities, it would make sense for the leak to be coming from the only person in this building who I know is aware of our project. That would be Marvin. I understand that all of this is speculation and am definitely not accusing Marvin of anything. But I can't rule him out either.

Then, of course, there is Jessica. She knows exactly what this is all about, and she has multiple motives to want to shut down my project. The most obvious is the utter disgust for it that she has made no attempt to conceal. Another motive could be genuine concern for the privacy of my mother. In some ways Jessica became closer to my mother than I myself did.

I suppose Jessica might even think she is saving Zeke from the shame and embarrassment of having a father who Jessica believes will be held up as either a crackpot or a villain. And Jessica could be driven by simple vengeance. She clearly feels that I have done her wrong, trivialized her own professional work, abdicated my responsibilities as both a husband and a father, and destroyed her dreams of a happy family life. This is one angry woman.

Lisa remains another potential concern. She knows about every facet of this project except the fact that the human brain I've surgically removed and downloaded was that of my mother. She had clear religious qualms about the whole project even though eventually she overcame them.

It would also help her job search enormously to be able to describe the breakthroughs to which she contributed, particularly her discovery that the holes in the membrane of each picobe are one-way valves partially blocked by disks. She might even be tempted to exaggerate her own contributions to the theories and outcomes that preceded and followed "her" discovery. All my instincts tell me that Lisa is innocent, and I will be heartbroken if I'm proved wrong, but I can no longer afford to assume the loyalty or the confidentiality of anyone.

If any of those individuals – Marvin, Jessica, or Lisa – has breached my confidence, there's any number of people they could have shared the information with. They include my department head and also the NIH. Either would be very interested to know the use to which their funding has been put, and I haven't forgotten that on the very same day, they had both told me my annual reports were overdue and had to be submitted immediately. It's hard to imagine they are not acting in collaboration with each other. But whether or not they are, it's certainly possible that one or the other is working closely with Marvin, Jessica, or Lisa.

Thursday, June 4, 2026

I don't want to become so caught up in my worries over security that I get distracted from my main mission, which is to decode the memory data and finish this project once and for all. But I've been thinking about this some more, and the evidence of a possible leak is slowly mounting.

As I mentioned in an earlier entry, I now drive my car to work every day rather than walk. I park the car in the garage beneath the building that my lab is in. This morning, as I was walking from my car to the garage elevator, I saw a woman standing by the elevator. When it came, she glanced at me about 50 feet behind her, darted into the elevator quickly, and instead of holding the door open for me, let it close behind her.

I didn't get a close look at her, but she looked *very* much like Jessica. She had the same color jacket that Jessica wears and seemed to be approximately the same height. If Jessica has been leaking information about my project to, say, my department head, he could easily have made a key to my lab so that either he or Jessica could sneak in when I'm unlikely to be there and gather whatever information would be useful to them. They probably don't realize how early I arrive or how late I stay.

Obviously I can't be sure. This could all be in my head. And maybe that woman wasn't Jessica, and she decided not to hold the door for me because she didn't feel like waiting. Or maybe she was scared of me. After all, I was a stranger and there was no one else around. But I can't get past the fact that she looked so much like Jessica.

That's not all. As soon as Marvin arrived this morning, he came over to chat. This was unusual. He's ordinarily much too busy – and uninterested – to spend time on small talk.

"So, how's it going?"

"Fine, Marvin, and you?"

"Oh, fine, though my wife is still pretty upset with my hours. I've been telling her that the work is really important and that these long hours are only a short-term problem, but I think her patience is starting to wear thin. For the moment, though, we're working it out."

"I understand. My wife wasn't happy with my work hours either."

"You said 'wasn't.' Has that changed? I'm sorry if I'm getting too personal."

"No, it's OK. I guess I might as well tell you that Jessica and I split up a few weeks ago. It wasn't just the long hours. Our relationship had been deteriorating for a while."

"I'm really sorry, Jason. I didn't know."

"It's for the best. But let's change the subject. Any progress on the decoding?"

"Actually yes. I've been focusing mainly on the conversation between you and your mother at the time of your father's passing. More and more patterns are emerging. I could be getting close to translating a handful of the series of bytes."

"Wow, that's fantastic news! When did this happen?"

"It's been a gradual progression over the last few days. I didn't want to create any false expectations, so I figured I wouldn't say anything until I was far enough along to feel that this is serious. But you asked, and I couldn't resist letting you know. It's still very possible that these data will be a dead end, in which case I'll try a whole different set of data."

"No, I'm glad you told me. I'll try not to get too excited, but this sounds hopeful."

"Well, we'll see. But actually I just wanted to check in and see how you were doing. I know you've been concerned about some of those events you were describing."

"I am, but it's probably nothing. I think I'm just letting my imagination get the best of me. Probably not getting enough sleep."

"Yeah, those events didn't seem like anything to be concerned about. I agree – maybe shorter hours and longer sleep would do a lot of good, but of course you know your own body better than anyone else."

"Well, yes, but I appreciate your concern. We should probably get to work now."

"Right. See you later."

And with that, Marvin returned to his cubicle. Today I've been puzzling over this whole conversation. He never – I mean never – stops by to initiate any conversation, much less one that doesn't directly affect his work.

And he went out of his way to persuade me that I'm just imagining things. That's standard operating procedure when you're trying to deceive someone who might be on to you and you think you can convince them that they're crazy – that none of the things they've seen with their own eyes and heard with their own ears ever happened.

If that's what is occurring now – and again, I'm not saying it is – I wanted to be sure I didn't reveal that I was on to what he was trying to do. So I tried to make it sound as if he had convinced me that my imagination was just getting the best of me. But the truth is that his continual "reassurances," coming on the heels of this morning's glimpse of a woman I believe to be Jessica, serve only to fuel my suspicions further.

All that said, it also sounds as if Marvin might be getting close to filling in the first piece of the puzzle. Fingers crossed.

Tuesday, June 10, 2042
Today was a *very* big day. A little after 10:00 a.m., Marvin practically sprinted over to my cubicle.

"I have some news."

"Yes?"

"I think we have our first break. Remember last week I told you that I might be closing in on translating a few of the numerical series?"

"Of course! Don't keep me in suspense."

"Well, I'm virtually certain that I've now done it. By last night I was actually pretty confident that I had accurately translated parts of the memories your mother had during that conversation with you on your first day of high school, but I still worried about telling you prematurely and then later finding out I was completely wrong. I just wanted to do one more thing, which was to test out this translation on other memories that were formed years later, to see whether the same correlations would produce the same results. And they do. Exactly. Look at this."

Marvin then showed me a printout with two columns. The left hand column showed a series of bytes in a specific order. The right hand column displayed the words or concepts that those numerical permutations signified. But he still wanted further confirmation. He continued:

"OK, so here's what I recommend we do next. This is your copy, which I'll leave with you. Would you have time to read this over and tell me whether the memories that I've translated these numbers into are consistent with the conversation as you remember it? I know it was a long time ago, and of course all you were privy to were your mother's words and demeanor, not what was going on silently inside her head. But you might nonetheless have a sense of whether the memories that I think I've distilled seem realistic."

"Absolutely. I'll do this right now. I'm very excited, Marvin. Great work."

"Thanks so much. But you should probably reserve judgment until you have a chance to see whether I'm in the ballpark."

Marvin left, and the job he had assigned me didn't take long. He had translated only isolated parts of this set of memories. There were no real surprises, nothing the printout said my mother was thinking at that moment that didn't fit perfectly with my own recollections of what she had been saying, the emotions she had been displaying, or the thoughts I would have expected would be bouncing around in her brain upon learning that her husband had suddenly died.

Most impressive of all, the printout even included a couple small kernels of information that I could recall but which I had forgotten about and therefore had never shared with Marvin. For example, on the bookshelf behind the guidance counselor's desk there had been a large blue book that teetered on the very edge of the shelf. I had noticed it at the time, thinking it could fall off any second, but I had forgotten all about it.

My mother apparently had noticed the same thing, because her memory of it was included in the printout. There was no way Marvin could have made that up. It had to have come from my precious picobes.

I can't believe it. I'm practically jumping out of my seat as I write this. Not only does it give me the confidence that this project will ultimately succeed, it also takes a giant step in that direction.

As soon as I finished, I walked over to Marvin's cubicle. At first he didn't see me. His eyes were glued to his computer monitor, and his back was to the entrance. So I startled him when I called his name. In my most dramatic tone, I told him his translation was perfect. I even told him about the detail concerning the blue book.

He was ecstatic to hear this, because he was well aware that I hadn't told him anything about the blue book, so he knew that if I could confirm even that one detail he could be nearly certain that we were on our way. He then proceeded to fill me in on the observations that had led him to this pattern.

"Do you remember, several months ago, I was telling you about the techniques that Champollion used to decipher the hieroglyphs on the Rosetta Stone?"

"I do, yes."

"Well, his major breakthrough was discovering that the hieroglyphs were of two different types. Some were ideographs, which are pictorial representations of particular concepts. One character represented a whole concept. But most of the hieroglyphs were phonetic characters. They made certain sounds that together produced a word. They were letters in an alphabet. My hypothesis was that our numerical sequences would similarly represent both ideographs and phonetic characters. At least I didn't want to assume the opposite – that all the numerical series were ideographs or that all were phonetic. And that hypothesis turns out to be true. Some of your mother's memories of that 2021 conversation were analogous to ideographs, while others were analogous to phonetic characters."

"Interesting. Were there patterns as to which types of memories were stored as ideographs and which ones were stored as combinations of phonetic characters?"

"That's exactly what I was about to say. The visual images in her mind were stored as ideographs. The same is true for the sounds she heard. All the emotions that I could detect were all expressed as ideographs as well.

"The ones that showed up the most clearly in this data set were sadness, shock, fear, and a couple times even physical pain. When she hugged you, the data revealed the physical sensation of touch and the emotional memory of comfort, or maybe relief. I'm guessing that other physical sensations, like itching, tickling, pain, and so on are also ideographic, though we'd have to look at other memories to confirm that. The same for the various pleasure sensations.

"But the part that surprised me was that the verbal communications all seemed to be stored phonetically. As she was speaking to you, and as she was listening to you, she was picturing the actual words, as if they were written down somewhere. When she said or heard the word "father," she wasn't just picturing your father's face, though she was surely doing that as well. She was also picturing the letters "f-a-t-h-e-r," written out just like that.

"Of course she wouldn't have been conscious of this, but unconsciously she had a mental picture of each word she spoke and each word she heard you speak. That's how they got stored."

"Marvin, this is amazing. I am so grateful. And so impressed. But actually, one other thought occurs to me as a result of what you've found."

"Yes?"

"The part about the blue book. The first reason I was so excited about that was that this was a fact you couldn't possibly have known, so it had to have come from my mother's memory data, not from your unconsciously reading that into the data.

"But now I realize it has additional significance. This was an extremely mundane detail, one that I'm sure my mother wouldn't have kept coming back to throughout her life and continually reinforcing. Yet it was still there when she died and even afterwards, clear as day and readable from a portable drive. This never-ending debate over whether the brain permanently records every memory or just those that are periodically refreshed? Well, I think this blue book thing is pretty strong evidence that every memory, even the most trivial, is permanently stored."

After this conversation, I began to feel guilty that I had been doubting Marvin. Apart from being too hard on him in terms of work hours, I now think there's very little chance that he's been disloyal. He seems to want this project to succeed as much as I do. If there have been leaks – and I still worry that there have – Jessica and Lisa are more likely sources.

I'll still be judicious in what I share with Marvin. But I think he at least deserves the benefit of the doubt.

Wednesday, June 10, 2026

It was especially hard to sleep last night. I got in a couple hours, but the excitement over yesterday's breakthrough was too much, and I ended up getting out of bed at 2:30 a.m. and arriving at the lab before 3:30.

The first thing I did was study the printout Marvin had given me yesterday. Its contents reminded me of the French language textbook I had used in high school. It was like a vocabulary list for lesson 1. The numerical sequences in the left column were like the French words, and their English translations appeared in the right column. Once I knew what those French words meant, seeing them in a written passage enabled me to figure out from context what some of the other French words in that passage had to mean.

Same thing here. Adding these new words to my brain-language vocabulary will help me translate still other passages. The more my vocabulary grows, the easier it will be to discern the meanings of other new words.

For this project we had an additional advantage that I hadn't had in my French class. When I started reading a new French language passage in high school, I had no advance knowledge of the story I was about to read. My only guide was the vocabulary that I already knew.

But with my current project I have starting points. I already know about specific memories that my mother had on specific dates and specific times. And thanks to Marvin's discovery of the metadata, I now also know the exact dates and times that the numerical data on the portable drive were recorded in her brain.

That's the good news. The more ominous news is that suspicious things continue to occur. This afternoon my phone rang once and then stopped. When I looked at the list of recent calls, I could see that this one had a Washington, DC 202 area code. At the time I assumed someone had dialed the wrong number, quickly realized it, and hung up. But when the same thing happened an hour later, I became curious.

So I got on the web and visited a site where you input a phone number and they tell you who that number belongs to. This number was unlisted, however, so the website could not provide the name of the caller. My only option was to call that number back myself, which I did. There was no answer and no recorded message.

The mere fact that the number was unlisted would not have aroused any suspicions on my part. Lots of people, especially these days, prefer to block their phone numbers just to preserve their privacy. But the blocking of the number, combined with the fact that the person called twice and hung up after one ring each time, and further combined with all the other strange and worrisome events I've already described, did get me thinking.

Up to now, my suspicions have focused on Jessica, Lisa, and possibly Marvin as the original source of leaks – and on my department head and the NIH as the recipients of the leaked information. I had missed an obvious alternative possibility – the government of the United States.

I am not a conspiracy theorist. I've always dismissed those folks as people who are one Big Mac short of a Happy Meal. But think about it. Suppose any of my potential leakers – or for that matter, any of the potential recipients – have contacted the government. They would have every reason to do so if they think the government is likely to shut me down or monitor my progress.

The government, in turn, would have plenty of motivation to monitor me. They might actually want me to succeed, at least up to a point. The law enforcement and intelligence agencies – the FBI, the NSA, the CIA, the National Counterterrorism Center, any of them – might have major uses for the memories stored in the brains of certain deceased individuals. If they could exhume the bodies of dead criminals, for example, they could use my discovery to learn the identities and maybe even the whereabouts of the higher-ups in a large criminal organization. Criminal prosecutors could download the memories of murder victims to find out who killed them. And if the CIA could access the brains of dead foreign spies or dead terrorists, they could learn the secrets of the enemy organization.

On the other hand, they might want me to fail, for fear that their own agents could be compromised if the invention were to fall into enemy hands and the enemy has captured U.S. agents, either dead or alive.

They might even be worried about whether I myself am in contact with enemy agents.

And there's still another possibility. They might speculate that my invention could work in reverse, enabling them to upload new memories into the brains of either live subjects or deceased individuals. If so, then they could deliberately upload disinformation into brains that they allow the enemy to capture.

I'm sure there are still other possible government uses that I haven't even thought of. Under any of these scenarios – whether the government wants me to succeed or fail – they would have ample reason to keep me under surveillance.

I know this is reading a lot into two truncated calls from a blocked phone number. But the combination of all these recent events is troubling. All I can do is take every precaution to safeguard the secrecy of the project and keep my eyes and ears open for any further signs.

One precaution I'm taking immediately is to keep this journal locked away in my desk whenever I'm not adding to it. From the start I've been printing hard copy of each installment as I go along, mainly as a backup in case anything happens to my computer. Since the earlier episode with my old office laptop, I haven't felt comfortable relying exclusively on electronic files. I've taken Tim's and Lisa's advice, and I religiously back up everything.

But now that I have reason to fear government monitoring, I'm especially relieved that from the outset I have been typing this journal on a private computer that I have disconnected from the web, the network, and everything else. It is completely self-contained. I needn't worry about anyone hacking into this computer. And with my double security of two complex and independently essential passwords, even someone who managed to obtain physical access to my computer would be unable to open any of my files.

I'll also need to secure the separate binder that contains my handwritten notes of my mother's interviews. I'll keep that one locked away too and will instruct Marvin to do the same with his copy. He will react with the same patronizing skepticism and will again think I've lost my marbles, but better that than risk prematurely exposing the whole project.

Thursday, June 11, 2026

I need to be systematic now. In addition to the binder full of poorly organized notes of the interviews with my mother, I have hundreds of my own memories of things that would also be in my mother's memory bank. Those are my basic reference points.

So today I made a preliminary list of all my mother's memories that I know about and can think of. I'll add to it as new ones come to mind, and I'll worry about perfect chronological order later, but here's the starting list that I compiled today, with dates or approximate dates that I either know or could find out with some digging:

- Mother's various early childhood memories, related to me during interviews
- Mother dates Robert Navin during junior year of high school, 1971-72
- Mother goes to junior prom with Robert Navin, first drinks alcohol, April 1972
- Mother's parents ground her for one week, April 1972
- Mother goes to senior prom with Mark Toricelli, April 1973
- Mother goes off to Swarthmore for college, August 1973
- Mother learns, approximately Oct. 1974, that Robert Navin died a year earlier during military basic training
- Mother graduates from Swarthmore, May 1977
- Mother starts medical school at University of Rochester, August 1977
- Mother graduates from medical school, May 1981
- Mother's and father's tenth college reunion, they make out, April 1987
- Mother and father make various trips between St. Louis and Philadelphia, roughly last half of 1987
- Mother and father start living together in St. Louis, approximately Dec. 1987 (don't know exact month)
- My father's father dies, approximately June 1988 (don't know exact month)
- Mother's and father's wedding, June 11, 1989

- My father's mother dies, spring 1991 (don't know exact month)
- My birth, July 9, 1991
- Mother moves kitchen gadgets to high shelf to put them out of my reach, at my age six
- Mother's and father's conversations with friends about my fixing the electrical short, at age 7
- Mother's comment, when I was a child, about my father not being "ambitious"
- Various visits with mother's East Coast siblings
- Conversation with my mother in the high school guidance counselor's office on the day of my father's death, Aug. 22, 2005
- Mother expresses concern that I am too obsessed with there being no afterlife and encourages me to seek professional help
- I graduate from high school, May 2009
- I go off to college, Aug. 2009
- Mother's parents die in car accident, February 16, 2011
- Funeral for mother's parents, Feb. 19, 2011
- I return to college after funeral, Feb. 21, 2011
- I graduate from college, May 2013
- I start medical school at University of Rochester, Aug. 2013
- I graduate from medical school, May 2017
- My and Jessica's wedding, Aug. 5, 2017
- Zeke's birth, Sept. 30, 2020
- Mother's visits to our house every Christmas Day

- Mother phones me in March 2025, leaving voicemail message
- Mother phones Jessica about two days later
- Mother's 70th birthday, and party with friends, Aug. 27, 2025
- My return phone call to mother, Sept. 6, 2025
- Mother receives cancer diagnosis, Dec. 11, 2025
- I drive mother to hospital for cancer surgery, Dec. 15, 2025
- Doctor tells mother her cancer is inoperable, Dec. 15, 2025
- Meeting with oncologist, Dec. 17, 2025
- Mother tells me she has decided to forego treatment, Dec. 17, 2025
- I tell mother she should stay with us, Dec. 17, 2025
- Mother's last Christmas, Dec. 25, 2025
- Oncologist meeting where mother learns she has less time left than previously thought, declines hospice, Jan. 5, 2026
- Jessica spends day with mother, Jan. 6, 2026
- Mother experiences nausea, Jan. 6, 2026
- Mother makes comment comparing me to my father as a husband and father, Jan. 6, 2026
- Mother admits to some disappointment about my father, Jan. 6, 2026
- Mother hints that she has done or thought things she's not proud of, Jan. 6, 2026
- Nurse's aide, Doris, arrives and meets mother, Jan. 7, 2026

- Mother has severe chest pains, learns cancer has spread, gets very depressed, Jan. 22, 2026
- Mother's pain worsens, more medication, breathing labored, ambulance ride to hospital, visits from Jessica and me, Jan. 29, 2026
- Mother discharged from hospital, Jan. 30, 2026
- Aunt Betsy visits mother at our house, Jan. 31, 2026
- Mother has more breathing problems, Feb. 2, 2026
- Mother dies, having lost consciousness before I could get home to see her, Feb. 2, 2026

Friday, June 12, 2026

I think the cumulative effects of sleep deprivation are beginning to catch up with me. Often, especially right after lunch, I get extremely sleepy. I almost feel as if I've been drugged. On occasion I've been able to close my eyes and doze off briefly in my chair. It's usually only for a few minutes, but I get a good burst of energy.

Today, I not only dozed off but had a dream. I was a kid again, back in the high school guidance counselor's office with my mother. Mom was telling me my father had died, and as she was talking I noticed the blue book dangling on the edge of the shelf. But this time, Marvin appeared in my dream. He was standing in the open doorway listening to my mother's words.

As I was waking up from the dream, I could see Marvin slowly backing away into the hall until he had disappeared from sight. That was strange enough. Even stranger was that once I was fully awake I couldn't tell whether Marvin had really been part of my dream or whether he had actually been standing right here, in the opening to my cubicle, watching me as I slept.

Later that evening, as I was reviewing the vocabulary list that Marvin had prepared, I started thinking about that blue book again. I had been excited about that detail, because I am certain I had never mentioned it to Marvin, which meant he had to have gotten it from the memory data.

But now that I think some more about it, how would that have been possible? It's not as if there was a known memory that I had related that had something blue in it, or a book, or something falling, or a bookshelf. So how could he have distilled that memory just from the numbers that appeared on the portable drive?

And then I remembered my dream. I had been picturing the book falling, and in my dream Marvin had been standing by the door. Might I have been talking in my sleep? And if so, might Marvin have been eavesdropping? Could he have heard me talking and come over specifically for that reason? Is that how he found out about the blue book – not from translating the picobes?

Even if that were the case, would that necessarily suggest anything sinister? Or might it simply be that Marvin saw this as an opportunity to gather additional reference points that could potentially speed the decoding? If it was the latter, I would expect Marvin to share that information with me tomorrow. If he doesn't, that will be a strong indication that he is not entirely on my side – unless, of course, he wasn't there at all and his presence was just part of my dream, or, I suppose, if he really was there but didn't learn anything useful.

Moreover, the sinister interpretation doesn't make sense chronologically. Marvin discovered the memory of the blue book several days ago, so it's not as if he could have learned about the blue book only by overhearing my sleep-talking moments ago. On the other hand, I might well have had the same dream earlier on, and he could have overheard me talking in my sleep back then. It's not unusual for people to have the same dream more than once or for people to forget having had their earlier dreams.

And the more benign assumption – that Marvin's appearance was merely part of my dream and that he wasn't actually there at all – still leaves me where I started: How would Marvin have been able to translate the numerical sequences that relate to the blue book balanced on the shelf, without any obvious reference points?

This is where I need to remind myself to get a grip. Sometimes my mind seems to play tricks on me, perhaps because of all the sleep deprivation. There's a perfectly innocent explanation that should have occurred to me much earlier. Marvin said he had discovered that the brain language was a combination of phonetics and ideographs, but mainly the former.

So his reference point wouldn't have had to be something blue or falling or a book or a shelf or any other concrete, visible thing. It could have been the letters, b, l, u, and e, and the letters b, o, o, and k, and so on. And those letters could well have come from matching other numerical sequences with known memories and distilling patterns from those matches.

True, the vocabulary list he gave me had the numerical brain sequences in the left column and only words or concepts – not letters – in the right column. But that might just have been the final results of his work, not the internal matching of numerical sequences with letters that he used to derive those results.

Still, wouldn't he have shared the latter with me as well? He has to know that those would be valuable to me as I do my own searches.

Maybe he doesn't especially want my help with the matching, because he would prefer to do the whole thing himself and needs me only for whatever known memories I can supply as we go along. Or maybe, as I have feared, he's planning to appropriate these results and claim them as his own.

That would be a giant betrayal by someone I've entrusted with my most important secret. It's also something I would never do. I have always planned to give him credit for his contributions and for that matter attribute Lisa's contributions too. That's only right.

This is getting crazy. I think I'm getting carried away here. The most likely explanation is also the most innocent: He just didn't think to include the internal logic that led him to these results. When he gets here tomorrow morning, I'll ask him for the translations of numerical sequences to letters.

Then again, if I'm being too trusting and he really is purposely squirreling those letter translations away for himself, I'll have tipped him off that I've figured it out. But that's a risk I'll have to take. I absolutely need those translations if I'm to make any progress in identifying additional matches.

This also affects my end goal. Champollion didn't merely decipher the short passage on the Rosetta Stone, though that alone would have been amazing enough. He used the patterns he discovered from the Rosetta Stone to develop a whole glossary of hieroglyphics that he then used to translate still other ancient Egyptian texts.

I want to do the same thing. I don't just want to decipher the memories in my mother's brain. I want to use the patterns I discover from that brain to develop a universal glossary that can be used to translate the numerical sequences representing the memory data in other people's brains. That's what will make this a lasting scientific contribution and the equivalent of eternal life for all humans who want it in the future, not just my mother. And for that, since so many of these data are phonetic, I'll need to be able to translate data into letters, not just into whole words and concepts.

Saturday, June 13, 2026

Shortly after Marvin arrived this morning, I wandered over to his cubicle.

"Marvin, a quick question. You explained to me the other day that a lot of the data, probably most of it, is phonetic as opposed to ideographic, right?"

"Right."

"OK, the vocabulary you gave me has been extremely useful, but I realized last night that all of the entries match combinations of numerical series with whole words or concepts. But if so many of the data are phonetic, I'm guessing you must have relied heavily on being able to translate many of those numerical series into letters of the alphabet, not just words, correct?"

"Yes, absolutely. Actually I should give you those as well. I should have done that right at the outset. I hadn't thought of it, because I was so focused on the words and concepts that those letters produced, but knowing how to identify letters will help you a lot as you look for additional patterns."

"Thanks, yes, that's what I was going to ask you."

"Right, I'll gather that together today."

"Perfect, thanks. I should have thought to ask you for this. I think sleep deprivation is starting to get to me. I don't know if you've noticed, but every once in a while I nod off in my cubicle for a few minutes at a time. It seems to help."

Marvin didn't say anything. That means either he had noticed my naps and didn't want to embarrass me, or he didn't want to let on because I was talking in my sleep and he was benefitting from the information. Or he simply hadn't noticed my naps at all. So I tried to pry a little more.

"Jessica used to tell me that sometimes I talk in my sleep. I hope I haven't been doing that here. That would be pretty distracting to you as you're trying to work."

"No, I haven't heard a thing. So if you're talking in your sleep, you're doing it pretty quietly. Really, no worries. If short naps help you, what's wrong with that? Anyway, back to the grind for me. I have a few computer runs I want to do that I hope will unearth a few more patterns."

That was the end of our conversation. I didn't learn very much from it. He had been unresponsive when I mentioned that I sometimes nap in my cubicle. I would have expected him to say something like "I hadn't noticed" if indeed he hadn't. Not until I wondered aloud whether I had been talking in my sleep and distracting him did he feel compelled to respond, and he claimed not to have heard me.

That might well be true. The problem is I have no way to know, and that also means I might never know whether Marvin's doorway appearance was real or part of my dream. All the more confirmation that I cannot let my guard down, ever. Which isn't easy when you're sleep-deprived.

At any rate, I was able to put most of this out of my mind the rest of the day and get some good work in. I devoted most of today to going through my list of known memories to identify a few where I knew the exact dates of both the original events and my mother's specific recollections of those events.

A few of these seem particularly promising. In chronological order:

1. Mom's fifth birthday party would have been on August 27, 1960. She recalled this during the January 9, 2026 lunchtime interview.
2. Mom and Dad began a romantic relationship at their tenth college reunion. That was on April 18, 1987, at a reception/dinner that began at 6:00 pm. (I learned this by calling the Swarthmore alumni office and explaining that my mother had died and that I was compiling a history of her life.) She recalled this during the January 6, 2026 lunchtime interview.
3. Mom's and Dad's wedding was on June 11, 1989. She recalled this during the January 9, 2026 lunchtime interview.
4. Mom gave birth to me on July 9, 1991. She recalled this during the January 9, 2026 lunchtime interview.
5. Dad died on the morning of August 22, 2005. It would have to have been right around 12 noon, because Mom gave me the news while my 2:00 class was in progress and said that the accident had occurred about two hours earlier. Mom recalled this on February 16, 2011 when she phoned to tell me her parents had been killed in a car accident. She recalled this again during the January 9, 2026 lunchtime interview. So for

this memory there are at least three specific reference points to compare.

6. Mom's parents died on February 16, 2011. She recalled this during the January 9, 2026 lunchtime interview.

7. Zeke was born on September 30, 2020. She recalled this during the January 9, 2026 lunchtime interview.

CHAPTER 9
RESURRECTING MOTHER

Tuesday, June 16, 2026

Since last Wednesday I have meticulously stored the printed copy of this journal in a locked drawer. The only time I take it out is at the end of the day, when I'm adding a new entry. And then I'm always meticulous about putting it back and locking the drawer. I have the only key to that drawer, except for one duplicate that is hidden at home in a place that no one would ever think to look. I'm not going to disclose its whereabouts in this journal.

But when I woke up this morning, I suddenly realized I had somehow forgotten to put this journal away last night when I was done. I had inadvertently left it on top of my desk, where it would be in plain sight.

With my heart pounding, I skipped breakfast, threw on some clothes, and raced to the lab. I even drove through a red light, seeing no one on these deserted streets in the middle of the night. I parked the car in the garage, sprinted to the elevator, pressed the light, and waited seemingly forever for it to arrive. It's an old elevator, and it also seemed unusually slow as it inched its way up to the fourth floor, where my lab is. Leaving the elevator, I ran to the lab, nervously dropped my key as I was trying to get into the lab too quickly, picked it up, made my way in, and ran over to my cubicle. To my relief, I could see that the journal was still lying there, apparently undisturbed.

Or so I thought. Something occurred to me. Since I'm right-handed, I keep my printer in the back right corner of my desk. Between my computer and the printer is a space, about two feet wide, where I normally put any hard copy that I'm reading or writing or have just printed. Yet this morning I found my journal on the left side of the desk. It's possible that I moved it there when I was finished printing yesterday's installment, perhaps to make room for something else. But I don't remember doing that, and it seems unlikely. If I were going to move it, I would have moved it directly to the locked drawer.

Then again, the fact that I forgot to put it back in the drawer is an indication that I must have been unusually tired. And in that condition, I suppose I could have moved it for some reason and forgotten that I had moved it. Besides, I was out of the lab only from about 11:00 last night until my arrival at 4:00 this morning. That's a pretty narrow window for someone to enter the lab and read this journal. It's possible, though, and if they really are intent on monitoring me, there would have been enough time to photocopy the whole journal. They wouldn't have had to read it right then and there.

So I have to think about who could get access to the lab. The cleaning crew could have come through last night, but I quickly dismissed that possibility. For one thing, the only reason they would have moved my journal – or at least the only innocent reason – would be if they wanted to dust the area where it originally lay. I could see that that area had not recently been dusted.

Besides, the cleaning crew comes to the lab only once a week, and it's always on Wednesday night, maybe Thursday if there was a holiday early in the week. And they're always finished by about 9:30 pm at the latest, never here between 11:00 pm and 4:00 a.m.

But just to be on the safe side, I decided I would call the cleaning supervisor upon his arrival later this morning just to confirm that the Wednesday schedule is still in effect. And I did call him, at around 9:30 a.m. I asked him about the current cleaning schedule for my lab. He confirmed that they tidied up my lab every Wednesday night. He thought perhaps I had a problem with the cleaning, but I assured him I didn't and made up a lame excuse for my inquiry.

Marvin has a key and he knows my work schedule. But I find it hard to picture him getting up in the wee hours to do this. And if he did, his wife would find his behavior very strange unless he made up some story about an urgent detail he had forgotten to take care of and that he needs to repair before his boss gets to the lab. Then again, if he has told his wife about our project, he wouldn't have had to lie to her about anything.

My department head would also easily be able to get hold of a key, as would the FBI or some other government law enforcement or intelligence agency. I wouldn't have expected them to slip up and leave the journal in a different place, however. They would be more sophisticated than that. Also, why would they, or Marvin for that matter, just happen to choose the one night when I had left the journal unprotected? They would have had to know this, which they couldn't have.

Unless they have planted a hidden camera! I could inspect my cubicle and the ceiling carefully to ensure that there's no camera, but that would be risky. If there is one, it will see me searching for it and alert them that I'm aware of being watched. That's the last thing I would want them to know, because they might then feel obliged to take more drastic action. God knows what these people are capable of.

So this morning I made two decisions. The first one is that I would inspect my cubicle but with the pretense of hanging pictures on the walls, all the while trying to glance inconspicuously at the ceiling. I don't actually have any pictures to put up, but I have old memos and other papers that I could tack to the walls, purportedly so that I would have easy access to them. To make that look credible, I'll have to stand up occasionally and look at the various papers, as if they're helping me with a task that I'm working on. I just have to make sure the papers I post look relevant enough to my work to appear credible, because the camera would presumably be capable of zooming in on them.

Anyway, I did end up tacking a bunch of papers to the walls, occasionally stealing a glance above me as I tilted and scratched my neck so that it wouldn't look as if I were examining the ceiling. This cursory inspection didn't reveal any signs of a camera, but that doesn't mean it's not there.

The second decision is one that I could never have imagined myself making, but drastic circumstances call for drastic precautions. If the FBI gets wind of my being on to them, they could possibly decide that in the interest of national security they need to eliminate me. I have to protect myself.

So this afternoon I drove to a small gun shop. I knew about it because I pass it every day on the way to work. I don't know the first thing about guns, but the proprietor was extremely helpful. He agreed that nowadays there's just too much crime and that it would be foolhardy not to have a gun available in case I needed it. He helped me choose a suitable weapon and showed me how to load it.

He couldn't sell it to me right then and there, because a year ago "the bleeding hearts in Congress who have nothing better to do with their time" had passed a law that requires more extensive background checks. These now take over a week. But he said he'd let me know when it's ready to be picked up.

That was a bit worrisome, because if the FBI really is watching me, they might notice that a gun shop is doing a background check on me. I'll have to hope that the left hand doesn't know what the right hand is doing. I don't really have a choice.

Also, in case my phone is tapped, I don't want the proprietor calling or texting me. And I don't want him emailing me in case they're hacking into my office computer. So I told him not to contact me. I said I'd stop by next week to check. He seemed to think that a bit odd but said that would be fine as long as I gave him a cash deposit of $200, which I did.

He also advised me to take a gun safety course, but I doubt I'll do that, as the risk of the course registration revealing to the FBI that I have a gun is probably greater than the risk that I'll use the gun incompetently if the need arises. I'll keep the gun loaded but in the briefcase that I will now carry with me at all times. That way I'll be protected both at home and at work, and the gun will stay safely out of view.

I know this might all start to sound a bit paranoid, especially the precaution of buying a gun. I'm fully aware that carrying a loaded gun around can be highly dangerous. But I will be extra careful, and if the need to use it actually arises, I'll be glad I have it with me. And if I'm imagining all this and it turns out no one has me under surveillance after all -- as I'm grounded enough to acknowledge is quite possible -- then no harm, no foul.

Monday, June 22, 2026
I'm still working on the very first of the potential leads that I had assembled last week. This is the one that involves my mother's fifth birthday party. Based on the date and rough time of that party, I'm pretty sure I've found the numerical sequences that describe it. In addition, I've found the almost identical numerical sequences in the data that correspond to our

January 10 interview, when she recalled that memory. The two sets of numbers aren't 100% the same, but I wouldn't expect that, since these memories are always edited somewhat when they're recalled.

I'm virtually certain that I'm seeing the edited version of the same memory. And since my mother described a few specific things that she recalled about the party – the picnic, her back yard, lots of kids, lots of moms – I think I'm on my way to being able to match some of the numerical sequences to the corresponding letters, words, concepts, feelings, and phonetic characters.

The one major distraction today was Jessica's call. It has now been over a month since I've seen Zeke or even called. The truth is, she claimed to be sad to say, he no longer seems to miss me. He doesn't ask about me at all. He appears to have moved on, and thanks to my showing absolutely no interest in my own son, I'm slowly becoming an irrelevancy in his life. If I'm happy about that, then there's nothing more I need to do. But if I want my son to be part of my life, I need to call him promptly and start regularly spending time with him. For my own sake, not just his. One day I'll regret allowing him to slip away. And so on. You get the drift.

It came as a surprise that it's been that long since our last visit, but I glanced at my calendar while she was berating me, and I have to admit she was right about the dates. As usual, though, she is exaggerating everything. I don't believe for one moment that Zeke has forgotten me or that he doesn't care about seeing me.

I explained patiently that, as I had told her earlier, I'm under a great deal of time pressure at the lab, the work is absolutely vital, the exceptionally long hours are temporary, and once I am at a point where I can slow down I will again be spending heaps of time with Zeke. Until then, I made emphatically clear, I have literally no time for anything but work. When time does become available, she will be the first to know. To convey the seriousness of my work responsibilities, I told her what my lab hours are these days. She gasped. "This is even more insane than before," she advised me.

I ignored that last comment. This isn't mental illness. It's called prioritizing. It's called social responsibility. I asked her not to call me again unless there is some kind of emergency. I would call her when I'm ready. And I hung up. Without a trace of guilt.

Thursday, June 25, 2026
This morning the comparison of the two known memories of my mother's fifth birthday party – the original event and her January 9, 2026 recollection of it – paid off. Using the common sets of numerical sequences for the two dates and times, I was able to match a couple of them with specific letters of the alphabet. I'm reasonably confident I've even matched some of the numerical sequences with ideographic concepts – visual images of the other children, their

mothers, and possibly, though I'm not 100% sure of this, the green lawn in the back yard. I've added those translations to the list that Marvin started and have shared it with him.

I'm now going to start studying some of the other memories for which I know the dates of multiple recollections. Particularly promising are those that relate to my mother's giving me the news of my father's death, in the high school guidance counselor's office. For this, I have three known dates and times, not just two – the original conversation, my mother's recollection of it when she phoned several years later to tell me about her parents' deaths, and the recent interview. There should be a snowballing effect in the making. The more letters, words, physical sensations, and emotions we can translate the numerical sequences into, the more context we'll have to translate still others.

Friday, June 26, 2026
Marvin made an interesting observation this morning. At the beginning, we had converted the time markers on the portable drive into the actual calendar dates and clock times when the memories had been recorded or edited. To do that, however, we had had to assume that the brain times that we uploaded to the portable drive were linear. For example, if 1000 units of brain time in the early stages of my mother's life correspond to one minute of real calendar/clock time, we assumed that the same ratio would hold during the later stages of life.

The results that we've obtained to this point now confirm that our assumption was correct. We know how many brain time units there were between the first recorded memory and the last, and we also know when my mother's life began and ended. That gives us the ratio of total brain time units to total calendar units. It turns out that same ratio holds for the period between my mother's fifth birthday party and her recollection of that party some 65 years later. This is important, because it gives us confidence that a given time marker on the portable drive will provide a very close estimate of the actual date and time of the corresponding memory.

Meanwhile, since my gun was supposed to arrive sometime around now, I went over to the gun store after lunch. It had arrived, and with the help of the proprietor I loaded the gun and stashed it neatly in my briefcase so that I'll be able to access it quickly if the need arises.

The proprietor told me I'd chosen the perfect weapon for someone who has not had previous weapons experience and who wants the gun only for protection. He said he hopes I enjoy it and again advised me to take a gun safety course. To humor him, I assured him I intended to do so.

Tuesday, July 7, 2026

For some reason, it took me longer than expected to draw any additional patterns from my mother's three known memories of the conversation about my father's death. But I'm glad I was patient, because over the past couple days I've unearthed some fantastic patterns. I figured out the translations for a few more phonetic characters. Even more important, I'm certain that I now have the translations for several ideographs. I can identify my mother's general visual image of the guidance counselor, her physical sensation when she hugged me, and her sadness.

For his part, Marvin too has been productive. He's been working on the last two items in my list of seven – my mother's known memories of her parents' sudden deaths and of the birth of her grandson. He wanted to work on those simultaneously, thinking that the contrast between her deep sadness in one context and her joy in the other would reveal patterns leading to the translation of various other emotions.

In the process, he found several new phonetic patterns as well. Some of those were the same as the ones I was independently distilling, a nice confirmation that our conclusions about those characters were reliable.

But I smile when I realize that even without mathematical training I've actually discovered more patterns than Marvin has. I'm sure that fact hasn't been lost on him. He probably felt a little embarrassed when I shared my recent findings. Of course he was smart enough to at least pretend that this isn't a competition and that he was happy about my discoveries. Who knows what's going through that mysterious mind of his?

Wednesday, July 29, 2026

Between the two of us, we've now gone through almost all the items in my list of seven. Our vocabulary has been growing by leaps and bounds. We now have over 150 confirmed translations of phonetics and ideographs. And the more we accumulate, the faster we find still more translations. Our list isn't just growing. The process is actually accelerating.

I now have no doubt – none whatsoever – that we will ultimately be able to translate, and therefore re-live, literally every memory that my mother's brain has ever recorded and that we have time for. Soon she will be alive again in practically every sense of the word.

All this should probably prompt me to slow down and try to get more sleep, secure in the knowledge that my end goal is in sight. But these successes have had precisely the opposite effect. I'm too excited to sleep. I can't bear to delay the thrill of crossing the finish line.

Meanwhile, though, there have been some new worrisome developments on the security front. Until today I had decided not to record them in this journal, mainly because I had been uncertain whether they were significant. It's clear to me now that they are highly significant.

A couple weeks ago, I went down to the snack bar in our building to get a croissant. I've worked in this building for several years now, so the people who serve food in the snack bar recognize me. And they're a friendly, cheerful group, always greeting me with "Hi, professor" or "How are you?" or other innocuous expressions.

But on this one occasion, after the lunchtime crowd had dispersed and things were quiet, the man who waited on me was chattier than usual. He asked me "So how are things in the lab?" I replied that they were fine, but he didn't stop at that. He asked: "Out of curiosity, what are you working on?" I gave a vague answer, and that was it. At the time, this seemed like a natural question and I didn't give it a second's thought.

But a few days later, I got a call from one of the university's public affairs professionals. She said, as I knew, that they like to keep up with the research of their most eminent faculty and publicize their achievements. Could she interview me for an article in the university's weekly newsletter?

Of course I declined, apologetically, using as an excuse that I'm now at a critical juncture where I'm not sure yet whether my current project is going to pan out. I said I would be happy to get back to her when I have more certainty. She understood and thanked me.

It's perfectly normal for Public Affairs to reach out to faculty, so even that conversation didn't raise any strong suspicions. Until today. My phone rang. It was a number I didn't recognize, but I answered it.

"Hello, I'm trying to reach Dr. Stramm."

"Speaking."

"Dr. Stramm, my name is Arlen Fried. I'm a freelance journalist. I'd be grateful if you could spare a few minutes for an interview about your work. I've heard some impressive things about the research you're doing, and I'd love to do an article about it. It would take only a few minutes of your time."

"I'm curious. What exactly have you heard about my research?"

"Well, as I'm sure you know, people in your building are aware that you maintain an unusual level of secrecy and security in your lab. The rumor I've been hearing is that you're hoping to discover time travel. That would be quite a spectacular discovery, and you deserve the recognition that comes with an achievement of that magnitude. My article would give you that exposure."

I had to pause to process this. I was fearful of his probing into my project. I was also stunned to hear that the intense security precautions in my lab were a matter of common knowledge. Of course, the rumors about time travel were laughable, though I suppose in a way I am a time traveler. By re-creating memories of events that occurred long ago, I'm traveling to the past, kind of.

Apart from all that, I felt humiliated. If people really think I'm working on time travel, they're probably laughing at me behind my back. I'm sure now that instead of my image being that of a distinguished academic researcher, they picture me as eccentric at the least and more likely a mad scientist. But most of all, I worried about who his source was.

"Dr. Stramm?"

"Sorry, you've caught me by surprise. Out of curiosity, where did you hear this rumor about time travel?"

"I'm sorry, I can't say. As a journalist, I have to respect the confidentiality of my sources. But is the rumor true?"

What I wanted to say was "Oh, no, I haven't invented time travel – just eternal life." One day I'll be able to say that publicly. Today I had to answer differently.

"Let me assure you I am not working on time travel. That's the stuff of science fiction novels. People have fertile imaginations, though I can't imagine how a rumor like this could get started."

"Thanks for setting the record straight. I appreciate it. So what exactly are you working on? I'm sure it's something very interesting."

"Mr. Fried, I'm afraid my research is pretty boring. I'm doing routine, traditional investigation of how the human brain processes memory, just like thousands of other neuroscience researchers around the world. And at the moment my project isn't advanced enough to report anything tangible. I'm flattered that you called, but I'm not ready yet for an interview about any of this. Sorry."

He accepted this explanation, thanked me for my time, and encouraged me to call him down the road when I reached the point where I could share information about my project. And that was the end of the conversation.

Coming on the heels of the exchange in the snack bar and then the call from Public Affairs, and all of that on top of the series of earlier episodes, his call unnerved me. And not just because the rumors he cited would be humiliating, or even because the rumors about the tight security and the time travel could imperil the secrecy of the project.

No, there is a more ominous danger. It might be that no such rumors exist and that the caller was not a journalist at all, but an undercover FBI agent. Posing as a journalist would be a clever strategy. By leading me to think that I am rumored to be working on time travel, and knowing that as an eminent scientist I have a reputation to preserve, the FBI might have figured that I would instinctively dispel the rumors by spilling what the project is really about. Thankfully, I had enough presence of mind not to take the bait.

I immediately searched the web for "Arlen Fried journalist." Multiple links came up, some biographical and others containing articles he has supposedly written. So his story holds up.

But that tells me nothing. The FBI is smart enough to know I might check out his credentials. I assume the articles were real; the FBI would know that a little research would quickly expose the whole plan if they weren't. But they could easily have recruited a real journalist to take this assignment for them, especially if they were willing to compensate him.

As a scientist, I'm always open to alternate hypotheses and committed to reach whatever conclusions the objective evidence points to, even if that evidence negates the result I wanted. You'll recall that as much as I have long wanted to believe that picobes exist, I was fully prepared to give up this whole project if my research had shown that hypothesis to be implausible. Even when it became clear that Jessica and Lisa were both finding me repugnant, I accepted that obvious reality.

So I'm not one of these people who is emotionally incapable of handling either professional or personal bad news. I don't go into denial just because the hard facts are unwelcome.

I need to summon that same objectivity to assess my own mental state. Might Jessica – and others who think it but haven't said it, or at least haven't said it to me – be right? Am I losing touch with reality? Is it possible that no one has revealed my project to anyone and that my worries about security breaches and being monitored are just signs of a growing paranoia?

Yes, it's theoretically possible. But I also know what I've observed. And there is now just too much cumulative, consistent, hard evidence to ignore. It is highly probable that Jessica, Lisa, and Marvin are no longer the only people who are aware of what we are doing in this lab. This is not paranoia. It's reality.

Thursday, August 5, 2026
Jessica called me at the lab this morning.

"I know you said not to call you unless it's an emergency. This isn't urgent as far as timing is concerned, but there's something very important that I have to talk to you about."

"Yes?"

"Jason, we both know our marriage has been dead for the past few years. I think it's time for us to move on."

"I thought we'd already done that. We've been separated for months."

"Well, I believe it would be best for everyone if we finalized it. I saw a lawyer yesterday, and I'm going to file for divorce."

"That's fine. I think that makes sense."

"You're OK with that?"

"Of course. Why shouldn't I be?"

"I'm glad you agree. I don't want this to be contentious. We had some wonderful times together, and I want to remember those times and not dwell on the more recent ones."

"I agree, Jessica. This catches me by surprise just because I hadn't really thought about it, but it's a good idea. We both need to get on with our lives."

"Just so you'll know, I don't want any alimony or child support or anything like that. Our practice is doing very well, so financially I'm in good shape. The one thing I want is sole legal custody of Zeke. I think joint custody arrangements tend to be messy. You know I would never try to separate the two of you. You'd be able to visit with him and take him places any time you want. It would just be a matter of coordinating our schedules."

"That all sounds fine too. I won't obstruct any of this."

"Thanks, Jason."

"I'm curious. Are you seeing someone else?"

"No. I'm not seeing anyone and I haven't seen anyone."

"It would be perfectly all right if you were. I realize you need to move on."

"No, really, there's no one else. There never has been."

And then she started to sob. It took a good 30 seconds for her to collect herself, and then she continued.

"You know I really did love you, Jason. Actually, I still do. This is so terribly sad for me. It's just that I don't think our relationship can be mended, and the healthy thing for all of us is to get on with our lives, as you just said. And I wish you all the happiness in the world."

She then began to cry again.

"I wish you the same, Jessica. And if this has to end, I'm glad it's ending in a kind way. I know I've caused you a lot of pain, and I'm sorry for that. I really am."

"I'm sorry too, Jason. You're a good person, and I've said some terrible things to you these past few years. I'm so sorry."

Then there was a long, awkward, painful pause. I badly wanted to get off the phone.

"Good-bye, Jessica. I'll try to get together with Zeke as soon as I can. In the meantime, just let me know if there's anything I need to do as far as the legal stuff goes."

"I will. Good-bye, Jason."

I should have a highly emotional reaction to all this, but for some reason I don't. In fact I can't remember the last time I have felt so calm and collected.

I'm glad, of course, that this is ending on a positive note, with a civil conversation. The truth is that at this moment I am not feeling one ounce of animosity toward Jessica. The good wishes that I conveyed to her in return for her own were genuine. Her conciliatory tone and clearly sincere warmth and regret managed to melt all the anger and resentment that I had been feeling for some time. As we spoke, I even felt some residual affection for her.

But if past is prologue, the reality is that this won't last, as much as I wish it would. After so many nasty arguments and their ice-cold aftermaths, we've had several thaws and even moments of tenderness, only for the vitriol to reemerge unexpectedly yet again.

And the more I think about it, she could apologize every day for the rest of her life and that wouldn't erase the indescribable anguish she has caused me with all the horrible things that she's said and that I know I'll never be fully able to forgive her for. After practically every important milestone in my world-changing project, I deserved to revel a little in a sense of accomplishment, fulfillment, even elation. She cheated me of that. Instead of ever once crediting me for a brilliant discovery that will transform humankind in unimaginable and wonderful ways, she consistently chose those very moments to ridicule my life's work and make me out to be a monster and a mental case. For this I was and remain deeply resentful and probably always will.

Also, I still can't let my guard down. I simply have no way to know how much I can trust her with my secret.

She's divorcing me? I should be divorcing her.

Monday, September 14, 2026
It's been about six weeks since my last journal entry. We've been making rapid progress, but it's all been of the same kind, so there's been no one specific development worth recording. Hence the long hiatus. We've now milked my list of seven for all that it's worth.

You might recall that before preparing that list, which consists of memories for which my mother had multiple recollections that I knew the dates of, I had compiled a much longer list of other memories my mother would have had. That longer list included memories for which I didn't know the exact dates, as well as memories for which I wasn't aware of my mother having any specific subsequent recollections.

Now that the list of seven has yielded an extensive vocabulary, we've been able to use that vocabulary in conjunction with my longer list to translate massive amounts of additional memory data. As a result, our vocabulary has grown exponentially.

The plan now is to continue along the same path until we've exhausted all the independently known memories from the long list. I think we're no more than a couple weeks or so from that point, as we're pretty far along already. Once we get there, we'll have a strong enough foundation to start translating the remaining data and begin a complete re-creation of my mother's life, from her earliest memories to her last.

As we near the finish line, I'm again feeling a heightened sense of urgency. I've been able to sustain my 4:00 a.m. to 11:00 pm work hours this whole time, partly by occasionally allowing myself to doze off for a few minutes in my cubicle and partly by upping my coffee intake to about 9 or 10 large cups per day.

I'm definitely feeling the physical effects of this regime – muscle weakness, shakiness, a drugged feeling, sometimes bursts of anger and even rage at unexpected moments or upon minor setbacks. I'll have bursts of lucidity followed by lapses in concentration.

Marvin tells me that a little more sleep would make me more efficient. He feels that the increased mental acuity would more than make up for the loss of a few additional hours. He might or might not be right. I can't be sure what number of sleep hours would be optimal in terms of my productivity, but it doesn't matter, because I am constitutionally incapable of slowing down. My mind and body keep racing and I can't stop them.

Still, I'm relatively young, and the human body adapts to its needs. With a little caffeine, I can keep this up for a while more as long as I don't let it become a permanent lifestyle. And as we approach the final leg of this marathon, that's what I fully intend to do.

Jessica's lawyer has filed the divorce papers. I received the notice in today's mail, along with some information about the papers I'm supposed to fill out and send to the court in response. I'll have to take a look at this eventually, but I'm in no rush to do the paperwork when I'm under these kinds of time constraints with my project. She's just going to have to wait. If she thinks she can bully me into dropping everything and investing time in *her* lawsuit, she's badly mistaken.

Tuesday, September 29, 2026

Jessica called to remind me that tomorrow is Zeke's sixth birthday. She has organized a party for him at the house and hopes I'll be able to come. I told her that of course I would love to, but I won't be able to break away from work. She pressed me, saying that it's important to Zeke and that even if I can't stay long, it would still be great if I could just stop in for a short time.

I asked her how it could possibly be important to him. She had told me weeks ago that he barely remembers me anymore.

On top of all that, every minute is critical to me right now, and, as I had told her earlier, I really don't have time for anything but work. I also reassured her that as soon as we reach the next phase of our project the time pressure will ease and I'll be able to rekindle my relationship with Zeke. Until then, he has his mother.

Jessica was clearly disappointed, but she refrained from saying anything nasty. She did, however, ask me whether I had had a chance yet to look at the divorce papers. All I need to do is fill out a couple forms and return them to the court. Until I do that, the court proceeding is stalled, so if I could take a few moments to get to it, that would be appreciated. I told her that I've been too busy even to think about that but will do so as soon as I can.

Monday, October 5, 2026
Today Marvin and I finished going through all the known memories on my original long list, so we're ready to begin the systematic translation of the vast store of remaining data. Marvin will start with my mother's early childhood memories, and I'll start with her early adult years.

Wednesday, October 7, 2026
Digging out additional memories is proving to be a slower process than before. Translation is harder when we don't have specific dates and known memories to search for. On the other hand, we have more vocabulary to work with than we did earlier, and as that vocabulary continues to grow, I expect our successes will start to snowball once again.

Marvin has made a striking observation, one that should have occurred to us weeks ago. Our earlier confirmation that the brain times are linear leads us into some very interesting territory. Since we know how many brain-time units there were between my mother's first memory and her last, and we also know the ratio of brain-time units to actual number of calendar days, we can calculate how much calendar time elapsed between those first and last memories. And since we know my mother's exact age at the time of her death, this in turn means we can now pinpoint the time of my mother's very first memories almost to the day.

It turns out that that first memory was recorded twelve weeks before my mother was born – that is, when she was in utero, about a week or so into the final trimester. Amidst the passionate debates over abortion, one empirical question not yet conclusively resolved is the age at which a human fetus first becomes capable of experiencing pain. Earlier researchers had similarly estimated that point to be at the beginning of the final trimester, approximately 24-26 weeks after conception. That is because it is only then that the neural connections to the cerebral cortex have been developed, a necessary condition for feeling pain.

Our data now provide the most reliable confirmation of those early findings, though I suppose it's possible that sentience – in the form of either pain or pleasure – could have occurred earlier than the brain functions that permit the recording and the storage of those memories. At any rate, these are only metadata. Marvin has not yet translated those early memories, so we'll have to wait to discover their content.

Still, this is impressive. I myself have no *conscious* recollection of anything I experienced before approximately age five and certainly not while I was in utero. I expect most people's conscious memories similarly go back only about that far. This means, once we translate those early childhood memories, that we'll be able to know what my mother was thinking and feeling even before she reached the age at which she herself would have been able to consciously retrieve those memories.

Perhaps more important, this will give us the first-ever meaningful glimpse into what a fetus experiences, feels, thinks, and understands – and when. The medical implications are limitless, the social and ethical implications perhaps even more so.

Tuesday, October 13, 2026

I've now managed to translate a large portion of the memories my mother recorded on the day she left for college at Swarthmore. I have found the memories of when her parents dropped her off at St. Louis's Lambert Airport for her flight to Philadelphia.

She sees both of her parents mist up as they say good-bye to her, and she pictures her parents' faces as she walks to the back of the security line. Then she notices that the line is very short. The data reveal her quickly changing focus to getting her boarding pass and driver's license out of her backpack, then placing her backpack and purse on the conveyor belt, walking into the booth, raising her hands above her head, exiting the booth, waiting for her belongings to come out of the tunnel, craning her neck to see the opening of the tunnel and spotting her backpack as it slides through, reaching down to pick up her backpack, slinging it over her shoulder, picking up her purse, and then walking along the concourse to her gate.

All of this is vivid, as if I were watching live action. She is thinking C16, presumably the number of her gate and looking at the first gate sign she sees, which is C1. She sees the faces of people walking toward her and the backs of people walking in her direction in front of her. She notices a young girl, probably about three years old or so, straying from her parents and the father shouting to the child to come back. She identifies with the girl. She smiles, thinking about how they're both taking a step toward independence.

Having now completed the practical tasks that got her to the gate, she has time to think about her arrival at college. At that point the memory data reveal what appear to be a combination of excitement, anxiety, and homesickness.

I won't try to record every individual memory, and in fact I wasn't able to translate all of them, but this should be enough to illustrate the level of detail that our expanded vocabulary now allows us to obtain. For a while I found myself forgetting the task at hand, fascinated instead by the spectacle of watching my mother as a young woman almost 50 years ago and having a window into her thoughts and feelings. In a way, I got to *be* my mother as she traveled through the airport and on into adult life.

It was a little like starting to clean out your basement but getting continually distracted by the nostalgia of long-forgotten photos and other memorabilia, except that in this case I was being distracted by somebody else's nostalgia, not my own. This also helps reaffirm my initial instinct that the brain records and permanently stores every memory, conscious and unconscious alike, even those so trivial that the person has no reason to refresh them.

Today was also the day that Marvin succeeded in translating many of the memory data that had been recorded in utero. Obviously there were no phonetic characters at that stage, and even many of the ideographs were new ones that he has not yet figured out how to translate. But some other ideographs were reliably identifiable, bearing surprising resemblance to the more sophisticated emotions and sensations experienced by adults.

He saw that in that last trimester my not-yet-born mother had a visual image of the darkness in the womb but was also aware of the less extreme shade that the darkness assumed when it was daylight out there in the free world. She could also hear sounds, especially the digestive and excretory sounds that her own mother's body would make, as well as the sounds of her mother's vocal cords vibrating as she spoke and her lungs contracting and expanding as they inhaled and exhaled. Marvin believes he also detected certain emotions, such as familiarity and security, as well as physical comfort, but he was not as certain about those.

Thursday, October 15, 2026
I won't keep recording these minute details, but today, for the first time, I translated most of an actual conversation, word for word. It was mother's conversation with her college roommate, Rhonda, when they first met. Just to give you the flavor of it, here's a sample of what I could make out:

Mother: "Hi, I'm Martha."
Rhonda: "Hi, Martha, it's great to finally meet you!"
Mother: "Me too. Did you just arrive?"
Rhonda: "Actually I got here three days ago. I have relatives in town, so I came early to spend time with them."
Mother: "Do you [Incomprehensible]"
Rhonda: "Yeah, I think around 8:00. That's if [incomprehensible] on time."
Mother: "Have you had dinner?"
Rhonda: "No, and I'm starved. I'm not sure what's open now, but Charlotte next door will know. Have you met her yet?"
Mother: "No, you're the first person I've met in the dorm."

Rhonda: "She's very nice. She's from Belgium. Her English is good, but she has a thick accent and I don't always understand her."

Mother: "We can invite her to [incomprehensible, but most likely 'join us for dinner.']"

And so it continued. Even with the occasional gaps, I was amazed that I could decipher actual conversations word for word, as if they were happening right in front of me.

Friday, October 16, 2026

Marvin too has more translations. He's been working on the memory data recorded at the time of my mother's birth, and the information he retrieved is phenomenal. We weren't surprised at how traumatic an event the birth is for the baby, but the more specific experiences that Marvin was able to identify from the data were extraordinary.

During labor, as my fetal mother was slowly edging closer to the doorway to St. Louis, she recorded memories of fear, confusion, movement, increasing light, and the clenching of muscles in her hands. As her head emerged, there were new memories – a blinding light, more fear, the movement of the muscles that release tears, the sound of crying, the wetness of the tears on her cheeks, and complete confusion.

She then recorded memories of being touched and lifted into the air, the cold of this new lower-temperature environment, the feeling of her flesh against the warm chest of her mother, more sounds that she could not understand, the feeling of her mouth latching onto her mother's breast, the contractions and expansions of her facial muscles as she sucked, the taste and smell and warmth of the colostrum, and the movement of the muscles that permit swallowing.

More would come. Marvin successfully translated the data that conveyed memories of someone poking and prodding, pressing flesh and metal against her, sensations that brought on more fear and more confusion. We are speculating that all this related to the brief physical exam that the doctors performed immediately after birth.

After that, she felt warmth and wetness, presumably as she was being bathed but possibly peeing on herself, we can't tell which. There followed the sensations of something soft and pleasurable touching various parts of her body – most likely the experience of being dried by a warm towel. Then there was a tugging and jostling sensation accompanied by something soft, presumably a diaper, fitting snugly around her buttocks. Then more softness, probably her other clothing, followed quickly by a feeling of warmth and security.

More movement followed, in particular a feeling of being raised up and then lowered down to her mother's chest again. A while later, there were sensations that Marvin could not identify but which he is speculating might be sleep.

Saturday, October 17, 2026

I hadn't thought about this earlier, but Marvin had. All along he had assumed that once the vocabulary we were constructing was large enough -- and now it is -- he would be able to computerize the remaining translations. He would do this by writing software that resembled the many existing foreign language translation programs. He would input the translations that we had already manually deduced, and the software would use those to produce English language translations of the entire data set.

At first, he emphasized, there would be lots of numerical sequences that we didn't have English translations for. But the output would in turn enable us to distill new vocabulary that we could periodically add to our database before re-running the software. Marvin was already familiar with the techniques that had been used to write foreign language software, and he felt confident he could pretty quickly extrapolate those techniques to our emerging "language."

He cautioned that this won't be a cure-all. Just as with the existing foreign language programs, there will be places where the translations of individual words don't make sense. For many of the numerical sequences, there won't be any preexisting translations to work from. Even when the computer knows all the words that constitute a given memory, the computer will be very literal, putting those words together in a way that alters or obscures the meaning.

So there will be many limitations. I understood this but was still impressed and excited at the avenues this would open up. I told him to go for it.

Monday, October 19, 2026

On Saturday afternoon I began experiencing tremors, most likely from cumulative sleep deprivation and perhaps too much coffee. They continued through the weekend and today, but so far they haven't slowed me down. Marvin noticed it this morning and suggested I see a doctor, which of course is the last thing I have time for right now. If it gets to the point where it's impeding my work, I'll have to think about getting a little more sleep, which might also reduce my need for continuous coffee. For now, I'll soldier on. There is so much more to translate.

I've also accepted the obvious reality that even with the computerized translation that Marvin is in the process of creating, I will never be able even to read, let alone translate and type out, literally all the memories from my mother's brain. The sheer size of the total memory bank is too great. Each memory that my mother's brain recorded in a split second would take at least several seconds for me just to read. If the memories were ones for which the computer could not spin out complete, comprehensible sentences or images, then it would take much longer still to translate them and type out. And she has 70 years worth of those memories. Marvin and I working together would have to live and work hundreds of years each to do a comprehensive rendering.

That's OK, though. My mother's memories are still preserved in a form that will permit all her thoughts, feelings, and physical sensations to live indefinitely even though I myself won't see every one of them. They're still here, on our portable drive.

So I have to start thinking about which parts of her life to prioritize. It was useful and interesting to eavesdrop on her trip to college, as she left home to set off permanently to begin her adult life. And of course Marvin's translations of her fetal and earliest post-natal moments were fascinating. But now I have to be strategic.

Since I still don't know whether Jessica ever told my mother about the plans I had in store for my mother's brain, I'm going to look for indications that my mother was aware of my plans. The earliest she could have known was January 2 of this year, because that's the day I first informed Jessica. But this would be a big enough deal for my mother that, if she knew, she would have thought about it repeatedly during her remaining days.

So I think the most efficient way to proceed is to start with the moment of death and work backwards, with no need to go back any further than January 2. If my mother knew of my plans, then the memory would almost certainly have been refreshed at least once, probably many times in her last few days, and most likely on many prior occasions as well.

Thursday, October 22, 2026

The tremors haven't stopped, and they are annoying, but they're no more frequent or severe than when they started and they still aren't interfering with my work. My hands are a little shaky, and I spilled a little coffee the other day, so I've taken to filling my cup only halfway and just making more trips to the coffee pot. As long as it doesn't get appreciably worse, I don't see any reason to change my routine or see a doctor.

My search of the memory data for my mother's last few days hasn't turned up any surprises. She understood that she was dying, and there were the expected emotions of sadness and worry, especially about me. She was continually convinced that I am mentally ill, and I don't think there's anything I could have said that would have disabused her of that belief. She worried about it during my teen years and apparently never stopped. And her conversations with Jessica served only to reinforce that belief. Apart from that, my mother's steadily increasing physical pain was also evident from those late-stage memories.

The bottom line is that I've seen no evidence that she had any idea about my intention to extract her brain. She remained blissfully ignorant of my plans.

That's a relief, and not just because I wouldn't have wanted my mother to worry. It also means that there's still no evidence that Jessica was, in general, loose-lipped about my secret. It's still entirely possible that she was willing to share it with someone other than my mother, but I think what I've seen to this point at least reduces the odds. I'll continue to search this time period for a while longer.

Friday, October 23, 2026

Having searched many of the memory data that my mother had recorded in the final stages of her life, I suddenly had a startling thought. We humans have long wondered, but have never known, what people experience as they pass from the world of the living to the world of the dead. Do they have momentary visions of their bodies suspended in the air above them, as some who have had near-death experiences claim? Do they see the pearly gates of heaven? The fires of hell?

My mother died at 1:45 pm on February 2, *2026*. I know this because I had to enter that information on the death certificate. So now I immediately zeroed in on the minutes that led up to that moment.

It took several hours of translation work to understand just the last five minutes of her life. Given the special importance of this time span, I went meticulously through every numerical sequence recorded during those final minutes.

There was nothing noteworthy. No suspended body, no pearly gates, no raging fires. Just fatigue, sleep, and a slow, gradual fading of my mother's final visual and other sensory images. I wish I could report something more dramatic, but I can't. It's just what I expected. The end of existence.

Wednesday, November 4, 2026

Today Marvin completed the computerized translation program that had been occupying him these past few weeks. He again stressed the limitations but said this software would be "mega-times" faster than our manual searches, to use his terminology.

Using a combination of his new software and some manual tweaks, Marvin has been coming up with some interesting glimpses into my mother's early childhood. The pre-school years are especially interesting, because our data contain memories that my mother herself was never able to recollect consciously – turning over in her crib, smiling at her parents, crawling, cruising, walking, saying her first words, tasting ice cream for the first time, and so on.

Most of these memories were decipherable because of the words she could hear her parents saying, like "Look at you crawling!" or "This is ice cream! Do you like it?" She would not have understood all of those words at the time, but they were recorded in her temporal lobe and are still there.

On a totally unrelated subject, I had an intriguing idea today. I have always assumed that Lisa had no interest in me, at least not the kind of interest I had in her. And that very well might be the case. But it's also possible that her religious and moral compunctions about having an affair with a married man were all that were holding her back. Perhaps she had feelings for me that she would have acted on had I been single.

Well, now that I'm in the process of getting divorced, it wouldn't hurt for her to know that. I could simply call her, pretending it's just to ask her how the job search is going and whether there's anything I can do to help, and then casually mention the divorce during the conversation. I'm curious how she would react to the news.

Probably she would just say something generic like "I'm sorry to hear that, Jason. I hope everything works out for both of you." But even then, I could put out feelers. For example, I could ask about her and Manny. If there's any encouragement in her response, I could urge her to take a trip to St. Louis to get together and catch up.

I need to think this through a little more so that I don't screw it up. In the meantime, though, I have to fill out and file the court papers at some point anyway, so I did that today. Now, when I call Lisa, I'll be able to say the court process is well under way and we're just waiting for a hearing date. She needs to know this is definitely happening.

Thursday, November 5, 2026

I couldn't wait any longer. I've got to find out whether there's any chance with Lisa. So I called her at 8:00 a.m. my time, 9:00 her time. As usual, I got her voicemail. To make sure she returned the call, I blurted out that I had some very exciting news and asked her to please call me back right away. That wasn't what I had planned to do. I had wanted to sound casual. But when I got her voicemail and listened to that amazing voice of hers, I couldn't help myself.

She called back immediately.

"Hi, Jason, it's Lisa. I just heard your message. What's up?"

"I just wanted to tell you that Jessica and I are divorcing. It's a definite thing. We're already well into the court process, so it will become official very soon."

"I'm sorry to hear that, Jason. I hope you're all right."

"Oh, I'm fine. Actually more than fine. I feel a sense of liberation. The truth is that we had been drifting apart for a long time. This is absolutely the best thing for both of us. And now I'm free to explore other relationships."

Here there was a bit of a pause. I waited for her reaction, but after several seconds of silence my nervousness got the better of me and I started to jabber.

"I mean, Jessica had said some really cruel things to me, and I would often end up responding in kind."

"I see."

"Anyway, how are things with you and Manny?"

"Fine, thanks for asking."

"So are you kind of thinking of this as a permanent thing, this relationship?"

"I don't know, Jason, probably. But I need to go. I have a lot of work to do today. Again, good luck to you with everything."

"Wait, Lisa, I was just thinking that if you can free up some time, it would be great if you could manage a trip to St. Louis. I sure would love to see you."

"Oh, thanks, but right now things are really hectic. Thanks for the thought, though, and take care. Bye, Jason."

That was it. I had clearly made a total fool of myself. Calling her to share the "exciting" news of my pending divorce was odd enough. But then talking about how I'm now free to explore other relationships, and following that with questions about her relationship with Manny? Not very subtle. My motives were transparent and my words were surely offputting.

Predictably, just like last time, she couldn't wait to get off the phone. She wants nothing to do with me, and if there was ever a chance of that changing, I'd have to be an idiot to think that possibility still exists.

I sat in my cubicle, suddenly feeling as if all the life had just drained from my body. I became aware that my tremors had worsened. My left hand, in which I had been holding the phone, was shaking like a leaf. I realized that I'd been clenching the phone very hard during the whole conversation and afterwards, so in addition to the tremors I was actually feeling some pain.

Why did I have to do what I just did? That was beyond stupid.

Then again, when I asked her about her relationship with Manny, she didn't say it was great, or terrific, or they're planning to get married, or anything that would indicate a deep love or permanent commitment. All she said was that it was "fine." That doesn't exactly sound like a ringing endorsement. I guess I don't really know what to think at this point. Probably I should let this sit for a while before calling her again.

Friday, November 6, 2026

Accepting the reality that in this lifetime I'll be able to examine only a small fraction of the memories stored in my mother's brain actually frees me to begin work on those components of the project that I would otherwise have put off until my mother's entire brain had been entirely decoded. One of those components is finding out how universal the results of this project really are. How much of what I'm discovering is limited to the particular individual – in this case, my mother – and how much can I safely assume will apply to all human brains?

Certain elements are clearly universal. I know that all human brains contain picobes. I know that these picobes store memory data in the form of electrical energy. I am now reasonably confident that they store all the memories the person ever recorded. I know that as long as the brain tissue is chemically preserved, those memory data remain trapped inside the picobes. I even know the cellular and molecular physics that explains why they are trapped.

I also know how to free the memory data from their picobes and how to capture them on a portable drive. None of those discoveries is unique to my mother. They apply to all human brains. I know this because we originally observed all of those things when working with the brains of other dead humans.

What I don't know is whether the decoding is universal. When the memories were transferred to our portable drive, they were recorded in combinations of bytes – numerical sequences of eight bits of information in a prescribed order. I cannot yet say whether identical memories in another human brain would translate into the same numerical sequences on a portable drive. And even if they do, I don't yet know whether those numerical sequences in turn would translate into the same phonetic characters and ideographs in the brains of all humans.

Even if the patterns aren't universal, all the work we've done up until the decoding stage would still be a giant breakthrough. It would mean that anyone's memories can be preserved after death, though the decoding would have to be individualized. But if it turns out that even the decoding is universal, the breakthrough would be more gigantic still. The foreign language dictionary that we are compiling would be for a language common to all humans, not just a language unique to my mother. And in the decades to follow, other researchers would be able to expand that vocabulary.

So we'll need to test our vocabulary on other human brains. That kind of testing is analogous to what Champollion did after deciphering the hieroglyphs on the Rosetta Stone. Using the glossary of phonetic characters and ideographs taken from the stone, he sought out other ancient Egyptian writings. He found the same patterns.

That discovery not only confirmed the accuracy of his translation of the Rosetta Stone, but also gave him new words and ideographs to add to his glossary. I'm not so concerned with the latter benefit, because my mother's brain contains heaps more information, and therefore permits a much more extensive vocabulary, than the few lines of the Rosetta stone.

But just being able to confirm that the glossary itself is universal would be major. Marvin and I have been working full-time on the decoding phase for more than seven months now, and we're still a long way from the finish line. If the glossary we end up with turns out to be universal, then anyone who wishes to discover the memories of a deceased loved one in the future would have an enormous head start. And even aside from timing, it would avoid potentially prohibitive research costs.

With all this in mind, I asked Marvin to shift gears for the moment. I told him to put aside his continued probing of my mother's childhood memories and instead begin work on uploading and decoding the memories from the brains of other human cadavers.

As we talked about how best to go about this, he brought up an issue I hadn't thought of. Much of our existing vocabulary, in fact most of it, is phonetic. And phonetics, of course, vary from one human language to another. We have to assume that even if the translations are universal in all other respects, they would vary depending on the individual's primary language. At least the phonetic portions would vary, a little bit even in languages that use the same alphabet and radically in languages that don't.

In contrast, translations of the emotions and physical sensations might well be universal. We're all human, after all. Culture and other external variables can influence what emotions will be felt in the first place, but once the same emotion is felt, there's no obvious reason it should be represented by a different set of numerical sequences on the portable drive just because the person has a different native language.

One immediate problem is that we normally don't know the identities or backgrounds of the now-deceased individuals whose brains we're extracting memories from. In particular, we don't know what their primary languages were. But if we see identical patterns in multiple brains, then we know that at the very least our glossary is universal among individuals with a common primary language. And if the data that we're able to read actually reveal that the person's primary language is not English, and the patterns remain identical even then, we can generalize further.

To be clear, the searches of other brain specimens won't be nearly as exhaustive as the search we've been doing with my mother's brain. Time doesn't permit that. All we want is enough information to determine whether the glossary that works for my mother's brain appears to work for the brains of other humans as well.

We discussed one other problem. The way to test for universality is to see whether identical memories in two different people translate into the same numerical sequences and ultimately into the same letters, words, images, emotions, and physical sensations.

But different people have different memories to start with. If the memories aren't identical, patterns become harder to establish. It will be immensely helpful if at least the metadata that mark the timing of the various memories turn out to be universal, because then we could probably hone in on those memories that are somewhat close to universal at the same point in the life span, such as the visual images and sounds in the womb.

In addition, we could think about a few major news events that we can assume were likely to trigger similar emotional reactions on roughly the same dates. This is not easy, though. If we don't know the person's age at the time of death, it will be much more difficult to translate the metadata that reveal brain-time into calendar dates and clock times, even assuming the metadata are similar enough to be comprehensible to us.

We talked about one additional level of universality. Could some or all of what we have discovered actually extend beyond humans, to the brains of other animals? Or at least to the brains of other mammals?

That, I have to admit, I'm skeptical about. We don't even know whether any other animals have picobes, let alone whether any picobes they have would possess the same properties that permit us to transfer the electrical signals to a computer. And even if all that were the same as in humans, there would undoubtedly be no phonetic translations, and perhaps not even similar translations of emotional and physical experiences.

So we decided that as interesting as it would be to try to discover what non-human animals are thinking and feeling, that kind of experiment would be beyond our present capacity. Figuring out how to decode all human brains will be enough of a challenge for us. We'll let other researchers worry about other animals. After all, we have to leave *something* for them to do.

Sunday, November 8, 2026
With everything else on my mind, I didn't need the extra aggravation of a phone call from the same obnoxious reporter who had tried to interview me about my research a few months ago.

"Hello, Dr. Stramm. I'm not sure if you remember me. Arlen Fried. I had called you a while back in the hopes of interviewing you about your work for an article I'd like to write about you."

"Yes, I believe I told you then that I'm not at a stage where I have anything noteworthy to report on."

"Right, I understand, and I'm sorry to disturb you. But the reason I'm calling you again is that those rumors about your trying to invent time travel are resurfacing, and this time I think they're more widespread. I know those rumors are stupid, and I'm thinking that an article about the work you're actually doing would help put an end to them once and for all."

"No, those rumors aren't worth dignifying, and I'm still not ready to talk about my research. Thank you."

"Are you sure you wouldn't want to share a little bit about the general drift of your research? I would hate to have to say in the article that you refuse to disclose what it's all about. That would just further fuel the rumors."

"I said no! I don't mean to be rude, but no. No, no, and no again. Am I making myself clear? I don't have time for this shit. Do not, I repeat *not*, call me again. I mean it."

And I hung up. This guy has now progressed from an annoyance to an insidious bastard. His snide comment about how he would "hate" to have to write that I wouldn't talk was clearly a veiled threat. I won't be blackmailed. Let him write whatever the hell he wants to write. If he credits any of the time travel rumors, I'll sue him for defamation, for every cent he's worth.

Well, not really. If I did, the truth about what I'm really researching would probably come out, and in any event I certainly don't have the time for a lawsuit. But I still absolutely, positively, unequivocally will not allow that son of a bitch to blackmail me.

I also still don't know whether he's just a sleazy reporter or an undercover government agent, but if it's the latter, I will be damned if I'm going to let my own government treat me this way. There are real criminals loose on the streets, making me fearful of walking to work in the darkness, and the government is spending its time harassing an innocent, eminent scientist who is trying to bestow the most amazing gift imaginable on an unappreciative society. If it weren't so sickening, this would almost be comical.

Not only that, I just realized that he called me on a Sunday. As it turns out I was working, but he had no way to know that. He just figured he would call me anyway on a day that he had every reason to assume was my personal time.

I don't know about cause and effect, but when I hung up I noticed that my tremors had worsened. That creep really upset me. And that's going to decrease my concentration, my typing speed, everything. Which in turn will create even more stress and probably more tremors. This is getting awful.

CHAPTER 10
BE CAREFUL WHAT YOU WISH FOR

Monday, November 9, 2026

The problem with exploring the unknown is that some discoveries are unpleasant. Today I stumbled upon some numerical sequences that I hadn't seen before, and when I got to the point where I had a confident read, I realized that the memory I was translating was that of my mother on the toilet.

I won't write out the graphic details. I'll just say that I had no desire to continue with that passage. I'm not sure whether it was because I found the image so unpleasant, embarrassing, and unsettling, or because I felt I was violating my mother's privacy, as Jessica had once warned me would be the case. Whatever the precise reasons, I didn't like it at all.

Thursday, November 12, 2026

The last few days, I've been hunting around in my mother's memories of college years. I had earlier recreated her first day of college, but I was curious to find out who she was, and what her experiences were, during those formative years of real adulthood. Most of the memories were pretty mundane – going to class, studying, waiting for grades, receiving grades, eating meals, walking around campus, chatting with her roommates and other friends, and so on.

But I got more than I'd bargained for when I stumbled upon another combination of numbers I hadn't previously encountered. This was in the middle of her first semester freshman year, and I was able to figure out that these were sexual fantasies. For me, this was even more embarrassing than my earlier discoveries of her memories of using the toilet, so I skipped ahead several days.

It got worse, as I then encountered memories of what appears to be actual sexual activity with someone named Roy. She never mentioned him to me during our interviews.

As a scientist I should be able to read, translate, and record these sorts of things clinically and dispassionately. But as her son, I simply don't feel comfortable being privy to these aspects of my mother's life. And I'm now becoming gun-shy, afraid to translate any memory that has an unfamiliar combination of numerical sequences.

The problem is that I can't avoid doing so. It's precisely the numbers I haven't seen before that I have the greatest need to decode.

After this I skipped far ahead, into the spring of her sophomore year. I caught up with her as she was studying for the last of her final exams, the one for her organic chemistry course. There were useful discoveries there, as I could see memories of my mother struggling with a complicated organic chemistry problem. I had to smile at that, because I know the issue well and wished I could have sprung into her life at that moment and explained it to her.

And then things got a little disturbing. As my mother was sitting at her desk, she began thinking about other things. She was recalling the exam she had taken three days earlier in her partial differential equations course. Her recollection was of sitting next to Jamie Cohen, a friend and excellent math student, and covertly reading his answer to one of the questions. She copied the relevant part onto her own paper.

I can't believe that I had just caught my mother cheating on a college test. That wasn't all. Her recollection of having cheated three days ago triggered a further recollection of her having cheated on another exam the previous semester. And those recollections, in turn, generated an emotion that I was able to translate as shame.

I remember that during one of our interviews my mother had alluded vaguely to having done things she was not proud of. I wonder whether this is what she was referring to. If it is, it doesn't mean she's a bad person. The fact that she felt ashamed even at the time, and still felt that way decades later, shows she's wasn't pathological. She was very young and did something she should not have done, but the important thing is that she recognized her failing and sincerely regretted it.

Still, I didn't know whether those were the incidents, or the only incidents, that she had been referring to in our interview. So now having identified the numerical combination that indicated shame, I decided to use it as a search tool for finding any recurrences of the same emotion.

I immediately located a few later recurrences, and they turned out to be recollections of exactly the same cheating incidents. That was a good sign. It confirmed that she really did feel guilty about what she had done.

It's also better than if these numerical sequences had corresponded to other lapses. I think of my mother as a very good person, and although as a scientist I must accept whatever conclusions the evidence leads me too, I'm hopeful that I won't find evidence of any other moral lapses. And at least for the moment, I don't plan to look for any.

Friday, November 13, 2026
Starting today, I began searching for memories that specifically involved me. There were thousands and thousands of these, many of them duplicative, and many of them inconsequential. It would take forever to study all of them, so I did random spot checks. Again and again, I found memories that confirmed what I have long known – that my mother loved me.

I so wish I could sit with her now and pour out all my sadness and frustrations and fears and anxieties and listen to her reassure me that things will work out. But I can't. She's gone. Her old words have been preserved, but she can no longer create new ones. Anyway, I have a strong premonition that things *won't* work out, that my life story is never going to have a happy ending no matter what my mother would have said had she still been here.

Love wasn't the only positive emotion that this search revealed. Pride was another. I was able to uncover many instances in which my mother either thought quietly about how proud she was of me or communicated that pride in the things she said to me or to others. Among those others was my father, and it was wonderful to encounter memories in which my mother was hearing my father talk about how proud he too was of me. They especially liked to talk about my mechanical and electrical talents when I was a child.

I should have quit while I was ahead, but I continued searching for memories that involved me. And one that recurred with particular frequency was worry. During my teen years, my mother worried incessantly about my "preoccupation," as she called it, with there being no afterlife. I can remember her worries myself, because she talked with me about the subject at least twice, but until today I had no idea how persistent this worry had been or how much it had dominated her life. She thought about it on and off all day, practically every day.

So I decided to search specifically for any memories that contained both the numerical indicators for the worry emotion and the numerical indicators for me. I found a large concentration of those starting with the days when I began to work long hours at the lab. The concentrations became even denser as my hours continued to increase. Her fear was that I had become "obsessed" and that I would refuse the counseling that she was convinced I needed.

Skipping ahead, I could see a different emotion involving me, occurring on, and for a while after, her

70th birthday. That was the one that I had missed, because of its coinciding with brutal time pressure at work. The first emotion I could distill was hurt that her son would think so infrequently about his mother.

There was one more. I remembered my mother's interview comment encouraging me to be as good a husband and father as my own father was. At the time, I hadn't known whether this was simply a straightforward positive statement about my father, to make up for her having let slip that she was disappointed in his lack of ambition, or whether her comment also reflected a corresponding disappointment in me for my perceived failings as a husband and father.

The memory data left no doubt that it was the latter. She was clearly disappointed in me and wanted to turn my life around.

This one really hurt, because I feel – no, I know -- that I have been an excellent, loving husband and father. A temporary high priority on work during unusually critical stages of a major project isn't inconsistent with either responsibility. And although our marriage didn't last, I refuse to accept the blame for that. That's 100% on Jessica. She forced me to choose between her and my work, and she had neither the need nor the right to force that choice.

I still haven't exhausted my search for the shame emotion, but it has gotten extremely late and I am now mentally, physically, and emotionally spent. That's where I'll pick up tomorrow.

Saturday, November 14, 2026

Today was a disaster. As usual, I got to the lab at 4:00 a.m. The first thing I always do is make a pot of coffee. The machine makes six good-size cups, which normally last me until lunchtime.

This morning I found I had left the coffee-maker on overnight with no water in the tub. The motor burnt out. That is not supposed to happen. How much intelligence does it take to design a coffee-maker so that it doesn't heat up when there's no water in the tub?

Jesus, I do not need this. I am getting very little sleep and I depend on coffee to get my work done. And I don't have time to go shopping for a new coffee-maker. Even if I did, the stores probably don't open until 9:00 or so. And of course this had to happen on a Saturday, when the fucking snack bar in this building isn't open. Because, of course, who ever heard of a professional working on a Saturday? Christ!

I decided that as soon as Marvin arrives I would tell him to go out and buy a new coffeepot. He doesn't drink coffee himself, but he knows that I need it and our work is a joint project, so if one of us has to lose time on shopping, I don't think there's anything inappropriate in my expecting it to be him.

Still, what the hell was I supposed to do until I got the coffee that I needed in order to function? I couldn't sleep and I couldn't work. All I could do was check my email, which took all of about five minutes, and pace back and forth around the lab with periodic glimpses at my watch.

Of all the days to do this, Marvin chose today as the day he would come in late. He's supposed to be here by 7 or 8, and he didn't get in until about 9:30.

"Christ, Marvin, where have you been?"

"Nowhere. I just got a slightly late start today. Is something wrong?"

"As a matter of fact, yes. Something's wrong. Something is god-damned, FUCKING wrong. The coffee-maker is dead."

"Maybe we can extract its brain and see what it remembers."

"Is that supposed to be some kind of joke? I've lost five hours of work because of this. More by the time we get a new one and I can make some coffee. I need you to go out and get a coffee-maker. I can't function otherwise."

"OK, I can do that for you. I want to get a couple hours of work in first, though, since I just got here."

"No, you're going now, not in a couple hours. Did you hear a word I said? I can't get anything done until I have some coffee. And it's not 'for me,' which is what I hear you implying. It's for the project. It's for you just as much as for me."

Marvin didn't say a word in response. He could see I was angry. He just nodded and started walking toward the lab door. I didn't know whether this meant he was going out to get a coffee-maker or was walking out on me as a show of independence or indignation.

"Where are you going?"

"I'm going out to get a coffee-maker. Just as you commanded."

He clearly felt wronged, though I'm still baffled as to why. I'm his boss, and I needed something in order to do my job. Is there something I'm missing here?

Marvin returned about 90 minutes later. I don't know how it could possibly have taken that long, and I didn't bother to ask. But at least when he returned, he took the new coffee-maker out of the box and set it up. This "favor" that he did me, however, didn't come without some gratuitous advice.

"Jason, I know you're upset, but I don't feel I deserve to be spoken to in the way you just did. I'm not angry. I'm concerned. You've been sleep-deprived for months now, and you're compensating with coffee. Please don't get mad at me. I'm saying this as your friend and colleague. I think you need to get some sleep. And I'm not a psychiatrist, but this problem has reached the point where I think you need to talk to a trained professional."

"You're absolutely right, Marvin. You are not – absolutely, positively are *not* – a trained psychiatrist. And until you become one, I suggest you refrain from offering any further unsolicited, patronizing, amateur psychiatric advice to an eminent scientist who happens to be your boss. And I might add that instead of admonishing me for working too many hours, it might be more constructive if you were to show a little more dedication and put in the hours you need to put in to make some speedier progress on our decoding. We talked about this once before, and I had assumed, mistakenly it appears, that that conversation would have some effect on you. I can't do this single-handedly."

"Single-handedly? My contributions are worth zero? Jason, from the moment I arrived, I've been working six days a week, from early morning into well into the evening, with scarcely even a coffee break, much less a lunch. I have literally no life outside the lab. None. And instead of thanking me for what anyone else would think of as unusual dedication, you're trashing me for not working even longer hours. At the same time that my wife is on me all the time to cut back. And you know what? She's right. I'm not willing to sustain this level of tension or continue to jeopardize my marriage. Starting today, I'm scaling back my hours. We're making steady, rapid progress on the decoding, and at this stage what we're doing isn't time-sensitive. The data are there and will be there forever. I'm made my decision. I'm sorry if you don't like it."

And he walked back to his cubicle. Not only was he utterly unapologetic, he was doubling down. His strategy seems to be to make me feel guilty, first of all, and beyond that, crazy. Dedication to one's work, apparently, is evidence of insanity.

Sadly, he has all the leverage and he knows it. It's plain as day I'm not going to get any more hours out of him than I'm getting now, and firing him is out of the question. With his skill level and his accumulated knowledge of the decoding and the project generally, there's no way I'll get someone who could step in and accomplish more or accomplish it faster at this point.

He also knows that if I were to fire him, nothing would prevent him from leaking our project to the government, the media, or anyone else. He holds all the cards. I can't believe this is someone I've trusted and mentored.

I tried to get back to the decoding work, but I couldn't keep my mind on it. This is all too upsetting. For the rest of the day, I avoided him and he seemed to intentionally do the same. I heard the lab door open and close at 5:00 pm as he left without saying good-bye. It made me wonder whether 5:00 is going to be his new departure time.

Suddenly I had a worse worry. Had he merely left for the day, or had he actually walked away for good? I rushed over to his cubicle and, to my relief, all his personal things were still there. So obviously he's coming back, though I still don't know whether he will simply come back to collect his personal items or cool off by Monday and return to the job.

Sunday, November 15, 2026

Marvin never works on Sundays, so I wasn't expecting him to come to the lab today unless he had decided to quit, in which case this would have been a logical day for him to return to collect his personal effects. Since he didn't, I'm assuming at least for the moment that he is not planning to quit, though hopefully I'll get a better read tomorrow.

In the meantime, I need to focus on the decoding process. Yesterday I allowed the altercation to distract me from my work the entire day. I can't let that happen again today.

One stage of my mother's life that until now I hadn't probed much is her time as a single adult, especially from the end of her medical residency to the beginning of her romantic involvement with my father. So I began to target that period.

I could immediately see that during that time she was heavily occupied with her dermatology practice, though she had a social life as well. I could see and read conversations she had with friends, as well as private thoughts about dating, movies, restaurants and other common social activities and interactions. This period spanned roughly her 28-32 age range, when not surprisingly she would frequently think and talk about her desire for a permanent relationship and eventual marriage and children. And, of course, sex.

During these years, she had at least three different relationships that I could identify, but all for fairly brief durations – two months, ten months, and again two months, with some isolated dating in between them. I found one conversation she had had with her friend Gretchen, who had married while in college at age 21 and who by age 29 had already had three children. In that conversation both my mother and Gretchen seemed to feel some envy for the life of the other one. At least that's how my mother was internally interpreting Gretchen's carefully-phrased words.

It's interesting that decoding my mother's memories has a kind of domino effect. Through her perceptions of other people's actions and statements, I'm learning something about those other people as well.

I'm sure they trusted my mother to keep these conversations to herself. They couldn't have known that one day I would be retrieving those confidential utterances from my mother's brain without their or my mother's knowledge. But anticipated or not, I have just learned something about Gretchen that she might not have wanted to share with the world, just as earlier decoding had revealed things about my father and even me -- or at least my mother's perceptions of my father and me – which in turn had resulted from her interactions with us.

Monday, November 16, 2026
Marvin arrived on schedule today and walked directly to his cubicle. I listened for sounds of his packing his belongings or doing anything else unusual, but fortunately all I could hear were the beeps from his computer booting up.

Later this morning we passed each other in the common area of the lab, and we nodded to one another without exchanging verbal greetings. I think this is going to be awkward for a while, but hopefully the damage to our relationship will be short-lived and he will stay on for the duration.

I'm still not happy with the things he said on Saturday – or with the fact that he acts as if I'm the one to blame when it is clearly his conduct that precipitated all this. But I'm starting to appreciate that he's been under a lot of stress as well. I can tell he's getting a lot of flak from his wife, who from the sound of things has the same self-centered view of the universe as Jessica and the same willingness to pressure her husband to skimp on his professional responsibilities. His reaction the other day was immature, but I'll cut him some slack.

I resumed work today on my mother's single adult years. Another unsettling episode came to light.

Upon completing her medical residence, my mother joined a dermatology practice. A few weeks into the job, she misdiagnosed a patient's melanoma, mistaking it for something harmless. Three months later, when examining a patient with a similar-looking growth, she called in a more experienced colleague, who recognized that second patient's growth as very likely melanoma and immediately referred the patient for a biopsy.

The memory that my mother recorded that day included a flashback to the earlier patient whom she now realized she had misdiagnosed. She panicked. She knew that the right thing to do would be to call that patient immediately for another look and most likely a biopsy. But she was fearful that it might now be too late and that she would be blamed for the original misdiagnosis, one that might now prove fatal. She didn't contact the patient.

I could recognize the memory of the same shame emotion that I had found in her college cheating incidents. But this one proved to be much more serious.

My initial impression was one of shock. It appeared to expose a profound moral failing, one that I would never have thought my mother capable of. And when I looked for the next few occurrences of the same shame emotion, I learned that indeed she received word that that patient had died four months after she discovered her faulty diagnosis. She wondered whether he would have lived had he received the correct diagnosis originally or, more importantly, had she at least contacted him when she first learned that her original diagnosis had been incorrect. I saw many repetitions of that same question in her mind and repeated feelings of real shame, staying with her for the rest of her life.

On further reflection, though, I'm not so sure that her response was immoral. She had a difficult judgment call to make. If she had contacted him upon discovering that her original diagnosis was faulty, she would have risked two things – a lawsuit and the destruction of her professional reputation.

The lawsuit alone would have taken up massive amounts of her time, which she could otherwise be spending on helping other patients. And if she were found to have been negligent or irresponsible, she might have lost her medical license, and with it the ability to help countless other patients.

On top of all that, there was no guarantee that these sacrifices would even accomplish anything. For all she knew, by the time she learned of her misdiagnosis it might already have been too late to save this patient. It must have been an agonizing dilemma for her, with no clear-cut moral answer.

I haven't found any specific memory data that show that this was her actual thought process, but it very well might have been. And in the end, after all, she went on for decades helping thousands of patients over the course of her career, saving countless lives in the process. Moreover, she clearly felt a deep lifelong guilt, an emotion that an amoral person would not feel.

I need to be more understanding about the college cheating episodes that previously triggered similar feelings of guilt and shame. They actually don't seem all that bad. They helped her and didn't hurt anyone else, so I shouldn't be questioning the moral fiber of the mother whom I knew personally as someone who consistently felt and practiced kindness toward others.

Still, I have to accept that other people – especially those who didn't know my mother – might interpret these incidents differently. They might not take the time to consider her reasons for acting as she did. I have no desire for the general public to think ill of her, especially since she doesn't deserve it.

I must admit that all this is causing me to re-think the privacy and ethics implications of releasing my mother's innermost thoughts. I had dismissed those concerns when Jessica kept harping on them, and I still think her obsession with them was a bit hysterical. But now that I'm coming face to face with my mother's clear expressions of guilt and shame, I can see that there is a germ of truth to what Jessica was saying.

Thursday, November 19, 2026

Marvin has now done enough work on the brains of other subjects to confirm what we had both hoped and expected. The vocabulary that we have distilled from my mother's brain is proving to be universal, at least to a point.

Using the EOSF, Marvin has extracted memory data from four different brains. For three of them, he was able to confirm that a given combination of numerical sequences translated exactly the same as they did in my mother's brain. And that was true for both phonetic and ideographic characters.

With the fourth brain, Marvin again confirmed the identical translations for the ideographic characters and even for most of the phonetic letters, but not for all of them. He could discern from those same translations that this brain had come from a person whose primary language was Spanish. So the result wasn't surprising, given the common but not entirely identical alphabet for the two languages.

Marvin will do a little more testing to make sure these same patterns hold. But barring some unexpected results, we will assume from this point on that our translations are universal with respect to ideographs. For phonetic characters, they appear to be universal for people who speak the same primary language and nearly universal for people whose primary languages differ but share a substantially common alphabet.

There was another scary incident at the lab tonight. It occurred at 10:15 pm. I heard footsteps out in the hall, and they stopped at the door to the lab. The door is wooden and windowless, so I couldn't see anything. I waited for the person to walk away, but after several seconds that didn't happen.

I quietly reached for my briefcase, which I keep just to the left of my desk, opened it, and pulled out my gun. I held the gun nervously in my right hand, ready to use it if the intruder entered the lab and approached my cubicle. It took another ten seconds or so before I heard the footsteps of the person leaving. I kept the gun out for a few more minutes while listening intently for any sign of the person returning. He did not, and I carefully put the gun back in my briefcase.

This was especially scary, because even in the unlikely event that someone else would still be in the building for a legitimate reason, there is no possible explanation for why that person would linger right outside my lab door for as long as this person did. I'm guessing that he could see shafts of light underneath the door and had stopped to listen for the sound of someone being there. The light alone would not have been conclusive, since people often forget to turn out the lights when they leave.

But it doesn't make sense. I didn't make a sound, so it's not as if he would have learned that I was here. Then what was the point of stopping to listen? If his plan was to scurry away if he heard a sound but to break in if there appeared to be no one present, then the absence of sound was the best sign he could hope for. Yet he still didn't try to break in.

It is now my usual 11:00 departure time, and I am about to leave. In the event that anything happens to me tonight, I wanted to complete this latest journal entry so that you, the reader, will have as current a picture of my life as possible.

Friday, November 20, 2026

Last night, before leaving the lab, I unzipped my briefcase just enough that I could easily have reached my gun quickly had I needed it. I exited the lab slowly, looking carefully both ways before stepping out. There was no sign of anyone in the corridor.

I walked to the elevator, constantly glancing back and forth in both directions, and waited nervously for the elevator to arrive. When it reached my floor and opened up, I was relieved to see no one was in it. I stepped in, turned around quickly to face out, pressed the button for the parking level, and continued to stay alert until the door closed.

On reaching the parking level and walking to my car, I was exceptionally nervous, but nothing eventful occurred. I drove home and parked my car in my assigned spot in our apartment's outdoor lot adjacent to the building. There was no one in sight, and I walked rapidly into the building, again glancing frequently in all directions until I was inside.

I continued into the apartment elevator, up to my floor, and along the hall into my apartment. When I entered, I turned on the light and inspected every room and every closet carefully. Everything seemed to be in order. I locked the door and got ready for bed. As an extra precaution, I kept my gun on the night table next to my bed and within easy reach.

But I couldn't sleep. My mind was racing as I tried to make sense of what pretty clearly had been an attempted break-in to the lab and what it portended. All this has kept me on high alert. As mentally and physically exhausted as I was, I could not sleep a wink. The harder I tried, the more frustrated I became.

When my alarm went off at 3:15, I sat up and turned on the light. I listened intently for any sign that the intruder had entered the apartment during the night. Hearing nothing, I got up and again inspected every room and every closet, just as I had done when I first got home. The door to the apartment was still locked and the chain was still in place. Everything appeared undisturbed.

I remained extremely nervous as I made my way to the lab, but I arrived safely and locked the lab door behind me. Before doing anything else, I inspected every nook and cranny in the lab. To my relief, everything appeared to be in place.

As I turned my computer on, I noticed for the first time that my tremors had returned. This was upsetting, since I hadn't actually been conscious of them the past few days.

And then I realized that I had left my gun in the apartment. I was now completely unprotected. Real panic set in. It was even more severe than what I had been experiencing over the preceding few hours.

I debated whether to go back and get it. In the end, I decided that another trip back and forth in the dark of night would be riskier than just waiting until Marvin was here, when I could make the trip in daylight.

When Marvin arrived, I told him I had to do an errand. I drove home with my empty briefcase, retrieved the gun, placed it back in the briefcase (leaving the briefcase unzipped in case I needed to access the gun quickly), and returned to the lab.

I told Marvin about the footsteps and reminded him of the need to be vigilant for security breaches and to keep the lab door locked at all times. He seemed puzzled that I would be concerned, but he couldn't offer any innocent explanation for why someone would linger at our door in this way. Nonetheless, he promised he would remain attentive and would let me know immediately if he saw anything suspicious.

All this has fortified a decision I've been thinking about for a while, albeit for different reasons. I've discovered that I truly don't need other people in order to feel fulfilled. Right now the *only* thing that matters to me is completing this project, and I'm devoting every waking hour to doing exactly that.

I don't miss Jessica at all, and to my surprise I'm not even missing Zeke. I haven't seen him in six months, and that's OK. He's getting plenty of attention from Jessica and his friends and teachers at pre-school, and there will be lots of time for me to see him once this project is finished.

Truth be told, I'll be glad when I no longer need Marvin. He's a good person, and he has contributed a great deal to the project to this point. But since he's now the only thing that stands between me and the solitude that I need to focus on my work, I'll feel liberated once he's gone.

It's not just that I need my solitude in order to get more work done. Last night's events have only heightened my concerns about security. Every human interaction I have is one more opportunity for someone to pick up on something that tips them off to my project. There are already enough people who know exactly what I'm doing and whom I can't trust – Jessica, Marvin, and Lisa.

Any of those three could also have told others – my Department head, the NIH, Marvin's wife, or, most ominously of all, the government. Any of the latter in turn could have spread the word to still others.

I obviously can't avoid all human contact, but I'll keep it to an absolute minimum from now on. I have to work with Marvin, but I'll be judicious about what I tell him. I have to stay in touch with my Department head and the NIH, but only when they contact me or I know a report is due. I don't want to miss any more deadlines and give them an excuse to dismiss me or cut off my grant. No contact with Jessica or Zeke or Lisa unless they contact me.

No need either to go out for lunch. I'm going to keep a stockpile of peanut butter and jelly here in the lab and have PB&J sandwiches every day for lunch and for snacks. They're perfectly healthy, as peanut butter is a good source of protein. Jelly has a little sugar, but that's all right, since I really don't eat very many sweets. I'll also have to stock up occasionally on bread, but I can buy it in bulk and freeze it at home. Coffee is an absolute necessity, but I'll drink it black. I don't like powdered milk, and regular milk doesn't keep, so if I drink my coffee black I won't have to go to the supermarket nearly as often.

For dinner I'll continue to go to the Mexican restaurant every evening, but no more conversations with the waiters except to order and exchange greetings. If they ask me "How are you?" I'll politely say "Fine, and you?" That's all.

Today I also slightly changed the focus of my research. Lately I had been translating memories that my mother had formulated during her years as a single adult. I'm now moving ahead to the period when she was with my father – from the tenth college reunion that marked the beginning of their relationship up to the time of my father's sudden death.

Some of these memories, particularly those that convey sexual attraction and especially those that involve actual sex, are too intimate and embarrassing for me to want to see the graphic details of, let alone write about in this journal. So I'm skipping over those when I encounter them. They pop up really often, though, a lot more than I would have guessed. I'm not making a moral judgment when I say this. It's just that it's a little icky to think too much about your mother's sexual desires and acts.

By early afternoon, I couldn't keep my eyes open. Getting no sleep last night, on top of the cumulative sleep deprivation before that, left me feeling drugged. Without meaning to, I fell asleep in my chair and stayed that way for more than an hour. I suppose that was a good thing, but it did wipe out an hour of productive work.

I'm starting to worry about my tremors. Hopefully they're just an indication that I need more sleep than I've been getting. If that's the case, there will be plenty of time for that once my project finishes.

But if they're a sign of a disease that would shorten my life, or even if it's something lesser that would require me to cut back on work and spend time on doctor visits or hospital stays, that would be a disaster. As it is, I'll never have enough time to do everything on this project that I would ideally like to do. I absolutely can't afford to lose whole chunks of time and have to leave even more of my mother's memories untranslated.

As soon as I awoke I downed another cup of coffee and got back to work. One thing I learned came as an utter, complete shock. Soon after they started dating, my father told my mother that he had been married once before. His first wife was one of their college classmates. My mother vaguely remembered her name but hadn't really known her and couldn't quite place her.

My father's first wife became pregnant about a year into their marriage. They were both excited about starting a family, but she suffered a miscarriage seven months into the pregnancy. Both were devastated, and she careened downhill fast – mentally and physically. The relationship suffered, things kept getting worse, and they ended up divorcing three years later. They had not seen each other since.

It amazed me that I could fail to know about something so important in my father's life. It also made me wonder what else I don't know about him.

I skipped ahead to their wedding day. I could easily translate my mother's happy conversations with the wedding guests, including her parents, her siblings, her mother-in-law, and her and Dad's friends. It was just as she had described it in our interview. I could also pick up on her love for my father and the joy she felt on this first day of their marriage.

There was, however, one fly in the ointment, and it recurred on multiple occasions that day. It was a sense of doubt. She worried about my father's lack of motivation and initiative. It clearly bothered her that he had no inner drive to do anything substantive beyond being a husband and father. And it scared her to think she could be making a big mistake, marrying someone she loved deeply *today* but who might bore her or disappoint her as the years wear on.

She even worried that one day she would lose respect for him. And then she would either be stuck in a relationship that wasn't satisfying her and maybe even leaving her resentful, or have the marriage terminate, with all the pain that divorce would entail for both of them and for the children they planned to have.

I guess none of this should have surprised me. From comments my mother had made when I was a child about my father not being an "ambitious" man, to her more explicit admission during our interview that she was "disappointed" in him, I had known that this was something my mother had long had on her mind. I was a little surprised, though, at how many times that worry would manifest itself on her wedding day alone.

And if it bothers me that a normal thing like sexual intimacy would invade her privacy when I observe it – and certainly if I were to share it publicly – then the negative thoughts she had about my father raised still graver privacy concerns. Aside from wanting to safeguard my mother's privacy, I also wasn't wild about advertising my father's deficiencies to the world.

This isn't causing me to have any second thoughts about the project. But since practical time constraints alone will already force me to be selective in deciding which memories to translate, I'm going to prioritize those that I don't think would violate her most privately-held thoughts and feelings.

Saturday, November 21, 2026

Today I searched for follow-ups to the disappointment and worries that she felt on her wedding day. I was looking for similar combinations of numerical sequences at various points in time during the course of the marriage. There were hundreds, and they translated into precisely the same disappointment. There were also conversations that my mother would initiate with my father about his general life goals and his specific short-term plans for seeking work.

It was clear that her disappointment deepened as the years went on. It was also breeding frustration – annoyance with him directly, and with herself for being unable to turn him around. I do not like this at all. I loved my parents, still do, and miss them terribly. This is very, very upsetting.

Around lunchtime today I did the supermarket run that I had planned out yesterday. I bought ten jars of peanut butter, ten jars of jam, ten loaves of whole-wheat bread that I had the bakery department slice, and ten pounds of coffee.

When I checked out, the cashier gave me what seemed like a strange look. At first, I interpreted her expression as a sign of suspicion, and it occurred to me that she could well be working for whichever government agency is the one that is spying on me.

But I dismissed that possibility right away. There were at least six checkout lines, so there's no way anyone could have known to plant her in this one. For that matter, I myself didn't know which line I would end up choosing. I ended up laughing at myself about this. Of course she would look at me strangely. Who buys ten of each of those things all at once, and nothing else?

This was a useful reminder that I can't allow my genuine, realistic worries about government monitoring to turn into paranoia. Not everything suspicious has a sinister explanation. Realizing that I'm capable of distinguishing real threats from imagined ones was reassuring, as I had started to worry that I was losing my mind.

Anyway, since I don't have a freezer in the lab, I drove home and stored most of the bread and coffee in the large freezer compartment of my refrigerator. The rest of the supplies came back with me to the lab, along with a knife to spread the peanut butter and jelly and a plate to put the sandwiches on. These provisions will last me for several weeks, enabling me to avoid all supermarket trips during that time.

Monday, November 30, 2026

I've been on this peanut butter and jelly regime for nine days now. I had initially worried that after a while I would get sick of eating the same thing for lunch every day, but so far that hasn't been the case at all. To the contrary, I find myself not only looking forward to these lunches, but snacking on additional peanut butter and jelly sandwiches during the day.

My only remaining concern is that if I keep snacking on these sandwiches during the day, my supply will run out more quickly and I'll need more frequent supermarket appearances, which means that much more unwanted and potentially risky human interaction. And I can't solve the problem by buying any more at a time than I did during my first run, because the amount I stored in the apartment freezer last time filled it to capacity.

I guess if I have to make more frequent trips to the supermarket, so be it. I'll just be extra careful to minimize any conversations, without appearing unfriendly or doing anything else that could attract notice.

When I first decided to minimize human interaction until my project is finished, I had also wondered whether I would start to miss it. We humans are supposed to be social animals. So far, I haven't missed it one bit. I love the solitude and the freedom it gives me to focus laser-like concentration on my work.

And after all, I still see Marvin every day at the lab. Although we talk only when it's absolutely necessary, those occasions are not all that rare. In addition, I continue to have dinner at the Mexican restaurant seven days a week, and each time I exchange greetings with the waiter, order the usual, and pay my bill. All of these things require at least minimal conversation, and that has been more than enough to satisfy any need for human contact.

Somehow, even though I don't miss the human interaction as such, I feel fear when I consider how alone I am in the world. While the rest of the world is socializing and partying and leading normal lives, I'm out there on a self-made island watching them at a distance. Even with my lifelong professional dream now in sight, I have never felt so thoroughly afraid. It even makes me question the whole premise for this project. If life is this unhappy, why in heaven's name would I want to eternalize it?

The one thing I do miss about human interaction is dialogue about the project itself. Lisa and I had many, many stimulating, productive conversations about our research strategy, and so have Marvin and I.

But even as to that, I'm finding that what made those sessions so productive was not so much that it was two minds building on each other's thoughts. It was more the fact that the dialogue format itself is stimulating and engaging. And I can replicate that through the age-old technique of talking to myself.

I know that sounds odd. When we see people talking to themselves, we usually assume they're either mentally ill or elderly and demented. But as I work in solitude, I find that having actual conversations with myself – even arguments with an imaginary foil – helps me solve complex problems. And since I started doing this, I have found it to be quite natural.

If anyone overhears me -- and Marvin probably does from time to time, as do the waiters at the restaurant – they probably think I've gone off the deep end. They probably mock me behind my back. But I frankly don't care what they think, and in any event they'll banish those thoughts once they see the end product of what I'm now almost done producing.

Tuesday, December 1, 2026

This morning I received the annual email from my department head reminding me that my annual progress report is due by the end of the year. I'm not going to miss my deadline, as I did last year, and give the department any excuse to terminate me. I also recall well that on the same day that I received what he called his second reminder (and I'm still not sure there ever was a first reminder), I received a similar request from the NIH. So this year I'm going to prepare and submit both of those progress reports ahead of schedule, before I have a chance to forget.

I had a slight problem. These things are called progress reports for a reason: they're supposed to demonstrate progress. And I've certainly made progress, dramatically so. But it's the kind of progress I can't share yet, not without risking losing my job or losing the NIH grant money that is essential to maintaining the lab.

So once again I had to fudge the descriptions of my mission, my research methods, and my findings. It's just that it was harder to do this today than it had been a year ago, because last year's reports had highlighted certain accomplishments, and I can't just repeat those same accomplishments in this year's report. This meant I had to invent some fictional breakthroughs that built on my previous fictional breakthroughs.

Rather than let this hang over my head, I decided to do both reports today. I re-read my reports from last year. In those, I had said that I had been using the

EOSF to locate areas of the brain that had properties most conducive to housing picobes in live humans. So in this year's reports to both my department head and the NIH, I wrote that I have now definitively identified those areas and that the next steps would be (a) running more tests to confirm those results; and (b) then using the brain scans of live patients to search for electrical signals in the areas where I now expect them to reside.

In truth, of course, I've long since accomplished step (a) and much more. And I'll never have any reason to go back to the live scans that I'm referencing in step (b). But by the time I have to file my next reports a year from now, my project will surely be completed and I'll already have published the results. They will then discover that my reports were not 100% accurate, but at that point I will be the most famous scientist in the world and they will be thrilled with the publicity they will receive as a result of my work. And if they're upset, it won't matter, because I'll have the clout to work anywhere I want.

Wednesday, December 2, 2026

I spent most of today continuing to look at the memories that my mother formulated during the course of her marriage. What I stumbled upon this time reduced me to rubble.

In July 2003, fourteen years into their marriage and roughly two years before my father died, my mother attended a three-day medical conference in London. By this time her disappointment in my father had become quite marked, and she knew he could sense that.

On her first night in London, she went out to dinner with another St. Louis physician, a man named Walter who was also attending the conference. It was an innocent get-together, but there was clearly a mutual attraction.

They ended up spending a good deal of time together over the course of the three days, and they arranged to sit with each other on the plane on their return to St. Louis. At one point she started to doze off, and he leaned over and kissed her on the cheek. She smiled back at him but told him that was not a good idea, and he apologized.

Back in St. Louis, they would occasionally meet for lunch. He made clear that he wanted theirs to be a romantic relationship. The memory data show that my mother was strongly attracted to this man and, to my embarrassment, had sexual fantasies about him. To her initial credit, she insisted that she would not violate her marital vows and that if he wanted to continue seeing her, the relationship would have to be strictly one of friendship, nothing more.

Over the next several months, however, they began getting together two or three times a week. They even arranged to both go to a medical conference in Chicago, staying in the same hotel but in separate rooms.

On the first evening of the conference, they had a drink together in Walter's room. At one point they kissed passionately, but my mother then pulled away and said "I can't do this, I'm sorry" and returned to her room. As far as I can tell from the memory data, my mother had to fight hard against her very strong desires but throughout her stay held true to her convictions, and they did not see each other again at that conference.

Their get-togethers resumed once both were back in St. Louis. My mother was clearly in love with Walter, and she believed, probably correctly, that he was in love with her. There were on-again, off-again periods, but I followed these events all the way up to the date of my father's death.

From London on, I don't think my parents ever had anything resembling a normal marital relationship. When they first married, she had been torn between love for my father and disappointment in his lack of ambition. But in these final years of the marriage, it seemed to be all disappointment and no love.

That is not to say she wasn't fond of him and appreciative of his many fine qualities, and she certainly wished him no harm, but the romantic love she had once felt was now a thing of the past. Although she never told him that in words, she knew that my father understood this. She even knew that my father strongly suspected she was having an affair, though he never confronted her.

This led her to feel sad for him, guilty for allowing herself to fall in love with someone else, and resentful that she was trapped in a marriage that blocked her from pursuing the relationship she most wanted. She thought often about divorce but could not bring herself to "do that" to either my father or me.

Yet she still continued to see Walter and they would sneak around and do "everything but." She persuaded herself that as long as they didn't have actual intercourse she could feel that she had remained "faithful" to her husband.

Mom, that was a lie, and you knew it. I can forgive you for the college cheating. I can even forgive you for your selfish decision to protect your professional reputation at the cost of a patient's life. Yes, I know I had earlier tried to come up with moral justifications for all these actions.

But this, Mom? Cheating on my wonderful father? He would never have done that to you. Not ever. He adored you. All he ever wanted to be was a great husband and father, and he was both of those. If that was enough for him, shouldn't it have been enough for you?

But worst of all, worse than any one of these individual failings, is the pattern they reveal. They expose a moral depravity that I had no idea lived within you. You are not the mother I knew and loved. I understand now what you were referring to when you told me you had done things you weren't proud of. But I never imagined anything like this.

Oh, Mom, I feel as if an evil spirit has just crushed my body and sucked out all the life that was once inside it. You're dead now and will never know what you have done to me. But I'm still physically alive and am the one who suffers for your sins – and always will.

When I discover memories like those, I'm not just torn apart because of the distress that it causes for me. As angry as I am at my mother for doing these things and thinking these thoughts, I find myself constantly coming back to the privacy implications and my own responsibilities as a human being – and as a son. I want to be an ethical person. I don't want to be like Marvin, who thinks only about math and computers and science, with scarcely a thought for the larger moral questions.

Then again, I suppose the very fact that I'm thinking about these moral questions is something I can be proud of. Not everyone does. At every stage of this project I've carefully balanced those ethical concerns against the huge benefits for society. Or if I hadn't thought about them enough until recently, at least I'm consciously thinking hard about them now. And it just seems to me that as long as I exercise some judgment in deciding which memory data to report on, the right thing to do is to see this project through to completion.

"Jason, you say you've carefully balanced all the competing moral interests, but have you really? Are you sure you're not rationalizing? Remember all the things Jessica said? Shouldn't you respect the wishes of your mother? She, and only she, has the right to decide which of her private thoughts she'll share with other people -- and *which* other people. She certainly wouldn't have wanted to share all her private thoughts with the world."

"But that's exactly why I'm being selective. I'm not going to publicly disclose graphic bodily details, or any other thoughts she had that I'm certain she wouldn't want disclosed."

"Then why did you include so many of those things in your journal, which is what you plan to circulate to the public? You included all the information about your mother's college cheating, her cowardly and totally selfish decision not to contact the patient whom she had misdiagnosed, her disappointment in your father, and now even the details of her cheating on her husband, your father. You wrote all of that down. Obviously, you meant for the public to see it. And I don't hear you suggesting that you now plan to delete it. You can't possibly think she would have wanted that to be shared."

"OK, maybe some of the memories I'm including are ones she wouldn't want shared, but those are essential. They help provide a complete and realistic picture of my mother. Readers will understand that no one is perfect. I included a lot of positive information as well. And don't forget that I've already omitted the most intimate and embarrassing things, the kinds of graphic bodily things that Jessica was all lathered up about."

"Come on, Jason. Even as to the items you omitted from the journal, sure, the general public won't see them. But you did. You knew you were looking at something very private and intimate, even embarrassing, and you continued to look. Do you really think your mother wouldn't have felt abject humiliation had she known you would be peeping at her while she had every reason to think she was alone, or with no one but her husband? Or Walter? Don't you think this would have caused your mother profound distress?"

"Would have? Yes, if she had known. But she didn't know and never will."

"And what she doesn't know won't hurt her?"

"You're starting to sound like Jessica. And the answer is that that's right. What she doesn't know won't hurt her. How could it?"

"OK, and what happens after your discovery is shared with the scientific community and the world? At that point, and thereafter, everyone will know that their most private thoughts and actions might one day be read by the entire world. People will be afraid to think. While they're still alive, they'll know this can happen after they die."

"Anyone has the right to decide how his or her body is going to be disposed of. If you don't want your memory data shared with others upon your death, all you have to do is say that in your will. That's the law. And that will be the end of it. Complete privacy."

"Oh, come on! Not everyone takes the time to make a will, and even if they do, how many people would even think to include that?"

"They'll think about it once this discovery becomes famous. And if they don't, they have only themselves to blame."

"And what if they want to share a particular thought with one or more other people whom they're close to, but not the whole world? Once they tell those individuals, the memory will reside in their brains as well. No one can control whether all the people they've spoken to will be sure to specify that their brains are not to be downloaded when they die."

"But that's true already. Even now, you can never know with certainty that a person you confide something to will keep the secret forever. That's the risk you take when you choose to share something in confidence. This is the same thing."

"And Zeke? You don't mind his finding out, after you die, about your secret love for Lisa while you were married to his mother, or about any other embarrassing thoughts or desires you had while you were alive?"

"I wouldn't mind in the least. Remember, I never acted on those desires, the way my own mother did. And if I decide that I do mind, I can elect to be cremated and make clear my brain is not to be extracted."

"You didn't give your mother that choice. In fact, you made a conscious decision to conceal the purpose of your interviews from her, even as she was suffering and in the process of dying."

"I had no alternative. If I had told her, it would have inhibited her from sharing with me the kinds of things I needed to know in order to have a decent shot at decoding the data."

"Please. You know perfectly well that that wasn't your real reason. You didn't tell her because you knew she would never have agreed to let you cut up her body and violate her in the way you have. Admit it."

"That's enough. I'm done having a conversation with an imaginary foil. This is all very confusing for me. I'm very, very tired, but I can't sleep until I come to grips with what I should do. Truth be told, I'm not always sure these days what's real and what's just in my head."

I started to work again, but I still had tremors, and they were now starting to slow down my typing. If this turns out to be a permanent condition, I'm screwed. I have far too little available work time as it is and can't afford to be less than 100% efficient with the finite time that I have.

I suddenly had a powerful urge to see my baby. He's in the crawling stage now, and it's so much fun to crawl around the house with him and chase Jessica, who always laughs when we catch up to her. She pretends to be startled, and that starts Zeke laughing too. But I realized it was late at night and that Zeke is now asleep, so I'll put that off until tomorrow.

Friday, December 4, 2026
Marvin told me today that he has decided to leave. The job, he said, has been taking a huge personal toll on him, to the point of jeopardizing his marriage. He said he would remain for two more weeks. And

without my having to ask, he assured me that he understands how critical the secrecy is and will never tell anyone about our project until it's finished and I've gone public with it. He hoped that his contributions have been helpful and was confident that now that the heavy computer programming was done I would be able to complete the rest of the project on my own. And he thanked me for the privilege of working on such an important project, which he said he had found really interesting and educational.

I wasn't terribly bothered. Marvin was quite right that the IT and mathematical knowledge that had been so essential at earlier stages of the project is no longer needed. From this point on, it is just a matter of laboriously reading and translating additional memory data.

But his decision did take me by surprise. Since our recent argument, he had cut back his hours to 9-5, five days a week, just as he had said he would do. So I would have thought that the long work week was a thing of the past as far as he was concerned. The timing seems awfully odd.

I have to think he is not being straightforward with me. Maybe the real reason he's quitting is that I hurt his feelings when I criticized him for not working more hours than he then was. If that's the case, he's going to need to grow a thicker skin if he wants to get anywhere in this profession.

Or maybe he thinks I'm crazy. He certainly implied as much the other day, when he advised me, condescendingly, that I should see a "trained professional," meaning a psychiatrist. Apart from the fact that his amateur medical diagnosis was so off base, I don't see why he would quit even if he believes I'm completely wacko. I'm not a serial killer. It's not as if he has any reason to think I would harm him in any way.

I know it sounds paranoid, but I must again consider the possibility that his real reason is that he plans to blab. It would be a major feather in his professional cap if he could persuade the mathematics community that he was the principal architect of this project, or at least the parts of the project that involved designing the software for transferring human memory data to a computer and breaking the code needed to translate those data into English.

For all I know, he could well be the source of the leak to that obnoxious reporter -- if indeed he was a reporter and not an undercover government agent, as I increasingly suspect. He could even have something to do with the mysterious late-night visitors, either the one who followed me to the men's room a while back or the one who lingered outside the lab door more recently. Marvin had taken pains to discount both incidents. That would be consistent with his being directly involved in them.

Puzzled as I was by Marvin's sudden announcement, I didn't question him about his reasons or try to talk him out of leaving. The truth is that I really don't need him anymore. In addition, he won't be able to spy on me, gather more details about the ongoing work, or conspire with others. That's assuming he has been doing those things, which of course I can't be sure of.

So when he told me his plans, I just said that I understand, that I've appreciated all his contributions, and that I wish him well. He seemed a bit surprised and perhaps disappointed that I didn't encourage him to reconsider, but the exchange was cordial and we both went on with our work.

Tuesday, December 22, 2026

Since the last journal entry it's been hard to muster the motivation for this project or for adding new journal entries. I'm feeling mounting anxiety about the privacy issue. It's also hard to concentrate when I increasingly feel as if I'm being watched. I haven't seen any additional signs of this, but I'm sensing a presence even though I can't see or hear it.

Beyond all that, I am really, really tired. The sleep deprivation is cumulative, and the coffee that used to compensate for it isn't having as much effect. I need more and more caffeine every day just to stay awake and on task. I'm now up to about 15 large cups a day.

Nonetheless, I have maintained my 4:00 a.m. to 11:00 pm schedule. It's the only way I can be at least modestly productive. And I have continued to dig into the memory data that correspond to my mother's married years, uncomfortable as that has been.

In my fatigue today, I found myself suddenly questioning why I was doing all this and whether it's really worth it. I'm physically and mentally spent, I've been on an emotional roller coaster, I'm stressed every minute of every day, I've destroyed just about every personal relationship I cared about, I'm possibly in physical danger, and I no longer have any semblance of normalcy in my life. So why?

Is it really, as I've been telling others, my fear of eventual nonexistence and my consequent craving for eternal life – not just for me, but for the good of humanity? Is it my need to understand what made my parents tick and my desire to enable others to do the same? Is it the noble thrill of scientific inquiry and discovery?

Or, as I ask myself in my most honest moments, is it a crass desire for fame? Deep down, I know that I badly want to be recognized as the most famous scientist in the world. But that's not because of ego. It's because, if I succeed in pulling this off, I'll *deserve* that level of recognition. That's not ego at all. It's a matter of simple justice.

Anyway, Marvin's last day was this past Friday. He spent his last two weeks writing up what he had done since his arrival and preparing an electronic manual that contains all the information I would need to run or modify his software. His software programs – including both his program for recognizing and recording the electrical signals from the EOSF and his program for translating the resulting numerical data into English -- were all attached as appendices. I've made a note to myself to be sure I include his software when I publish all this. I also have his phone number, and he generously told me that I was free to call him if I had any questions.

Meanwhile, Jessica called me this morning. She wanted to remind me that Friday is Christmas. She told me I needed to buy a gift for Zeke and invited me to their house for a gift exchange and brunch on Christmas Day. This had been our tradition in past years.

I thanked her but explained that I was still on my seven-day work schedule and had to adhere rigidly to this routine if I didn't want to get sidetracked. Once I start making exceptions, I'll never finish.

I asked her if she would do me a favor and pick up a gift for Zeke and tell him it's from me. I also let her know that I was now getting very close to the finish line with my project and that once I crossed it I would be back in Zeke's life and working normal hours. She then said "That's good, Jason, good-bye" and hung up. I tried to say "Wait, are you going to get that gift for Zeke from me?" But I couldn't get the words out in time and didn't feel like calling her back. So I really don't know whether she's going to do this.

I returned to my research, but I was having trouble focusing. I'm finding that most of the time I'm perfectly lucid but that I have these bouts where I get confused.

Friday, December 25, 2026

This day got off to a terrible start. Last night I came down with what I'm sure is the flu. I'm running a fever and I have chills. So of course this had to be the day we had a massive blizzard. Almost thirty inches of snow fell during the night and the roads were blocked everywhere. In addition, the falling snow had turned to freezing rain, and the roads and sidewalks were slick. There was no possibility of driving to work unless I waited several hours, and I wasn't willing to lose that much precious time. I had to walk.

I must have lost my way with all that snow, because the route to work kept getting less and less familiar. I felt as if I had suddenly been transported to a foreign country, and there was no one around even to ask for directions. I tried to figure out how to get to the lab, but the more I tried, the more lost I got. I started to cry, and in those freezing temperatures my tears became icicles. Everything hurt, and I felt very weak, as if I were going to faint.

Somehow, by sheer luck, I found myself at my lab building around 7:00 a.m. I have no idea how I got there. I must have been out in the freezing temperatures for more than three hours.

In the lab, I knew I needed to warm myself up, so I immediately went to the coffee machine. By this time my tremors were by far the worst they've ever been, and it was very hard just to spoon out the coffee and pour in the water. I spilled a lot of both but eventually got the machine started and waited by the radiator while the coffee brewed. I still couldn't get rid of the chills, but as soon as the coffee was ready I drank two large cups and that made me feel better, at least for a while.

As best I could, I got back to the memory data. I started accessing and reading the memories that had been recorded on the day my father died.

When she received the call telling her that my father had been in an accident and had died in the ambulance on the way to the hospital, my mother's initial reactions were exactly what you would expect – shock, sadness, tears. Her distress was genuine, that seems clear. But it was immediately followed by a surge of relief.

Relief! I understand her growing disappointment in my father, even though I think she was wrong to feel disappointment when he had so many wonderful qualities that I would have thought would more than offset his lack of professional ambition. But relief that he was dead? If he had died after a long and painful illness, I could understand that relief would be part of the emotional mix. But upon hearing that he had suddenly and unexpectedly died, and at such a young age, there should be no emotional space for feeling relief. She should be feeling pure grief, nothing else.

That evening she called Walter to tell him her husband had died. It appears that Walter was very comforting, and he offered to come to the house and sit with her. She declined because that might be inappropriate so soon after her husband's death, and in addition her son would likely find it odd, since he had no knowledge of their relationship.

I jumped ahead to the weeks and months following my father's death. Walter called frequently asking to see her, but she declined every time. It wasn't for lack of interest. Her sole worry was what people would say if she were to connect with Walter so soon after the death of her husband. She didn't want scandal. Down the road, she told Walter, there would come a time when they could be together. She continually asked him to be patient but offered no estimate as to how much more time she would need.

After eight months, Walter apparently got tired of waiting around. He called her to say that he had begun seeing another woman, someone who would not "jack him around forever," as he put it. He would not be seeing my mother again. She was devastated, but she didn't beg or plead, and that appears to have been their last conversation – though hardly the last time she thought about him.

The fact that my mother sustained such strong feelings for Walter even in the immediate aftermath of my father's death – and that the only reason she deferred their getting together was fear for her reputation – was another dagger through my heart. I really can't take any more of this. My tremors are now severe, making it extremely hard to type or do much of anything.

When I found myself in the men's room a little later, at the sink washing my hands, I glanced in the mirror. The 35-year-old man I saw looked almost elderly. He was very thin, and his once thick red hair was now sparce and mostly whitish. And he was shaking.

I returned to the lab but had trouble opening the door. I had locked it, and my tremors were now at the point where it took some time and effort just to get my key in the lock. I had to clasp one hand over the other to keep them steady. I finally succeeded, entered the lab, locked the door again, and made it to my cubicle, collapsing into my chair. I felt a new wave of exhaustion, but I was too hyper to sleep, which I'm *craving* more than anything else.

But I've got to resolve this privacy issue. It's tearing me asunder.

I'm now thinking of privacy a little differently. I had been thinking that it just meant I shouldn't invade somebody else's privacy interests, and they shouldn't invade mine. But I now think it's a different kind of two-way street. When I violate my mother's privacy, I'm not just going against her interests. I'm also going against my own, because there are things that I myself am better off not knowing about her. The things I'm learning about my mother are destroying *me*.

And yet I can't seem to help myself. Maybe I should never have started down this path. But now that I have, I feel as if someone is pushing me down a steep hill and I'm out of control.

There's also a cruel irony here. Just as I'm peering into the private thoughts of my mother, the government is spying on me to gain access to thoughts that I want to keep private at least for now. They have no right to do that. They're spying on me spying on her.

"Jason, if you don't want the government spying on you, there's a simple solution. Stop spying on your mother. Stop the project before it goes any further."

"I told you, I can't. It's beyond my control now. They're forcing me to continue."

"No, you're continuing because you want to. No one is forcing you to do anything. There is such a thing as free will."

"Just because I can't see or hear this force doesn't mean it's not there. I can feel it. I'm not capable of stopping. I'm so close to replicating eternal life. This is the most amazing scientific discovery ever. I just wish I didn't have to take such liberties with my mother's privacy."

"If you're so concerned about her privacy, why are you recording her memories in a journal that you plan to share with the world? You want to have it both ways. You're feeling self-righteous about wanting to respect your mother's privacy, but you have every intention of violating it. You're a hypocrite. To make matters worse, you want the fame that will come from publishing this. That's what's really driving you, isn't it?"

"No, that's not it at all. Of course I want the recognition. I'm only human. But that doesn't make me a hypocrite. My discovery will give humanity something people have wanted since homo sapiens first appeared on earth – eternal life. Benefitting the world and achieving personal fame aren't inconsistent."

"And the price you're willing to pay to achieve this is exposing your mother's most personal thoughts to the entire world, something you know with absolute certainty she would never have consented to."

"It's painful. You can see how much suffering I'm enduring because of this. But yes, the enormity of the benefit the world is going to get from this, for the indefinite future, is more important than the interests of any one individual."

"Fine, let's assume you can justify your actions on utilitarian grounds. Don't you still think it's just a little hypocritical to complain about the government spying on you while you're perfectly willing to spy on your mother?"

"I'm doing it for the good of humanity. How many times do I have to tell you that?"

"So is the government. They probably see their activities as protecting national security."

"It's still different. My mother is being spied on only after she's dead. I'm being spied on now, while I'm alive."

"But I thought the whole point of your project is that you claim to be preserving life eternally. It's as if she is still living, through the preservation of her thoughts and feelings. Isn't that what you've been saying all along?"

I didn't want to argue with my imaginary foil anymore. I wanted to talk this through with someone I can trust. I decided that perhaps I had been too suspicious of Lisa. She has always been someone I can talk to.

So I walked over to her cubicle, desperately hoping she was in, but her cubicle was empty, the light was off, and all her belongings were gone. I looked around the lab, but she was nowhere to be found. I guessed she had gone home. But why would all her belongings be missing? I returned to my own cubicle more confused than ever.

I don't know what to do. But I know I have to get a grip. I'm a scientist. I'm trained to be logical. So I got out a piece of paper and a pen and decided to write down my options for dealing with the privacy issue. Here's what I wrote:

Options
1. Keep on going just as I have. This is science. I should not deny myself or the rest of the scientific community the benefits of a major breakthrough, or withhold any relevant information.
2. Keep going as I have been, except don't include in the soon-to-be-public journal any information that I would be embarrassed to include or that I'm certain my mother would have wanted to keep private – even if that information has scientific value.
3. Same as 2, but in addition to not affirmatively including the embarrassing information in the journal, actually delete those memories from the portable drive.
4. Edit the memories on the portable drive, not just by deleting the negative ones, but also by adding some positive ones. Now that I know the basic vocabulary, I could just change the numerical sequences so that if someone else later translates them, they will provide a kinder picture of my mother. Some people would

consider this dishonest, but it wouldn't really hurt anyone.

5. Publicly release the vocabulary, but destroy my mother's brain and destroy the database that contains her memories. That way, the scientific community will be able to translate the memory data that it obtains in the future from other people's brains, but my mother's private thoughts will always remain intact. I'm not wild about this option, though, because researchers will need to see my proof, not just the ultimate results. And biographers will need to see my step-by-step process.

6. Destroy everything, including this journal, and pretend this whole project never happened.

I pondered these various options for a good part of the day. For a while, despite the tremors, the sleep deprivation, and what has now becoming a raging flu with worsening chills, I felt unusually lucid. I had real options now, and it was just a matter of choosing among them.

But by late afternoon I was again starting to feel confused. I tried to focus on the options, but they all seemed to blend together. More than anything else, I think it's now the deciding that is so excruciating. I wish I never had to make another decision. I wish someone else would tell me what I should do.

I suppose I could ask Jessica to decide, but I know what her decision would be. I could leave the decision to Marvin, but with all his technical brilliance he's clueless about the larger philosophical questions. Lisa would be great. She's thoughtful and open-minded and has a lot of common sense. But I don't dare let on to her what I've done to my mother, because I can't bear her thinking ill of me in any way. She might think that I'm wicked, or deranged, or just too weak a person to make this decision myself.

At about 7:30 pm, I looked up from my computer and saw a large man standing at the entrance to my cubicle, watching me. I panicked. I didn't have time to reach for my gun. He just smiled – in a kind of mocking manner -- and started to walk away. I immediately sprang to my feet and stood at the entrance to the cubicle to see where he was going, but in the two seconds that it took me to do this, he disappeared. Just like that.

How the hell did he get in without my seeing or hearing him, and more important, how could he disappear into thin air? I searched every inch of the lab and there was no sign of him. I checked the door, and it was still locked. I don't know whether he somehow managed to get in and out quickly, or whether I really am losing my mind as others have seemed to imply.

Then, at about 8:00 pm, I heard footsteps in the hall outside the lab. I'm assuming it's the same man. Just like the other night, the footsteps stopped as the man reached my door. And just like the other night, he lingered there. I quietly slipped the gun out of my briefcase and held it in my right hand, ready to use it if I needed to, even while fully conscious of the tremor that was preventing me from holding the gun firmly.

After about ten seconds, I heard the footsteps gradually recede as the intruder slowly walked away from the lab door. Then there was complete silence. Just like the other night.

I was now really frightened. I moved my chair to the cubicle entrance so that I could watch the door, in case the intruder returned and tried to enter the lab. I stayed seated in that chair for a full hour, holding the gun the whole time. Nothing happened.

Halfway through this vigil, at 8:30, I called Jessica. Keeping my eyes trained on the lab door, and holding my phone in my shaky left hand and the gun in my even shakier right hand, I talked with her for several minutes. She seemed surprised to receive my call and wished me a Merry Christmas. I had totally forgotten that today was Christmas.

I told Jessica I just needed to hear her voice and I wished her well. She asked me whether I was all right. I said I had a bit of a cold but was otherwise fine. She seemed worried and encouraged me to come over to the house and get some sleep. I told her that I couldn't but thanked her for the offer.

Then she put Zeke on the phone. I had forgotten how sweet his little voice was. He seemed very quiet and more than a little shy. I told him I was sorry that I have not been able to see him for a while because I've been too busy at work, but that I think about him all the time, I miss him terribly, and I love him very, very, very much. And then I said good-bye.

By 9:00 I had been training my gun on the lab door for an hour. There having been no new activity, I felt it was now safe to roll my chair back to my desk and put down my gun. I started writing today's journal entry.

At about 10:00 I finished this journal entry and am about to insert it into the looseleaf binder where I keep all the other days' entries. I took a deep breath and exhaled. I looked around my cubicle. I saw my desk, my chair, my computer, my briefcase, this journal, and the papers I had tacked to the walls. And my gun.

CPSIA information can be obtained
at www.ICGtesting.com
Printed in the USA
FFOW01n1522181217
44087501-43388FF